The Lightning Ridge Ladies

FIONA McARTHUR

www.fionamcarthurauthor.com

CONTENTS

DEDICATION

FOR LIGHTNING RIDGE – an outback town built on dreams and filled with characters.

CHAPTER ONE

BELLA

A decommissioned cement mixer by the side of the road was the only indication for Bella Grey to turn right and exit the Castlereagh Highway. It was exactly where her sister-in-law, Riley, had mentioned it would be. The sky-blue improvised sign shouted 'Lightning Ridge' across the stationary vehicle's belly. Below that, the words 'Black Opal Country' gave the reason for the town residing in the middle of baked-dry nowhere.

Bella pulled in at the layover stopping bay, winding her window down to let in the heat – plenty of that – so she could stare at the words on the bulge of the tumbler chassis.

While she sat here, soaking in the fact she'd arrived at the last place her twin brother, William, had been seen alive, the silence shattered with the *potato, potato, potato* noise of a black Harley Davidson gliding around the corner towards the town. Her gaze jagged on the enormous shoulders of the driver leaning back in the seat. Her older brother, Konrad, had a motorcycle once, and she'd loved the few times she and William had been allowed to ride pillion, but that bike had been nothing like this Harley.

The rider disappeared and she returned her gaze to the sign and sighed. Eight hours driving to find a sign she'd dreaded seeing.

She'd lived in this place too many times in her nightmares, and it spoke of her family's enormous loss.

Lightning Ridge. The town where William had taken his own life, nearly three years now – and the town Konrad now wanted to move on from to build a life with his new wife elsewhere. Like their parents, he wanted to accept William was gone forever. He'd even suggested holding a memorial service for the third anniversary of William's death. Even though they'd never found his body. Even though they'd buried an empty coffin. He would have been thirty now, like her.

She couldn't blame Konrad; he'd spent almost three years in Lightning Ridge, including the months before William died when they'd all been worried about him. But here she was, knocked out of the fog she'd been in since William's death by her big brother's plans, and she sure wasn't letting William go without her own investigations.

Here was the reason she'd agreed to take over Konrad's patients and this medical practice in outback New South Wales.

He needed to go on sabbatical and a belated honeymoon with Riley before they moved to Sydney. Much to her parents' horror that she'd head outback – especially to the place that had stolen their youngest son.

Unlike Konrad, she wasn't ready for a memorial service.

She needed to see his body. Find out the whys. William wasn't dead, she told herself yet again. He couldn't be. Too young to die.

But sadly it just didn't sound as convincing anymore. Especially looking around the hot, desolate landscape scattered with mounds of sunbaked rocks. How could anyone survive being lost out here for years?

She needed a breakthrough and moving to Lightning Ridge seemed like her best hope. As she eased back onto the road, the hot breeze brushing her cheek like a whisper of regret, a sudden loud crack of nearby branches caught her attention. Not the sort of breakthrough she'd expected. The crack heralded a whirlwind of motion as a huge emu sprang from the sparse scrub behind her and sped along the road beside her window, making her heart jump in her throat.

Good grief – the emu was so close, with all that muscle and speed and brown feathers waving around its stout body. Bella tightened her hand on the wheel as she took her foot from the accelerator. Right there. The emu was right freaking there! Huge feet slapping the dirt beside her like whip cracks, yellow beady eyes pointing straight ahead. Yet it seemed to be watching her with a side eye, so she didn't trust it not to veer her way.

Thankfully, the flightless bird swerved in the other direction and crashed back through the bush to disappear. Silence.

Her heart pounded. Freaking emus. Now Bella wasn't game to take her eye off the tar in case another one jumped out of the scrub.

She was a city girl – or at least a big-town townie from beach-side Port Macquarie, and compared to that, this place felt desolate, de-hydrated and downright dangerous. Rarely, very rarely, she'd had kangaroos jump out at her back home, but not freakin' emus.

William would have laughed to see her hands still white-knuckling the steering wheel.

Maybe she had been mad to say yes to replacing her older brother, but it was too late now – she'd already volunteered. And she'd just received a nice wildlife welcome for the new principal doctor at the Outback Practice at Lightning medical centre.

Maybe coming here would jerk her back into living again.

Maybe – hope flickered, perhaps unrealistically – but, dammit, maybe she could be the one to uncover some clues to William's dis-appearance. Not that she'd said any of that to Konrad or her retired doctor parents. They'd just 'Poor Bella' her.

When no more emus appeared and her heart rate settled, Bella accelerated past the scenery again. Low, barren hills and scrubby trees. Lots of touristy posters and signs attached to said trees at the side of the road, advertising opals, accommodation and tours.

Driving into Lightning Ridge was like coming into an outback Las Vegas . . . with emus.

Bella glanced at her fuel gauge. She'd fuelled up in Moree, but needed more now. Heck, her AWD had never driven eight hours in a day before – but she had to admit to feeling a smidgeon lighter away from the lingering grief at home.

She should never have moved back in with her parents after William disappeared . . .

Bella batted that thought away. Her life had been put on pause for the last few years, and she'd thrown herself into work to numb the pain – cutting off friends and any hope of a relationship.

Strange how the isolation of the drive had also felt confronting, heading out alone into the open landscape, long, straight roads in front and behind as she drove with few cars on the road with her.

Plenty of big cotton trucks. Fewer people. Houses even rarer.

But change was good. Wasn't it?

As she hit the town proper, Bella glanced up at the latest advertisement – this time a van lodged in the fork of a tree,

certainly different – and pulled into a high-roofed fuel station that looked normal.

Through the window of the office an older woman with white hair nodded once, and Bella nodded back. Riley had clued Bella in about Desiree, too. Apparently, the white-haired woman in the servo, known as the engine whisperer, knew everything about everyone in town.

Bella climbed out of her AWD, and the full weight of the outback sun hit her as she leaned out of the shade to fill the car.

Mid-spring afternoon and the hot air already shimmered over thirty degrees Celsius, even though it was only October.

She replaced the fuel cap and glanced across the road to her right as she headed for the mini-office. There was nothing familiar about the setting: cranes and strange mining trucks, and derelict cars in a paddock, and that weird tree-van parked up high in the leaves behind her. The back of beyond was how this place felt. She pulled her shirt collar off her sticky neck and walked into the cool air-conditioning inside.

As soon as Bella stepped inside, Desiree murmured from behind the counter, 'Doc Konrad's sister.'

Riley had been right. Bella smiled. 'You picked me. You must be Desiree. I'm sorry I don't remember much from the wedding.'

The whole event had been a blur with Bella stuck on William not being there with her, but Riley had been chuffed the Lightning Ridge contingent had come to Sydney for her nuptials.

Bella's turn to come to them. 'Yes, I'm Bella. Do I look like Konrad?'

The service-station owner looked like she'd spent her three score and ten years in the sun around here. 'No, actually. More like William.' As soon as the words left her mouth, the other woman winced as she took the credit card from Bella's suddenly stiff fingers.

Bella let out a breath and forced another smile. 'Well, he is my twin.' Was. She should have said was. But she hadn't. She pushed past the painful moment – something she had a lot of practice at by now but that still felt hard. 'Nice to meet you again, Desiree.'

Desiree looked relieved. 'Just arrived?'

'Yep.' Bella took back her card.

'Receipt?'

'No thanks.'

'Then welcome to the Ridge. See that yellow crane across the road over there? Drive up that street. The OPAL docs is on the corner before you turn left at the top. Park round the back.'

Bella nodded. 'Thanks. That's very helpful.'

'My pleasure. We'll chat more when you've rested after the drive.' Which meant, Bella assumed, she looked as tired as she felt. Desiree added, 'We'll miss Doc Konrad and Doc Riley when they go.'

Bella would, too. 'They'll be back,' she reassured Desiree. She hoped. Very much. She waved to Desiree and walked back to her car, climbed inside and started the engine.

Looking both ways, she drove across the deserted main road – no hold-up during peak hour traffic, then – and up the street Desiree had indicated.

On her left, she passed an opal boutique on the corner, with big windows and a wooden verandah, classy yet rustic in design, which fit with an opal town. Alongside the store were some small cottages marching up the street towards the slight hill where she could see the surgery's sign. The old-machinery-packed paddock she'd spotted earlier lay on the right.

She approached the Outback Practice at Lightning sign, snorted at the OPAL acronym, and drove around the back of the surgery to a motel-style row of units her brother had apparently renovated in the last few months. Even before she'd switched off the car, one of the back doors opened to reveal Konrad, who gave her one of those I-see-your-face waves he was so good at.

Her family were all blond. She and William had more honey hues than the platinum Konrad. Both their parents had been white-blond as well in their youth, but Konrad still seemed more Germanic-looking than the rest of them, even though Bella didn't know of any Eastern European roots in their family history. Riley had once told Bella he reminded her of Thor, or at least the Aussie actor who played him in the movies.

'You look like some wild-haired Viking,' Bella said to him in greeting. It was true – especially with his fjord-blue eyes and his chiselled face. Warmth suffused her. To Bella, her big brother was a giant softie at heart.

'Baby Belle, welcome to the Ridge.' Konrad was already there as she climbed from the car, and she was engulfed in his big arms.

'I am not a small round cheese,' Bella retorted as she tilted her head up at him. She pushed away thoughts of those Edam pieces wrapped in rubicund wax.

'Oh, come on. You're even wearing red.'

She laughed and hugged him back again. 'Bella to you.'

'Is he teasing you?' Riley murmured as she joined the group hug. Riley stood tall, too – not like Konrad's skyscraper, but she beat Bella's height by a good hand's width. Her styled cap of ruby-red hair hung in a straight line under her ears, and her green eyes travelled over

Bella, clearly assessing her for mood, tiredness and general wellbeing. Clinical Riley. Konrad might be the best guy she knew, but Riley was the smartest woman Bella had ever met. She loved them both to death.

Death. William hadn't called her Baby Belle. He'd called her Tinkerbell. Bella sighed and pulled back as the good vibes faded.

'Hi guys. Nice to have arrived. You both look well.' And didn't that sound stilted after the warm welcome, Bella thought to herself.

Riley's eyes narrowed; she hadn't missed the emotional down-swing, either. 'Come in, I'll make tea. Give Konrad your keys and he'll put your cases next door in unit number three and lock the car.'

Bella handed the keys over and grabbed her phone before following Riley into the second unit. The peppermint living quarters were modern, with a huge lounge and kitchen area on one side.

From what Konrad and Riley had told her of the renovations, Bella knew the bedroom and bathroom would be located through a doorway that used to be the next-door motel unit.

Riley filled up the huge teapot by the kitchen sink. 'You're coming in and I'm going out. Me packed and you unpacking. Sorry I can't stick around.'

Riley worked one outreach women's clinic in the Ridge every six weeks, while mainly working in Sydney, and was senior partner at a high-profile obstetric research practice. She'd even been asked to present a paper on infertility in Hawaii at this year's WCGO, the World Congress of Gynaecology and Obstetrics. Bella suspected her sister-in-law would have quite a bit to do in the next week instead of babysitting Bella's arrival.

'Bet you're looking forward to after, though.' Riley and Konrad were itching for that long-delayed honeymoon after the conference.

Riley blew out a breath as she carried the teapot over to the table. 'So true. Heaven, I can't wait for the down time.'

Bella hadn't been able to get here earlier due to work commit-ments in Port Macquarie, so they were pushing deadlines with one week to go. 'I really appreciate Konrad staying in the Ridge a few extra days, Riley. It'll be much easier to settle in when he's here to show me the ropes.'

'I'm glad he is, too. The least we can do when you're taking over the practice.' Riley poured the tea. 'So how are you, Bella?

Not regretting the move here already?'

Was it that obvious? 'Do I look like I do?'

'Something's going on.'

Bella shrugged her shoulders, feeling that weight again. 'Can't say thoughts didn't cross my mind on the drive. Coming here makes me think more of William. Of course it hurts.' She huffed out an unamused laugh as Konrad came inside and put the car keys on the table beside her. 'Even without Desiree saying I looked like my twin the minute I arrived.'

Riley blinked in surprise. Her gaze lifted to her husband's, though she spoke to Bella. 'Desiree said that? Very unlike her – she must have been knocked off balance when she saw you. She doesn't usually put her foot in it.'

Konrad nodded. 'True. Maybe something else happened to throw her off kilter. I'm sorry if she upset you, Bella. Wouldn't have been intentional.'

Bella lifted her hand. 'No problem. I'd rather people remembered William than forgot about him.' The unspoken memorial service rattled between them like an old bone.

Konrad's voice was soft. 'I need a closure for here, for me, yes, and that was why I suggested it.' The siblings' eyes met. He'd read her mind.

Riley patted his shoulder. 'Sit, my love.' She smiled at Bella.

'You take lots of milk in your tea, isn't it?' She put a mug full of tea in front of Bella.

'Good memory. And perfect. Thanks.'

'Remembering things is part of my modus operandi.' She sat beside her husband.

Bella glanced around the surprisingly large unit. 'I love your living space. It's more airy than I expected from the outside.'

Riley nodded. 'The motel room Konrad used to live in here was small. When we knew we were both going to spend more time in the Ridge, we had fun making them bigger. Six rooms into three units. Furnished with mostly online purchases.'

'All Riley's designs,' Konrad said, waving his hand at the room, 'I'm just the muscle.'

'And marvellous muscles they are, too, my love.' Riley patted his bulging biceps, then looked back at Bella, her eyes kind. 'How are the parents, Bella?'

'Good. They said they'll come out and visit when I'm settled in.'

She knew they wouldn't come until she invited them, even though they worried about her moving to the place they'd lost William to.

Riley's phone buzzed. She glanced apologetically at Bella and slipped out of the main room into the adjacent space where the bedroom must be.

But Konrad's face had brightened at the mention of their parents. 'That's a great idea. We have the three double units finished now. You could show them around the Ridge. Don't worry, I'll give you a good tour on Sunday, so you'll have found most things before they come.'

Konrad's phone rang. 'Sorry. Me too.' He stood to answer the call, walking over the window and leaving Bella alone.

Alone. Yup. When Konrad was gone at the end of next week, there'd be nothing to distract her from being alone after-hours. She might end up inviting her parents here out of sheer desperation.

So why had she agreed to come? Apart from the fact all country towns needed doctors, she knew there was another reason. She forced her shoulders not to slump with the never-ending ache for her twin. The lost part of her. The answers to William's unhappy ending were here somewhere, and she was going to find them.

Of course, now her eyes were stinging, and the heel of her hand went to her chest to rub the place where she felt the broken con- nection every day since William had disappeared over two and a half years ago. Thirty-two months, one hundred and thirty-nine weeks, nine hundred and seventy-three days.

Disappeared. Died. Suicide. Leaving behind nothing but a note saying they would never find his body. And they *hadn't* found his body among the deserted mines of the Ridge, despite the many searches. So how could she accept he was truly gone?

Bella missed William like a limb. Public opinion said twins had a special connection, but Bella knew that was a massive understatement. Except she hadn't felt the exact moment he'd gone like in all the books. No moment of sudden understanding they'd shared as kids – like when both knew the ice cream the other would choose or when one of them was hurt. Or how she knew when the phone was about to ring with a call from him. He hadn't called for nearly three years.

The silence in her heart meant she couldn't deny he'd departed.

She ached with the loss every day, dreamed of conversations with him most nights, none of which helped the need to find out: Why? When? How?

She needed to understand. Forgive. And one day, perhaps, to accept that her twin had left her. At least being in the last place he'd been alive, she could search for more information, she hoped.

Konrad had never discovered the catalyst for William's death either. She knew Konrad had searched endlessly for the body.

Paid for drones to comb mineshafts. Hired miners to methodically examine the fields. All to no avail. There were just too many old, disused mines. Too many opal fields in every direction. Bella – and all of William's family and friends – had been left with so many unresolved questions after the suicide note.

Konrad had told her in the early days after William's death he'd dreamed of his pale hand reaching out to him from the darkness.

As if he'd failed the brother he'd moved here to support. But even though nobody blamed him, Konrad blamed himself for failing to prevent the tragedy.

Konrad deserved his happiness with his new wife. He'd shouldered the most guilt and was now ready to move on with his life, but that still didn't mean Bella was ready for a memorial service.

Which brought her back to why she was here in Lightning Ridge.

Konrad deserved a honeymoon. A life. She would never complain about her big brother's departure. She hadn't been happy in Port Macquarie. Hadn't been happy for more than two and a half years since she'd lost her twin. And she certainly wasn't helping her parents recover with her own distress reminding them of the loss every day.

At least in Lightning Ridge she could talk to people who knew William, who remembered him, and maybe find out what really happened to her brother. She was determined to find at least one solid fact before a memorial service broke her.

CHAPTER TWO

MEESHA

Tamika Kerrison, Meesha to her friends and customers at The Iridescent Opal, lifted the precious gem tray out of the safe in the workshop at the rear of her jewellery boutique where she kept the rough opals. Most of the shimmering gems on the tray she'd cut and polished herself. A few were still nobbies of dirt and colour, claystone with tantalising possibilities she'd explore another day. Some were seam opals, sliced and glittering.

Meesha screwed up her face as she ran the tips of her fingers over the candidates.

'Darn it,' she muttered as she rolled the selection of sparkling light and colour around. She'd have to rethink her ideas for the centre-piece.

She needed a unique gem for the pendant she was picturing and none of these had the right shape for the focal she'd envisaged.

She wanted to create that piece in her mind. But she'd have to do another design until the right opal found her.

Frustration made her frown again. Seriously. When she'd first started her business in the Ridge, the quality and quantity of opal she'd been able to acquire had been astounding.

Right now, she desperately needed to find more raw opal stock from the local miners to boost her jewellery portfolio, especially if she was angling for the chance of attending the US trade fairs to showcase her wares this year.

A dream, sure, but she'd also dreamed she'd open an opal and designer jewellery store in Lightning Ridge, and here she stood three years down the track as a solo entrepreneur. It might be lonely, running The Iridescent Opal, and she barely had time for any sort of social life or friends, but it was certainly professionally satisfying.

Bless Grandad and his love of prospecting, his lapidary tumblers and his hole-in-the-wall jewellery shed back on the coast. In his will, he'd left his tools, collections and love of opals to Meesha, and his house in South West Rocks to her older sister Luci. Meesha had never doubted she'd got the better deal.

Lightning Ridge was the home of the rare black opal – had always been that – but lately it hadn't felt like it. She just didn't understand why the raw opal supply had dwindled to a trickle.

For some reason, an uneasy silence pervaded the air whenever she asked anyone in town about where the stones had gone.

She'd have to talk to Desiree again on Friday night, at the Lightning Ridge Ladies gathering. She knew everything, as everyone always said, though even Desiree had grown more reticent over the last twelve months or more. Or she could ask TJ, the big miner with a reputation for toughness she bought a lot of her stock from, but he was someone who didn't believe in conversation.

For now, Meesha picked out the largest cut opal on the tray, and three smaller stones of the same electric blue hue. She placed the potential pieces on the worktable under the swivel light before putting the tray back in the safe and spinning the dial. She turned back to the bench and felt the familiar tingle of excitement rise in her chest.

She loved this part.

Her mind jumped with impatience and her drawings sketched the bones of the piece, allowing her to absorb the colours and the emotions of the stones as she semi-finalised the design in front of her. The finished piece would be set in silver, she decided, not gold.

Her phone burst into a loud rendition of 'By the Seaside'. That would be Luci.

'Hey, sis. How's the ocean?' Meesha's usual greeting since Lightning Ridge sat almost seven hundred kilometres from the waves where Luci lived.

'Noisy last night. Crashing for hours. How's the rough dirt?'

It was Luci's normal answer. But something didn't sound right. Meesha frowned.

'Still rough. I'm just starting a new piece. You sound sad, though. What's happening with you?'

'Big life changes.'

'Oh?' Crap. Meesha chewed her lip. Luci had had enough big life changes recently for six lifetimes. She was already pregnant with an unexpected baby; she didn't need more upheaval.

'Batte's gone back to Brazil.' The determined finality clear in her words, but the brittleness in her tone made Meesha suck in a breath.

'Going?'

'To his mother. It's over. Four years wiped away.'

Bat-eh. She sounded it out in her head. She'd always thought it was a weird name. 'Aww, crap. I'm sorry, Luci. What can I do?'

'I think I need you.' Luci said quietly, and Meesha knew she too needed to hug her sister close. She would always be there for her.

'I'm here. Ask me anything.'

Luci whispered, 'Would you mind if I came out to stay with you for a while?'

Geez, wouldn't it be amazing to have her sister here? It was the only thing Meesha didn't like about the Ridge: no Luci. 'Of course, please come. I'd love it. Stay for as long as you want. Move in forever...' She thought about that for a moment. 'You'd have to leave for the birth, though, and then come back.'

'I know. I was thinking I could rent your other duplex. Adapt it for the baby. Rent out my house here and decide about what to do with it later.'

'You don't need to rent from me.'

'Yes, I do. I'll be getting rent from my place. It's only fair. I'm not a charity case.' Luci had always been sensitive to pity. Not that Meesha blamed her, and she would never pity her sister. Admire, empathise, love to the moon and back, though, absolutely.

'Okay,' Meesha conceded, But she wouldn't charge much.

'Good. Especially if I do some renovations.'

'Sure. Of course. Whatever you want.' Meesha thought about Eric, the friend who'd helped her so much with renovating the shop fittings. He'd happily help Luci. 'I know someone.' Gently, she asked, 'How did it end, Luci?'

Luci sighed. 'The baby, Meesh. Batte couldn't cope with the idea of having a child. I couldn't cope with him not coping. I just won't have time to baby two peple. So . . . I told him to go.'

Meesha closed her eyes and shook her head. 'I can't believe he left you both.'

'He didn't just leave.' Luci snorted but there was pain in the sound. 'He bolted when I gave him the option. Said it was for the best. Barely said goodbye.'

Meesha rubbed her chest. He'd been high maintenance, but she'd thought he'd really loved Luci. 'I'm so sorry.'

Luci huffed. 'Yeah. Well. It's been building for a while now.'

'Okay,' Meesha said, switching into practical mode. 'So, you're coming here. You and Pluto flying in, then? When?' She needed to get the caravan park cleaners in to help her spruce the second duplex from top to bottom because she needed to be in the shop for most of the day. In a stroke of luck, the previous renters had left last month – they'd been great tenants, but she still needed to sort the place.

Holey moley. Luci, her guide dog, Pluto, and a new niece or nephew coming soon. Meesha couldn't wait.

CHAPTER THREE

BELLA

Bella crossed the small courtyard from her new home to the back door of the surgery at exactly a.m. on Monday morning.

Day one. She pasted on her I'm-ready-for-work smile as Konrad stepped out of his unit beside her. 'Morning.'

'Morning, Baby Belle.'

She paused in the act of preceding him into the reception room, but before she could say anything to admonish him, he held up both hands in the universal apology sign. 'Sorry. Teasing.'

He grinned at her. 'Couldn't resist. It's just so good to have you here.'

She couldn't help smiling back. He had always been her and William's childhood hero. Annoying, but a hero. 'Yeah, right.

Only because you can leave me holding your precious baby.' She gestured to the pale peppermint walls and empty waiting room chairs of the surgery as they stepped into the reception room.

She took a second to look around and admire the curved mahogony reception desk and the polished floorboards. The place was roomier than she expected. And more welcoming. A few desert artworks adorned the walls and a potted ficus in the corner made it feel homey.

Konrad's lips twitched. 'We don't have babies in Lightning Ridge.'

The sound of a key working in the front lock made them both turn to see the wheels of a large, old-fashioned English pram push through the now open door.

Konrad grinned. 'Except for Teddy.'

Bella watched as a young woman and her large perambulator cruised inside and shut the door behind them.

'Good morning, Mel. I was just saying to my sister' – he gestured to Bella – 'that we don't have babies born in Lightning Ridge. Mel, do you remember my sister from my wedding?'

'Of course.' She grinned up at Konrad. 'You were saying no babies except for Teddy?' Mel smiled at Bella and held out her hand. 'Nice to see you again, Dr Grey.'

'Bella, please.' She took the woman's small hand and shook it.

The slight and smiling young mum's honey-blonde hair was pulled back in a no-nonsense ponytail. 'I know you're the wonderful Melinda my brother raves about.'

Mel blushed and dropped her head, but Bella could tell she was pleased. 'Just Mel.'

'And here's the famous Teddy,' Bella added, peering into the pram. She'd heard all about Teddy's precipitous birth in the Ridge's tiny local health centre last year.

Teddy had been under the care of a specialist in Sydney for his gastroschisis but his birth had come early and quick, with some of his intestines on the outside of his body instead of tucked inside where they should be. Everything had gone remarkably well, despite the remote location, because Riley had carried that load as the visiting obstetrician and expedited him out. All of Teddy's needs had been repaired by the specialists now, of course, and he was as healthy as any other toddler.

Bella met his bright blue eyes and he gave her a plump-cheeked grin. 'Oh, he's adorable.'

'He is.' Mel smiled with maternal pride, then glanced at Konrad and back at Bella. 'It's still okay that Teddy comes in to work with me, isn't it?'

Konrad was quick to reassure her. 'Bella is fine with that, aren't you, Bella?'

'Absolutely. I'm looking forward to getting to know you both better!'

Konrad and Riley had been there for Mel when she'd been going through a difficult time, Bella knew, but now . . . well, Mel was nine years younger than Bella at twenty-one, and she appeared to be loving life and motherhood. And apparently she was a whiz at reception, too. A win-win as far as Bella was concerned.

'We'll be the A-team, Mel, don't you worry.'

'Mum's on the team, too,' Mel said.

'We won't forget Greta,' Konrad reassured her, then said to Bella, 'Greta's coming in to see you at twelve-thirty.'

Bella mentally searched for the reference. Ah – the caterer and cleaner Riley had raved about. Mel's mum-in-law. Another person she should have remembered from Konrad and Riley's wedding.

Konrad went on. 'She brings our lunch daily, though often there's enough to reheat for dinner later as well.'

'That sounds amazing,' Bella said sincerely. She wasn't much of a cook and Konrad knew it. Rumour had it that Greta's food was amazing, though.

He whispered, 'She said your first lunch is free – a sort of tester in case you want to order every day.'

Bella shook her head at Mel. 'No free lunch needed. I'm in.'

Mel smiled. 'I'll make some coffee. How do you like yours, Bella?'

'Milky, no sugar. Thanks, Mel.'

Konrad laughed and waved Bella towards a doorway. 'Come through to Riley's office. Yours now.' He added over his shoulder,

'I'll warn you, though: Riley said, "Lucky she didn't bring a cat to swing." So you're welcome to take my room if you prefer. It's slightly larger.'

Konrad pushed open the door to the office. The consulting room held two chairs jammed opposite a desk with a large computer screen, and an examination table was tucked behind a new-looking gold curtain against the wall. A small bookshelf took up the back ten inches of the desk, loaded with books and models of lady parts, and reached up to the low ceiling. It was tight.

Nothing like the spacious, tastefully decorated office she'd had at her parents' practice at Port Macquarie.

She grinned at her brother. 'I want to see your room later to compare. Maybe I'll want to swap after you go.'

Mel reappeared with their coffees and by the time she'd put one in each office, the front door of the practice opened to admit a large man in shorts, a word- *bleep*-word T-shirt, and bare feet.

He'd indulged in interesting tattoos that swirled skyward on his neck.

Bella glanced at the clock on the wall. Almost eight-thirty.

Mel greeted the man without surprise. 'Good morning, Cyrus. Please take a seat. The doctor will be with you shortly.'

In Bella's consulting room, Konrad swooped forward, turned her computer on, wrote a password down on a notepad and tore the sheet off. He folded it, gave it to her, and stepped back. The MedicalDirector program opened on the screen in front of them and displayed the waiting room list.

'Change your password when you get a chance, but your first patient is here.' Konrad's blue eyes twinkled with amusement.

'Welcome to the Ridge, Dr Grey.'

Bella's first patient – Cyrus Pinkerton, according to the list – nodded and smiled politely as he came into her office. Konrad waved him forward as he passed the man on his way out.

Cyrus beamed at her. 'So, you're Doc Konrad and Doc Riley's little sister.' He took up most of the doorway where he hovered until she gestured him to the seat with not a little trepidation that it might break under his weight.

Cyrus looked to be a hairy but jolly giant with distinct ink work that made him stand out. The black-headed snake tattooed up the side of his neck seemed to shimmer as it disappeared into his ear. Bella forced her eyes away from the red flicking tongue.

'Please take a seat, Mr Pinkerton. I'm Dr Grey. How can I help you?'

'Call me Cyrus.'

Right then. 'How can I help you, Cyrus?'

'Well, Dr Grey.' Cyrus exposed his missing teeth in delight.

'I've got an itch.'

By lunchtime, Bella had the lay of the land. Her first patients had been a series of amusing older miners – possibly just here to check out the new lady doctor – matrons who needed their scripts updated, and kids with immunisations due. All routine and uncomplicated cases, with not an entitled client in sight – as far as Bella was concerned, that was a lovely change.

A tourist suburb like the one she'd just left in Port Macquarie hadn't always meant charming clientele, but every person across the spectrum at the Ridge she'd seen today had been delighted to introduce themselves and make her feel welcome. Maybe this hadn't been a bad move.

She glanced down at the framed photo of her and William, heads together, hands on hips like a mirror image, their last day at high school. The photo usually sat by her bed at her parents'

house. She'd brought it with her and placed at the back of her desk. Not unusually, she spoke to it. 'I've got this, William.'

Leaving her office after the busy morning, she found Konrad chatting to a small, blonde and busty woman cuddling Teddy in the reception area. Mel watched fondly from behind the reception desk. The woman might just have the warmest smile Bella had ever seen, plus, the aroma coming from the staff kitchen made Bella's belly rumble. This had to be Greta.

Konrad pulled her over. 'Here's Bella.' He added in a theatrically deep voice, 'Bella, you remember Greta? She's our gastronomically gifted chef.'

Bella raised her brows. 'That's a mouthful, brother.' She held out her hand to the other woman. 'Hi Greta. Lovely to meet you again, and something out here does smell very good.'

They clasped fingers briefly, exchanged a howdy-do over Teddy's head and stepped back. 'It's Macaroni Monday today, spaghetti bolognese this week, though I've kept yours in separate pots to assemble when you're ready – I wasn't sure about allergies or dislikes.'

'Oh yum. A favourite. Thank you. No wonder it smells great.

And just so you know, I eat anything I don't have to cook, so that means everything, Greta.'

Greta smiled. 'That's what your brother said but . . .' She shrugged. 'Just checking.'

Bella thought about logistics. 'Keeping them separate to assemble is great, though. Then I can make them fresh and have the other half for tea.'

On Thursday, Bella turned into the Lightning Ridge airport at the end of Opal Street, where it became Fred Reece Way out of town.

While the Air Link flights left for Dubbo twice a week, today the airport looked deserted at five o'clock in the afternoon.

'Thanks for dropping me off, Baby Belle.' Despite the joking words, Konrad wore that frown he always sported when he was thinking of William.

She tried to lighten the mood. 'Just because you're leaving don't think you get away with that name.'

'My bad.' The humour left his voice and loving concern replaced it. 'You're sure you're going to be okay here, Bella?'

'Of course I'll be okay. Busy, busy. Won't have time to scratch myself with all your patients.'

Konrad blew out a big breath. He added softly, 'At least think about the memorial service.'

Bella screwed her face up and turned away from him, looking out over the scatter of locked-up buildings. The place sported a barren gravel forecourt and fenced runway without any people moving about. 'Sure.'

He rested his hand on her forearm. 'Bella? You're not thinking of digging into William's life here are you? Leave it alone. Try to use the time to move on.'

Like you are, Bella thought, but she didn't say it, and really, she didn't mean it. Konrad was everything that was good. 'I'll be fine. You fly your little aircraft safely to Sydney and have a wonderful delayed honeymoon with your wife. You both deserve it, and I've got your Lightning Ridge baby all sorted. Mel and I will manage beautifully.'

His concern brushed her again and she leaned across and hugged him. 'It's okay, bro, I've got this.'

She used to say that to William all the time.

When Bella steered out through the gate, Konrad's private aircraft hung like a speck in the rear-view mirror and the droning noise of its engine had already disappeared.

In less than two hours he'd be in Sydney. The sun would still hang around for his landing since it was mid-October, so he'd be there before dark.

Six weeks on her own before he would even come back for the promised visit.

The silence in the car echoed, too lonely, and Bella turned on the radio, huffing when she only found static. Grumbling, she hair-pinned left onto the orange dirt of the detour road, the usual straight tarred road to town currently blocked for some reason.

Which meant her car would be orange-tinted with dust by the time she steered through all the miner's camps and white tailing heaps on the winding road back to town.

Even mid-spring the heat was shimmering at thirty-one degrees Celsius outside.

Chapter Four

BELLA

Taco Friday today, Bella thought, as she pushed open the rear door to the surgery for her first solo day as the principal doctor. It meant she was already looking forward to lunch, later. Good food bonus after Konrad had flown out yesterday – she couldn't help feeling a little lost without her big brother in the background. Not surprisingly, Konrad's departure made her miss William even more.

The aroma of great coffee greeted her in the reception area, which meant Mel had turned the machine on. Selfless of her, because her receptionist had been confirmed pregnant yesterday, and she'd mentioned to Bella the smell of coffee 'made her tummy go queasy'.

The young woman had gone on to say it had been like that during her first pregnancy, too. 'Which just goes to show, it makes a big difference knowing I'm pregnant at six weeks instead of finding out at thirty-five weeks like with Teddy.'

Bella couldn't imagine having only a couple of weeks' notice before giving birth to a baby – good grief – but Mel seemed to cope well with everything, even the smell of coffee on a nauseated tummy. The young mum was a whizz at sorting patients and admin at the OPAL medical centre, not to mention looking after Teddy at the same time. Luckily, the laidback kid just played in the waiting room in his playpen or slept in his big pram beside his mother's desk, and he made Bella smile every time she looked at him. As far as Bella was concerned, Mel and Teddy were a package deal she was extremely lucky to have.

The first patients of the day hadn't arrived yet, so she had some time to soak in being 'the doc' in charge. *Whoopee*, she thought nervously.

'Happy Friday, Mel.' She forced a warm smile and strangely began to feel better. 'How did Toby and Greta take the news of the new baby coming?'

'We're all very excited. Though' – she glanced at her son on his play-carpet in the pen – 'I'm not sure how Teddy will find sharing his parents.'

Teddy, the cutest part of the furniture in the waiting room, baby-talked to himself and turned at the sound of his name. He sent his mother a toothless grin and waved at Bella.

He's such a darling, Bella thought as she waved back. 'No doubt Teddy will take it in his stride like he and his mother have done with everything else. Greta must be thrilled.'

'She said she is,' Mel said shyly. 'And Toby is acting a bit silly, running all over town telling people. He can't keep the news in. He's so proud he'll be a real dad.' Mel's expression softened remembering his joy. 'Oh.' Suddenly, she seemed stricken. 'That wasn't what I meant. He's Teddy's dad now, of course.'

Ah, Bella thought, catching Mel's meaning. *Not biologically, but in all the other ways that count.* 'Of course.' Bella waved that worry away. 'He's a wonderful dad already. But a new baby is exciting, too.' Though it was the last thing Bella wanted for herself, maybe not ever.

She took the coffee Mel handed her. 'Thank you. Do we have any practice management issues I need to know about?'

Mel shook her head. 'I updated the software for MedicalDirector yesterday, and the pathology and X-ray results are working again online.'

'You're a star.' Mel had started explaining the background running of the medical practice management to her, and Bella hadn't realised how much she needed to learn if she wasn't going to totally rely on Mel now Konrad was gone. It had become curiously interesting and satisfying to get a handle on the logistics of a medical business.

'Mum said don't forget the Lightning Ridge Ladies tonight,' Mel said. 'Though tonight the party's at Meesha's store, The Iridescent Opal, not at Desiree's servo like it normally is. Everyone's excited to see you again.'

Bella kept in the sigh. Meeting strangers, or people she didn't remember, meant more joy. 'No idea where that is.' She hadn't ventured further than the surgery all week except for a couple of late evening walks and to drop Konrad at the airport. She probably needed to get out more.

A hand wave from Mel. At least she didn't seem to notice Bella's lack of enthusiasm. 'Walk down to the bottom of our street.

The jewellery store is a few doors up from Desiree's service station towards town. Meesha's celebrating three years in her shop and we're all going to support her. You'll hear the party.'

'So, this Meesha, she's another of the Lightning Ridge Ladies?'

Mel nodded, her ponytail bouncing. 'I only go every now and then, but Mum said Meesha joined a few months ago now.

She's about your age. They're not all old.' Mel looked horrified for a minute and covered her mouth. 'Um. I shouldn't have said that.'

Bella grinned at her, teasing. 'I'm happy I don't count as old.'

She should go to the party, and she did want to ask Desiree about William. Her mood dipped at the thought of her brother. 'What time is the party again?'

'Six.'

'I'll be there.' The front door opened and a weathered miner stepped in. Time to work.

At six o'clock, Bella changed into a blue swing skirt and a sleeveless white top with sandals in deference to the warm evening. It wasn't too hot – they hadn't come into the dry, baking heat of summer yet. More delight to come. Thank goodness for aircon was all she could say.

Despite the heat, she needed to walk more. She wasn't a runner like Konrad and Riley, but she enjoyed a slow amble to burn off the emptiness of missing her family. Next week she would start a routine stroll in the mornings before work, she decided as she left her unit.

But tonight she'd have a little time to explore the streetscape of the Ridge on her way to Meesha's. She smiled at herself with her use of the local vernacular. Never Lightning Ridge to the locals – just the Ridge.

The shops would all be shut, of course. She hadn't made it into town during business hours since she'd spent the last week in the office reading up on patient histories, but she and Konrad had gone for a couple of walks in the evenings to check out the lay of the streets and have dinner at the Italian restaurant.

Of course, it was a small town, so the whole place closed at five except for the pub, the one Italian restaurant and the club. Or the Club in the Scrub. Her mouth twitched at the name of the bush venue her brother had taken her to last Saturday night at Grawin, forty-five minutes away. She could just imagine how many emus would jump out at her if she drove there one evening on her own.

Not at night, Tinkerbell. The ache returned so harshly she had to rub her chest at the memory of her twin's teasing name for her.

She set off down Onyx Street, past the paddock of mine machinery and ancient abandoned cars. The smell of freshly mown grass wafted in the air as she passed the little cottages.

Her gaze drifted across the street to the well-lit opal store on the corner she'd seen on her first day in Lightning Ridge, all board-walks and big windows on the grey corrugated iron walls. Opals everywhere – it made sense for an opal town. She wasn't sure she even understood opals. Would they run her out of town if she admitted this in public? They were pretty, sure, but she preferred a classic sparkly gem, like a diamond or a sapphire. Perhaps she'd best keep quiet on the matter.

As she turned right and crossed the road towards the store, she peeked at the darkened service station.

According to Greta, on Fridays the Lightning Ridge Ladies would usually be out the back of the servo as soon as it shut on Friday afternoons. Bella thought about Greta and Mel making sure she had social contacts and pushing her to mix. It was sweet of them. Bella sighed. She'd see how she went tonight before she thought about next week.

For now, she continued along the main street towards the bright murals, enjoying how they popped up on large concrete walls here and there. She could do with the brightness of them – the happy, the cheerful.

Another opal store appeared on her left – all shiny panes of windows, bright lights and a huge sign: The Iridescent Opal. This had to be it. Music spilled out of the open door, and despite herself she hummed the familiar tune about pineapple cocktails.

The party looked to be swinging. Bella girded her loins, preparing to be social. It had been a while. *Practise your smile, girl, and lift your chin.*

'Hello,' a female voice called out. 'Do I know you? Oh! You must be Bella Grey. Mel said you were coming. I'm Meesha.'

Bella stopped by the doorway and smiled tentatively at the young woman with red curls holding a tray of champagne flutes in one hand and waving with the other. Gorgeous hands covered in rings, sporting bright nail polish, and demonstrating great balance with that tray. Meesha's vivid pink silk shirt and turquoise harem pants highlighted her cheerful personality. Bella felt underdressed in her boring skirt and white blouse.

Meesha set the tray down on a handy pedestal beside the shop door – some of the glasses wobbled but none of them tipped over – and she threw an arm around Bella's shoulder in an exuberant hug.

'Welcome to the Ridge. GPs are like gold around here. How are you settling in?'

So, this was Meesha. Bella experienced an unexpected feeling of connection, which was weird, but not unwelcome. One of those instantaneous things that were so rare. And precious.

'Work is good.' Bella smiled tentatively but didn't elaborate.

'What about you? Have you lived here long?'

Meesha's arms opened wide to take in the street. 'Feels like it.

I love it. Crazy place.' She gestured back at the shop. 'But then, I'm addicted to opals.'

See, someone is! Bella mocked herself. 'Wow,' she said. Socially inept or what? 'Go you.'

She glanced around the busy shop behind Meesha, all glass display cases, varied handmade furniture and interesting artwork.

And lots of people. Actually, the shop looked even more amazing now the door was open. 'Your shop?'

Meesha glowed and nodded. 'All mine. We're having our third birthday celebration. It's just customers, my sister and suppliers.

And my friends,' she added with a wink. 'So, welcome.'

Friends – Bella probably needed some of those. At home she would have avoided this opportunity to meet others, holing up at her parents' house or working long hours at their practice.

Isolating herself in her grief. Here she had Greta and Mel, pushing her to come, and they were harder to say no to than her parents.

Meesha patted her chest mock-importantly. 'I'm an opal buyer, cutter and jewellery designer. Opal entrepreneur, I like to say.

Come on in and see my fabulous displays.'

They stepped through the doorway and the noise of voices, clinking glasses, background music and laughter grew louder. But the actual display cases were filled with opal treasure the likes of which Bella had never seen. So many colours! 'This is super impressive,' Bella managed to say as her arm, and the rest of her as well, was dragged into Meesha's eclectic – and judging by the range of dress codes, probably eccentric – crowd.

Wow, this place popped – so vibrant and happy. Again, Bella thought, she could do with some happy. Her new acquaintance oozed satisfaction and pride, along with a bundle of bonhomie that had her introducing Bella everywhere. It felt warm and wonderful, and in a good way – not overwhelming.

Meesha shouted over the music and voices. 'Hey, everyone.
This is Bella, the new doc in town. She's just moved to the Ridge.'
'Hi Bella!' the voices cried. At least, it hadn't been overwhelming
until then. Bella felt like running when all eyes turned her way, but
somehow the crowd's friendly and welcoming faces calmed her. She
took a glass a tall bloke with an easy smile offered her, and a cheese and
celery stick offered by a heavily pregnant red-haired woman a little
older than Bella, who held onto the man's arm with one hand.

She sipped. 'Thanks. Nice wine.' She sipped again. Her gaze travelled around the room, smiling and waving the cheese stick at people
who waved back. Thankfully, none of her patients appeared to be
here. Konrad's clientele tended to towards older miners and young
families; Meesha's friends fell into a different demographic it seemed.

Here, everyone looked to be in for a good time, or a happy business
event, at least.

Except maybe for one huge, brooding guy lurking in the corner.
Her eyes caught on him and held. Black shirt. Black jeans.

Expressionless face. He drew her gaze like an unexpected puzzle.

There wasn't anything discordant in Meesha's beautiful,
colour-coordinated, spectacular jewellery shop – except him.

Meesha tugged on her elbow. 'Come see Desiree and the girls.
They're over in the corner.' She dragged Bella further into the
room. 'Greta would have told you the Lightning Ridge Ladies'
weekly soirees are usually out the back of Desiree's.'

'She did.'

Meesha said. 'They gave up the old petrol drums and wire chairs
and came here this week to help me celebrate, which is great.

You'll love these women. They're a cluey lot, and a crack-up.'

Bella followed Meesha across the room. 'I met a lot of them at my
brother's wedding in Sydney but that was bit of a blur for me.

So I'm meeting them all over again. I already know Greta.'

'She's Desiree's best friend. And the best cook in town.'

Bella chuckled in agreement. 'I have firsthand experience there.'

She remembered Riley saying the chance of exposure to germs from Greta's café was more remote than the town was from Sydney.

Privately, Bella thought that both Mel and Greta had struck gold when the younger woman married Greta's son. Two beautiful women finding each other – a precious thing.

Greta and Mel stepped forward as they approached the group of women, and Greta hugged Bella. 'I'm so glad you came. Mel did well with directions, then.' She nodded at her daughter-in-law in approval.

Greta turned to the white-haired woman from the fuel station and dragged Bella forward. 'Desiree. You remember our new doctor, Bella Grey?'

Desiree stood about a foot shorter than Bella, obvious now she wasn't sitting behind a counter, and looked amused. 'We've met again at the servo. Doc Konrad's sister. How are you?'

Bella smiled. Desiree who knew everything. 'Hello again.'

'Your brother looked happy you moved here.' Desiree brushed a strand of white hair away from her face with a callused hand.

Her stark white hair was tied back with a shoelace. 'All settled in now? And I see you've met Meesha. Reckon you girls will be up to mischief together.'

Meesha laughed and Bella decided there was something unpre-ten-tious and solid about Desiree she hadn't picked up on during the meeting at the servo.

'Yes. Everyone is friendly.' Then she remembered Riley had said Desiree was a single mum whose daughter struggled for a long time to fall pregnant. 'I hear you're enjoying your new grandson, Desiree?' She'd met Desiree's family, too, at Riley and Konrad's wedding – another blur.

The older woman's face transformed, now all softness and joy.

So much so it made Bella appreciate her lovely sister-in-law even more. 'That I have. Thanks to Riley's fertility clinics here. He's a bruiser like his dad.'

The other ladies in the group crowded in, waving their hands like a swarm of flies had arrived. 'Nooo! Don't start her on the golden child – she'll never stop.'

Greta laughed and said, 'Don't you mind them, Desiree. I'll listen anytime.'

'Ha. You just want to talk about your own golden child,' quipped a silver-haired woman in black trousers and western-style shirt.

'And the new baby coming in your house, too,' another said.

Everyone laughed and teased.

So, the news is well and truly out about Mel's pregnancy, Bella thought as she took another hand, warmly held out to her.

'I'm Selena,' the woman in the western-style shirt said.

'And I'm her cousin, Sarina.' This came from a woman in jeans and a lilac silk top. The two women did sort of look alike – both dark-haired, dark-eyed and slim.

Bella shook more hands. As the cousins stepped away to continue teasing Greta and Desiree, Meesha whispered, 'Watch out for the rivalry between those two. One runs the only pub in town and the other manages the bowling club. They both reckon their establishment is the better venue.'

Bella grinned at the picture of the two cousins battling it out.

'I haven't been to either so can't get in trouble.'

'That's what you think,' Desiree declared in no whisper at all, then waved at two new arrivals, both women simply but elegantly dressed, one in muted greys and the other in fawn colours. 'Here's Gerry and Elsa. They run the local arts-and-crafts emporium, with a jewellery section, too. Mostly opal, of course.'

Gerry, in her late fifties, sporting an intricate rope of banded opals around her throat, smiled and waved at Bella. 'We promote artistic expression in others, so if you have a need to learn about painting or needlecraft, come see us.'

She gestured to the tall woman next to her. 'Not sure if you remember my partner, Elsa.' Also quietly elegant, Elsa had brown eyes and an enigmatic smile that made Bella's lips twitch in response.

'Though, she comes and goes once a month for a stand-up comedy routine. A very prestigious comedy club in Melbourne won't let her leave.'

'Which is a joke,' Elsa said, deadpan.

Bella lifted her hand. Amused. 'Lovely to meet you both, again.' She sipped her drink, feeling happy and at ease, despite all the unfamiliar people. 'I'm glad I came.'

'Good.' Meesha said. 'You can't stay cooped up in that surgery all the time.'

'Not healthy,' Desiree agreed sagely. 'Good to see you, and we expect you at the servo next Friday as well.'

'Thank you.' Bella steeled herself to push through with the request that had been on her mind all week. 'And I would like to catch up privately sometime, Desiree, to talk to you about my brother.' And then, even though her throat threatened to close, she pasted a smile and continued. 'William. Not Konrad.'

'Ah.' Desiree's face grew solemn, and she looked away. She seemed to shrink as she said quietly, 'William. That was a bad business. Must be hard.'

Bella lifted her chin. 'It has been. Still is. But I was hoping while I'm here I might be able to shed some light towards the end of William's life.'

Now her eyes stung, and there was obvious empathy from Desiree, and sympathetic silence from the other women, but she swallowed the lump in her throat and went on. 'Did you know William well?'

'Knew him as far as him buying petrol and being polite. He was a gentleman like Konrad. Though he kept to himself. You can come talk to me during the week. Before five if you can get away.

Quietest time at the servo.'

Desiree looked uncomfortable, as if reluctant to talk about this in front of the others. She turned her back on the ladies and stepped away. Bella followed.

Desiree paused for a moment longer, then finally said, 'I seem to remember he was pretty good mates with . . .' She frowned, narrowed her eyes and stared past Bella's shoulder. Bella turned and caught a glimpse of the guy dressed in black in the opposite corner of the room, but when she turned back, Desiree had shut her mouth.

Then Desiree promptly changed the topic. 'Konrad get away all right?'

'Yes, thanks. Yesterday.' What the heck happened there?

Talk about being shut down in the middle of a possible lead – so frustrating.

Before she could ask who Desiree had been about to name, the other woman said, 'Gotta go talk to someone. Hope to see you at the ladies' night next week.' Then she disappeared into the crowd.

Before Bella could ponder Desiree's sudden departure, Meesha was back and handed her another glass. She took the empty one and handed it off to the red-haired pregnant woman who still seemed joined to the twinkling man from earlier.

'This is my older sister, Luci,' Meesha told Bella. 'Just moved to the Ridge as well.'

'Hello, Luci, nice to meet you. I love your belly.' Bella noted that Luci didn't make eye contact with her.

Luci patted her belly. 'The little one is growing beautifully.

There's a story in that. But not for tonight. Nice to meet you, Bella.' She nodded and eased away through the crowd with the glass and her escort in hand. Slow but confident.

'She's gorgeous,' Bella said to Meesha.

Meesha chinked glasses with Bella. 'So good you came.' She nodded at the departing Luci. 'My sister is legally blind, so if she doesn't recognise you by the sound of your voice, you'll need to say who you are when you meet her again.'

Bella had suspected that might be the case. 'Has she always had issues with her sight?'

Meesha sighed. 'Most of her life, since she was seventeen.

Though she can see the occasional dark shape.' She chewed back on something as if she'd changed her mind. 'But I'll let her tell you about that herself if she wants to. It's fabulous to have her move here, though. Especially with the baby coming. I've missed her.'

'What a woman. Babies are challenging, especially for a new mum. Let me know if I can help at all.'

Meesha's face softened. 'Of course. Thank you. I think that would be great.'

Bella lifted her glass in a toast. 'Well, thank you. You've made me feel so welcome.' And tipsy already. She hadn't had a glass of wine in years. But . . . it was nice.

'Makes my day.' Meesha pulled back her hair and shook it, as if feeling the heat and weight of the thick waves that tumbled and rippled past her shoulders. Vibrant red – vivacious like Meesha herself. Bella wondered if she should add a streak of colour in her own blonde hair and brighten the heck up.

Meesha looked thoughtful. 'Mel works with you, yes?'

'And Mel's baby, Teddy. He's a cutie.'

Meesha nodded. 'That's right. We must make sure Luci meets her – they can talk about all things babies and motherhood.'

Sounded like a good idea but Bella had one big question.

'Hope you don't mind me asking, but seeing your sister, it makes me wonder about her baby when the time comes. Lightning Ridge doesn't have a maternity ward, does it?'

Meesha glanced her sister's way and then back at Bella. 'No. But Moree does. We'll go to them for labour.' Meesha's eyes brightened with the obvious progression. 'Luci should go see you, as her GP, anyway. She was asking me if there were any female doctors in town.'

'Of course. I'd love to welcome her as a patient,' Bella said sincerely. Then her gaze caught once more on the shadowed man in the corner, the man Desiree had stared at before she'd left. Meesha kept burbling, and all the while the man's striking dark eyes bored into Bella's until finally she blurted, 'Who is the guy in the corner?'

Meesha glanced that way and laughed. 'Oh. That's TJ. He's the sexiest and possibly the crankiest miner in town.' Loudly, she added, 'Want an introduction.'

'No.' Heck no. Definitely not. Bella felt her cheeks heat at the thought.

But Meesha grabbed her arm and dragged her across the room until they stopped in front of him. Bella stared, unable to look away. Black hair. Surely not black eyes, but very dark brown or blue – hard to tell in the lighting. Black brows. Tanned skin.

He towered over them both and not just physically. The guy had a presence Bella could almost taste. Dark and dangerous and decadent.

Decadent? Not where she'd expected her brain to drift tonight.

Or ever.

Meesha seemed oblivious to the guy's shadowy attraction. 'TJ, this is our new doc, Bella Grey. She's at the OPAL centre.'

TJ muttered, 'Yeah. I heard.'

Cranky had been the right description. Bella might have turned and run if Meesha hadn't let out a peal of laughter and poked him in the chest. 'Be nice.'

Another rumble. 'Since when?'

Even Bella found that amusing, at least until someone in the crowd called out to Meesha, and she tapped Bella's shoulder, saying airily as she dashed away, 'I'll be back.'

Bella would probably have edged away with her if he hadn't held out his hand to shake hers. He rumbled, 'TJ.'

Automatically, she held out her hand, too. 'Bella. Though, really, it's Belle with an "e".' Why had she said that? It was a very strange impulse to clarify, because everyone called her Bella.

When TJ's long callused fingers closed around her much smaller ones, her hand disappearing in his, the room seemed to fade, noise muted, light dimmed, and all she could feel was his cool rough skin and a quiver of awareness that zinged up her arm and then down low in her belly.

His dark eyes hinted that he just might be interested too, but with a blink that changed, his expression wiped clean.

TJ. No name. Bare initials. Dressed in black. Watching the world from the shadows.

He still had her hand though, gripping it strongly as he searched her face.

Bella eased his heated palm free of hers. 'TJ.' She inclined her head and stepped back, reassuming her professional confidence.

'So.' She gestured at his black clothes. 'You're a minimalist?'

He laughed. A short, sharp bark. 'Yeah. That's me. Well, Tinkerbell, you're nothing like I expected.'

She blinked.

His smile disappeared as if it had never existed. He straightened, towering over her even more. She had the strange impression she'd annoyed him. Or maybe he'd annoyed himself. Then TJ gave her an ironic salute, two fingers touching his pierced eyebrow, spun on his booted heel and walked away.

A big man, moving fast like an assassin on the hunt, and the rowdy crowd instinctively parted and closed behind him like Moses and the Red Sea so he could get to the door. A strange image, given they were in the western desert, and nowhere near the ocean.

But he'd disappeared. Poof.

Tinkerbell? Her skin iced over. She whispered, 'William?'

The only person to ever call her Tinkerbell had been her twin.

Had TJ known William, then? Had he been close enough to William to have him talk about her? Or had it been just a random play on her name?

But he'd said she was nothing like he expected – so somebody had mentioned her to him before. Described her. Called her Tinkerbell.

There was only one answer to that: William.

Bella pushed through the crowd after TJ. When she finally made it outside – which took far more time than it had for that freakin' black-clad Moses – the street was empty. He'd gone. Disappeared.

But in the distance, she thought she could hear the muted sound of a motorbike . . . fading fast.

CHAPTER FIVE

TJ

Hell in a mine-basket. William's sister was here, and lust for her had slammed through him without warning. His worst nightmare.

Since TJ hadn't taken the time to unstrap his helmet when he climbed on the back of his Harley, his thoughts ground into him like the wind ground into his scalp. He pushed the speed limit until he hit the highway. He would double back via the old road after he'd ridden some fury out of himself. Why had he called her Tinkerbell out loud? He'd exposed his knowledge of her brother after only two minutes, breaking his personal vow to block out William's loss because it hurt too damn much.

At least his aviator sunglasses kept the bugs from splattering his eyes as the sun sank west in blood-red derision. He was an idiot.

William. TJ hadn't thought about him in . . . well, not very long. The guy was like a rusty windmill in TJ's mind. Noisy when the wind blew. Still creaking when it didn't.

Another bug smacked his cheek like a thrown rock, but he refused to wince. Hell. He'd tried his best not to think about William since his death, but his friend intruded on his thoughts at the oddest times. Like down a mine when he'd just seen a glimmer in the sandstone wall. Or late at night when a song tangled his soul. Or on the bike when he rode a lonely stretch of road.

In this life, especially here in the Ridge, TJ didn't have friends.

He didn't do mates – not since his time in the Tactical Response team, and that last horrific disaster when he'd lost Ree.

Then bloody William's death had almost broken TJ. When they'd met, first glance, the bloke had had a weak and lost vibe – not sure what that had been all about, because it wasn't true, or so TJ eventually realised. About the same time as he decided he wasn't looking for friends, he'd been strangely amused when William had accidentally exposed a quiet strength that struck a chord. They'd played too many games of pool with an escalating rivalry, and the guy's determination, his sheer stubbornness to not to lose, as well as his subtle black humour, had cut right through TJ's armour and made him smile, shake his head, and relent to giving the bloke the time of day. And worse – let him in.

Yes. William had been a real friend when TJ hadn't known he needed one. Which hurt even more, because TJ had let William down.

TJ, who thought he had his fingers on the pulse of the Ridge – knew the strikes, knew the best place to sell colour, thought he knew the ratters who did the worst – hadn't known how close young William had been to the edge. Hadn't picked up on the danger in time.

Then, despite weeks of fruitless searching, he hadn't even been able to locate his mate's body.

For that, TJ had never forgiven himself.

Now William's twin was in town. Shining with the same oddball, clever light that had defined her brother.

TJ wanted no part of it. No part of her. No part of whatever it was that caught at him like barbed wire and hung on, drawing blood.

William's Tinkerbell. Beautiful. Broken. Lost.

Even he could see that.

He didn't know why seeing her tonight had hit him so hard, but the agony etched in her eyes had tattooed on his soul. He could see her pain like indelible ink on his skin. Pain that was his fault, because he hadn't prevented William's death when he should have.

He hated that.

Hated the mark it left on William's sister.

Hated himself.

Beautiful Belle, who would want to talk about her brother.

Like her older brother had wanted to talk about him, too – but TJ hadn't connected with Konrad.

The inconsistencies were not his story to share. It was William who'd claimed to have depression and a drinking problem, although had TJ never once smelled alcohol on him. William who'd mumbled a strange request to look out for his family that TJ hadn't taken seriously at the time. William who'd disappeared and left a note for TJ to find.

No. He wouldn't break Tinkerbell's heart with his doubts and suspicions. Or tell her he was just as destroyed by William's decision to end his life. That was all he could give his departed friend now – no extra pain for his family.

Hell, TJ had his own secrets. A whole life full of secrets starting from when he'd been the only survivor in his mother's car when he'd been seven years old. Secrets from the foster homes. Secrets from when he'd pulled himself out of bad choices.

Secrets from his stellar career in the police force, and when he'd left. Secrets from Ree.

Women wanted to talk about secrets.

That was why he wouldn't have them in his life. But then, he didn't have anyone in his camp longer than needed.

Except William, who had come and gone regardless of what TJ said, like a willy-wagtail, hopping in and out, flitting about and blathering in TJ's face, ignoring the cold silences until TJ gave up and accepted that William would come when he wanted.

Hell, TJ thought. He wasn't a drinker, but he needed a drink.

CHAPTER SIX

MEESHA

Behind the glittering opal store, and the practical workshop where Meesha made her jewellery, in the bright, colourful kitchen of the first of her adjoining duplexes, everything was slowly being sorted after the party. Luci had finally finished repacking the cutlery and Bella and Meesha were washing up the plates and the glasses.

Luci turned her head in their direction. 'I've done my bit. This blind girl's going to bed.' She yawned. 'You girls need to finish up.

Night, Meesh. Night, Bella.'

Meesha smiled at her sister's comment. Embracing the sarcasm and irony of it, Luci had been calling herself 'this blind girl' since listening to a vision-impaired young woman in the UK on YouTube who used the same term for herself. It was fine for Luci, but Meesha would kneecap anybody else who called her sister that.

'Thanks for the help, Luci love. Sleep well.'

'Night Luci,' Bella called.

Luci disappeared through the doorway, heading to the duplex next door. She already knew every inch of the shop, the workroom and the two duplexes by now, and she moved calmly through them,

without needing Pluto or her white cane. Though, Meesha had appreciated that Eric had been there for Luci tonight in the crowd.

Meesha may have built her business in Lightning Ridge from scratch at thirty, but she still idolised her older sibling, as she always had.

'She's lovely,' Bella said as the door between the duplex houses shut behind Luci.

'Yes.' Meesha looked at her new friend. Blonde, beautiful, yet fragile in a way, her sad eyes a deep-sea blue. 'I know. She's only been here a week, and already found a part-time job on the phone that starts next month. I swear, everyone who meets her loves her. My mate, Eric, he's helping her turn next door into a baby-friendly home.'

'Eric. Tall guy, cute smile, hovering around Luci at the party?'

'Yeah, one of the local miners. But a carpenter as well. I'm betting he's already keen on her, but I reckon Luci just needs him as a friend right now. Again, her story to tell.'

'Wow. A move to the Ridge. And soon to be a single mum.

That's really taking the bull by the horns.' Bella turned back to the dishes.

Meesha shook her head fondly. 'That's Luci. When she lost her sight completely, she had to learn so many things all over again without visual clues. Cooking, make-up, choosing clothes.' Meesha shook her head again. 'I spent hours with her trying to be her eyes while she mastered a task by repetition. Made me learn what it meant to dig in. She'd have me try stuff with a blindfold and it was crazy hard. And frustrating.' Luci's skills with her other senses had always fascinated Meesha. Not that they were superpowers, just that Luci trained herself to use them to the max.

'I imagine it would be,' Bella said slowly. 'Even navigating everyday steps like pouring a cup of tea would be a learning curve.'

Abso-freakin-lutely. Bella got it, then – Meesha guessed a doctor would.

Bella put down the last dried serving dish and smiled. 'So how will you both manage with the new baby?'

Meesha shrugged. 'Won't lie, it was a shock when I found out Luci was pregnant. Our parents died a couple of years ago in a storm while sailing . . . and then our grandad passed. So it's just us.'

'I'm so sorry, Meesh.'

'Yeah, it was tough, but Grandad had health issues, and our parents were doing what they loved. That's what I keep telling myself, anyway. Without Mum, and with Luci pregnant now, we realised we know nothing about babies.'

She waved her hand at the door. 'Though, knowing Luci, she will manage beautifully, eventually. She's arranged through the Royal Society for the Blind to have a mothercraft nurse from Moree work with her after the baby is born. Nurse Humphries'

son is vision impaired, so she has the experience, and will be here with Luci for the first fortnight post-birth.' Meesha pointed to the door. 'Right there.'

Bella's mouth gaped. 'Now that's a fabulous idea.' She waved the tea towel.

'Yep.' Meesha nodded, 'She'll do the job Luci's ex should have been doing, and probably do it better, but . . .' She held her hand up. 'I'm not allowed to vent about him.'

Bella raised her brows, obviously curious but not asking questions, and Meesha smiled and shook her head. 'Matilda, Nurse Humphries, moves in as soon as Luci leaves hospital with baby.

She'll be available night and day from the beginning. That way Luci can learn slowly and have help with breastfeeding and bathing baby for the first two weeks. Or more if needed.'

'And Luci won't be the only one learning new skills,' Bella said. 'You'll be learning too?'

'I know.' Meesha felt delight course through her. 'I am going to have a baby niece or nephew sometime in the next two months. *Squeee!*'

Bella laughed. Flicked her with the tea towel. 'You're clucky?'

'God, no.' Meesha shuddered. 'I'll just agree with my sister's brilliance for thinking of a mothercraft nurse. We're both out of our depth here.'

'So, no plans of Luci's partner helping at all in the future?'

'They broke up. He wants to be kept in the loop, apparently, but he's not coming back.'

'More fool him,' scoffed Eric, arriving in the kitchen with the last of the heavy boxes from the party. He slid two cartons of beer onto the end of the kitchen table.

'Thanks, Eric. For everything tonight. And you were great with Luci, too, especially when she couldn't have Pluto in that crush,' Meesha said.

'Happy to help,' Eric said cheerfully, but his eyes were on the door to the second duplex. 'Has she gone?'

'Yep, to bed.'

Eric's face dropped. 'Then I'm off too. That's the last of the boxes.' He waved and left.

Meesha suspected her best mate had fallen hard for her sister. Men usually did. Luci was gorgeous. A petite, curvy red-head with lustrous hair tumbling around her shoulders, and a determined resilience that seemed to bring out a sense of protectiveness in men.

Meesha shrugged philosophically. Eric, a born and bred local opal miner, was tough when needed. He'd become a good friend to Meesha, and she knew he was loyal. She had her own curvy figure and red hair that often drew men in, but she'd never had any romantic interest in Eric. Or any man, lately. Eric was a great mate, though – platonic and cheerful. Just what she'd needed when she'd first moved to the Ridge.

'Thanks so much with your help cleaning up,' Meesha said to Bella. Eric was lovely, but a female friend like Bella – someone self-sufficient and smart – might be exactly what she needed in her life now. Her delight remained. 'Very cool of you.'

Bella smiled and shrugged. 'I had a great night. It's a long time since I've let my hair down. Your party was awesome.'

'Yup. I think it went well.' The celebration of The Iridescent Opal had been an enormous success. 'I even gained two more suppliers at the party through word of mouth. Good thing, too – I need more stones coming in.' TJ had said he'd follow up on her supply issues and ask around as well.

The two women washed and stacked the glasses back into boxes as the clock ticked towards midnight.

'It's going to be good to have you in town, Bella.' Meesha almost hugged Bella. She hadn't realised how isolated she'd been in her drive to make the jewellery store a success, but now with Luci and Bella here, she felt less lonely.

Bella hung the tea towel up on the rail by the sink. 'Looked like you had a lot of friends at the shop tonight.'

Meesha knew she did. But they were acquaintances. Not friends. Her fault – she'd been so freakin' busy. 'I have people in my life. Wonderful people. You know what I mean. But not a close friend. Not to get creepy here, but I feel I can talk to you.'

They looked at each other and grinned. Bella nodded. 'Me too.'

'Good.' Meesha ducked her head, laughing. 'Who knows? We might end up besties.' She almost cringed at herself; the alcohol was letting her say things she normally wouldn't.

Hugging thoughts rose again, and Meesha pushed them down.

She might just be a little tipsy but even she could see Bella wasn't ready for that kind of PDA from a woman she'd just met. 'Before Luci moved here, I didn't have women my age to talk to just for the fun of it. So maybe we could message each other sometimes, if we're both too busy to meet up.'

Bella tilted her face to the side. 'You're fun. Smart. I cannot believe you need friends in town.'

'There's Eric. He's my best mate. But he's a man. And except for the Lightning Ridge Ladies, I guess I've been too busy to work at it.'

'Sometimes women are easier.'

Too true. 'The ladies always welcome me, even if I can't make it to every Friday night. And it was so good of them to move the party here tonight. They're a supportive group.'

Bella glanced at the clock. 'Greta says that, too.'

Meesha watched her, mentally crossing her fingers. 'So, we'll see you at Desiree's next week?'

Bella looked back. 'Behind the servo? Sure. Riley also said I should go. Be better if I see you and Luci there, though.'

With bells on. 'Absolutely. Most of the ladies are a bit older than us but it's a hoot. And Desiree knows everything in town.

I swear the woman has more sources than ASIO if you want town insights.'

Meesha watched the flare in Bella's eyes and smiled to herself. She wasn't surprised when Bella murmured, 'I thought she might. Next Friday, then. Maybe you could drop by and pick me up?'

'I can do that.'

'Good.' Bella pinned her with an unexpectedly determined look. 'But you have to tell me everything about that guy, TJ.' Her voice lowered. 'I think he knew my brother William.'

Meesha felt her excellent mood slide just a little. They'd briefly touched on Bella's loss of her twin earlier in the evening and had both shied away from dwelling on the topic, but it seemed TJ had opened that wound again. 'Honestly, I don't know much about TJ apart from the fact he keeps to himself. And works hard at his mine. He's one of my main opal suppliers.'

It seemed that wasn't good enough for Bella. 'You must know something. Where does he live? What does TJ stand for?'

Meesha closed the lid of the last box of glasses. 'No idea on the initials. And as for his camp? I know where it is but I've never been there. Heard it's hard to find, but he left me directions in case I needed more stones.'

Bella nodded, so Meesha went on. Safer than not going on with this suddenly determined Bella. The thought made her smile. She liked strong characters.

'He's isolated. I hear his camp is behind a high wall. Someone broke in once and now it's a fortress.' She shook her head. 'He probably wouldn't even open his gate if you did go.'

There was that steely look again – that don't-mess-with-me expression Bella had hidden all night. The one that said, *I'm just gonna keep at you until you give in.* A bit like Luci when she wanted something badly.

Meesha grinned despite herself at the idea of Bella running up against TJ. Him the silent, brick wall type, and Bella, she now suspected, a willowy battering ram when she had her heart set on something.

She shrugged. Bella was a grown woman – what she did with the information Meesha gave her was her call. 'It's up Three Mile Road and down into the scrub. I'd have to give you a map.'

She felt around under the kitchen bench for a pad and paper she knew was hidden there. 'I'll write the directions down. They don't have house numbers or street signs up there. I could give you his phone number instead?'

Meesha glanced up at Bella. Her new friend shook her head.

'No. I don't want him to know I'm coming.'

There was a flat stare on Bella's lovely face and Meesha smiled to herself. If anyone could breach TJ's lair, she'd bet her priciest black opal on Bella.

CHAPTER SEVEN

BELLA

Bella spent the dark hours after the party in bed, tossing and turning at the glimmer of hope TJ would know more about William's last days. Something Konrad had missed, maybe?

TJ must have secrets – the guy had run from her!

Bless the weekend for no work, because suddenly she had time to chase this lead before Monday. She'd find him today. Something inside her said he had knowledge, if not all the answers. At this point, she'd take anything.

Following Meesha's map, Bella drove out at a.m. on Saturday morning, after stopping for bribes. Surely miners would be up early? And she'd get answers before she left.

Watch out, TJ, because here comes the school debate champion with a degree in psychology.

Not that she'd ever practised as a psychologist, but still, she knew how to glean information from reluctant sources.

Apparently, according to Meesha, TJ didn't like conversation.

Or visitors. Or people. Well, that just meant she'd have privacy to interrogate him, even if it was like drilling those precious black opals out of a mine in the dark.

Bella glanced at the page of written instructions on her lap.

No street signs up where the mine leases were. How funny.

Bless Lightning Ridge. There were lots of colourful painted car doors propped up at the edge of the road which led you to tourist sights – blue ones, yellow ones, red ones, but no helpful black ones that did a follow-the-doors trail to TJ's camp, sadly.

Bella's car rumbled down Three Mile Road – at least, it did if she was where the map indicated she should be by now. It was hard to tell. But so far, so good.

Turn left at the upended toilet bowl painted red and bump over two deep ruts. Tick.

Turn right at the white cross made out of cow horns and down another track. Tick.

Scattered tin sheds, old caravans, and the occasional container house on each side of the road. The distance between the broken clutter and equipment changed as Bella drove on, past some camps that lay exposed and others hidden by tall fences.

Turn right at the barbed-wire-wrapped flagpole with a skull and crossbones flying. Tick.

Ah, yes – there stood a wooden replica of a gun leaning against a pole. Final tick.

A wooden gun to mark TJ's driveway? So childish.

Eventually the long, winding two-rut track ran out and she parked beside black Colourbond gates and climbed out of her car. She pushed the heat-sticky hair off her forehead. The day was warming up already and she wouldn't mind some shade. But none of that where she stood.

In front of her loomed a two-metre wall of defence. Hmm.

Except for the seam where they opened, the gates were faceless, with no electronic or battery announcement pathway. No 'knock', 'press bell' or 'talk' instructions to help, either.

She'd have to shout over the top of the gates and hope he could hear her. All righty then.

The gates matched the fence and – surprise, surprise – what little she could see over the barrier was of a taller black dwelling, topped with solar panels.

This whole place didn't make her think *happy, happy, joy, joy*.

But the barrier did make her even more determined. She stepped up to the gate and called, 'Hello. You in there? TJ?'

No answer.

After ten minutes of one-minute-spaced repetitions and some banging on the gate – she'd grown up with brothers and knew how to be annoying and persistent – the sound of someone swearing on the other side of the gate cut through the forty-five-second silence.

She clearly heard him rumble, 'I'm going to kill you.'

Uh oh. She called over the fence again. 'Umm. I brought breakfast.'

'Don't want it. Leave.'

She narrowed her eyes. For goodness' sake. As if she'd done all of this only to leave now. 'Don't be a two-year-old,' she called out.

The gate jerked open and TJ, in nothing but black boxers that declared he was absolutely not a two-year-old, blew out an enormous, pained sigh. She almost keeled over from the smell of alcohol. And at the sight of his abs. And the front of an eagle tattooed across his chest.

Her heart went *boom* but it wasn't with fright. She had to be crazy but she still had to jam her jaw shut to stop her mouth falling open – and maybe losing some drool.

She was a doctor, for pity's sake, used to seeing males of all sorts, so why couldn't she be clinical with this specimen? Why couldn't she control her response? Who reacted like this to a cranky, hungover grouch?

'You. Are. So . . .' TJ spat. 'Like him.'

Her heart flipped and a gust of relief danced through her chest like a whirly wind, wiping away any scandalous thoughts. She'd been right. He'd known him well. Her William.

Finally, proof.

Her shoulders sagged. 'Thank you. And we'll talk about that in a minute.'

He threw his hands up in the air, which, she had to admit, made him look incredibly tall. Huge, actually. Like an angry – mostly naked – grizzly bear dragged out of hibernation.

TJ turned his back on her. *Oh my stars, his back.* Thickly muscled, tanned and tattooed with wings – his magnificent body sandwiched between the same enormous eagle, which rippled ink feathers as he walked away.

She needed to take a couple of deep breaths. More than a few.

But he did leave the gate open, so that was a win.

Bella picked up the silver thermal bag she'd carried from Greta's café in town – her bribes. She needed to eat soon, too, because her belly was somersaulting. A bucket full of crickets. Seriously jumping.

Just hunger. And anxiety about William. That was it.

The breakfast rolls had been teasing her nose for fifteen minutes now. The coffee she'd made and poured into the two Yeti coffee mugs she'd brought from home would still be hot.

She'd laughed when she made his coffee in her little kitchen.

Wondering how he'd want it. 'Black,' she had actually said out loud to the no one sharing her space. Definitely, without any hesitation. His favourite colour. Of course he'd drink it black.

She wasn't laughing now. Maybe coming here alone wasn't such a great idea.

Still, she stepped through the open gates, expecting to find the clutter and mess of the camps she'd passed on the way here.

Instead, she stared at . . . the epitome of order, regulation and discipline.

Except for a pale mound of freshly excavated opal dirt beside one of the shafts in the ground, the four-sided yard contained within the corrugated aluminium boundary fence appeared free of debris. Maybe everything was stored inside the one small black garden shed, shut and latched, or the roller-doored double garage.

Or under the long work bench in the yard.

Two concrete-rimmed circles – mine shafts – lay in the corner of the block, both covered with wire lids, one with a gantry and rigging above it and another with the ends of a ladder poking through the grate. No tools. No mess. No fuel tins to be seen, though Bella did spot an engine covered by a tidy square box beside the gantry. The long sorting table held neat piles of dirt.

Tall, empty painter's buckets sat under that bench like soldiers in a line. She was getting the idea.

No rubbish. Nothing out of place. Apart from the mine shafts, the yard was immaculate – if dirt could be immaculate. Seems it could be. *Control freak, much?*

TJ wasn't in sight. He'd already returned to the biggest shed in the yard – hopefully not back to bed.

On closer inspection, this second structure wasn't a shed but a prefabricated functional cottage with two windows on either side of the door. A door through which TJ had disappeared.

Guess that meant she had to go in, too. She doubted he was going to politely invite her inside. He would probably be quite happy if she stood in the yard with her indecision for the rest of the day.

Well, she hadn't expected to sit outside on a swing seat eating fairy floss. Lifting her chin, she reached out to pull open the screen door and climbed the two steps into the cottage.

TJ had thrown himself into a chair at the black chrome and glass kitchen table and sat slumped with his chin on his chest. Eyes closed. Breathing heavily.

His eagle-inked chest, bulging biceps and corded forearms were all still gloriously bare and overwhelmingly male. Interestingly, on closer inspection, his long fingers did appear to be gripping the table. Not asleep after all.

Her gaze flicked away.

From where she stood, she could see the cottage consisted of a bathroom, a bedroom, and a tiny kitchen, dining and lounge area.

Not much more than a three-car garage in size. Immaculate, except for the tousled bed she could see through the open door and something large – maybe piled boxes? – under a tarpaulin in the corner of the lounge. Shoved up against a wall, the pile looked untidily uneven and took up a quarter of the room – an eyesore that was completely out of place for this man.

Her gaze flitted back to the bed. Black sheets. Were they silk?

Nah, of course not. But she'd probably never look at black sheets the same after seeing them in TJ's house. Imagining TJ climbing out of them . . . imagining herself climbing in.

Whoa. She hadn't thought of bedroom antics in nearly three years. Absolutely not the time, not when this man might have information about William.

William.

She crashed back to earth.

Bella put the silver carry bag on the dining table without speaking and unzipped it. Pulled out the two Yeti mugs, set one in front of him, and lifted out two of Greta's bacon and egg rolls wrapped in foil. Placed them beside his mug. Rounding the table, she pulled out the chair opposite him and sat down.

The silence continued, so she lifted her own mug and sipped.

The coffee was still tongue-scalding hot, so she put it down and removed the lid to allow it some cooling time.

When TJ still didn't say anything – though he did lift his lids, his gaze burning as hot as the coffee – she tried for an airy, 'Maybe we should eat first.'

'Why?' he growled, glaring at her from under his black brows.

'So, I don't eat you?'

Oh boy. Anger and innuendo – she could see he still hoped she would run. Not happening. 'They say that's very nice, but I don't know you well enough.'

He closed his eyes, dropping his chin back on his chest. The incredible chest that was still bare, still as imposing as heck, and which began to expand until she thought it would explode.

The eagle grew bigger. Held. And held. Was he counting to ten?

He blew out the bated breath.

This time, thankfully, not in her direction.

TJ examined her. Eyes hooded like the bird on his chest, he studied her from head to table height. The same expression she'd last seen at Meesha's party crossed his features. The appraisal that spoke plainly of a heated interest but that also insisted he had enough self-control not to act on it.

Instead, he said, 'What do you want?' His voice came out like the back of a shovel over gravel. Grinding. Grating. Goading.

She sipped her coffee again, then put the mug down. 'Well, we both know what I want.' She peeled open her breakfast roll.

Steam and an enticing bacon aroma puffed out, the aluminium foil making little ticks of sound as she unfolded it. She'd thought the rolls would be tepid by now, but nope, they were still fresh and warm. Aluminium foil was way underrated.

Before she took a bite, she said quietly, 'I want to know about William.' Then she put the roll to her mouth, tore off a chunk and chewed.

TJ removed the lid from his own mug and took a sip. He shuddered violently, then sighed. Took another sip. The reaction more of a twitch this time. Took another sip and slumped as if with relief.

'Of course you do.' His voice was quiet. Resigned. Tinged with bitterness. 'You may as well go. Because, no, I'm not talking about your brother.'

Bella sat back. She'd known it wouldn't be easy, but the stark refusal stumped her for a moment. But then, it was acknowledgement that he knew *something*. That William had shared stuff with this man. She would take anything. She didn't care how small the morsel. 'So . . . he told you things.'

TJ was the first lead she'd had to her brother's last days, and she needed that information more than the breath in her lungs.

She swallowed the roll that now wanted to stick in her throat.

'And why won't you tell me?'

She got the flat five-hundred-yard stare. Close up, his eyes were so dark, his face so hard, he could have been dug from the earth outside. Or jackhammered out. 'I refuse.'

She blinked. 'You can't refuse. I'm here. I'm his twin.'

'So?' He looked at her coolly. 'Uninvited. Unwanted. Unimpressive.'

She flinched.

He sneered. 'You going to cry?' Harsh. Daring her to be weak.

Goading her again, as if he could make her run away and leave him alone. And that just made her more determined to stay. He had no idea what she was like once she was riled. And she *was* riled.

Oh yeah, tough guy. That isn't going to happen. Meet me – tougher woman.

'No.' Bella blinked back the sting in her eyes, absolutely no way would she ever weep in front of this man. 'And you don't know me or what I'm capable of.' She shrugged, pretending to be non chalant. 'I'm going to keep coming back, uninvited, unwanted' – she did not include the unimpressive – 'and I'm going to keep on asking until you spill what you know.'

He raised one brow. 'I'll borrow a guard dog. The dog will eat you.' He raised his hand and made biting movements with it.

'Chomp. Chomp. Chomp.'

Bella rolled her eyes. Unphased. 'Were you my brother's friend?'

She watched the battle rage behind those dark eyes. The fact he knew things. The fact he wanted to lie. The fact he didn't want to engage in any conversation with her, and she didn't think it was only because he was hungover. So why not?

'Sometimes,' he said finally, reluctant and grim.

Bella hadn't thought he would answer at all, and a flare of hope ignited, even if it was only a tiny flame. 'What does that mean?'

TJ looked away – to the window and the light outside. 'It means a real friend would have known he was desperate, and I didn't.' He shrugged, face still expressionless. 'So, sometimes I was his friend.

And when it counted, I wasn't.'

He stood up, towering over her even more than usual because she was seated. 'Now you can go.'

He drained the mug of the scalding coffee and put it on the table in front of her. 'Take that. Take yours. Don't come back.'

She rose from her own seat and lifted her chin. 'I'll be back.'

'No. You won't.'

He leaned towards her, but she darn well refused to cower.

'Yes, I will.' She jutted her chin. 'I'll be back tomorrow.'

Silence. Finally, he shrugged again. 'I won't open the gate.'

She smiled and it wasn't a friendly smile. 'I'll knock. And call.

Then come back next Saturday and next Sunday as well.' She held the smile. 'And the following Saturday and the following Sunday.

Until you tell me what I want to know.'

He didn't say anything, though she could feel his dark glare burning into her face as he read her intentions.

TJ turned his back on her, stormed into his room and shut the door.

She stared at the closed door. Blinked. What in the universe was she supposed to do now? She looked around the room again.

He hadn't touched his bacon and egg rolls. She picked them up and carried them over to the fridge. Put them inside to stay fresh.

Took another bite of her own. Forced herself to chew, even though her appetite had fled. And as she swallowed – difficult, given the lump in her throat – she thought about her options.

Bella searched the kitchen until she found a piece of paper and a pen. She wrote down her name, her phone number, the surgery's phone number and a short note. *If you think of anything, phone or come find me. Otherwise, I'll see you tomorrow. B.*

She picked up the coffee mugs and, taking one last searching look around the tiny black house, somehow diminished without its owner, she left.

CHAPTER EIGHT

TJ

The next morning TJ made sure he was working when Bella arrived. He'd covered himself up with a shirt, jeans and boots, and had already been down the mine and sent two new buckets up.

He couldn't handle the yelling if he locked her out, and he certainly didn't want her inside his house again. She'd worn a floral perfume yesterday, something sweet and light and lingering, and it had driven him mad all day. He'd almost doused the room with fly spray to drown it out but in the end he just . . . hadn't.

When TJ had stood on the other side of his bedroom door yesterday, he'd heard her moving around. Had wondered what was she doing in there, leaning his shoulders against the door and pushing the back of his head into the wood, his eyes shut, his head pounding. 'Damn it, William, you didn't tell me she was part terrier,' he'd muttered. And not a female terrier. She had balls, he'd give her that. He'd tried to intimidate her with his size – of course, that would have been more effective without the stupid hangover – but she'd had none of it anyway.

She was the kind of woman who took no prisoners when she was looking for weakness. Or answers.

He didn't know her, but that much he did know.

She'd looked so slight yet fierce, like a belligerent bird.

A blonde, blue-eyed, leggy bellbird haunting the bush with its echoing cry. Haunting him. Belle Bird. Yep, that was her.

He'd shifted to the window when he heard her leave, watching her car back away from the gate and turn. A Range Rover Sport.

Like Konrad's car, only gold. A gold car for the princess. He'd almost scoffed out loud.

So, this morning, he made sure he was sorting opal dirt at the bench in the yard when the gate opened. He'd left it ajar, meaning he didn't have to greet her when she arrived.

He'd had no doubt she'd turn up. Had guessed that much about her. It tallied with the tales he'd been told by William. How she was the one who'd always got her twin into trouble as children. Even dressing up as William, hiding her long hair under a hat, to pull pranks around the house as if she was him. But mostly, William had called her smart as a whip – medical degree, psychology degree.

Annoyance degree, too, probably.

Anyone who could get through medical school, not to mention survive the death of their twin, had determination. Tenacity.

Stubbornness.

TJ expected all of it in spades. But it didn't matter. He would not lose his walls.

Today she wore skintight jeans and a stare-worthy T-shirt he had to drag his eyes away from. Of course she carried the silver bag of bribes, the same as yesterday, and he mocked himself when his belly growled.

'Morning, TJ.' As if she were a tea lady who worked for him, doing her regular morning delivery.

She strolled over to his sorting table and put the silver bag on top of his dirt. Unzipped and pulled out two mugs. Put one close to her and one near to him. He tried not to sniff the aroma.

Out came two more bacon and egg rolls for him. They'd been excellent yesterday – he'd wolfed them down after she left. Then, casual as you please, she reached under the sorting table and pulled out one of the empty buckets, which she upended and sat on.

Saying she was staying – with her butt.

He took the coffee mug and removed the lid. 'Thanks. But I don't need you to feed me.'

She shrugged. 'I can afford it. Since I want something from you, it's the least I can do.'

She wanted something he wasn't going to give. He didn't look at her, just kept sorting his haul. He flicked anything promising, anything with a hint of colour, into a separate pile from the others, to take more time poring over later. Didn't want to miss anything valuable in the wash. 'Hmm. Won't do you any good. I'm not talking.'

She took the lid from her own mug. 'You will. Eventually.

I believe I mentioned yesterday I've got time and patience.'

He sipped. The coffee was perfect. Again. 'You'll need a lot of both.'

'Marking time is all I've done since William left that note.

Konrad showed it to me.'

TJ winced. That note. The note TJ had found taped to his gate when he'd come back from town the night William disappeared.

With Konrad's name on it. The secret note only TJ and William's family knew about. A message, telling them all William had taken his life.

When you read this, I'll be gone, and you'll never find my body.

William gone. Never seen again. And they hadn't found his body.

TJ had no idea why he'd been the recipient of the tragic thing.

He especially did not want to talk about the horror he'd felt when he found that note. Lifting the mug to his eye level, he changed the topic. 'You make this or buy it?'

'Made it. The mugs are mine. I hate cold coffee.'

Hell yes. He sipped again. 'Me too.'

She pounced on that. He'd known she would as soon as the words left his mouth. Stupid, dumb comment. Of course it would encourage her.

'Something in common already. Wow. Nice.'

He turned his head. Kept his face hard as he eyeballed her. 'We have nothing in common.'

There was no way TJ could have anything in common with this fine upstanding young woman. Beautiful, blue-eyed Belle. No world anywhere where she was his. Ever.

'We both cared about William,' she said and sipped her coffee.

'That's another thing.'

'No.' He needed to close off those thoughts. He didn't care.

And he didn't want her to think he did. 'I said I knew him. We talked. Didn't say I cared.'

He turned his head so she couldn't see his face and closed his eyes. He couldn't listen to this. Couldn't sit here with William's sister and their matching coffee mugs and their polite bickering.

He drank the steaming coffee as fast as he could, ignoring the burning of his mouth, and put the cup down empty.

When she looked away to follow a passing bird's flight, he scooped up the rolls and shoved them inside his shirt. If he didn't, she'd probably go inside his house and put them in the fridge like yesterday, leaving more perfume in her wake. 'Thanks for breakfast.' Then he glared at her, putting all the nasty he could into the words and the look. 'Don't come back.'

He heard her suck in a breath just before he strode across the yard to his mine, shoved the safety lid off it and swung over the hole and down the ladder.

The heated silver foil sat warm against his chest. He hadn't even known he was cold. *Don't come back.*

She had to understand that solitude was the only acquaintance he could risk having in his life. Anyone he'd come close to had died. He brought bad luck to everyone around him and he refused to direct his Grim Reaper abilities in her direction.

He'd already jinxed her brother.

He couldn't be anybody's friend, or their family. The price was too heavy. A price he wouldn't pay. She couldn't force him to be a part of her world, and he knew well and good that he had to stay away from

Belle Grey before he infected her with his karma like he'd infected her brother.

Ree, the only woman he'd ever loved, apart from the vague memories of his mother as a kid, had died. And she'd had big brass ones like Belle, too. He should have saved Ree. Taken her bullet.

Taken all the bullets for his team. But he hadn't been quick enough.

His head disappeared below the level of the yard, and he resisted the urge to check the expression on Belle's face as the circular sandstone wall surrounded him. She wouldn't be happy.

Nor would she give up. Yet.

But she'd see eventually. She'd be working again by tomorrow.

So, he had a week to hopefully figure out a better way to stop her coming before the weekend came around again.

Climbing further down the ladder into the shaft, stillness surrounded him. Isolated him. When he made it to the sandstone floor, he stepped off the ladder but kept gripping it with one hand.

Closing his eyes, suddenly he was back in the past. With William.

TJ was driving home from town earlier than planned – the pub had been too packed – still amused by the one close game of billiards he and William had played. William had pretended to sulk because he'd been beaten by TJ again, both of them now keen for a slow beer in the quiet of TJ's camp. After, William would most likely swag it on the floor for the night.

Except the gate to TJ's yard sat ajar, a strange tray-back ute parked outside. William leaned forward in the passenger seat of TJ's F-and they glanced at each other before TJ turned off the ignition and doused the lights.

'Ratters.' The mongrels would be down in his mine gouging out his new promising seam. Grabbing as much colour as fast as they could. TJ's anger surged like a cold wash though his system.

'Got your back,' William said. 'Don't kill anyone.' TJ appreciated it and felt the rapport for real. Ratters weren't worth going to prison for, but he would still make sure they'd be sorry.

'Won't. Might just wish they died, though.' His voice was low and icy as he rolled his truck to the side. He reached under the seat and removed a baseball bat, giving the second he kept for real emergencies to William. Switched off the auto interior glow before he opened the door, exiting without closing it. Somehow William was already out and by his side. Like he'd done this before but with discipline. The armed forces? Police?

There were three ratters and they never had a chance. TJ took out the useless lookout first – two fast swings, the wrist of the hand holding the gun the first fractured casualty, then both knees, and the man was down, screaming. TJ emptied the bullets onto the dirt and pocketed the weapon.

William ghosted to the mine, then whispered loudly down the shaft, 'Someone's coming.' He stood in the shadows to one side of the shaft as TJ stood on the other. They let the ratters scamper up and out, and then broke more bones. One ratter they recognised, Bane, and they left him still capable of driving. The other two they picked up and threw in the back of the ramshackle ute where they moaned noisily.

Afterwards, TJ and William had a fast beer and talked about security changes to TJ's camp for the rest of the night. No police arrived to complain about them damaging some men. Unspoken rule around these parts not to complain if you got caught with your hand where it shouldn't be.

A month later William brought an opal to TJ to keep safe, an opal he said he planned to send to his twin, Bella. For her birthday.

A week later he was gone.

Later that night, after a solid stint in the mine with his jackhammer and bucket, TJ rested his weary body at the dining table, elbows supporting his hands and chin. He sat staring at the tarpaulin-covered mound in the corner of the room. He'd buried it there the day he moved in, not knowing where to put the thing, wishing he could sell it but knowing he couldn't.

Instead, he'd hidden it beneath an old tarpaulin. Nothing showing. A forcefield that allowed him to ignore the memories that cut like razor blades if he let them in. An odd, untidy mound with a bulge on top where the stool lay on its side. The asymmetry of it all a nagging reminder of his failures.

'Ah, Ree,' he said out loud. She'd bought it for him the second year they were together, his thirty-first birthday because she'd missed his birthday the year before. Not her fault – he didn't celebrate and hadn't shared the occasion even though they'd been together for months by then.

TJ took a swig of his beer and shook his head, his chest hurting, a wry smile twitching. Ree had been wild. Spitting chips at his reticence, she'd vowed to buy him something ostentatious to make up for all the birthdays he'd refused to recognise, and for a few months there after that, he'd thought his life had finally changed for the better.

'Fool.'

He'd allowed himself to feel loved for the first time in years.

Even started to think about family, though Ree hadn't made it to that point.

Then everything was blown away. Ree was blown away. Four years ago in December. When TJ became The Jinx.

He stood up and walked over to the mound. Put his hand on the bulky cover. Imagined the cold of the polished wood underneath. He hadn't touched the gift since she'd died and he didn't want to touch it now, but he couldn't banish the memories of losing himself in the music after a bad day or even a bad month.

He could still picture Ree's face when he finally sat down and began to play. Soft and happy.

One of his earliest memories as a kid before his life went to crap had been his gentle mother, Mary, playing the piano. Teaching students the piano to pay the bills. His dad had died before he'd been born, and she'd named TJ after a brilliant young concert pianist she'd seen once in London, Terence Judd, before the guy had died at twenty-two. So, he'd become Terence Judd Jefferies.

After Ree's death TJ wondered at his namesake's fate and if he'd been The Jinx even then, before he was born.

But his first memories were of being lifted to sit beside his mother on the long piano stool, when his legs had been too short to climb up himself, while she taught him scales and finger exer-cises and then small pieces. He liked to play more by ear, but once he started school his mother made him learn the music, made him practise, made him do exams.

Before his life changed for the worse, just before the car accident when his mother died, he could play uncomplicated classical pieces from sheet music or pick up a tune and replicate it by instinct alone. Ma said he had the ear of a piano player. Strange, then, that he didn't play for more than twenty years after that.

When he met Ree on the Tactical Response team, he'd been might-ily attracted to her, though she'd shunned him. He'd been silent and serious in those days, but when she claimed he had no softness to him, no soul, he'd crossed to the pub piano in front of all the guys and played a Joe Cocker song about her being so beautiful to him.

It had been a bit of a joke, but she'd come home with him that night, and most nights after that when they weren't on duty.

When she'd bought him the baby grand, he'd pretended to be horrified. Odd thing for a tough policeman to have in the corner of their small house, but secretly, inside his chest, he loved it.

When work turned tough and they were both exhausted, mind-wrecked and doubting their sense of humanity after what they'd witnessed, they'd both disappear into the music, and she'd close her eyes with that gorgeous smile on her lips. Precious, soul-fill-ing times.

He stepped back and stared at the tarpaulin. So, there it was.

Mocking him with all he'd lost. All the way back to his childhood.

He should have sold it. A mining camp was no place for that kind of music – or sentimentality. Not normal. Not right.

The camp had been a place to hide after he'd packed everything up after Ree's death and escaped to Lightning Ridge. Nothing soft, or nurturing, or loving about the sandstone, the lack of power and fresh water in the camps, or the hard, physical labour of jackhammering, shovelling or drilling a shaft.

His mining lease gave him a channel of direction he'd desperately needed, though he hadn't realised the search for opal would take hold of him with such sharp teeth. Yep, he suited his life. His solitude. His claim.

The last thing he needed was William's annoying sister – the one he had no doubt would return on the weekend – making him dwell on the tarp-covered skeleton in the corner.

CHAPTER NINE

Meesha

Meesha threw open the door to see who was knocking and found herself face to face with a flint-eyed Bella.

'That man is so infuriating.'

Meesha laughed. 'Which man? TJ?' She turned, wondering if she should have changed out of her night-time cow-print onesie before she opened her door. She decided not, then grinned at her grumpy friend. 'Early bird. I have coffee on. Come in.'

'Thanks.' Bella tilted her head at Meesha as she followed her inside and shut the door. 'I've just realised you're right.'

'About what?'

'How much I need a friend. How lonely I've been. I'm really glad you're here, Meesha.'

Meesha smiled at her. They'd only exchanged two texts since Friday night, but she totally agreed. 'What *have* you been doing?'

Bella sighed. 'Rushing in where even angels fear to tread.

I went out to see TJ yesterday, frustrating, and bright and early this morning. Even more frustrating. Things didn't go so well.'

Meesha's brows had climbed as she studied Bella. 'You went back?' *Ha*, Meesha thought. *With that look in your eye, of course you did.*

'Well, yeah, he didn't give me what I wanted yesterday.'

Meesha pealed with laughter. 'Serves him right, then. I suspect you could be a very stubborn mule. But he spoke to you?'

'All I've got so far is that TJ is someone that William talked to.'

'You got that much?' She received a grimace for that comment.

'Then, after sharing "the crumb"' – Bella made air quotes with her fingers – 'I had to watch his head disappear into the earth when he bolted down his mine. I swear I wanted to throw his empty coffee mug after him.'

Meesha grinned. 'Maybe it would have fallen through the opening and hit him on the head.'

Bella sighed. 'His thick head might have dented the mug, actually, and I like those cups. Damn the man.' She gritted her teeth as she glared at the print-covered wall in Meesha's house.

Meesha didn't think Bella was really looking at the bright abstract pictures. *Don't laugh, don't laugh*, Meesha warned herself.

'I'm surprised you didn't go climbing down after him.'

'I thought of it. I tell you.' Bella's eyes narrowed. 'But I don't know enough about mines to be safe, and the last thing I need to do is endanger either of us.'

Meesha compressed her lips to stop the bubble of delight escaping. 'Such a sensible and responsible doctor.'

'Yeah.' Bella shrugged. 'So, I let him go and replaced my temper with logic.'

'Danger, Will Robinson.'

'Yes,' Bella said thoughtfully. 'Though, today, he was in a much better mood. Some progress. He was almost civil until he told me not to come back. He even said thanks for the breakfast.'

'You brought him breakfast?'

'Coffee and Greta's bacon and egg rolls.'

This time, Meesha laughed out loud. 'You crack me up. This is better than watching an episode of *Home and Away*.'

'Except here I am. Him disappeared down a hole. Me no further advanced.' Bella glared at empty space again. 'I'll have a week to think of a new tactic before I go back.'

She glanced at Meesha. 'Thanks, by the way. You're right. I don't think I could have found his place without your directions.'

Meesha took her hand from under her chin where she been watching, rapt, as Bella debriefed about her weekend, and shook her head. She crossed to the kitchen and filled an extra mug with coffee. 'Well, if you've managed to find the place and get inside the yard, I'm impressed he spoke at all. It's hard to get more than half a dozen words from that man, even when I want to buy his opals.'

She stirred a dollop of cream into her coffee and lifted it to Bella in a question.

Bella's brows rose. 'Cream in coffee? Decadent. Yes, please.'

Meesha stirred both cups while Bella came to stand beside her.

'So. I need your help. What else do you know about TJ?'

'Zip. Nothing to spill.' Meesha shrugged, with just a touch of frustration. 'Nothing more that I said before.'

'No idea what the initials stand for? Maybe I could search online to find some clues.'

'Nope. Nobody else seems to know.'

'No one? What about Desiree? You said she knows everything.'

'Nope. Not even Desiree knows what it stands for. Or any of the Friday ladies, because I asked.'

Meesha trailed across the room in her onesie and slippers and perched on a stool. 'I hear it's a fortress out there. Even deliveries sit outside on the road until the delivery man leaves. He actually opened his gate for you?'

'He opened the gate. I guess I was lucky, then,' Bella said.

'Twice.'

Meesha shook her head. 'No idea why he'd even answer you once.'

'Might have been because I yelled outside for ten minutes, without stopping, and he had a hangover.'

'Who knew there'd be this much fun introducing you! Talk about pulling the tiger's tail.'

A shadow crossed Bella's face that Meesha couldn't interpret.

What was that? Interesting, but she didn't comment.

Meesha regarded Bella over the top of her mug. 'You got away in one piece. I'd take the win. A couple of ratters who tried to break in a few years ago ended up leaving town with their tails between their legs. Word is they were limping for a while. If not forever. Bad choice to target TJ's mine.'

'What's a ratter?'

'Low-life mining thief, with his ear to the ground for other people's strikes.'

'Thieves?'

'The worst kind. They watch people's camps and sneak in as soon as the lucky shaft is unattended, try to grab as much as they can as fast as they can on the off-chance they'll get a high-bearing haul before the owner comes back.'

'Hard to feel sorry for a ratter, then.'

'Yep. There's rumours that with some of the tougher miners, ratters who are caught might never be seen again.'

Bella widened her eyes.

Meesha shrugged. 'But then everyone considers ratters the lowest lifeform in a mining town. People without morals or honour.'

'That does sound unsavoury.'

'True.' Meesha waved the talk of ratters away. Curiosity took hold of her. 'Did you get inside his house?'

Bella tilted her head at the question. 'Once.'

'Inside? You did?' Meesha clapped her hands like a child.

'OMG. Tell me – what's it like?'

'As if.' Bella rolled her eyes. 'I need to be able to go back, and if I shared that, he'd be right to bar me.' She waved her hand as if distressed at the thought of TJ knowing she'd betrayed his privacy.

'Sorry, Meesha. I can't.'

'Not worth your life to tell me anything.' Meesha nodded seriously. She gave a little shiver. 'True statement.'

'No, I don't think that's true at all,' Bella said, surprising her.

'But even an idiot can see TJ jealously guards his solitude. It won't serve me in any way to be untrustworthy after any visit.'

Curiouser and curiouser. Meesha wondered if there was more between her friend and the reclusive miner. Maybe even attraction?

Was Bella an upstanding person who wouldn't share others' secrets on principal, even with a friend? Or was she attracted to the man and wanted more?

'So, you're planning on going back?'

'Absolutely.' Bella's chin tilted up. 'Every weekend until he gives me what I want.' Her chin dropped and the ire faded.

'But . . . sorry. I've been whining since I got here and I'm probably ruining your peaceful Sunday.' She shook her head. 'And you gave me a delicious creamy coffee while I did it.'

'My pleasure. Wouldn't have missed this story for the world.'

Bella laughed. She looked calmer and happier than when she'd arrived, and Meesha took that satisfaction as her due.

'Okay, enough about me,' Bella said. 'What were you planning on doing today if I hadn't dropped in and complained for the last half an hour?'

'Well. Eric's coming to wallpaper the nursery for the baby, so Luci will be with him.' She glanced at her watch. Sugar! She needed to move. 'And the shop opens in an hour and closes at four, so that's the day, done, really.' She thought about the design she was working on. 'And I've got a new jewellery project I'll probably work on tonight.'

Bella's hand came to her chest. 'Do you work seven days a week?'

What's the problem with that? Meesha thought. 'Pretty well.

The shop needs to be open for tourists and for me to make a living. Sometimes people only come to the Ridge for the weekend.' She shrugged. 'I want them to fall in love with my jewellery and not someone else's.'

'Okay. I get that part. But don't you have help in the shop?'

'Not really, though Luci's been nagging me to hire someone.'

Boy had she. But, well, Meesha was still building a business here. She had to see the store successful, keep designing creative and unique pieces. Especially if she wanted the best chance to go to shows and find a bigger market for her wares. 'Sometimes it gets busy on my own.'

'I'll bet.'

'Until Luci came here, I didn't really have a life.' Meesha waved her hands towards the front and back of where she was standing, indicating the store and her opal-cutting workshop. 'This is my life.'

'So, you're in there seven days a week, every week?'

'Technically? Yes.' Meesha lifted one hand. 'One of the miners' wives, Gillian, comes in if I need to go somewhere during shop hours. She's great, too. I know she'd probably take permanent part-time work if I offered it. But I'm building towards something.'

'You just never thought of taking time off?'

Truthfully? No. She loved this place. 'I've shut the shop a couple of times to go to trade shows.'

'A couple of times in three years? And don't those trips still count as work?' Bella was shaking her head. 'Meesha, you need some work/life balance. I'm prescribing at least one day off a week.

And I understand if it's not Sundays, with penalty rates you'd have to pay . . . but Meesha? Burnout!'

'I know.' Or she should know. 'But I've got a goal, Bella. One day I'm going to sell my opal pieces at the trade fairs in the US.

Vegas. Tucson. New York. We have the most beautiful black opals in the world here.' She stared towards her beautiful shop on the other side of the duplex. 'When I can get them, anyway.' She glanced at her watch again and Bella stood up.

'I'll let you get ready for work. Though, I might wander back this afternoon for a proper look around your cabinets. I didn't get much of a chance Friday night, and your jewellery is glorious.'

'Aww, thank you. Come after three. And then we can have a glass of wine after I close the shop. Eric will have finished wallpapering the nursery by then, and if it's okay with Luci, I can show you what they've done.'

'Sounds great. Thanks for listening, Meesha.'

'My absolute pleasure, Bella. I'll be laughing about your TJ story until you arrive this afternoon.'

Except Meesha saw TJ before she saw Bella.

He walked into her shop after lunch, looking grim, as usual.

'Hey, Meesha.'

His purposeful stride took him right past her, over to the glass-topped counter at the rear of the shop she used for showcasing her best pieces.

On a mission much? 'Hey, TJ,' Meesha said to his back and tried hard not to grin at his antics.

She turned away, put a piece into one of the standing display cabinets where it didn't belong, but that she meant to fix later, and struggled for control. Bit her lip. Drew in a deep breath and settled.

Wiped that smile right off her face.

Once she had regained her composure, she followed TJ to the counter, walking around it to stand behind the glass top and faced him. 'You got some opal for me?'

'Well.' He sighed. 'I have, but it's more of a commission than a sale.'

That made her blink. 'Okay. That's different. Commission?'

'Yeah. I didn't actually find this piece. A friend of mine did.'

He looked away and then back again. Met her eyes briefly. Then glanced away again.

She waited for him to continue. It looked like it might take a while, but hey, she had no other customers just now. Though it had been a good day for sales.

He finally went on. 'When something happened to my friend, I forgot that I still had the stone. I shouldn't have, so . . .'

He blew out a breath and Meesha began to suspect where this was heading.

You are kidding me, she thought. She kept her mouth shut but knew she was grinning.

TJ narrowed his eyes at her grin. 'Yeah. Right. As we both know, his sister turned up,' he said drily. He shook his head, then continued. 'So . . . I thought the least I could do was ask you to make it into something spectacular so she could wear it. If she wanted. Instead of just handing her a box with an opal.'

Oh, my, goodness. Meesha had to restrain herself again, just stopping herself from begging, *Show me, show me.* The opal had to be big if he was this dithery. Instead, she said quietly, calmly,

'Geez, TJ, you've really got me fascinated. Show me the opal.' She clenched her hand open and shut.

When the bag appeared out of his pocket and he tipped the stone gently onto the display tray, the one she always kept on the glass counter for showing off a piece, her breath caught somewhere between her lips and her lungs. She stared. Rubbed her chest, tried to suck in a breath. Finally managed it.

When she could talk again, she whispered reverently, 'Is it solid colour?'

'Yeah.' He flipped the large, odd-shaped opal over, and instead of the usual naturally forming black back, the gem was clear through to the colour. Solid opal. 'Opaque. I was thinking something freeform and simple, just using the stone itself for everything.'

'Hell, yeah. It's a beauty. The depth.' *It needs a bit of carving to remove imperfections*, she thought, *but . . .* 'Look at those colours.' The mirage of greens and golds and blues was astounding. 'Shimmering like the sea in the sunlight.' *My lord.* She thought of the design she'd had in mind for weeks. The one that might just seal her spot at the US trade shows, if she showcased it at the Brisbane conference next month, where the winning nominees would be announced. The one she needed a spectacular opal for.

This was it. This stone. It was the best she'd seen in three years in Lightning Ridge, and she'd seen some beauties. 'If Bella says I can enter it in the upcoming awards in Brisbane I'll do it for free.

You just pay for the platinum claws. Hell, I'll pay for the claws and the chain, if she'll let me show it.'

'Up to her. But I'll pay if needed. Will you do it?'

'Hell yeah.'

TJ blew out a breath. 'Don't tell her. But I need it ASAP. She should've had this years ago. William asked me to mind it for her, and after everything happened, I forgot. I feel bad.'

It was the most words Meesha had ever heard him say in one go. 'I'll do it, TJ.' She smiled at him. 'One condition.' He gave her a flat stare. 'What does TJ stand for?'

He opened his mouth and shut it again. One corner of his lip twitched. 'She ask you that?'

No flies on our boy. '*Yep.*'

He waggled both his brows. 'She can ask me herself.'

Chapter Ten

BELLA

Bella's Sunday afternoon at The Iridescent Opal began with soaking in the shop's treasures as she slowly drifted around the tall, four-sided glass cabinets in the middle of the room and past flat-backed shelves along the walls. Brilliant mixed opals – every colour, size and price – were displayed in varied settings, each more intriguing than the last. The stock in the shop blew her away.

Long necklaces in silver, rose and gold dangled off fingers of wood. Bracelets, rings and pairs of earrings decorated chunks of beautiful stones like glamorous islands. Some displays were opal free and relied on the beauty of the silver jewellery to make their own statement. There were table-height stands with handmade pottery plates, vases, mugs and jugs, all in sky and earth colours, with the story of the artists detailed on small cards to explain their origin.

In another corner of the shop hung screen printings, bold earth and Aboriginal designs, and scarves embroidered with landscapes.

Tablecloths. Tea towels. All covetable and perfectly arranged.

Bella could have gazed at everything for hours.

By the time the last customer left, she'd seen every display and been stunned by the quality. Now she stood in the centre of the room and shook her head. 'Meesha. This is magnificent. Magic.'

She shook her head again, unable to find to words to capture the store's beauty. 'It's so much more than I expected. I missed the depth when I was here the other night for the party.'

Meesha flushed with pleasure, her pink cheeks matching the rose of her striped smock. 'It's a lot to take in. I tell my customers to come at least three times. See it at different angles and times of the day.' She glanced around. 'I'm proud of it all.'

'So you should be. Everything's stunning. Can you explain the prices, though? These pieces over here look as pretty as the ones over there. But they're a quarter of the price. Sometimes even more vibrant yet cheaper. Some are a tenth of the price of others the same size over here.'

'Yep, that's the most frequently asked question. It's easy – the most expensive ones are solid opals. The colour goes all the way through, with the darkness of the black opal enhancing the colour.'

Meesha moved to the round island table in the centre of the room and pointed to a sign. 'These ones are doublets. Doublets are a slice of opal with a layer of backing. The slice and the backing are joined together with jeweller's glue, and if you look at them from the side you can usually see two layers. The dark backing that's added makes the colour pop.'

Bella took the pendant and turned it on its side. 'Ah yes, I can see the layer.'

Meesha nodded. 'Look at these ones over here,' she said as she went to another round island bearing a sign saying 'triplets'. 'Here our slice of opal is even thinner and has blackunderneath – again, might be black glass or something else. Plus, on top of the opal slice is a piece of curved clear glass or resin, or maybe even quartz to make a dome. Three parts. A triplet.' She handed it to Bella to turn on its side. 'So, like a doublet with an added protective layer.'

Bella peered at the gem and nodded. 'I see. But it looks so bright and pretty. And it's cheaper.'

'It's only a sliver of opal. Which means, yay, the beauty of opal is available for everyone. But there is much less opal in this piece, even though the resin or glass magnifies the colour. It almost jumps out at you with the brightness.'

Bella thought so. 'Doesn't seem a bad thing.'

'Nothing wrong with triplets. They give people pleasure. But, though the dome protects the thin layer of opal and seals it all into one piece, it is fragile. You need be more careful with doublets and triplets as they hate water and can separate or go cloudy and be ruined.'

She walked over to one of the glass display cases and removed a glorious blue pendant. 'This, on the other hand, is solid opal.

Isn't porous, so it doesn't hate water, and the darker base is naturally occurring black opal. It's whole and it's precious. This is not just a beautiful piece of jewellery – this is an investment.'

Bella watched the intense concentration Meesha gave to the stone in her hand and saw the passion of someone who loved and understood her work. That glimpse made her appreciate Meesha even more. 'You really love this, don't you.'

'I do. I'll show you my workshop later – that's where I get really excited. Creating settings that showcase the particular opal I'm working with, that's the best part.'

To think Bella hadn't known anything about opals before she came here, and yet Meesha lived her life surrounded by them. 'It's fascinating, Meesha. Thank you.'

'I'll have you dreaming about opals in no time,' Meesha said and grinned. 'Now let's lock up, grab a glass of wine. I want to go see what the neighbours have achieved today.'

Eric and Luci were in the kitchen of Luci's duplex when they arrived. Both turned when Meesha knocked and entered.

'Bella and I have come for food, laughter and gossip,' Meesha announced. 'And to see the new baby's room.'

'Hope that's okay,' Bella added, feeling just a little like they were barging in.

'Excellent. The more the merrier. You show them.' Luci waved Eric away. And the tall, red-headed miner moved as bid, with a twinkle in his eyes. 'I'll get some snacks out.' She turned towards them, her smile warm. The more Bella spent time with Luci, the more she saw of Meesha's sister in general, the more she enjoyed her company.

'I'll come soon,' Bella promised Meesha, and hung back while her friend followed Eric to the nursery. To Luci, she said, 'Can I help?'

'Pour a glass of this real wine for Meesha and yourself. Saves me measuring it out.'

Luci had a little fluid measure she clipped on the side of her glass. The clever level gauge beeped when she poured her non-alcoholic wine using one hand for the bottle, resting the rim on the glass, which she held with her other hand.

Luci reached out for Bella's arm. 'Meesha says you've been hanging out a lot with big bad TJ.'

That was unexpected. 'He's big but I don't think he's bad,'

Bella said, squirming just a little, because she didn't want to break confidences.

Something had hurt TJ. She felt that instinctively. She knew from her own experience with William's loss that she hadn't wanted people to talk about her – or even talk to her – while she'd been lost in her heartbreak. Which made her think again that there must have been something dark in TJ's past for him to act in a similar way to her own behaviour.

She understood TJ's wish for privacy. But she was struggling too with what she might find out about William's disappearance, if and when he did finally give in and answer her questions.

Luci's voice interrupted her thoughts. 'And apparently he's hot!'

'Well, yes.' Bella laughed. 'He has the whole chest, abs, and arm thing going on.' She blew out a breath.

Luci grinned at her. 'You could be a little more descriptive for me,' she teased. 'But I guess I can imagine it well enough. So, what's the story with him? Did he know your brother well?'

Bella felt the stress of the last few days well up inside her, and suddenly she wanted to explain everything to Luci.

'When my brother disappeared, all we found was a suicide note. He said we'd never find his body.'

Luci winced. 'That's so horrible. For all of you. I'm so sorry.'

She screwed her face, then her hand reached out and she touched Bella's shoulder. Squeezed. 'I think I'd rather lose my sight than my sister.'

Bella turned her face and rested her cheek against Luci's hand.

'She hasn't annoyed you enough yet.' But the weak joke fell flat because it wasn't amusing by any stretch.

Luci bumped her shoulder.

'But you like TJ.'

Meesha arrived, catching the end of the conversation. 'We talking about TJ?' In a sing-song voice she crowed, 'Bella likes him, all right.'

Bella bit down on her smile and glanced around to see who could hear them. 'Shhhh. Eric will hear you.'

Eric appeared behind Meesha, the picture of innocence. 'Who me? Hear that you fancy TJ? TJ who?'

'And you better keep to that,' Luci warned, and Eric touched her cheek gently.

'For you. Anything.' And his eyes said it all.

Unabashed, Meesha studied Bella's face with an intensity Bella could have done without. 'You've got a bit of a sparkle happening here.'

'Shut up.'

Both Meesha and Luci laughed, but Bella heard their affec-tion in the sound and her embarrassment eased a fraction. She had friends. She had support. These women would be here for her no matter what. There was comfort in that.

CHAPTER ELEVEN

BELLA

On Monday Bella paused with her morning coffee in her hand and watched as Mel settled behind the reception desk.

'Mel? Don't suppose you know a miner called TJ?'

Mel sucked in a breath, paling, and Bella frowned. Damn. She winced at her own folly. Konrad had said Mel suffered from PTSd after she'd been a victim in a bank robbery. She'd developed a phobia about large men as a result. Of course, TJ fit that bill.

Mel took a deep breath as if calming herself. 'Not lately. I used to see him at the back of the pub when I lived there after my pop died. Sometimes I'd help out with the cleaning, and TJ would go there and play pool. I felt like a mouse next to him.'

'Yes, he's a large-boned person.' Bella tried very hard not to be side-tracked with thoughts of his musculature, lean in the right places, broad in others. 'But he seems nice.'

'Nice?' Mel gave her an incredulous look. Then shook her head as if warding off that ludicrous description. 'Anyway, yes, I saw him back then. Until Dr Konrad said I could move to the units out the back here when I started working for him. But I wouldn't say I know TJ.'

Bella touched her arm. 'That's okay. No worries. It just seems he knew my brother, William. Before he died.'

'Oh. I'm sorry.' Mel looked even more stricken. 'Suicide is so sad.' She whispered, 'You know my Toby almost took his own life, too. Dr Konrad and Dr Riley helped there as well.'

Good grief. Upsetting Mel was not the optimal way to start the week. Bella needed to think more before she spoke.

She swallowed the lump in her throat and hoped Mel could swallow hers, too. 'Thanks, Mel. For telling me about TJ. Just let me know if you think of something else.' She so wished she hadn't started this conversation, but she hadn't realised it would be such a minefield.

Mel lifted her chin. 'That's okay. He's always been polite to me.' Her forehead crinkled. 'You know, now that you mention it, I might have seen William with him a couple of times. William worked as bar staff there sometimes.'

'Oh?' Wow. That was news to her. Their parents had been disappointed when William hadn't gone into medicine like his siblings – he'd had the Australian Tertiary Admission Rank needed for medicine, but he'd chosen the police force instead. William had been happy in the force until, unexpectedly, he'd told them he was leaving. Moving to the Ridge for no apparent reason. That's where all the drama had started. The secrets. The odd moods. The lack of contact when suddenly he stopped taking calls. Not taking calls from his twin!

Their parents worried so much that Konrad had offered to do a locum up here, so he'd come to Lightning Ridge, too.

And William had worked at the pub? She hadn't thought working the bar in a mining town would be his dream job, but who knew? The confusing man her twin had become certainly hadn't shared any of that with her.

Mel scrunched her face up, concentrating unhappily, and Bella felt worse. 'Don't worry if you can't think of anything more.'

The first patient arrived, and Mel straightened behind her big reception desk and lifted her chin to smile. Bella took herself to her consulting room and allowed the day to fall into routine.

On Wednesday afternoon, Bella rose from her desk, so happy to invite Luci and her beautiful yellow labrador, Pluto, into her consulting room. Luci had asked Bella on Sunday evening if she could take her on for shared antenatal care, in addition to her check-ups in Moree, and Bella had enthusiastically agreed.

Since then, Bella had shuffled through Luci's medical history – Mel had acquired copies of her antenatal records from the Maternity unit in Moree – and read them prior to the appointment today. Always a bonus to save asking the same questions that have already been answered, which left time to spend on anything extra Luci wanted to talk about.

Her new patient looked amazing – pink cheeked, head up, big belly out with the lovely Pluto in his guide harness beside her as she came into the consulting room.

Bella cast a glance around the room as Pluto guided his mistress inside. 'Welcome, Luci. It's so great to see you and Pluto. There's a chair just behind you to your left.'

'Hey, Bella.' Luci reached out a hand behind her and she felt for the chair back, then eased herself gracefully into the seat.

Bella gave them a few seconds to make sure Pluto was settled and Luci looked at her. 'How was the walk up here? There isn't a path, is there?'

'We walked on the side of the road. There's some lovely roses on the way I could smell, so it was pleasant. It's not too rough, and close to home, so no problem. I'm sure it will get easier each time we do it.'

'You and Pluto are a great team. I'm officially inviting you to come visit me socially in my unit anytime. I've been to your house, now, so only fair.'

'You're on.' Luci clapped her hands.

Bella remembered the lovely space she'd seen for the baby at Luci's duplex the other night. 'It must be good to know the nursery is ready for the new arrival.'

Luci's face softened. 'The wallpaper feels amazing, and I love the feel of the big koala stickers on the other wall.' Excitement flashed.

'And one of my friends sent me a children's picture book in braille with print over the top – I can't wait to read to my baby.'

'It's a beautiful room for a baby.' Bella had run her hands over the pressed paper, marvelling at the detailed design. 'So good to see you here. Just reminding you, I do have basic obstetric training, and I can share care with your routine antenatal appointments, but I don't deliver babies. Right? Moree will still be your primary carer.'

Luci nodded. 'Sure. I get that. It's just so good to have a female doctor in town, even for after baby.' Her hand drifted down unerr-ingly to scratch Pluto's head.

Mel had also said that. 'One of my other patients, also pregnant, mentioned the lack of women doctors, too. And having to go to Moree for her antenatal checks. Still, it's great to establish rapport with the midwives there before you go into labour.'

'Sure.' Luci shrugged. 'They're lovely, but it's so much better cutting down on travel for half the visits.'

Shame it was so late in the pregnancy, Bella thought, or she could have been more useful. 'How long does it take to get to the maternity clinic?'

'It's a five-hour return drive.'

Bella shook her head. 'That's huge. Especially with a pregnant belly. What's your plan for labour?'

'Meesha said she'll take me to Moree as soon as I want to go. She'll shut the shop if she has to.'

'From what I've gathered, I think she's feeling blessed, having you and Pluto with her. She's told me several times how glad she is you're here.'

Luci lifted her chin. 'Yes, well. We'll see how it goes. I'll be a single mother with my baby in her space.' She lifted her chin. 'But we'll manage with bells on.'

Bella risked a pun. 'Literally? I did read that unsighted parents sometimes put bells on their children.'

They both laughed and the tension eased. 'Probably. When he or she starts to crawl around.'

Luci was a practical woman, all right. 'Meesha said she didn't think the baby's father would be coming back at a later date?'

'No. Not at all. He's gone home to Brazil, though he said he will help with maintenance. If he does, I'll bank it, and the baby can have it at eighteen. Maybe when the baby is grown they might want to meet him.'

Wow. 'I guess you know where you stand, then.' Bella managed to keep her voice level. 'What made you choose to settle in the Ridge? Do you think being this remote will be a problem?' She wanted to say it was far away from services and the Royal Society for the Blind, but she didn't say it.

Luci shook her head. 'No. I've spent too much time in cities already. I'm a country girl at heart. The RSB are amazing' – it was as if Luci had heard her thoughts – 'but I don't need to be near services like that. Pluto and I have been together for four years now, and the rest I'll just have to learn as I go along. It was always a train wreck with Batte once I was pregnant, even though we'd talked about it and how it could work. He just wasn't coping with the incoming responsibility. I don't have the headspace to worry about him as well as me and the baby, so I gave him an out.'

Tough love, Bella thought. 'Was he relieved or devastated?'

'Sadly, he sounded quite relieved. Left quickly. There was no doubt about that.' Luci looked rueful for a moment before she lifted her chin. 'Better to find out now than later.'

Bella agreed but again didn't offer her opinion. She waited for Luci to continue.

'Anyway, I think the Ridge will work. Meesha said she wanted us here. It's a small town, so it's easier to navigate than busy city streets, and she swears the people are unlike any she's met before.

In a good way.'

'I totally agree.' Bella did. 'Seems it doesn't matter if you're local, just passing through, or the prime minister. They make you welcome.'

'Yep.' Luci nodded. 'I've felt the warmth here and it's not just the weather. I think it's a good move. Plus, Meesha has always been someone who relishes a challenge.'

'Sounds like you're very much the same.' Both sisters were such strong characters. 'Well, I'd love to help with your medical care.

Apart from saving you the trip to Moree once a fortnight, is there anything else I can help with, antenatally?'

'Meesha says you're smart, practical and tough. I need that in my GP.'

'Thank you.' Bella smiled. 'Ditto on my friends. Put me on speed dial.'

Luci's own smile lit up her beautiful face. 'Thanks. Eric's still helping me remove as many hazards as we can and set up for easy baby care at my place.'

'I love what you've done already. And I want to hear more about the things you've learned. Maybe I can help some of my older patients who have low vision as well.'

'Sure.'

'Wonderful. But this appointment is all about you.' She sat back. 'How about we start by checking your blood pressure, and then your baby's growth compared to your gestation, and we'll have a listen to this little passenger you have inside.'

Later that afternoon, when Bella opened her surgery door to let out her second last patient, Mel's message pinged on her computer screen with the final patient's arrival. Bella's lips quirked when she saw it was Cyrus – the miner would give her a smile for the end of the day. He needed his scripts renewed for his blood pressure tablets, and she had to grin. Cyrus had established himself as a special character of the area.

She stood at the door to welcome him inside. 'Hello, Cyrus.'

She glanced over his not yet trim but certainly slimmer physique.

'Wow. You look good.'

His ears actually turned pink. 'I've been doing my walking,' he said proudly, a grin of his own splitting his face as she closed the door after him and gestured for him to take a seat.

'That's good to hear, Cyrus.'

He sat heavily in the chair and it creaked ominously. 'I'm feeling pretty good. I reckon Doc Riley would be happy with me.'

'I'd say she would be, Cyrus. I'll let her know. I might be talking to her quite soon. Let's see what your blood pressure is doing.'

She pumped up his massive arm with the sphygmomanometer and watched the mercury fall. Bella shook her head once in delight as the beat finally commenced at one forty and left at eighty-five.

'That is so impressive.'

As she unwrapped his arm, Cyrus said, 'I've been doing the bore baths as well. I think that helps me blood pressure, too.'

'I think everything you've been doing has helped your blood pressure, Cyrus. Great work. Keep going.'

'You been to the mineral baths yet, Doc?'

He was such a sweetie. 'No, I haven't, Cyrus. I must do that.'

There was a cheeky grin on the old man's face. 'You should get TJ to take you.'

Bella blushed. Maybe not such a sweetie. She wanted to say, 'I don't know what you're talking about, Cyrus,' but she knew it wouldn't fly. This town. Everybody knew everything. She laughed and gave in. 'Maybe I will.'

He nodded. 'And I hear Meesha's sister Luci's having a baby, and you'll be here for her, just like Doc Riley was there for young Mel.'

Who said old guys didn't care about others? 'You really have got your finger on the pulse of this community, Cyrus.'

'Maybe. Best place in the world to live.'

The rest of the conversation had to be steered away from him extolling the virtues of Bella's sister-in-law, who had worked briefly as a GP in the Ridge last year, even though she now only came occasionally for outreach women's fertility clinics. If Bella wasn't mistaken, Cyrus had a severe crush on Riley.

On his way out, Cyrus turned back at the last second. 'Did I tell you she saved my life?'

'You did. I'll tell her you asked after her.' Bella kept her face blank as Mel closed her eyes to contain her amusement. She held up three fingers. 'Three weeks, please, Mel.'

Bella's gaze returned to Cyrus. She said very quietly, so Mel couldn't hear, 'I do think, Cyrus, that Riley will be thrilled to see you've taken off all those kilos in two months.'

He froze. 'You think?'

'I really do.'

'Right.' He nodded decisively. 'I'll keep up that walking in the morning. That helps takes it off, too.'

Bella suppressed a grin. 'Excellent.' In her normal voice, she said, 'I'll see you again in three weeks to check your blood pressure and your weight again. I'm sure Riley will ask me.'

As Cyrus left, clutching his appointment card and scripts, Bella smiled at Mel. 'Another successful day at the Ridge. How did you two go?'

'We had a good day.' Mel smiled at the empty playpen where her sociable son had spent the day, usually with a block in one hand, before Toby picked him up in the afternoon. He seemed to be constantly building things. 'Teddy's loving the new felt activity board Greta made him. And the blocks. He's such a good little boy.'

'He's an absolute champion. You head off and see him and I'll lock up.'

'Thanks, Bella. See you tomorrow.' The young mother stood and gathered her bag. 'I put your dinner in the fridge. Toby dropped it off when he picked up Teddy.'

'Thanks. I'm spoilt.' Bella suspected Mel still worried too much about having Teddy in the surgery, even though Bella truly didn't mind. Between Mel doing all the admin and Greta cleaning and sending lunch and sometimes evening meals from the café, Bella's needs had been met with a smoothness she hadn't expected. And the financial arrangements suited them both. Spoilt indeed, with no downside. 'See you tomorrow.'

Bella glanced at the empty office across the room. She still missed Konrad. In the winter, Adelaide Brand, Riley's awesome mother, a miner and semi-retired nurse, worked at the OPAL

centre one day a week so Konrad could have a nurse assistant for minor surgeries. Bella might continue that arrangement if she could.

But Adelaide and her husband were back in their home in Sydney and wouldn't return to the Ridge and their off-grid camp until April, even though Adelaide's husband had really taken to the mining life, too.

Bella suspected Konrad and Riley were hoping Bella would fall in love with the Ridge and stay forever.

Bella wasn't sure about that, but it was becoming more of a possibility every day. The Ridge was more remote than she'd expected. But she'd been welcomed in town. And between Meesha and Luci, she might have found real friends and possibly another reason to stay here longer than she'd intended.

Konrad had briefed her about the patients and explained the intricacies of living away from a major centre – how to contact the small, but very efficient, local health and emergency centre, plus the Royal Flying Doctor Service when necessary. Running an outback medical centre like OPAL meant being aware of the little things, like delayed pathology collection, and having to order special prescrip-tion drugs to arrive by mail or plane to the one local pharmacy.

Today at work, she'd found herself smiling with anticipa-tion when her patients returned for their follow-up visits, because already she'd become invested in their families and concerns and begun to appreciate the rewards that could grow exponentially with her clientele.

Which, of course, had been why she'd gone into general practice in the first place – until after William's loss when she'd lost the desire to connect with anyone too deeply.

Sure, there was a lot of responsibility she couldn't shift to anyone else, but it wasn't as onerous as she'd thought it might be.

Besides, she used to enjoy a challenge, and she needed to get back to that mindset.

Thinking about long term, she considered her own self-contained flat out the back of the surgery. It was lovely, but lonely.

So thank goodness she had evenings with Meesha and Luci to keep her sane.

She had no idea how Konrad had managed on his own for all that time before Riley, but she planned to talk to her dad about arranging locums. He had connections at UNSW School of Clinical Medicine at Port Macquarie who might be able to help organise it.

Even if each new resident could come for only a month, that would be an enormous help.

Funny to think about sustainability and longevity, Bella thought to herself. She liked the Ridge. But she couldn't work these long hours indefinitely and still have work/life balance. She needed to take the advice she'd given Meesha. Now that she was getting her life back, she decided she wanted to enjoy more of it.

She'd figured that even help with simple consultations like script renewals would be a huge bonus and allow her to slow down the consultations she felt she was rushing through now. Bella had been one of the favourite mentor doctors in Port Macquarie before William's death, and she suspected the uni would be interested in her offer to mentor again.

Accommodation wise, locums could take turns staying in the spare units behind the surgery.

But those were plans for later.

Right now, Bella had work she enjoyed and a home where she could relax. A very comfortable and chic home, thanks to Riley.

But now, with Konrad and Riley on their belated honeymoon trip, it was sinking in that the only permanent family would be the ghost of William.

Her phone vibrated with a text from Meesha.

Hey Bella. Wanna start walking just before the sun comes up each morning? If yes, am at my shop, out front tomorrow?

The loneliness retreated two steps.

That's right. There was Meesha. And Mel. And Luci. And, of course, the enigmatic TJ, who wasn't a friend – more a puzzle she still needed to solve. And the Lightning Ridge Ladies on Friday nights.

Mel who was such a champion at work, Meesha who might teach her about opals, and Luci who reminded her to be strong.

The women were easy companions. TJ, not so much, but she smiled at the idea of future confrontations.

Life wasn't empty. Far from it. It was just beginning.

For their first morning walk, Meesha took Bella down the town's divided main road and around the corner, past a huge swimming pool and diving complex on the left as they walked out towards the cactus garden.

'That's a huge area!' Bella craned her head as they passed.

'Built with an Olympic-sized diving centre and pool. Plus, a water-park for kids,' Meesha explained.

'I heard it hits forty degrees out here.' Bella turned and walked backwards for a few paces before facing the front again. 'Still, a swimming complex like that seems big for the size of the town.'

'One of the reasons I always felt comfortable coming to the Ridge to start my business.' Meesha spread her arms wide. 'This place is built on dreams. Good place for me to dream, too.'

Bella smiled. Walking with Meesha made that happen often.

'Sounds like a story?' Like a lot of the conversations had been on the walk so far – about who lived here, how that particular town business started, how often it seemed to start with finding an opal.

Meesha inclined her head backwards briefly as they strode on, the slight still-cool breeze ruffling their hair. 'The Lightning Ridge aquatic centre started as a dream in by five local schoolgirls and a few boxes of lamingtons.' She grinned. 'The project grew exponentially over the next ten years and was actually designed based on the Homebush Olympic Pool in Sydney.'

'Wow. Local schoolgirls?'

'The town backed them. They had huge support, and it took ten years and a lot of hard work, but I was told the US diving team has even trained here, and that Aleks Popov guy used the pool.'

'This town.' Bella shook her head. 'I believe you. Crazy place.'

They passed the dirt racecourse and followed the road as it turned to dust. All dirt roads now, with a few camps, scrubby trees, and tracks leading off in different directions. Meesha kicked a rock.

'It's down here somewhere your sister-in-law tripped and fell down a mine. So don't wander off the road if you come this way on your own.'

'No way.' Bella shivered. She imagined Riley, alone down a deserted shaft overnight, in and out of consciousness. 'Not me.'

'Good. More fun to be had out of the mines, I say. So, when are you coming to my workshop for your first lesson in opal cutting?'

Bella perked up at the idea of a new challenge. 'You're on. Sell me a bag of poor-quality claystone I can't ruin and we can start tonight.'

The accumulation of white-looking, washed tailings of clay and sandstone hopefully contained traces of opal colour. Bella's job was to shape and clean them one at a time on the shop's rough wheel.

She savoured the quiet comfortable time and repetitive action while Meesha worked with her jewellery, and Bella began the process of learning to prepare and cut her first opal from the rough sandstone.

Luci slipped in quietly with Pluto to sit with them in Meesha's workshop and crochet with her braille-marked crochet hooks and audio pattern. All three of them concentrating on their separate industries, relaxing and serene.

Looked like they'd all needed a friend, Bella had thought more than once. She'd found good ones.

Meesha had focus. Something Bella had lost after William's death, but she could feel her own connection to the world clawing back.

Meesha ran her opal business with an exuberance and skill Bella could only admire.

Bella had begun to realise it took persistence and patience, not to mention time, to gently remove the biggest inclusions, clumps of sand and grit that housed the promise of colour inside the claystone.

She'd also picked up the mantra 'Don't waste the carat', because, as Meesha repeated constantly, with opals, it was all about carat weight.

'Go easy.' Meesha had come up behind her. 'You're losing too much stone.'

Bella hid her smile.

The next morning, Meesha and Bella trekked in the other direction up the main road, out to the artesian baths, past the health centre and ambulance station. Bella felt more familiar with the layout of this side of the town, as she'd walked this way with Konrad before he left.

Meesha piped up. 'The bore baths are only closed between ten a.m. and midday for cleaning. That's weekdays, otherwise they're always open and free to enter.'

Bella stared at the big parking area and the steam rising through the gate beyond. 'We should come out one night after work then. Have a swim.'

'Let's.' Meesha grinned. 'I've heard the locals say a few times that clothing is optional after midnight.' They turned around to walk back. 'I started these morning adventures, so you organise that.'

Bella glanced at her watch. Ninety minutes until she started work. 'I'll do that. Before midnight. Watch this space.'

Chapter Twelve

Bella

At the end of her next week in town, Bella arranged to meet the Lightning Ridge Ladies at their usual haunt behind the servo with her newfound friends. Right after Meesha and Luci checked out her new home.

'Oooh,' Meesha said as she stepped inside Bella's unit, 'the peppermint paint is soothing.'

'It's the same colour as the surgery.' Bella held the door open for Luci and Pluto, the guide dog beside Luci as she headed towards a chair. 'There's a round table and chairs to the left, Luci, if you'd like to sit down while your sister checks everything out.'

'I expect a running commentary,' Luci said as she put her hand out and found the back of a chair.

'It's a two-room,' Meesha called as she dipped between both living areas. 'Pretty, and efficient with a bathroom and sleeping space on one side, and living and kitchen on the other.'

Bella pulled out her own chair and sat at the dining table with Luci, letting Meesha have her way. 'Apparently, my brother went all DIY master and helped Toby, Mel's husband, transform the six tiny units into three larger ones. The second bathrooms were turned into kitchens when everything was gutted and rebuilt.'

'Oh, look-ee here! That's not fair.' Meesha was in the kitchen now. 'Your coffee machine is better than mine.'

Bella laughed. 'That's thanks to Riley. State-of-the art everything – dishwasher, all of the kitchen appliances possible, and new aircon.'

Meesha's gaze roamed. 'The unit has a full lounge area that could seat six people, Luci. Floral lounges with grey cushions.

Lots of white edging and a white desk in the corner.' Her voice faded as she wandered away to check out the bathroom, then came back. 'Oh, my goodness, this shower is huge! Luci, you and Pluto could walk in here together. There's even enough room to bring Eric.'

'Eric is just a friend,' Luci said mildly.

'Bet he'd still like to shower with you.'

Luci pushed back. 'My focus is on the baby – anything else would have to wait, and Eric knows that.'

Bella hid her grin and changed the subject. 'Not sure why it's so big, and with two shower heads, too.'

Meesha snorted. 'I'm sure Riley could tell you if your brother won't.'

That made Luci laugh.

Bella blushed. 'Oh. Okay. I didn't think of that, and now I'll have to go find distracting thoughts every time I shower. Thanks, Meesha.'

Her wicked laugh came closer as she returned to the main room. 'This place is way bigger than I thought it would be. Very cool. Thanks for letting us check it out. Are we ready for party time at Desiree's?'

'I'll just grab the ravioli.' Bella went to the fridge. 'And I think we should claim a bottle of Konrad's good wine from his unit. Just pull the door shut when you come out, please,' Bella said and slipped next door with Konrad's key.

Soon the three of them, plus Pluto, were walking down the street towards the servo, Bella carrying the wine and Meesha the food.

For Bella, walking slowly beside Meesha and Luci felt so different to the recent times she'd spent with her parents at Port Macquarie, or even the evening walks with Konrad in the Ridge. Marvellous what a change making new friends had wrought in her insular life.

Had it only been a couple of weeks since she met Meesha and Luci? It seemed way longer. She'd already had a party invite, a Sunday store inspection and five morning walks with her new friend. And with Meesha teaching Bella to polish her own opals in the evenings, there was more than enough to keep even her mind busy in the first weeks of leaving home.

And she'd met others in the Ridge who were just as friendly, as well as her patients she admired. Of course, the one outlier was TJ, hidden like an ogre in his camp, but she wasn't going to think about him and his OCD home tonight. Or the fact she was going up there tomorrow morning to interrogate him again.

Still, her female friends were wonderful. And something she'd missed. To her surprise she felt at ease in a community that somehow felt more welcoming than the place she'd grown up. Felt like she was finally starting to appreciate her life again for the first time since losing William.

Yet, despite all that, threading through the new world she'd begun to build around herself, the challenge of extracting information from the reluctant TJ on the coming weekend still sat front and centre of her non-work-related thoughts.

'Hey. Earth to Bella. You ready?' Meesha's voice pulled her back to the here and now.

Bella straightened. 'Let's do this.'

The service station in front of them stood dark and locked, but the sounds of revelry came from the lighted backyard.

Wow, thought Bella, as she went through the gate after Meesha and Luci. The gravelly whisper of Meatloaf music added to the backyard barbecue feel of the gathering. The chairs and tables had a fun mish-mash of styles – 'Esso' and 'Ampol' wood-topped forty-four-gallon drums, versus wire chairs with grey cushions, park benches and half a dozen wooden-armed director chairs. The group of eclectic smiling ladies she'd met again at Meesha's party all waved as the three younger women arrived, sending out a chorus of hellos.

The homemade bar was a slab of old tree wood with a bunch of wine bottles and a plastic yellow bucket of ice, plus extra glasses.

Bella nudged Meesha. 'It looks more fun than I expected. You said old drums and wire chairs.'

'We had a working bee here a couple of weeks ago, even though Desiree protested all the way through, saying she liked the grunge.

But it was fun to add a few extra pillows and chairs that we all brought from home. The fairy lights are new, too.'

Meesha steered them towards the grouped chairs, past a long plastic folding table buried under small plates of food and takeaway dishes. Looked like Bella wasn't the only one who frequented Greta's café. Between every chair and the next sat a wooden-topped oil drum, probably from the original ladies' nights but newly spruced up.

Meesha tapped a heavy chair with wooden arms for her sister.

'Here's a spot, Luci.' Luci and Pluto headed towards the chair, and Meesha sat on a drum on the other side of her sister.

'She spoils me,' Luci said sotto voce.

Sotto voice back, Meesha said, 'I'm trying to get in good with her, so I can cuddle her baby, when it comes.'

'Hello, ladies. You're here.' Greta's blonde hair seemed to be catching the beams from the light string and her smile was as welcoming as always. This time Bella was prepared for the hug that wrapped her up. Greta squeezed tight. 'Congratulations on settling in, Bella. Mel says you've got everything under control at the medical centre.'

Bella returned the hug and then stepped back. She smiled at the crazy warmth of the woman. 'I think it's Mel who's got everything under control, Greta. But yes, it's been a good week. I have to say, the dining options have been amazing.'

'Good to hear. Ah, here's Desiree.'

A distant voice called Greta as she stepped away, and Bella thought it might have been Gerry, the lady who ran the arts and craft emporium she'd yet to visit.

Desiree lifted a hand. 'Hello! Welcome, Meesha and Luci, and of course Pluto. And welcome to you, too, Bella.' She raised her beer.

'Half expected you'd come down to see me through the week?'

Bella had been meaning to visit Desiree, to talk to her about William, but the timing just hadn't been right. She hoped tonight she'd get a chance. 'I really wanted to. But it's hard with the surgery closing late.' She gestured to the yard, took a breath and ignored the prickle in her throat. 'I'd love to ask you and the other ladies a couple of questions about William later tonight, if I could?'

Was it her imagination or did Desiree truly not look enthused at that suggestion? Though, maybe Desiree hadn't heard her properly, because the white-haired woman didn't smile or answer Bella, turning to Meesha. 'Good party the other week, Meesha.'

'Thanks, Desiree. Appreciate everyone meeting there for the night instead of here.'

Greta was back. Such a sweetie. Bella now knew Greta's miner husband had left her and her son, Toby, to search for the elusive find she suspected he'd never be satisfied with. Greta was warm, positive and the perfect person to settle beside. 'I had a great night,'

Greta said. 'Having one tonight, too. Come and sit with me, Bella. I'm over with Gerry and Elsa. They just asked me if you were from Port Macquarie. They've got friends there.'

And just like at Meesha's party, Bella allowed her shoulders to release the burden of loss for now. She let the constant gnaw of questions, the busyness of work, and the loneliness of her peppermint unit float away in the buzz of interesting feminine conversation, a glass of wine, and a plate of Greta's *fabulous* ravioli just for a few hours.

The fairy lights swayed in the evening breeze that cooled the warmth of the day's heat. Bella shifted in her director's chair, the wooden arms smooth under her fingers. The music had softened to the Eagles, making the snippets of conversation among the scattered groups of women more audible.

Desiree wandered over, beer in hand, and settled beside Bella's Esso drum. Funny how the old oil containers could look almost elegant in the dim light, topped with smooth wood.

'So,' Desiree said, taking a sip of her beer. 'You had some questions?'

Something in her tone made Bella peer closer. The older woman seemed . . . tense, despite her casual pose.

Greta appeared with a plate of sausage rolls, the smell making Bella's full stomach ache. 'Here you go, loves. Can't beat hot food on a cool night.' She sank into a wire chair opposite them, adjust-ing its cushion.

'Was just thinking,' Desiree said, her eyes catching Bella's in the fairy lights, 'how you remind me of someone else who used to sit right there. He had the same thoughtful look.'

'William?' Bella accepted the offer to talk now. Her brother's name lingered between them like the old drum.

'Mmm.' Desiree's fingers tapped against her beer bottle. 'Your brother spent a few weekday evenings in that very chair. Especially that last month. Sometimes TJ would show up with him.'

Greta leaned forward, a pastry in her hand. 'Those two had a strange friendship, your brother and TJ. Mel was talking about it tonight before I came here. Asking if we remembered anything odd before William . . .' She looked at Desiree. 'You reckon it all started with that business with Bane?'

From next to her sister, Meesha turned her head. 'Bane? Crikey, even I remember him. Tried to sell me a batch of stolen opals once.

Backed away when I confronted him about it. Horrible little man.'

'Horrible is putting it kindly.' Desiree snorted, reaching over to dip the pastry into the tomato sauce. Of course Greta had brought the perfect condiment as well.

Bella noticed Desiree's hand wasn't quite steady, and the doctor in her wondered if she had a tremor coming on.

Desiree said, 'Bane had a friend with a claim near TJ's, but everyone knew mining wasn't his real game.'

The breeze carried the sound of quiet conversations across the space, but Bella refused to be distracted. She leaned forward.

'What was his real game?'

The older women exchanged looks in the shifting light. Across the yard, someone laughed, and the music changed to something instrumental.

'Let's just say' – Greta lowered her voice – 'opals weren't the only things going missing when Bane was around. TJ caught him on his claim one night with a few friends. TJ and William arrived at the camp in time to catch them. TJ and your brother took out the lot of them. Heard some of them still don't walk properly.

Heard TJ tightened his security after.'

'I remember that night,' Serena called out. 'Was talk about it at the bar at my place.' She made her way over to join them, one hand waving her glass. She eased into another director's chair beside Greta. 'Not long before . . .' She shot Bella an apologetic look.

'Before William died,' Bella finished. In the dim lights, she caught something flashing across Desiree's face. Sadness? Guilt?

But why would Desiree feel guilty?

'Thing is' – Desiree set her beer on the drum, the stubby making a hollow sound against the wood – 'your brother was seen talking to Bane at the pub the next week, after TJ beat up those ratters. It was an intense conversation, by all accounts.' She spread her hands. 'Then Bane vanished right after William did.

Heard he headed down Coober Pedy way. Might have been to hide from TJ.'

'Yeah, the kicker being,' Greta added, her voice barely carrying over the music, 'TJ went looking for Bane after William's death.

For weeks, he was gone. Didn't find him apparently. When he came back . . .' She shook her head.

'He was different,' Meesha said softly, her hands wrapped around her glass. 'The way he pulled back. Barely spoke to anyone.'

The fairy lights blurred as pieces started falling into place.

TJ did know something. And who was this Bane? Bella set her glass down on the nearest drum, the wood cool under her fingers.

'When exactly did Bane leave the Ridge?'

Desiree's shrugged. 'Long time ago now, but interesting, isn't it? If someone wanted to know about Bane . . .' She let the words hang in the air.

Determination replaced the uncertainty that had been gnawing at Bella all week. She needed a drink and a think and a few minutes for both. The bottle of wine she'd brought was in the bar fridge.

At the thought of the award-winning shiraz, she smiled. Konrad would hate that she preferred ice with her red wine instead of drinking it room temperature.

'I'll be seeing TJ tomorrow, and you've given me plenty more questions to ask him. Thanks, ladies.'

Desiree murmured, 'Watch yourself with Bane if you find him.

Bloke like that, running from something? Could be dangerous to corner.'

'Don't worry,' Bella said, thinking of TJ. 'I'll make sure I have back-up.'

Bella stood up and went to open the bar fridge. Her mind racing, ideas coming and going. William had talked to Bane before he died. And Bane had left town immediately afterwards. Surely that couldn't be a coincidence – surely Bane would know some-thing about what was going through her brother's mind in those final days. As she filled her glass, the music paused between songs and, with that moment of silence in the night, she heard Greta's low voice drift after her.

'You didn't tell her everything.'

And Desiree's quiet reply, heavy with something Bella couldn't quite name. 'Some things, she needs to discover for herself.'

Standing with her back to the fridge, Bella couldn't shake the conviction that Desiree knew more than she was letting on. But how to get it out of her needed some thought, and it wasn't going to happen here. The music turned louder again and Meesha came over to the fridge to top up her own glass. 'Come and sit with Selena. She said William used to play billiards at the pub.'

By the end of the night, Bella didn't think she'd ever been a part of such an inclusive and warm group of women. They all had opinions – often hilarious ones. Especially Elsa and Gerry, and it made Bella want to fly down to Melbourne and see Elsa on stage at that comedy club. Which would be a real mission, considering she was in Light-ning Ridge, but she suspected the comedian would be world class if she did ever get there.

As she bid goodnight to Luci and Meesha at the corner of Onyx Street, she kissed their cheeks. 'You were right, it was a fun night. Thanks, Meesha.'

Bella moved in for a final heartfelt hug, because this had been exactly the tonic she'd needed. She couldn't thank Meesha and Luci enough.

'BFFs.' Meesha's hiccough made the letters sound funny but no less serious.

Luci smiled and she lifted one hand as they turned left down Morilla Street towards their duplexes. She and Pluto were the only sober and sensible ones, and it looked like they were in charge of seeing Meesha home.

Chapter Thirteen

Meesha

The room spun as Meesha twirled through her doorway, her foot catching until she stumbled to a stop. Okay, maybe twirling wasn't the brightest idea right now. But lordy, what a night. Luci's laughter still echoed in her ears from when she'd dropped Meesha at her door – more genuine joy than she'd heard from her sister since she'd arrived in the Ridge.

That heavy moment when Bella and Desiree had talked about William had cast a shadow, but then – who'd have thought? – Bella had bounced back, trading one-liners with Elsa that had the whole group in stitches. Such a change from the wounded woman who'd shown up at that first party at The Iridescent Opal.

The wine buzzed pleasantly in Meesha's system as she replayed the night. The way Bella had worked the group, drawing out conversation from even the quietest ladies with that GP charm of hers.

Though Desiree . . . something had been off there. Their usually down-to-earth hostess had been subdued, distracted. Not that Meesha could entirely trust her own judgment after sharing that bottle of Konrad's red.

But something had shifted for her tonight as well. Before Bella, even after Luci had joined her in the Ridge, Meesha had always felt like the odd one out among the older ladies. Tonight, though . . . tonight had felt different. Balanced. Like they'd finally found their groove as a group.

The tap water ran cool over her fingers as she filled her glass.

She took one long drink, then refilled it. Her reflection in the kitchen window looked flushed, happy.

God, she was grateful for both of them – Luci and Bella. Their little trio. Her mouth curved into a grin, thinking about Bella's determined face when she'd announced she was heading to TJ's tomorrow. Poor bloke had no idea what was coming. She could picture his scowl already, that mountain of a man trying to dodge Bella's laser-focused questions about William.

Her grin slipped a little. William. She hadn't met him, but then she hadn't gone out in those crazy first months setting up the shop.

How could someone so like Bella . . . No. Too depressing to go there.

She went upstairs, relishing the cool air that hit her skin as she stripped off, stepping into the shower's warm spray. Better to think about the good stuff. A niece or nephew, soon. Her hand drifted to her flat stomach, imagining Luci's baby. Those early worries about managing faded a little more each day. Between Bella's medical know-how and friendship, and Eric's growing attachment to Luci, and nurse Matilda coming, things were looking up. And Bella, well, it was great that Bella wanted to learn more about opals. The woman needed a hobby even if she didn't find a passion. For Meesha, the Brisbane conference was coming, a chance to replenish her supplies and showcase her talents among her peers.

Steam curled around her as she smiled into the spray.

Everything would work out. Perfectly.

CHAPTER FOURTEEN

TJ

In TJ's first dream of the night, William held the jackhammer against the wall down in his mine. Surprised again at the wiry strength of the guy when he'd thought he was such a lightweight.

So, he showed him how to fill the bucket with load and bring it up through the second shaft on the hoist. Showed him how to spread out the opal dirt, to sift through it and turn large pieces over, looking for a trace of colour that might flash briefly.

In the dream, they laughed about the stirrings of a passion for opal as it bit William hard, like it had bitten TJ.

Suddenly, in the dream, William appeared on a distant ridge, and TJ knew something was wrong. He watched in horror as William tumbled down a mine and disappeared. TJ broke into a run but couldn't get closer no matter how hard he tried. He searched and searched, frantic, but couldn't find him.

TJ woke gasping, swore, his heart pumping as he reached out and downed the water beside his bed. He rolled back onto his pillow and closed his eyes, chest heaving, hating the hopeless feeling that wouldn't go. Eventually, he gave up and got out of bed, watched TV for an hour, went back to his bedroom where finally sleep claimed him again.

This time he saw the man who had targeted the shoppers.

TJ groaned. Saw the killer aim his rifle, and TJ dived in a desperate attempt to intercept the bullet. But it hit Sergeant Rhiannon Carter in the throat. Between the armour on her chest and her helmet. Took everything out, a clinical side of his brain noted. He saw the exit wound as she spun with the force and fell. The spray of arterial blood. The light dying in her eyes. Then the killer turned the gun on TJ's comrades.

TJ roared, leaping forward. Landed. Rolled. Charged towards the mongrel, firing his own gun as he went. One. Two. Three. The bullets smashed the killer backwards but there was no satisfaction, no triumph for good, because he knew it was too late.

Ree was dead. His mates were hit. He'd been too late. Again.

'Hello? You in there? TJ?' When he heard her voice, it was like redemption from the dreams. He waded out of the stickiness of blood in those terrible memories. This time, being woken was a good thing.

'Thank you, Belle Bird. Your timing is impeccable,' he muttered.

Except then the memories of Belle's own loss crashed in.

Her loss was just like his. He'd come to Lightning Ridge, run here, to escape the past, the failures. It had been working,

too, standing on these featureless rocky plains like a solitary mesa among a scattering of other mesas in the distance. Alone.

Until William had pushed in. Talking, talking, talking. Interested in everything.

Like his sister was pushing in. Talking. Asking. Questioning.

A minute passed.

'Hello? You in there? TJ?'

She brought back everything he thought he'd shoved down, back into the daylight.

A part of him growled that the dreams were her fault. Another part sighed and said he deserved them anyway.

He threw off the sheets, pulled on his shorts, slid on his Crocs and grabbed a T-shirt on the way, the unexpectedly cold air pebbling his skin. He yanked the cool material over his head and pushed open the door.

He'd forgotten it was Saturday.

He'd been working like crazy down the mine. Following the ghost of a seam that promised . . . something. Tiny glimmers teasing him into too-long hours of dig, shovel, rickshaw, hoist.

Hour after hour. Diverting the memories. Diverting the spectre of Belle's return on the weekend.

With the generator going, it hadn't mattered what time of the day or night he worked, because it was always dark down there in the mine until the lights went on.

Working to exhaustion had got him through the week.

He strode across the yard and threw up the bolt to let the gate swing open.

He stared at her. No friendliness in his expression. Even though he already knew the answer, he snapped, 'What do you want, Grey?'

She studied him right back. Blonde hair loose at her shoulders, wisps floating in the morning breeze. Stubborn chin lifted. Sapphire eyes glaring back at him. A pair of ridiculous tree earrings dangling from her pretty ears. He towered over her, but she didn't even twitch. Of course she didn't. He suppressed his sigh.

'I want to know about the last time you saw my brother. And I want to know about a man called Bane.' The words were clear and held a hint of interrogation. Demanding. As if she was the monster and not him.

He dragged a hand through his hair. Screwed his eyes shut.

Opened them. 'Then you'll go? Stop showing up? Never come back?'

She looked away, clearly thinking about it. The silence between them stretched like an elastic band ready to sting his skin when it was released.

Finally, she said, 'Maybe. But probably not.'

At least she hadn't lied. He hoped like hell he hadn't really felt a tiny, insidious flicker of relief when she'd said that, though.

They stood like two prize fighters waiting for the bell.

Ridiculous disparity in their body weights. The air between them pumping emotion like his generator pumped power.

TJ ground his teeth. Who was he kidding? He'd lost this round to her the second he got out of bed. He turned and strode back across the yard towards the house. Of course she followed. He could hear her quiet footsteps like the patter of rain on his soul.

Ah, hell. He stopped at the screen door, pulled it open and stood back, expectant. The ghost of the gentleman he'd been before Ree's death had turned him antisocial – a simple politeness.

She carried her little silver food bag past him up the stairs and stepped lightly into his house. 'Thank you.'

Damn – that floral, wispy scent trailed behind her as he tried hard not to stare at her perfect butt cupped in tight jeans.

He inhaled. Followed. The door slammed behind him as he watched her put the two cups on the table under his frown. She removed the bacon and egg rolls from the foil, pulled out a chair and sat down like she owned the place.

He threw himself into the chair opposite and reached for the coffee mug she'd brought. Might as well get his name engraved on the side of it by this point. He stared at his hand wrapped around the buffed metal, not knowing where to start.

'Do you really take your coffee black? No sugar?'

Her question derailed him. He looked up to find her watching him, her blue eyes attached to his face like steel limpet mines.

'Yes.'

Her head tilted in a nod. A small twitch of a smile. Didn't see what was so funny, but couldn't help looking at her again. One hand under her cheek. Blonde hair falling to the side. Her face so familiar, too familiar for someone he'd only seen four times. Not that he'd counted.

He could convince himself it was only because she looked like William. Or that he was trained to remember faces, pick out distinguishing features, categorise body types and recognise movement patterns.

But it wasn't any of that. It was her. William's Tinkerbell. His Belle.

This was dangerous territory. He wondered what William would've thought about his twin sitting comfortably in TJ's house.

Or her older brother. That one was easy – Dr Konrad wouldn't be happy about it at all.

TJ mulled over where to start. How to keep it simple? How to give her what she needed without causing more pain?

'I met William in the pub. Over a game of pool. He was better than I expected, and real competition is hard to find.' He shrugged.

Bella smiled but her eyes filled with grief. 'Mum and Dad put a table in the games room when we were growing up – we were maybe eleven? We practised together. We always played each other.' Her eyes seemed to refocus on him as she pulled herself away from the past. 'Did he beat you?'

TJ heard the hope in her voice and couldn't help staring at this soft yet fierce woman who did strange things to his emotions. He remembered William's concentration as his opponent. The careful consideration of angles had always amused TJ, who banked on raw natural ability and a marksman's eye. 'He tried hard enough.

Came close.'

'Dammit. I want to play you, now.'

His gut stabbed with pain at the competitive spirit. Geez. She was so like William.

And in other ways, she wasn't. He tried not to but imagined her bent over a pool table. Bum out. Looking at him from under her brows as she lined up a shot.

'Well, you can't.' The words were harsher than he'd meant them to be, and she winced. God, no. She was behind his eyes too much already. Behind his walls. 'You want this story or not?'

She pressed her lips together, stopping words he suspected would derail him again and waving him on. Silent. Patient. She had more patience than William. A mountain more than TJ.

Get this over with, man, he thought. 'Something was riding him. Memories, I think. He'd drink too much, staying at the pub long after I'd call it a night. Though then again, he never seemed to be drunk or hungover.'

She nodded, mouth turned down. The grief was in her eyes again. 'Konrad said he was drinking here.'

Then she didn't need these details from TJ. He was just causing her more pain. 'He met a bloke. Bad. Not the sort he should hang with, but he wouldn't listen.'

'Bad in what way?'

In every way, TJ thought. The bastard had left town after William died, and he'd hunted for him but never found him.

Maybe he should have kept looking. 'One of those easily offended, entitled dicks you see on the street after the pub shuts.

Loud. Dishonest. A sometimes ratter. An obnoxious drunk. A little big man.' He glanced at her. 'You know the type?' He saw by her face she did. 'William wasn't perfect, but he was honest.

Don't know what he saw in this bloke, or why he gave him the time of day.'

'Bane.'

'Yeah.' He narrowed his eyes. Where had she got the name from anyway? 'That's his name – not a good person. But the mongrel was sure he'd found an ATM in William.'

'ATM?' Her brow crinkled. 'From what Konrad said, William didn't have any money to dole out. He was working casual, hardly making enough to live off. Mel said he worked behind the bar at the pub sometimes.'

'Not often.'

'He wouldn't take any money from Konrad, or from anyone, as far as Konrad knew.'

TJ huffed a harsh laugh. 'I think Bane was looking more long term than that. William had a brother who was a doctor in town.

He had rich doctor parents living in a coastal city. Future wealth. Bane latched on. That's the kind of leech he was.'

CHAPTER FIFTEEN BELLA

BELLA WATCHED TJ AS he spoke, letting the words drop over her one at a time. She had excellent recall, and she'd replay them again later.

But for now, she studied the hard lines of TJ's face, chiselled like the rocks on his bench outside, planes and shadows, sharp edges and dark hollows. A simmering darkness under the skin.

The man rarely smiled. And when he laughed, it was harsh and mocking, as if life had already played too many pitiless jokes on him. She wondered what the world had bestowed on him in the past to make him so bitter.

The doctor as well as the psychology student inside her said he overflowed with anguish. He'd tried to intimidate her with his size and his height. Not that it had worked. But it suggested he often used it as a defence. Or offence. Yet, she didn't think he was a bully. He'd shown her unexpected common courtesy today, opening the door for her, thanking her for the food. So, what was his core trait? His philosophy? Maybe he was a protector? Maybe that was something he'd failed at in the past and it haunted him?

She hadn't heard him swear except for 'hell' and 'dick'. He kept himself and his home clean and neatly ordered. The man was an enigma.

Worryingly, he fascinated Bella when she didn't want to be fascinated – she was far, far too busy finding out about William's last days for that – but then, it seemed there was something in TJ that had drawn in her twin as well.

That first day she'd come here, TJ had said he'd let her brother down. Which meant he cared. Or did it? She was so sick of guessing.

Was the tough loner image an illusion, or 'what you see is what you get'? Hard to tell when he only gave her specks of information – passing her one miserly, minute crumb at a time, like the grains from the shattered sandstone outside.

William had been drinking more – maybe. He'd met Bane, a man TJ disliked. That man wanted to use William for money, maybe take advantage of his family.

She needed to find Bane. 'So where is he? This man? This Bane?'

'No idea. I searched. He left at the same time . . .' He didn't finish the sentence.

The same time as William left the suicide note. 'Was it you who found the note? Konrad said one of William's friends brought it to him.'

Bella closed her eyes. She had no idea how she'd come to that conclusion, but Konrad had said William had few friends in town.

TJ had clearly been his friend. TJ would be reliable. It just seemed right.

She breathed in the pain and let it go. Opened her lids and found him watching her. Dark eyes darker with some emotion.

'What?'

'Yes. I found the note taped to my gate when I came home from town.' He hadn't told her that before. His face shuttered. 'Must have been the last place he went to before he . . . Must have already decided what he was going to do.'

For a second, just a glimpse, she saw the remorse, the horror, the regret that he hadn't been home to stop the tragedy.

'I gave it to Konrad,' TJ said, then shifted as if ready to stand.

'But I know nothing else.' He shook his head as he studied her. No doubt she looked as devastated as she felt hearing this. 'I'm not helping anymore. That's everything. You should go.'

'No. I waited all week to talk to you. I need more than the time it takes you to drain a mug of coffee and escape out the nearest window.'

'Not the window.' He gestured to the door. 'I've got work to do.'

She said quietly, 'It helps me to be here with you.'

'What?' He looked genuinely taken aback. Horrified, in fact. 'How could it?'

His shock matched her own. She didn't understand it either, but there was no denying the strange relief she felt when she saw him.

'There's no easy answer to that.' She squinted as if that would help her see more clearly, but it didn't. 'You make me feel . . . Less lost. Less alone without William.'

That got him out of the chair. He sprang from it like it was a slingshot, his hands spread wide. 'You really need to go. You're imagining it.'

Whoa there, excessive response. 'What are you afraid of, TJ?'

He didn't answer. The silence stretched between them. One minute. Two.

When he didn't answer, she huffed. 'And what the heck does TJ stand for, anyway?'

'TJ. The Jinx,' he said drily. 'So run along, little girl, before I jinx you. Like I jinxed your brother. Like I jinx everyone. I've got work to do.'

And he left, his broad back all she saw as he blocked the light from the door and pushed it open, leaving her in his house.

Somehow, she didn't think he was in the habit of leaving people in his house. Alone. Unsupervised. Unobserved. Unless he had a camera in here.

She glanced around but couldn't see any hidden observation point inside the house like the ones outside. So, that was twice he'd left her alone now, inside his home. Which suggested he trusted her. And if he trusted her, then it was likely he had trusted William.

This man might call himself 'The Jinx', but he wouldn't trust lightly.

At least she had a little more information about William, even if it was frustratingly scarce. But she was further along than she had been, and she could still try again tomorrow.

She took one last look at TJ's domain. No way did that 'J'

stand for Jinx. He was more like 'The Jungle'. Hidden. Mysterious.

Or maybe 'The Jaguar'. Something dark that could jump out at you at any time. Dangerous – but magnificent.

Good, grief. *Magnificent.*

She needed a safer word.

And she should get out of the guy's house.

She glanced at his bedroom where the bed was tousled, yet the ends still tucked in tightly.

'Sweet heaven, you have hospital corners,' she murmured out loud. Her gaze landed on the swathed boxes across the room.

Again, she thought they looked so out of place.

Though, from this angle, the mound didn't look like boxes anymore. She wanted to go over and inspect it, but she wouldn't do that without his permission. She had a feeling that was a line she shouldn't cross. And besides, that would really be snooping. She gathered up her coffee mugs. Noted that he'd taken the rolls again.

She stepped out of his house but couldn't spot him in the yard.

He'd disappeared down his hole like a . . . not a rabbit. Not a rat.

Not a snake. She was pretty sure that jaguars didn't go to ground.

Like a bear going back into his cave. Yes. She smiled at her own whimsy.

She walked over to the edge of his cave. 'Hey, TJ. You have to eat lunch. I'll be back at one. We need to talk more about Bane.'

His voice growled up from the depths. 'Don't bother.'

She grinned. Eyes narrowing. Challenge accepted.

CHAPTER SIXTEEN

TJ

TJ leaned his head back and bumped his helmet against the tunnel wall once. *Arrgghhhh*. That woman. He stared at the row of bare bulbs running along the roof, the uneven sandstone and the circular shaft with the ladder bolted to the wall leading to the outside light.

His eyes landed on the place where William had helped him start the new tunnel.

But in his chest, bizarrely, the world felt lighter. Even his hard mouth twitched. No wonder William had idolised his sister – she was an unstoppable, immovable force. And sexy as hell. She brought to mind thoughts he hadn't considered acting on with any woman for a long time.

The only wins he'd scored against Belle were when he walked away. Which had started the first time he'd met her.

'Pattern happening here, mate,' he growled to himself, and his voice echoed back softly.

Mate. Mate. Mate. The walls mocking him. He might have escaped her physical presence down here, but she was still with him.

She'd asked him what he was afraid of.

That one was easy: destroying her. Like he'd destroyed everyone else he cared about. But that answer wouldn't wash with Dr Grey.

His gaze travelled down to the jackhammer leaning against the wall. He remembered her brother in his dream, and memories from real life when William had come down the shaft.

Now he studied the tool with its tip resting on sandstone. Belle was like a jackhammer, he was the mine, and she was drilling away against his walls. And there was a distinct possibility that he just might cave.

Problem was, he doubted she'd be thrilled when she saw what came down on her head.

He couldn't stop her – no, that wasn't true. All he had to do was not open his locked gate. Not invite her into his home. Push away her ridiculous coffee and food that he fooled himself were the only reasons he'd let her in.

Instead, if he wasn't strong enough, maybe he should do what he'd warned her he would – get a scary dog. He wouldn't hear her calling down the mine and she wouldn't get through the gate with his pet guarding it.

Nope. Couldn't do that either. She could be stubborn enough to get hurt – or she'd probably be a dog whisperer like her twin had been.

What he wanted to do, what he'd already imagined in his dreams, was take her to his bed and unwrap her like a coveted parcel to get her out of his system. Because he suspected – he saw it in her smoky blue eyes – she wasn't immune to him either.

Them together would be wanton and wild. He wanted her.

Badly. Why not? They were both grown adults. Despite the sudden surge of hunger that had nothing to do with the food she'd brought, he knew that wasn't the answer, either. Dangerous, dangerous fantasy. Acting on it was the worst thing he could do.

He could go away for a while. Pack up, lock everything down.

Leave town. Leave Belle, so she couldn't jackhammer him anymore.

Logistically, though, what about the ratters? He had that new glimmer in his south wall, and they'd been sniffing around his camp since that last bag of coloured stone he'd sold to Meesha a month ago.

He had cameras. He had people he could call on. And he had street cred. Nope. They wouldn't breach his walls again after the last lot he'd caught. Including Bane. That incident had built him a dangerous reputation that had kept ratters away from his mine for almost three years.

Maybe he'd go off and try to hunt down Bane again. Might find him this time, if the last few years of peace had given the dirtbag a false sense of security. Odd that Belle had only been in the Ridge for a couple of weeks asking questions about her brother and she'd already zeroed in on a man he'd all but forgotten.

Finding Bane would feel good. He could use the skills he'd honed in the police force to track him down. Call in some favours.

And if he found the scum, what would he do? What could he do?

Rattle his brains. Shake him until the truth came out.

TJ sighed. The man didn't have any truth inside. He'd just scream whatever he thought TJ wanted to hear.

But he could bring him to Belle, and that might get her off his back.

He laughed out loud, one harsh, bitter snort. That'd sort Bane out, if he set Belle the jackhammer onto him. Ridiculous idea but amusing and somehow appealing to let someone else take the brunt of Belle's determination to find out the truth about her brother's death.

And what was the truth? Most likely scenario, William had taken his own life, just as his note had said, but . . . the more Belle questioned it, the more unease bothered TJ, too. Hopefully her digging wouldn't produce a scenario even more painful to live with. Still, she wouldn't give up until she'd solved it, he suspected. And strangely, his mood seemed seemed slightly restored after her visit.

TJ shovelled the freshly dug opal-bearing clay into the steel bucket to winch back to the surface. She'd said she'd return at lunchtime. One o'clock. She'd be on time.

Maybe his offer to leave and search for Bane would be an excuse to escape on weekends.

TJ worked a solid four hours in the mine, achieving more than usual in that time, and he had most of it hoisted topside up the other shaft by the time he stopped. He'd need to go to the dam and wash his loads soon and sort through everything properly.

But he could do that during the week when a certain visitor wasn't due.

Still, a satisfying morning had been achieved. He could do with a small break now. Maybe even stretch out on the bed until she came back.

Which was why he showered, he told himself. Put on clean clothes. Even considered putting on a dark blue shirt instead of a black one for a change. Or none at all.

Mate. He mocked himself as he glanced at the clock. Two minutes to one. He'd gone out three minutes ago and unlatched the gate.

Ah. There she was. The rattle of stones on the track and the purr of her engine outside his unusually open window.

Seems he even recognised her car now.

He'd given up on the idea of keeping her outside and eating at the sorting table, because it was just too hot. Inside, the aircon made it cool despite the blazing day.

He rolled off the bed and crossed the floor. Stood at his back door as she approached.

'Becoming quite the habit. You turning up here with food.'

He pushed open the door for her from the top of the steps, which meant she had to squeeze past him in her sleeveless top and tight jeans, her foil bag in one hand. Her scent and warmth sliding against him deliciously. Her body hot on his. Mean of him, but satisfying.

'I was just thinking that,' she said over one slim shoulder. 'It must be your turn to supply a meal.'

'I don't cook.' He did but he wasn't going domestic with her.

Not for her. That was one step too far.

'And yet,' she tilted her chin at him, 'I noted food inside your fridge when I put the rolls in there. Looked pretty stocked to me.

For someone who doesn't cook, that is.'

'Observant, aren't you?'

'Not as much as I could be. I pride myself on being circumspect.'

He laughed at that. Really laughed. Probably the first time since William had made him laugh that time in the pub when he'd said he'd run naked down the street if TJ beat him at darts.

William won but it had been close. He watched her eyes widen.

Yes, she was so like her twin. At the thought of William, his laughter died, like it should. 'You? Circumspect? When have you been circumspect?'

'I haven't snooped in your house.'

He raised his brows at that. 'I haven't snooped in yours either.'

And didn't that make a delightful thought. He'd like to see where she slept. Undressed. Bathed.

He blinked. Dragged that image away in haste.

'There's nothing worth snooping for at mine. But I am intrigued by those boxes in the corner there.' She pointed. 'Draped untidi-ness doesn't fit the rest of your aesthetic.'

Since when did he have an aesthetic? Unless the look was noir cop.

Yes, she was observant all right. He was not going there. No.

And interesting that she knew it annoyed him to see the shrouded disorder. 'What did you bring for lunch?'

She glared at him for a few long seconds then opened the bag on the table. 'Greta's roast beef. And gravy.'

As soon as she opened the zipped bag, he could smell it. Rich meat. Veggies. Gravy. 'There are certain advantages to you coming here,' he said, going to the fridge and pulling out two beers. He put one in front of her.

She nodded her thanks. 'Really?'

World changes, now he'd offered to drink beer together. 'Yeah,' he said. *Erudite as always,* he chided himself. He chose two knives and forks out of his tidy cutlery drawer. 'All of them have to do with food and coffee.'

'This is good. But I like iced water more than beer. And come on,' she said. 'You know you like to see my smiling face.' She laughed –

and what a laugh it was. Throaty and low. The hairs stood up on his arms and his gut clenched.

He shook his head at her, couldn't help glancing at her gorgeous face, and sat down. How had they got here, to this rapport? He was doomed.

She only stayed an hour, to eat, to ask about other times William had come here, and then she left.

After she departed, as promised, he made a few discreet inquiries at far-off places he thought Bane might have gone. He wouldn't need her for this. It would take a good nineteen hours on the road to reach Coober Pedy, but Bane had mentioned a cousin there who'd made a good find, and TJ's police friend had thought there was a man there who might answer the description.

Different name, though that didn't concern TJ. Who knew if Bane was his actual name? A slimeball like him could have an alias in every town. He'd try a couple of other places and if nothing came of it he'd just go to South Australia and see.

He guessed it could take days to hear back with a confirmation, and suddenly TJ didn't want to waste that time. The little snake had been obsessed with opals almost as much as he'd been obsessed with scamming newcomers out of their money, so a town where he could carry on his ratter predilection seemed the most likely.

TJ wondered about White Cliffs, another place he thought the weasel might have settled in. He didn't have any contacts there so would have to physically check – which meant a trip to the opal town, eight hours' drive each way from the Ridge, but he could do that tomorrow, and that way Bella wouldn't be able to come calling. Which was safer for her – and for him.

He thought about checking in with the dodgy miners Bane had hung out with here in town, but they were connections TJ didn't want to spook – not just yet.

Sunday morning, early, TJ drove his black F truck away from Lightning Ridge. Away from Bella and her breakfast and coffee before she arrived. Out through Bourke, Cobar and Wilcannia, dropping into each town once the bars opened to question the pub-licans, because Bane's ways made him memorable in a distasteful way to those who served drinks.

He hit White Cliffs at p.m., scouting the town and starting by chatting up the bartenders in the pub. Nobody had seen Bane.

TJ sighed, accepted it wasn't going to be a quick success, even though he hung about for a while in the bar but without luck.

Mentally, he prepared for the longer drive later in the week.

White Cliffs had character, with quirky underground motels and dugouts like Coober Pedy – not a bad idea since the weather had turned stinking hot with the approach of summer – but after a pub meal, he opened his swag and slept in the back of his truck for the night before heading home early on Monday.

He didn't bother going the extra distance to Broken Hill; if he was heading to Coober Pedy later in the week anyway, he'd go past the town on the way and could check then.

Of course finding the little weasel at the first stop would have been too easy. At least the size of the Cliffs meant it unlikely the man had been missed in TJ's search.

*

TJ spent the next three days securing his fortress back at the Ridge, and by Wednesday night he'd added two more cameras that would activate on his mobile phone if they picked up any trespassers. One pointing at the mine and one at the camp. He'd also thick-chained and padlocked the protective grate to the mine and secured the shed with all his equipment.

When he left town again, he could pull down the roller screen shutters on the house and lock the gate on his way out.

He was ready. Didn't need to wait till Friday. Just needed to drop his latest haul of stones off at Meesha's for cutting, because she was better at it than him and would give him a good price.

And see how she was going with that setting for Belle's opal.

Then he should leave. Without seeing Belle. No contact.

CHAPTER SEVENTEEN

MEESHA

On Tuesday night, Bella and Luci sipped tea in Meesha's lounge room after their now nightly sessions in the workshop.

Meesha had introduced Bella to opal preparation, and her new friend had seemed to find that absorbing, but tonight Bella's thoughts were not in a happy place.

Meesha didn't know how to help.

She wondered if she was brave enough to approach the elephant in the room. That's what friends did, right? They tackled the hard stuff. She'd try anyway, and if Bella didn't want to talk, that would be fine, too.

'You know, Bella,' she said carefully. 'We've never really talked about William.'

Bella looked up from the mug of tea she'd been frowning into.

'I don't usually.'

'I understand that, but know he's on your mind a lot. Especially with TJ not coming through with the information you'd hoped for.

Would it help, or is it worse if you talk about him?'

Bella tilted her head sideways, looking a little startled.

Thoughtfully, she said, 'You know what, Meesha, I think that's been some of the problem. Since we lost him, we – me and my family – haven't talked much about William at all. Maybe because of the way it all went down. We've avoided the subject because of the pain. The not knowing *why*.' She blew out a breath. 'But it does seem sad I'm not remembering the good times as a result.'

Meesha waited, but when Bella didn't go on, she said, 'I'm just gonna ask. What's it like to have a twin? I can't imagine a sibling that close.' She tilted her head towards Luci. 'Or one that wasn't older and wiser.'

Luci laughed. 'That's me. And I'd like to hear about your William, too, Bella, if you want to talk about him.'

'Umm. Okay.' Bella loosened her neck like a prize fighter about to enter the ring. There was a long silence, and Meesha almost said, no, don't worry, when Bella began. 'So. Having a twin was amazing. Wonderful and annoying in equal parts.' She smiled and shook her head. 'As kids we always played together. Games were fun, because you didn't have to explain stuff to your twin. Thoughts crossed, like seeing the swing-set outside when he wanted to go there. Or playing a trick on Konrad without having to explain a practical joke.' She smiled at the memory. 'Like me holding his attention while William popped a bag behind him to make him jump. We had lots of in-jokes between the two of us.' She waved her hand. 'We rarely fought, because it would be like fighting with yourself. He was always there.' She winced. 'Until he wasn't.'

Ouch. Meesha really considered dropping the subject now, but as if the lid was off Bella continued. 'I didn't always know what he was thinking, but when I did, I understood why he thought that. Does that seem weird?'

When both Meesha and Luci shook their heads, she kept going.

'And it was the same for me. William understood things that were important to me. He knew when I was upset and vice versa, even when we weren't together. But that lessened as we got older and spent less time together.' She studied her clasped fingers.

Meesha nodded, fascinated. 'I know you went to uni, to study medicine after you left school, but what did William do?'

Bella looked up. 'He didn't go to uni. He did well at school, chased girls, all normal stuff until he joined the police force. My father would have preferred another profession for him. Dad had a good friend who really struggled after spending his life around criminals and nice people who became victims, and Dad blamed this man's job for sucking the life out of him. But William was determined. He had this moral justice thing going on. Couldn't stand bullies. I guess a lot of police are like that.'

Meesha remembered Bella's distress at hearing how Luci had been let down by Batte. 'Gee. How unusual. I bet you're the same, Dr Bella.'

Bella smiled back, a real smile, and Meesha's relief grew as her friend's disclosures about her brother seemed to flow more easily.

Luci said, 'So, William believed in sticking up for people?'

'Strongly. When we were kids, Konrad would have to monster other kids to extricate us. We'd both go bowling in against bigger kids if we thought something was unfair. William was like me on steroids in that regard. I guess the police force was a natural progression for him. In the beginning, he loved it.'

'In the beginning?'

'That's the strange thing.' Bella paused, her brow wrinkling in thought before she continued. 'He was so happy at the start. Had a great flat, a girlfriend, good mates. After a couple of years, the girlfriend left, and he went quiet and not long later he left the force. He wasn't the same after that.'

Luci nodded slowly, and Meesha considered the information.

Broken relationships could skew people. 'Do you think he'd been badly hurt, then? Lost love? Did that make him change?'

Bella seemed to peer into the past. 'I don't think it was that. He seemed almost blasé about Jill. I tried to find out what happened, but he wouldn't talk about it. It wasn't a grand passion, was what I gathered. But after William died, Konrad was convinced that was where it had all started. I just didn't see him caring that much about her. I should have paid more attention.'

Meesha stood up. 'You were a new doctor, by that point.' She refilled Bella's tea and her own. 'You had a lot going on.'

'Thanks.' Bella tapped the mug. 'Sure. I was busy, had lots of exams, was working long hours as a resident, so I guess William and I sort of drifted apart more than usual.' She shook her head.

'I regret that so much, now.'

Meesha could see the depth of that sadness and her heart squeezed for her friend. Maybe talking about this wasn't such a good idea.

Luci added, 'Sounded like he drifted too. Not all you.'

'You're right.' Bella spread her hands. 'He left me with lots of unanswered calls. Then he moved out here, and Konrad moved temporarily, too – ostensibly to do a locum, but really to check on him. Then he ended up staying out of worry, because William seemed to be living on the edge. Alcohol. Pub mates. No real job.'

'Did he drink much before?' Meesha asked.

Bella frowned and shook her head. 'Neither of us ever did. Didn't care for it that much. But maybe he changed.' She shrugged.

'Started hanging with the wrong people, maybe. Stopped talking about his feelings. We just didn't know how to help him.'

So sad, Meesha thought. 'Must have been hard to watch.'

Bella gave her a crooked smile as if she knew what she was thinking. 'Yes. Then it was all over, too late. He was gone.'

Meesha waited and when Bella didn't say more, she asked carefully, 'What do you think happened?'

'I really don't know. Taking his own life is so out of character to be honest, it's why I'm here. Nothing adds up.'

'I totally get that.' The only thing strange about Bella coming to the Ridge was how long it had taken her to arrive. But grief wasn't linear, as Meesha knew from her own experience. 'Isn't depression and suicide out of character for anyone, though?'

'Yes, and I'm sure that's the truth for many families affected by suicide. But it was incredibly strange for William as far as I'm concerned.' Bella's voice grew determined. 'If . . . *When* I find Bane, I'll be looking at that.'

Meesha blinked at the change and savoured the mood lift. Yep.

That was the Bella she was coming to know. 'Okay then. How?'

'Don't know yet.' Bella stood. 'Now, I better go home. I need some shut eye. Big day at work tomorrow and more opal polishing tomorrow night.'

The three of them stood at that thought.

When Meesha opened the door for Bella, she was surprised when her friend gave her a long, extended squeeze. 'Thanks for asking me about William. I haven't been able to do that with anyone, except TJ, and he wasn't exactly open to it. So, thank you. It means a lot.'

Meesha felt the prickle of tears in her throat. She hoped she had helped and hadn't just stirred up the pain. 'You can talk about him anytime with us. That's what friends are for. See you tomorrow night.'

On Wednesday evening, before Bella arrived, Meesha closed the last claw on the pendant and checked the others were properly compressed towards each other to eliminate any gaps, ensuring the opal remained firmly caught in their grip.

Nope – perfect. It wouldn't loosen. She'd cut a small groove in each claw to seat and stop the stone from slipping before she'd tightened it. She used a magnifying glass to check if she needed to trim any claw edges to stop them catching or snagging, then polished the whole thing to finish. Then threaded the finished opal onto the long chain she'd chosen so Bella could slip it on and off without having to unclip it, and the pendant would fall to just above her cleavage.

Good to go. TJ would be happy – the piece glowed with green and blue fire from within the platinum surrounds, hanging true and eye-stopping from the white gold chain. Bella would love it.

Hopefully Brisbane would love it if Bella gave the okay. Meesha loved it. Not long till the awards.

She stood, stretched and reached forward to pull one of her designer boxes out of a drawer to package the necklace.

Straightened the presentation. Done.

As she stood to return the box to the safe, her fingers traced the dwindling stack of raw opals.

Not good. Tourist traffic had been mad lately – a blessing and a curse. Her display cases had begun to look sparse, the void making her stomach clench. She'd been on the phone all morning, suppliers hemming and hawing about selling stock.

Weird thing was, the Ridge was crawling with miners these days.

Opal wasn't a diminishing resource and its value increased every year. Heck, good-quality black opals were rarer than diamonds, but Lightning Ridge was the place for them. Yet despite the opal and the miners out there, there was less and less stock. Where was all the opal going?

Through the window, she caught a glimpse of Eric next door, measuring something on Luci's porch. Meesha had to smile at the way he kept sneaking glances through the window, probably hoping for a glimpse of her sister.

The big softie had started carrying around Braille flashcards in his work shirt pocket. He'd even bought a green plastic Braille writing board on Amazon to press Braille letters onto paper for Luci.

Between him, and Luci's alternating antenatal appointments coming up with Bella, keeping Moree trips to a minimum, Luci was blooming. Maybe some of that was Eric's attention. From Luci's actions, something might truly blossom there after the baby was born and Luci had settled into motherhood. Meesha had to wonder.

Speaking of Bella . . . Meesha looked towards the safe, then glanced at the time. Made her think of Sunday's visit when Bella had found TJ's gate locked.

She'd love to know what was going on between her friend and TJ on their weekend meet-ups. Her lips curved. Could be fun to watch, at least. Though, it made a girl think.

These quiet evenings with Bella and Luci were gold, but listening to their talk of Eric and TJ had stirred something. For the first time, her workshop felt almost empty, especially now Eric was always at

Luci's. Maybe she needed . . . no, not needed, just wouldn't mind someone of the opposite sex to dress up for, share a bottle of wine with at the local Italian restaurant. She snorted.

The Ridge's fine dining options were limited but male companions were too.

As if she had the time, anyway.

The sketch pad under her elbow sat filled with new designs and she couldn't wait to show Bella – because her friend's new enthusiasm for opal jewellery filled her with joy, reminding her of when she'd first fallen in love with opals herself.

But first she had to sort this staffing nightmare at The Iridescent Opal. If Brisbane came through and led to the American shows . . . Her heart did a little skip at the thought. Who could she trust to look after the shop? These days, her display cases held a small fortune in precious stone. Even with Luci's sharp ears next door, she needed someone solid. More than Gillian as a casual that was for sure. With a sigh, she picked up the new piece she'd set aside while she'd finished TJ's order.

A knock at the door had her setting down the new stone carefully again. Right on time. When she opened the door to greet Bella, the hug was automatic now, comfortable. 'Hey, Bella. How was your day?'

'Good. Busy. And yours?'

The memory of today's big sale flooded back, warming her chest. 'I sold that set of earrings and the matching silver drop pendant – you know, the ones like your earrings?'

'The blue opal one with the tree branch?'

'Yep.' Pride hummed through her veins.

'You star!' Bella pulled back and looked at Meesha, her face breaking into a grin. 'You had six thousand dollars on that set.

We should open champagne!'

'Sounds like an idea to me.' The laugh felt so good. 'Bubbles at least. I have two piccolos, so we won't drink too much – mustn't hurt our opals.' Her hand drifted to the stones still waiting to be cut. 'These things are precious.'

Chapter Eighteen

Bella

Thirty minutes later, Bella smoothed the opal on the end of her dop stick. *No, not opal*, she corrected herself. *It's a nobby*.

It was the third night this week she'd found solace working in Meesha's workshop. Not solace from William, though that pain was easing a little, too, especially after talking about her twin so openly the night before, but solace from a less painful, more aggra-vating annoyance.

Some of it stemmed from when she'd stormed home after her fruitless visit to TJ's on Sunday, her head spinning and full of a cold determination that she would work out the thought processes of that infuriating man one day soon.

Her mind had needed a diversion and Meesha had given her one.

She looked down at the irregular dome in her hand. The rough had been the size of a finger and she'd worked it down to a fat thumbnail-size. Bella had her own corner now at the rear of Meesha's workshop and she'd bought a bag of low-quality nobby stones to practise on. The first one had irregularities and large imperfections – a problem value-wise, but it excited her to know she was bringing the best out of material born of ancient sandstone, transformed through millennia of acidic weathering within sedimentary clay.

Right now, her goal was to tease this second faulty opal fully from its bed.

The whir of her polishing wheel filled the workshop and, surprisingly, Bella found clearing the grit and inclusions quieted her impatience with TJ. In the process she found peace and focus, channelling her efforts into something creative and absorbing that soothed her scattered emotions.

Not to mention this was a skill she could wave in TJ's face, one that even pertained to his own work. No idea why all roads led to TJ these days. Did that make it better? Or did it make her petty?

The last two nights, they'd just worked quietly from seven till nine like Meesha did every night, and then Bella went home to bed, soothed and settled. Simple. Opal therapy. She smiled at that.

Before she came over tonight, she'd resumed her education on opal cutting via YouTube, while scoffing down the other half of Greta's to-die-for pilaf. Next week she'd start the online course she'd enrolled in, too.

Tonight, here with her nobby, finally comfortable with it secured to her dop stick with wax, she felt she had good control for when she was on the wheel to finish shaping the dome. The intense concentration of rounding the perfect shape from the unpolished opal absorbed her. It was like a puzzling medical problem, seeking the core and life of the stone she worked with, something different yet similar to uncovering the clue to a baffling patient.

She'd needed a point of sanity, something she could concentrate on to keep her grounded when she thought of William's secrets and his final days. What had really happened? Was the note real, or was there more to the story?

Kicking herself now, she knew she should have asked these questions long ago. On top of that was the frustration with TJ – if he knew something, even if not everything – that made her want to march right back up to his black shack and force him to help her find Bane.

He hadn't been home on Sunday. Or he'd disappeared down his mine and hadn't answered her. Well, she wasn't planning on shouting outside his gate again.

She had time. A purpose. A home. She thought about the medical practice and smiled.

This move to Lightning Ridge was working. She enjoyed her flat, her work, her people. And right now, she had no plans to leave the Ridge.

Funny that. She appreciated her quirky patients more than she had for years in Port Macquarie, and she really enjoyed Meesha's and Luci's wonderful company. Heck, even Friday nights with the Lightning Ridge Ladies had been downright fun.

But she'd been here more than a month now and needed to ask her parents to visit, though a tiny part of her psyche worried it would bring back all the sadness and ennui she'd left at home.

Here, her world had stabilised in ways she hadn't expected.

Except for TJ.

So, when she looked up from her cutting wheel that Wednesday evening, and saw the tall, broad wall of him standing at Meesha's workshop door, she had an unexpected urge to poke his massive chest and demand that he help her.

His gaze rested on her with such weight she could feel the pressure from three metres away, his eyes shadowed and stormy with some emotion she couldn't read. Then he strode across the room and to her side. 'What are you doing here?'

She stood. It didn't give her much advantage, but it was better than sitting with him looming over her. She tilted her chin.

'I thought you were a miner?'

'I am a miner,' he rumbled.

She raised her brows. ' *Sooooo*, what am I doing, TJ? It should be obvious.'

'I see you two are still snarking at each other.' Meesha's voice came from behind TJ's shoulder.

'Yeah. I've had the pleasure a few times now.' He said it as if it was anything but. He gestured towards Bella. 'You got a new cutter, Meesha?'

'Bella's learning the trade. She can't be *just* a doctor all her life,' Meesha teased.

Bella loved this girl. 'I'm learning. Meesha's very patient with me.' She held up the stone on her dop stick. 'I bought a bag of poor-quality nobbies and I'm practising.'

He stepped back to study her, as if he hadn't seen her before . . . or at least hadn't considered she had this complexity in her. 'Playing in the dirt with your pretty hands?'

She raised her brows and held her hands up. Studied the backs of them, turned them over, looked at the palms. 'You think they're pretty?'

'Sure,' he said. Then he turned to Meesha. 'Got a bag of opal for you.'

Bella refused to feel slighted.

Meesha's interest shot out, the opal-obsessed businesswoman emerging. 'Yeah? A bag? Show me.'

TJ kept his back to Bella, as if they hadn't just been verbally sparring with each other, and strode to the table with the brightest lamp. He flicked out a square of thick cloth with one hand and slid a drawstring bag from his pocket.

Bella moved closer, scrambling for composure but also curiously satisfied with the brief clash. That was just sick, she mocked herself.

She watched as TJ widened the neck string of the bag slowly while he studied Meesha's expression, a flare of amusement creasing his eyes. The smile looked good on him. He tipped the contents of the bag onto the square of cloth in a controlled tumble and stood back. Lots of rough, but also enticing splashes of colour – iridescent green, blue and even a twinkle of red catching the light.

'Ohhhh. You found a seam,' she breathed.

'Wouldn't say that. Going away for a few days, so no word to anyone.' He swung back to Bella, and she nodded.

She held her hands up and wiped her finger across her mouth for good measure. 'Lips are sealed.' But where was he going?

His eyes darkened, seemingly caught on that finger as she touched her mouth. Her belly tumbled at his instant response.

Whoa. What? She did *not* just react to that.

'Well, you might have brought him good luck, Bella,' Meesha teased absent-mindedly as she passed her fingers through the stones, picking one up and weighing it in her hand. She rifled through them to see the strands of brilliant colour in the light.

Reverently, she added, 'You've even got a tiny bit of red on black! Must be important if you're leaving now.'

'I'll be back.'

Was he going to look for that man, Bane? Without her?

Suspicion took hold and Bella stepped closer, but Meesha had her business face on as she turned to TJ and threw her hand back towards the table in a wild gesture at the bounty. 'With that in your camp?'

He shrugged. 'Camp's secure. That's most of it, anyway. I'll be back soon.'

'Okay. It's your mine. But I'm thinking there might be an element out there taking the easy way to find stones. I told you something's going on. The opal's drying up.'

They stared at each other for long moments. Finally, he said, 'I hear you. Something I'll look more into when I get back.'

She nodded and then glanced towards the safe. 'I've finished that commission you wanted.'

TJ went still. Glanced at Bella. Back at Meesha. Back at Bella.

'You should give it to her now, then.'

Meesha asked quietly, 'Don't you want to do that?'

Were they talking about her? What commission?

TJ looked away. 'Not mine to give.' He rolled his hand at Meesha as if to say, *Hurry up and get it.*

When she returned with a black shop box but didn't say anything, he heaved a sigh and turned to Bella. 'Your brother gave me this. William,' he clarified. 'To mind for you. He was planning to give it to you. Before it all went down. After he . . . well, I forgot about it. Found it last week and gave it to Meesha to set because I felt bad.' He scrubbed his head. 'Sorry for the delay.'

Meesha handed TJ the box and he frowned at her but took it and handed it to Bella. 'From William.'

Bella sucked in a breath. Looked at the closed black box with Meesha's designer logo on top. She was almost scared to open it.

'What, was it meant to be like a going away present?' The horror in her voice made TJ shake his head fast.

'Absolutely not,' he snapped, throwing his hand up. 'I remember, he was excited about it. Didn't want it stolen. He planned to get it made into a necklace for your birthday. We talked about it a week before he . . .' TJ shook his head again. Cursed under his breath when he saw her expression. 'Anyway. I asked Meesha to fix it so you could wear it more easily.'

Bella lifted her head, tearing her eyes from the boxed treasure in her hand. 'Why would you do that?'

'I don't know.' He sounded testy now and scrubbed the back of his head. 'So, you wouldn't lose it. Hell, maybe just because the stone deserves it. And with apologies for not sending it to you earlier.'

'Open it,' Meesha said quietly, as if she understood how Bella battled with her emotions. 'It's a beautiful stone. You should wear it all the time.'

'You do that.' TJ shrugged half-heartedly. 'Thankfully it's not my problem now.'

When Bella opened the box, the luminous opal seemed to jump out with bottom-of-the-ocean-through-sunlight colours, all blues and greens. Like someone had captured the essence of the Barrier Reef in a gemstone. The opal was held in a swirling setting that made it look like a glorious sapphire starfish as it dazzled and shifted until it shimmered into a fog of tears. Bella blinked them back.

'It's magnificent.' And heartbreaking, she thought. The last gift from her twin. Her chest ached as she lifted the pendant out of the box and pulled the long chain over her head. 'It's truly beautiful.'

TJ's words came back to her. *He planned to get it made into a necklace for your birthday.* A week before William died, he'd been planning to give her a present? Their birthday had been months away.

That didn't make sense. William wouldn't commit suicide on a whim a week later, would he? Bella couldn't shake the feeling that something was off. Maybe TJ had the dates wrong. 'Are you sure it was a week before he died, when you talked about it?'

A stony glare. 'Yeah. I am. Why?'

'Doesn't that seem odd to you. Him being excited and planning to give it to me months later?'

'Should it?'

'Yes.' She'd studied suicidal patterns and statistics in uni, and this didn't add up. There were always anomalies, but still . . . it left her with more questions not fewer. She really needed to find Bane.

'I think there could be some information about William's last days that we're missing,' she said firmly. 'If you're thinking about looking for Bane, I want to come with you.'

He froze. 'Who said I'm looking for Bane?'

She tilted her head back and held his gaze. 'I do. You looked for him before, just after William's death. You didn't find him, Desiree said.'

'So?' He glanced at Meesha but she held her hands up and shook her head. Clever girl.

'Things don't make sense.' Bella spread her hands. 'You want to find him. I want to talk to him. Win-win.'

TJ shook his head. Backed up a step. 'How is this a win-win for me? Even if I *was* looking, which I'm not, you wouldn't be coming.'

She narrowed her eyes. 'Fine. Billiards. If I beat you in a game, you have to take me when you look for Bane.'

'Pool? That's my girl,' Meesha crowed.

TJ just laughed.

Okay. That didn't work. What else could he gain? 'If I lose, I'll never bother you again at your camp.' Which gave her every reason to play the best game she'd ever played in her life.

There was a long pause while he studied her, and she wished again she could read his facial expression, but there was none. Had she lost already? Wait – was that a flash of calculation? Was that his mistaken belief that she had no chance of beating him?

Finally, he growled, 'You'd never come back to my camp? Ever?'

'Never.'

'Done. The pub. Let's go – shouldn't be busy on a Wednesday night, so you won't get too embarrassed.'

She was *not* going to lose. 'Do I need to change?' She wore a black pair of lycra tights and a long navy-blue T-shirt with 'AC/DC' on the back – not quite appropriate for a night out, but she liked the way the plain blue front made the bright colours of William's opal jump out. 'I'd have to go home.'

TJ threw her a disgusted glance. 'No, you don't need to change. We'll go straight there. Oh.' He glanced at Meesha. 'Meesha polished and set the stone for free. She's hoping you'll let her borrow it for a weekend to show it in Brisbane for the competition – if you like the setting.'

As Bella passed Meesha, who had a hand over her smile, she passed her dop stick and opal to her for safe keeping. 'Of course you can show it.' She closed her fingers around the pendant. 'It's amazing. I love it.'

TJ muttered, 'She'll be back to fix all the stuff later.'

'Or maybe tomorrow,' Bella couldn't resist calling over her shoulder, and Meesha's laugh turned into a cough.

They made it out to the street at speed, and TJ looked up and down as if scouting for observers. Not that there was anyone around to notice her with him. It was dark. Deserted.

His Harley sat on the curb, and he pulled off the helmet strapped to the back, handing it to her. 'Put this on.'

'Ha. Your bike is big and black, of course.' She smiled as she slid the helmet over her hair and closed her eyes briefly, scent of him all around her.

'What?'

'It smells like you.'

'Yeah, well. Sorry.'

She rolled her eyes at him. 'Of your soap, man. It's nice.' And maybe she shouldn't have said that. Or even thought it.

She fiddled with the strap until she huffed with impatience.

'Hell,' he said. 'Here. Let me.' His hands lifted under her chin, rough-skinned, but gentle against her skin as he threaded the loop and pulled it snuggly. 'That okay? Not too tight?'

Their gazes met and held. It was like staring into the opal she'd just been playing with – all blue but way darker. The moment dragged out until he said quietly, 'You'll be the death of me, Belle.'

Then, barely perceptible, he added, 'Or I'll be the death of you.'

Sensing his angst, she said lightly, 'I thought we were playing pool. For a bet.'

'Bad idea we had,' he muttered.

It looked like some serious internal conflict was happening there, and almost unconsciously she reached up and tapped his shoulder. 'Come on. Let's go play billiards and then you'll take me to find Bane.'

'Or more likely,' he rumbled, 'I'll win and find some peace.'

He climbed on the bike and waited while she put one foot on the peg and lifted her leg over. Then she shimmied up behind him and wrapped her arms around his waist, her hipbones against his butt.

His back stiffened into rock at her touch.

This. Was. A. Crazy. Idea. But oh, this was nothing like climbing on a bike behind Konrad. Riding pillion with TJ was a sensual experience, Bella thought as her thighs squeezed tightly around his. She couldn't help pushing herself more firmly against him, her breasts into his back, her pelvis into his hard backside. Twining her arms around his muscular waist from behind felt decadent. Who knew?

Oh yeah, she had a new appreciation for motorbikes and their riders. Even if her sensible medical brain had cleaned up too many minced and broken bodies and said neither were safe.

The engine growled to life, sounding a bit like its master, and the thrumming pistons vibrated up through her body, through her legs, through to her centre – a totally visceral experience. She shifted her neck to settle the weight of TJ's helmet.

She clung to TJ as he peeled away from the curb, wanting to whoop. Oh heavens, she felt so alive. It had been years since she'd allowed herself to be sucked into a wild caper like this, and she'd keep hold of this feeling as long as she could. She'd ridden pillion on a bike before, so she knew when to lean and when to loosen. When to cling and when to relax back. But this was a short ride. Up the street, past the crossroads and Desiree's servo and into the parking area of the pub.

Far too short. Tragically short, in fact.

The engine died and she released her hold on TJ with reluctance and slid backwards to climb off the bike. She managed to deal with the helmet strap herself this time and clipped the clunky piece of protection back on its holder.

TJ stayed on the bike. Didn't turn his head. Just stared straight ahead.

She shifted to stand beside the front of the bike and found him frowning ferociously at the wall of the pub in front of him.

'Hello?'

When she raised her voice in question, he growled. 'I'll be a minute.'

And suddenly she realised, and grinned. Yeah, well. Luckily she didn't have any external signs of arousal – then she glanced down at her pebbled nipples. Oops. Right. She zipped up her jacket, a sudden giggle escaping her lips. She never giggled. But another one arrived, followed by a snort.

TJ turned his head and glared at her.

She backed away, holding her hands up. 'Sorry. But . . .

So funny.'

After another minute TJ shifted his bike onto its stand and eased himself off.

'Great. Keep going. Sadly, laughing at me helps,' he said in a dry voice.

Which made her want to snort again but she forced it back. He probably did have a limit to his control. 'You can have a handicap,' she spluttered, and he shook his head.

'Inside,' he muttered. But there was a crinkle at the corner of his eyes and his face had eased from its usual hard lines into almost amusement. 'You are the biggest stirrer I've ever met.'

'Me?' Her hand went to her chest in mock horror. 'I'm not a stirrer. I'm the respectable principal doctor from the Outback Practice at Lightning.'

TJ shook his head again, walked past and held the pub door open for her. When they entered, the place looked deserted except for the young bloke behind the bar polishing a glass with a rag.

'Hey, TJ,' he said.

'Dylan,' TJ returned. 'A beer, please, and a schooner of water with ice for the lady.'

'Never seen you with a lady before.'

TJ deadpanned him and Dylan hurriedly reached for a glass and began to pull the beer.

'This way,' TJ said over his shoulder – as if she couldn't see the green felt up ahead – and went to the pool table.

'Rack 'em up and I'll get the drinks.'

'You have such soothing social skills.'

He looked at her. 'I do. When I want to. I'm struggling tonight.'

He stalked to the bar.

TJ might be enjoying a little bit of revenge for her teasing after the bike ride. But then what was different about not being able to read the guy? And she was going to win a shot at finding Bane, no matter what. Possibly not good odds, but there'd been no odds before, so it was still an improvement.

She pulled the black plastic triangle from the end of the table and set it in the middle of the felt. Started emptying the pockets of the balls. Set up the numbered balls with the first at the triangle's apex, the black in the middle, a striped ball in one corner of the rack and a solid ball in the other corner. She picked up the white ball and placed it in the half circle.

By the time she'd felt the weight of three sticks and decided on her cue, TJ was back with the drinks.

He handed her the glass tinkling with ice. It was nice that he'd remembered she preferred water. Almost as if they weren't strangers.

TJ put his beer down on one of the round high tables nearby.

'Okay, show me what you got.'

'Here in front of Dylan?'

He didn't dignify that with a reply.

She shrugged, sauntered to the top of the table, leaned over just a little and broke the set.

The number three ball peeled off into the side pocket and the set scattered – a little harder than she'd intended, but still good positions. Definitely smalls.

'Five in corner pocket,' she murmured. *Clink.* 'Seven in side pocket.' *Thunk.* 'One in top pocket.' *Swoosh.* 'Two, same pocket.'

Click. 'Four in corner pocket.' *Clunk.* 'Six, top pocket.' There was a satisfying clatter of balls hitting each other inside the pocket.

And that left the black.

Turned out that she hadn't lost any skills in the last three years.

She glanced up at TJ who shook his head, but his white teeth were visible. He closed his mouth when he saw her looking.

'Where would you like the black, TJ?'

Where would she like TJ? The thought echoed through her belly, snapping her composure, and she stepped back and straightened before making the shot. Blocking him out, because she really, really wanted to clear the table. And find the man who might know more about her brother's death.

She leaned forward to pocket the black, and suddenly TJ's breath teased her ear. 'Wherever you like it, Belle.' Her butt warmed with his heat behind her, though he wasn't quite touching.

Close, though. Too close to concentrate.

She held back on the shot. 'You wouldn't be sledging me, would you?'

More warm breath on her ear. 'What's wrong? Can't you concentrate? I thought you liked to tease.'

She straightened slowly and he eased away. 'I might have a sip of water first.' As soon as he stepped back, she leaned down again and whispered fast and just loud enough, 'Black in corner pocket,'

as she slammed it home.

Slow clapping came from the bar.

TJ ignored Dylan, folding his arms over his chest, a small smile on his face. 'Impressive.'

'Thank you, kind sir. Your turn.'

TJ cleared the table in pretty much the same style, but with more speed and snap. Just before he sank the black, Bella brought her face down six inches behind the pocket and, locking eyes with him, she caressed her top lip with her tongue.

He laughed out loud and rolled the ball gently into the pocket, as smooth as silk. *Plop.*

Another slow clap from the bar.

'That was fun, but we still have no winner.'

TJ grimaced. 'Nobody's a winner with us, Belle Bird. Not even if I think you're a pool shark.'

'Me? A pool shark? You'll be reneging if we don't play again.'

She ducked under his arm. 'We need one more game to find the winner.' She had him and she knew it.

They stared at each other. She saw the refusal in his eyes and wondered if she could just follow him in her car all the way to Coober Pedy.

TJ's hand caught her elbow before she could step away. 'Hold on there, Belle Bird. First to three?'

She turned back, caught the glint in his eye. 'You remember the stakes?'

He spoke very quietly so Dylan couldn't hear. 'You win and I take you with me to find Bane tomorrow. We might not be back for three to four days. How are you going to sort that with your patients?'

Damn, she hadn't thought that through. She'd been too obsessed with finding Bane at all and hadn't factored in her work – not like her. Neither was giving up.

She could ask her parents to come and cover for emergencies?

Yeah, right. She could just hear herself. Hi Mum and Dad, I'm going off with a random guy to interrogate a potentially dangerous man in Coober Pedy about William's death. We'll be sleeping rough, gone about three days, and by the way, can you mind Konrad's patients until I get back? No, she'd just have to sort it herself. Cite a family emergency. Two surgery days. She could do longer hours to catch up next week.

Plus . . . she had to beat him first. Logistics later. 'And if you win?'

'You stay put. Don't visit. Let me handle it.' Bella's heart skipped. Could see there'd be no quarter, because he was adamant about working it his way. Getting his privacy back. Going alone.

She'd just have to play the best game of pool she'd ever played.

'I want to hear what he says when he says it.'

Bella studied TJ in the dim light, saw the tension in his jaw.

This mattered to him. Keeping her here. Probably thinking she'd be safer that way. The protector side of him screaming. But she needed to be involved, needed to hear confirmation of how her brother died, if there was any chance of that.

Finally, TJ nodded curtly. 'It's a deal.'

Dylan materialised with fresh drinks without being asked. Bella took a slow sip of the new iced water, watching TJ rack the balls.

His movements were precise, deliberate. No more playful banter.

'Ladies first,' he said, stepping back.

Bella lined up her break, but this time the balls scattered without dropping. TJ's eyes narrowed as he surveyed the table. He sank two striped balls in quick succession, before missing a tricky bank shot.

Bella worked the angles methodically, her focus absolute. The click of balls and soft scuff of chalk filled the silence. They traded shots, neither giving quarter, until Bella found herself staring at the eight ball with two of TJ's striped ones still on the felt.

'Black, corner pocket,' she called softly. The black sphere rolled true.

TJ's mouth tightened. 'Two to one.'

The could-be deciding game started tense and only got tighter.

Bella's hands were steady, but her pulse kicked as she watched TJ clear half the table. One miss – that's all she needed. When it came, she pounced.

Her last solid hung on the lip of the pocket, defying gravity for a heart-stopping moment before dropping. Okay. She could do this. Just the eight ball stood between her and the search that could reveal answers she'd been waiting to find for years.

She could feel TJ's presence behind her as she lined up the shot, but this time his nearness steadied rather than distracted her. The eight ball rolled home with quiet certainty.

'Looks like you've got yourself a partner tomorrow,' she said, straightening.

TJ's expression remained unreadable in the shadows, but he gave her a slight nod. 'First light. Don't be late.'

She lifted her hand to the bar, calling, 'Night, Dylan,' and followed TJ to the door where he stood holding it open. The perfect impression of a gentleman, despite the tension that radiated out of him.

As they walked out into the cool night air, Bella caught herself smiling. She'd won more than just a game of pool tonight. She'd won a piece of respect – and that almost felt like the bigger victory.

They walked past his Harley.

She turned back to look at it with regret as the distance grew.

'Are you leaving your bike here?' She'd had a definite desire to swing her leg over behind him again.

They passed through the carpark out front. 'Yes.'

'You said that grimly. Why?'

'A whim.' He snorted, not a sound she'd heard from him before. 'I'm not putting you up behind me again, not tonight.'

'Ever?' She glanced up at the stars, hard to see with the street lights and windows from the pub. The game must have gone to her head. She didn't need to flirt with the guy. She had what she wanted: the chance to talk to Bane. A man who quite possibly had played a part in William's final days.

When he didn't answer, she lifted her chin. 'You don't have to walk me home.'

'Will though.'

They'd reached the road and she grimaced. 'I don't need protecting. I'm a grown woman, TJ. Been out with boys all by myself and everything.'

He slowed under the streetlight, tall and powerful and . . . twitchy. 'Dr Grey. Please may I walk you home?'

Please? Oh my.

Then he said, 'You don't have to come. I'll bring Bane back here for you.' He gave a frustrated shake of his head. 'Should have done it back then for Konrad, and maybe myself, but I *will* find him this time. Then you can talk to him and get on with your life.

I'll get on with mine.'

'Nope. Where are we going to find him?'

'Broken Hill. Coober Pedy.' He shrugged. Looked away. Then surprisingly, he asked, 'What made you start opal cutting?'

She huffed out a laugh. 'I was trying to find something that stopped me pounding on your gate.'

He froze and then shook his head. 'You say the darnedest things.'

'Darnedest? Is that you swearing? What sort of badass are you?' She should not be teasing him, but his awkwardness was the best fun.

'The worst kind. I just don't swear around women.'

They were almost at the medical centre and her unit around the back.

'Don't you have a motion-sensor light?' His voice scraped across her skin with delicious roughness. Things had changed since she wrapped around him on his bike – a line had been crossed.

He was being delightfully bossy.

The darkness covered them both except for the rectangle of illumination from her door.

'I have an outside light.' She leaned back towards the doorway and depressed the switch. 'But not a motion-activated light.'

'You need one,' he said, 'but something for later.'

'Would you like to come in?'

One brow went up and she saw the glint of the stud in the streetlight. 'To see your stamps?'

'Or just a coffee? I don't have any beer.' She added thoughtfully, 'I must get some. What kind do you drink?'

'Belle Bird, this is not happening.'

'What?'

'Whatever you think is between us.'

She chose to misunderstand him. 'There's nothing between us.'

He said with stark force, 'Your brother William is between us.'

She thought about that. Then, slowly and quietly, she said,

'That is the strangest part of all this, TJ. Apart from family, you're the only man I've talked to about him. William isn't between us.'

'No?' TJ sounded sceptical. 'Because he's sure as hell riding along with me. Thanks for the offer but I won't come in.'

Bella tried not to feel disappointed.

'I'm leaving at seven a.m. I have a strong bullbar, but would prefer the wildlife is off the road, so we'll be waiting for first light.

Go to bed, Belle. If you're not out back here at seven on the dot, I'm leaving without you.'

She knew he would. And she had a lot of arrangements to make before then.

CHAPTER NINETEEN

TJ

Taking Belle with him to find Bane was crazy. Let alone the danger if that weasel had been mixed up in something bigger than TJ thought. There was an itch of worry about that. But that might just be paranoia from his time in the force.

He wanted to get on the road, find Bane, get her answers a different way so she could move on and leave him alone. The thought filled him with a sense of desolation, but he pushed the feeling aside. *It's for the best. For her.*

He must have been walking fast because suddenly he was on his Harley outside the pub with the wind in his face.

How many times was a man supposed to knock back a woman like her? Belle was smoking hot, gave as good as she got, and her mouth – heaven help him, just looking at her mouth destroyed him. And that honey blonde hair. And those deep blue eyes.

Watching her play pool had been enough to put him off his game for the first time in his life. He wanted her, hungered so badly to lift her up so her legs wrapped around him, to carry her inside her unit and savour her mouth and her body until he died of old age.

She'd probably laugh while he did it.

The beautiful doc drove him insane, and he had to spend the next seventy-two hours in her company.

Once home and through his gates, TJ locked his bike in the shed, bolted and locked everything else in preparation for the trip, and dug around for the spare swag he now had to pack.

Last time he'd used it, he and William had gone out to a party at Coocoran, William's idea, and slept under the stars because neither had wanted to be deso to drive home.

Funny that. For himself, once in the force, those drink driving rules never changed. Another thing about William he'd liked. He didn't break the law either. Except when he killed himself.

TJ narrowed his eyes and paused. With all this Bane stuff rearing its ugly head again, he knew now he'd been too quick to drop it all. Grief had screwed with his thought processes. What if William hadn't jumped into that mine? What if he'd fallen – or been pushed? Dangerous people without morals could make that happen.

His skin chilled. If that were true, the last thing he needed was William's sister tagging along with him to interrogate Bane. Like he could stop her now, though. Geez, he suspected she'd follow him anyway. More fool him for mentioning his planned route.

He tossed the extra swag into the back of his F-. The beast could do with another road trip. Shame he'd have an unwelcome passenger.

*

The next morning TJ pulled around the back of the OPAL medical centre at . a.m. His personal coffee deliverer stepped out of her front door juggling two Yeti mugs and a backpack and pulled the door to her unit shut before he could turn off the engine. A small but bulging black leather tote sat on the ground by her feet; he assumed it was her doctor's bag. At least she could travel light.

And she was on time.

He got out, picked up the tote and gestured to the tray under the tarp. 'You want to put that bag in the back?'

'Nope. All good. Behind the seat will be fine.'

He opened the passenger door for her because, well, she had no hands, and pushed the black bag into the space behind the seat before she handed him his coffee mug and slid into the vehicle. 'Thanks.'

'Welcome,' she murmured. He carried his cup thinking, so that's why I'd subconsciously decided not to have coffee at my place. May as well drink it now.

When he'd slid inside, too, she nodded at the dash. 'Nice ride.'

Her mouth kicked up as she watched him. 'And it's black.'

'F trucks don't come in pink.' He could smell those flowers on her. The scent she'd left in his house. Luckily, the coffee covered a lot of it, and he removed the lid so the aroma would steam out even more.

She smiled into her own coffee. That annoyed him too.

He really wasn't a morning person. Especially this particular morning.

When they hadn't spoken, passed a car or seen a house for half an hour she said, 'Are we there yet?'

He shook his head. Not to answer her question, but because she thought this was a joke. Then he pulled himself in. No. He was a dick. She'd lost her twin. Of course it wasn't a joke for her. She was just trying to make the trip more comfortable, and he could damn well do the same.

He blew out a breath. 'First stop, Cobar, another four hours.

Let me know if you need to stop sooner.'

'Doctors and nurses can go all day without a break,' she wise-cracked. 'I'll be fine.' She turned to look out the window.

Ten minutes later, he said, 'Emus coming up on your left.'

'Met one of those before.' She leaned her head against the window and he heard the smile in her voice when she said, 'It's a family. Oh, look at the chicks!'

He glanced that way, but his gaze stuck for a second too long on her profile before he jerked it back to the road. 'Yup.' Beautiful.

The last emu disappeared into the scrub, and the road stretched ahead like a ribbon of heat. Belle shifted in her seat, and he knew she was going to ask about her brother.

'Tell me about your friendship with William.'

He shot her a sideways glance, forced his hands to stay relaxed on the wheel. 'I told you. We met in the pub. Played a game of pool.'

The corner of her mouth twitched. 'And?'

'I was off my game.' He raised one brow and shot her a wither-ing look. 'He almost beat me.'

'Seems you were off your game yesterday, too.' That teasing note crept into her voice again. He swore she loved needling him.

'I might give you a chance to get your pride back against me anoth-er day.'

'Yeah, maybe.' That ship had sailed – or truck had passed, he thought, as a road train went by them in a swirl of dust sucked from the side of the tar.

She waited. He had no doubt she was letting the silence work for her. Eventually, when he was ready to shred the steering wheel, she said, 'You were telling me about your friendship with William.'

He drew in a breath and tried to think about the good things, pushing away the familiar self-condemnation for not saving the guy. Something he could give the sister that wouldn't hurt. Might even give her a smile. He could do that. 'When he first came to the Ridge, every time I turned around, he was there. He was different in a group, but when he and I were the last men standing, he made me laugh. Which not many people do.'

He fingers tightened on the wheel and he forced them to loosen.

'William was hard to dislike. Before I knew it, I looked forward to being amused by him. Considered him a mate. First real one I had since I came here.'

The admission hung in the air between them. He felt Belle still beside him, but that didn't stop him adding, 'Goes to show how dangerous it is if people get close to me.'

'That's just stupid.' The words shot out of her, forceful enough to make him frown. 'Whatever was going on with William had nothing to do with you.'

His jaw worked and he stared straight ahead. Why the hell should she care? He jammed a couple more bricks in the metaphorical wall between them to shore up the crack.

She changed the subject. 'How long have you been in the Ridge?'

He could answer that. 'Four years.'

'Where from?'

Oh, no you don't. 'Nowhere.'

'Spare me,' she muttered and let conversation lie for a good ten kilometres. Impressive. He could stay silent too. Eventually she murmured, 'Must say, that's a tidy set-up you have in your camp.'

'Thank you.' It helped to be orderly since his past was such a disaster.

Another five kilometres and she tried again. 'Tell me about William when he visited your camp. You said he came out there?'

Okay, a topic he could deal with. He'd been planning to give her good memories. They still had hours to go, might as well be civil. 'He came up on a Monday. Had tied it on the night before and I'd gone home, so I expected him to be hungover. He wasn't.

Never seemed to get sick with it. Never seem to drink as much as he said he did.'

She spoke slowly, as if mulling something over. 'It's strange to think of him drinking. Drunk. Even when we turned eighteen, we didn't get plastered at our birthday party. Back then he'd sit on a drink all night. We both would.'

'He had a drink in his hand every time I saw him.' TJ furrowed his brows. 'Not so much at my place. Anyway, he turned up that Monday demanding I explain what was so great about opals.'

It was a good memory – after they'd done the dance of TJ not wanting him to come in and William waving all that away just like his sister had. 'I showed him my mine. He liked the whole "swing over and climb down the ladder" thing. Liked the circular shafts carved out of sandstone. Liked standing at the bottom and not being able to see the end of the drive where it turned.' He could picture it now, the smile on William's face. TJ liked all that too. 'Liked looking up from the bottom to the circle of light past the ladder.'

'I want to see that, too.'

He glanced at her. 'A lot of people don't enjoy the closed-in feeling down there.'

'I might. Will you show me, one day?'

And what could he say to that? 'Maybe.'

She snorted at him. 'Come on. You can do better than that. Do I have to flog you again at pool to get down there?'

He slowed as another road train went past. 'You did not flog me. You distracted me.'

'Ha. You tried it, too. I'm just better at it than you.'

No argument there. 'Anyway, moving on.' He glanced at her with raised brows and when she flicked her fingers in a 'go on'

gesture, he said, 'I talked to your brother about looking for opal.

Showed him a nobby I'd found that morning. And then a slice of seam opal in the shaft. Put the torch on some silica on the wall to show him the glow.' He shrugged. 'William lit up. Done. Bitten.

After that he dropped by the camp a couple of mornings a week, would turn up and help for a couple of hours. Said he enjoyed it.

Wanted to learn about the whole opal-mining gig.'

Belle was quiet and TJ stopped talking.

'He was always curious. Insatiably so.' She stared fixedly at her hands.

'True. Wanted to know how you secured a good mine, how valuable different opals were, and the good places to mine about town.'

He felt her gaze on him and he flicked a glance at her. She looked sad but her mouth was soft. 'Thank you. I can imagine him being excited about that. It's a nice picture for me to keep.

Of him finding joy here, at least some of the time.'

They drove for a while before she spoke again. 'And the opal he wanted to give me?' Her hand drifted to her opal necklace, where it shimmered at her chest. 'Where did William find this one?'

'There's a story to that.' He could feel the amusement he'd felt that day William had come to his camp practically shaking with excitement. 'Typical William. There's a place in town, open to anyone who wants to scratch around and look for opal – more of a tourist attraction really. He'd gone for a walk after a heavy rain and ended up there. Did a bit of noodling. What they call fossicking, in the discard pile. That's when he found your opal.'

TJ shook his head. 'Seriously, hundreds of tourists had picked over that place. Just one of those random luck-of-the-draw things after the rain. It's not the first time it's happened, but it's still crazy luck.'

His voice dropped and Belle turned her head to catch the words.

'When he brought the stone to me, that amazing stone, I thought his face would split in two. So delighted.' He glanced at the opal on her neck. 'Said he trusted me to keep it safe. That's when he told me about you. His sister up there on the pedestal.

Dr Tinkerbell. Thirty minutes older. Someone he was so proud of and loved more than anything.'

Chapter Twenty

Bella

The words wrapped around Bella's heart like a warm fist. In the past twelve hours she'd spent too much time thinking about the man beside her. The last few trying not to watch his face, his hands, his heavily muscled thighs as he drove.

Now she stared out at the mirage wavering on the horizon, blinking hard, seeing William, her beautiful, impossible brother.

He'd always seen the best in everyone, even when it got him into trouble. Had this Bane been an example of not seeing clearly? Had Bane exacerbated William's mood swings as his drinking partner?

Or what else could it be?

Gears whirred in Bella's head. Things falling more solidly into place. Inconsistencies leaping out at her. 'I'll say it again.

Don't you find it strange he planned to give me the opal on my birthday? You said his face was splitting with delight. Does that sound like a man who would commit suicide a week later?'

'I did find it strange.' TJ sounded wary, and she guessed she had shot those questions at him rather than asked. 'Which is why I wanted to find Bane immediately after William's death to find out what else had happened.'

'Because,' she said quietly, 'you found it hard to believe he killed himself.'

'Yes,' he said flatly, staring straight ahead. She couldn't read his expression but his lips were pursed so she assumed he was thinking hard.

'That man standing in your mine, excited about opals. Did you think he would self-destruct? Did he ever show any signs of desperation?'

He blew out an enormous breath, his shoulders dipping forward before he inhaled again. 'Hells, Belle. Who knows? Sometimes there are no obvious signs for these things. He was drinking, hanging with the low set, and when I first met him, he looked flat and quiet, so maybe?' He sighed. 'I didn't really know him until later, so I can't say. Where are you going with this?' But the expression on his face said he knew.

'Same place you did. That he didn't commit suicide. That he might have been pushed, and maybe his body wasn't meant to be found.'

TJ's face didn't move when she said it. She could see he'd arrived at a similar hypothesis.

Finally, he said, 'Well. That's why we're going to see Bane, isn't it?'

The scenery changed again on the section from Wilcannia to Broken Hill. They'd been driving for seven and a half hours, and Bella wriggled in the seat trying to ease the stiffness in her hips.

They'd seen so many wild goats the last hour or so but it was still wearing.

'We're stopping at Broken Hill for the night, yes?'

'Yes.' They'd paused briefly for petrol at Cobar and again at Wilcannia, and now they were passing red sand and low bushes, until finally the run of hills that gave this outback highway its name – the Barrier Ranges – appeared on the horizon.

She felt worn. Bloody TJ looked as fresh as he had at seven this morning. Though, it was impossible to see his eyes under the dark wraparounds he had on – maybe he was human and had lines and dark shadows below them. She hoped so. Only fair.

'Broken Hill's only two hours from Wilcannia. Nearly there.

I have a place to stay on a friend's farm. It's an empty cabin. He's overseas at the moment, but I've access to stay anytime.'

Probably an isolated farm, then – funny how the idea of being alone with TJ didn't worry her. 'Handy.'

He didn't comment on that. 'I'll sleep on the porch in the swag. You can do the same inside.'

'I didn't bring a swag.'

'Yep. Noticed. I brought one for you.'

Nine hours and ten minutes after they left Lightning Ridge, TJ pulled into a Broken Hill servo and Belle eased herself out of the F-, stiff and hungry.

'How about takeaway pizza?' TJ suggested once she'd straightened out beside him and turned slowly around to look at the options. 'We could take it to my mate's farm – it's only a short hop out of town.'

'Perfect. I'll buy, since you've sorted accommodation. What do you want? I'm not fussy.'

He murmured, 'Still buying me food.' An amused pause. She didn't say anything. 'Supreme, no anchovies. And a bottle of real Coke, please?'

'Done.'

'Thanks. I'll fuel up while you do that.'

'And after we eat? What's the plan?'

'You think I have a plan?'

'Don't doubt it.'

He laughed. 'Right. I'll shower quick, we'll eat and set up swags. Then I want to duck back into town and check out the pubs. Too early yet for the clientele I want to talk to.'

This guy really did have a plan. Lucky, because she was flying by the . . . 'Who do you want to talk to?'

'Mostly the bartenders and miners. They'll remember him if he's here,' he said wryly. 'Not in a good way.'

'I could come.'

'Easier if you don't.'

Well, that was to the point. But then when hadn't TJ been blunt?

Maybe it would do her good to have some space from him. She could have a shower while he was gone.

'Boys club.' Not a question. 'I get it. I didn't really want to go trolling anyway.'

And she needed to phone Mel to see how she'd managed with cancelling the day's patients. Mel had said she'd be fine, but there might have been a medical issue for one of the patients while Bella and TJ were out of service, which they had been for most of the day. But she'd had no missed calls or messages come through when they'd arrived in town.

When Bella had told Mel she needed to leave the Ridge for a few days, she had agreed with citing a family emergency for cancelling Thursday and Friday appointments. They'd tentatively arranged house calls for people who needed to be seen soonest when Bella returned.

Urgent cases would have to go to another doctor or the health centre. A thread of guilt tugged at her, but still, she was glad she came. She needed answers.

'You kick back.' TJ's comment returned her to the present.

'Ten hours' driving ahead of us to Coober Pedy. I want to leave early enough tomorrow to set up at the motel before I start bar-hopping in town.'

Another ten hours in the cab with TJ. 'You're sure he's there?'

'No. But. A friend of mine thinks he is.'

'But he's not sure.'

'Nothing is sure, Belle Bird. Except that right now you'll get the food, and I'll get the petrol. But we'll sort it.'

Together, she added silently, and the idea settled her.

The crushed rock driveway that led to the overnight shack ended at a small hill overlooking a dry, red creek bed studded with ancient river gums. No other houses in sight.

The cabin itself perched on small rounds of wood, bordered on three sides with a rust-coloured bullnose verandah. Three wooden steps led to the front door. The walls were ancient wood slab, and the windows were the up-and-down sash type, painted white. The whole effect was rustic and solid. Water tanks covered the fourth wall, ready to catch any rain off the roof. Bella knew she'd better have a fast shower and not waste the water. Broken Hill was not often a high rainfall area.

TJ retrieved a key from somewhere around the back, handed it to her, and lifted the swags out of the F-'s pick-up tray. He tossed them on the verandah while she carried the pizzas to the cabin and put them on a table beside the door.

When she pulled the old screen door wide, the key turned easily in the solid front door, exposing a dim room with a big dining table on one side and a day bed opposite. It was a little musty, but she suspected it hadn't been shut up for too long. TJ came in and the room seemed to shrink, though it helped when he switched the light on.

'Yours.' He dropped her swag on the day bed, and her small back-pack beside it, then disappeared through a side door. His voice floated to her just before he shut her out. 'I'll shower and you set up the pizza.'

She did not need to imagine him showering ten feet away.

Unbidden, her eyes glued to the closed door, until she decided it was bad form.

'Stop it. Pizza,' she told herself out loud. She crossed to the kitchen, formica and chrome, washed her hands first then found two big floral plates and solid old silver knives and forks. She also found paper towels and an egg flip to dig out the pizza, because the quick look she'd given it said fingers weren't an option.

An efficient little cottage, really. But that wasn't the problem.

This quest to find information about William was morphing into something a lot more dangerous for her peace of mind and didn't that just make her feel guilty. It should all be about William.

Yet there was no doubt these past few hours in the car with TJ had ramped up the tension and awareness between them. It had always been there, since that first touch of his hand at Meesha's party – an alertness of him. Every time she'd looked over at his profile in the car today, the scent of danger grew stronger. The carved details of his face grew more embedded. Sadly, while the whole reason for this trip was William, she could feel herself becoming more alive and interested in the man driving.

She didn't even know what it was about TJ that drew her in.

Sure, he was a big guy – her dad and Konrad were, too, so she'd always felt comfortable around big men. But this was a lot more than familiarity or comfort – she'd known all along TJ was as sexy as all get out, but that hadn't been a true factor . . . until she'd jammed her body up against him on that Harley last night and she'd invited him into her unit, and not just for coffee. But that might have been the euphoria of beating him at pool. Or adrenaline from the fact she would soon be actively doing something dangerous that might solve the mystery of William's final days.

TJ was a complicated guy. He pretended to be mean – looked like he'd tricked the whole Ridge into believing that one. But he didn't feel scary to her. Just driven. A loner. And too darn sexy.

So what?

Was it wrong that together they could find some answers, maybe even some peace and resolution that helped them both?

She could see he was hurting like she was about William, had seen more of it as they drove out here, and she guessed something in his past had been exacerbated by her brother's death.

The bathroom door opened and she lifted her gaze to meet TJ's as a small billow of steam curled around his thick, slightly curly, wet hair. Five o'clock shadows on carved cheeks looking better than they should. His shirt a button-down with three open at the top. Long sleeves rolled up over those muscled forearms.

Boy, it was hot in here. Boiling. She needed a cool shower herself.

He dropped his gaze and strode to the table. 'I'll eat and go,' he said as he sat. The scent of soap and clean male wiped out the pizza for a scrumptious moment in time.

She blinked. Swallowed. Found her chair with her hand.

He lifted the egg flipper and put a piece of pizza on her plate before his. Then he tucked in, and she tried not to watch.

After the first enormous slice disappeared like magic, he held his fork poised in his big hand. It was a thick, droopy style of pizza, and the forks and knives worked well.

'Let's talk about Bane,' TJ announced. 'I've been thinking about that.'

Now? When they finally had a sense of almost-harmony between them? She moistened her lips. 'Yes, we need to.' She gestured to her plate. 'But can we eat first? It'd be a shame to let this get any colder.'

Bella didn't want to talk about William dying as she ate. Or about the horrid people who might have been instrumental in his death. Tomorrow might bring that and more, and she could feel her anxiety ramping up about the horror to come.

She lifted her own fork. They could just have a quiet meal together without bringing the darkness she knew would come when they spoke about the man they searched for.

TJ nodded, looked down at his food, and her eyes followed as he put the fork again to his beautiful lips. Closed his mouth, and then his dark eyes, as he savoured the flavour. Chewed.

A symphony of all sorts of musculature. Carved cheekbones.

Strong jaw. Masculine throat.

She blinked again. She shouldn't be watching, and sprang into conversation to cover her distraction. 'It's limp but the flavours are great.'

His long lashes fluttered as he blinked, too, and nodded. 'Needs more meat.'

'Strapping man like you should be having half a steer a month.'

What was coming out of her mouth? Good grief. She was an educated woman.

Startled, he laughed. That was the second time he'd really let go and laughed properly in front of her. It sounded like spring thunder in the afternoon. A deep, low rumble of amusement that swirled in her belly. Made her breathe him in. Smile back.

Admire him. 'You look good in that shirt. Nice fit.'

His fork stopped. 'What are you doing?' It was a jaguar- worthy growl.

'What do you mean, what am I doing?' Her cheeks felt a little hot. Her neck prickled. Belly heated. 'Having a conversation – small talk, you know, while we eat. You're not carrying much of it.'

He fixed his gaze on her and he wasn't smiling anymore. 'That's not what you're doing.'

She lifted her chin. 'What do you think I'm doing, TJ?' she asked, like she had at Meesha's when he asked about her opal work.

But she hadn't meant to lower her voice into a sexy purr this time.

He put his fork down quietly. 'Flirting.' He pushed his chair back with a scrape and her heart went *thump*. Cardiac organs should not lodge in throats, but hers had shifted skywards.

Standing, TJ growled, 'I think you're pulling the tiger's tail.'

'The jaguar's tail,' she corrected. 'A black one. TJ, The Jaguar.'

He blew out a breath and shook his head. She sat like a rabbit – definitely a rabbit in headlights – on the other side of the table.

Not quite quivering but almost.

'I'm trying to fight against this here,' he said, almost conversation- ally.

'Fight against what?' But she knew. Oh lordy, she knew.

He stepped around the side of the table, and she watched him move until she couldn't see him unless she turned her head – but she didn't, only stared straight ahead. Could only listen, catch the whisper of sound as he stopped behind her. Feel his heat.

Her heart thundered.

TJ leaned down and spoke softly in her left ear. 'Stand up.'

Bella felt the heat from that whisper sliding through her limbs like smooth, lush cream. Every hair on her body stood up before her legs managed the feat, but it wasn't from fear. Much more dangerous than fear. She tried to push her chair back, difficult when her legs felt so weak, and he helped by pulling the back of the seat, creating just enough space to leave a small gap between the table and the chair. She slid out from the seat and edged around to face him, her butt against the table, and him right in front of her.

His dark eyes stared down into hers. She knew now they were dark blue but right now they looked so black she couldn't distinguish between the pupils and the iris.

He slipped one hand around her waist and pulled her in against him until she was doused in warm, soapy, male scent. He didn't do anything else. Just waited to see if she pulled away, looked away, or even slid sideways.

She did none of those things. She breathed him in. Soaked in the heat and hardness like that dry creek bed outside would soak up rain. Stared into his face as he trained those hard eyes on her.

Head tipped back as she looked up at him. Defiant. Turned on. Daring him.

'Yep,' he said. 'Flirting.' His other hand snaked around her waist and cinched her closer so she was caught in a two-armed vice. He crushed her to him, and his mouth – his beautiful mouth – slanted down, hovered, and then drifted onto hers as if covered in silk.

She expected him to kiss her hard. But he didn't. He licked. Nibbled. Seduced. Gently sliding, slowly building the rhythm.

Building pressure. Building sensations until they were roiling inside her like soft sand in a sudden tremor. Shaking her. The perfect storm.

Her fingers reached up to tug his shoulders towards her. She wanted him closer. His mouth danced on and off her lips and she opened to him, because this was exactly what she wanted. His tongue touched hers. Exactly. That. Except . . . more.

The world outside TJ kissing her disappeared.

Time passed. A lot of time. A lifetime.

When he pushed her away from him, she'd been thoroughly, expertly, drug-inducingly kissed. So had he, she thought dazedly, but there was no doubt who had strength left in their legs, and it wasn't her. He directed her back into her chair, pressing her shoulder until she sat down, and then he went back around to his seat.

As if nothing had happened, he picked up the knife and fork and finished his dinner.

She watched him, seemingly oblivious to her as he devoured mouthful after mouthful. Her meal, forgotten. His plate, growing emptier.

Her heart thumped like a steam engine in her chest.

She'd had some defining moments in her life. Some good, some terrible. This, definitely, stood out as one of the good ones.

And the terrible ones.

Oh my goodness. Her temperature had to have soared to a hundred. She felt like she was on fire, and the blood in her veins rushed around all over her body trying to put it out . . . or make it hotter. And he just sat there. Eating. Ignoring her.

She could not read his reaction.

Chapter Twenty-One

TJ

TJ chewed the food he couldn't taste anymore and stared at the wall opposite, past Belle's shell-like ear. Hell. He shouldn't have kissed her. Hadn't been able to stop himself, which was a worry.

Now she was really in his head. But at least she'd stopped talking.

Inside, where his heart still beat like a drum from the taste of her, he groaned. He hadn't kissed a woman like that since Ree.

And Belle was nothing like Ree.

Which was a good thing.

Belle was liquid and heat, but fragile in a way, and he wanted to hold her in his arms and keep her safe. Inhale her scent and soothe her skin. Brush away the pain. Quieten the loss of her twin.

But he couldn't do any of those things.

He was a guy with too much baggage from a previous life, like so many of the miners back at the Ridge.

Men and women, hiding from the past.

But that wasn't the real reason. No. He needed to stay away from her, because around him she'd get hurt. Might even die, with his track record.

Being with him could end her. The beautiful Belle Bird. Not for him. He needed distance. A diversion. A task.

Wait – he had a task. He forced his mouth to move. 'About Bane.

If we find him, I need you to stay out of the way until I say so.'

He watched her face, emotions crossing it like a movie screen.

So readable it would be funny if it didn't pull at his heart. The heart he'd thought had turned to tailings years ago. But something inside him had shifted with that kiss. Cracked. Opened. Her fault.

There it was – disbelief, hurt, pique, determination, calculation dashing like starlings across her face. Oh yeah, she had a lot going on in there as she stared back at him. He could see she was trying to fit his words into the events of the last five minutes, and, bitterly, he wanted to laugh out loud.

Her turn. Not so much fun being derailed, is it? he thought.

But he didn't say it, because he'd lose ground admitting she had the ability to derail him, too.

A tiny pink tip of tongue curled out and she licked her top lip as if tasting the last of him.

His breath caught.

Not fair. So much power in that centimetre of pink flesh.

Heat slammed into him and fanned the blaze he'd forced down, blew it back into a roaring flame. No, he wasn't going there again.

Because next time he wasn't sure he'd be able to stop.

There wasn't going to be a next time.

He had to leave. Check out Broken Hill's nightlife. Give them both some space and sanity. 'I'll be back late. We leave at seven tomorrow. Shower and go to bed.'

He stood up. Picked up his empty plate and put the knife and fork in the sink. Turned for the door.

'You can't do that,' she said. 'You can't just kiss me like that, then finish your pizza and walk away.'

'Sure I can.' He strode towards the door, but she was out of her chair, in front of him, between him and the outside. He'd barely seen her move. So much for Tactical Response training. Fast little thing.

She poked him in the chest. 'You're not going to have anything to say about that kiss?'

Her eyes were narrowed and blazing, her brows drawn. Hell, she was beautiful. His hand wanted to lift . . .

No. He tried for a shrug, faking nonchalance. Not too bad.

'I'm not really interested in discussing it.'

Her face pinked right up. She didn't like that. Which was why he'd said it, hoping she'd storm off. Get out of his space, because he could still smell her. Wanted to lean in and drag in a lungful, touching his nose right there, to that soft spot under her delectable ear. Kiss her neck. Run his hand . . .

'Nothing about the kiss?'

The kiss. Yes. He wanted more of the kiss. And of course she was made of sterner stuff than he'd thought. Again. She stood her ground in front of the door.

He tried another shrug. Pasted a bland expression on his face to hide the hunger. 'The kiss was fine.' And something he was bound to repeat if she didn't get out of his face. He put one hand on each of her upper arms and squeezed to gain purchase. Lifted her in the air. Moved her out of the way sideways. Put her down.

'Stay with me. Go to town later.' Her voice was soft behind him and his arms prickled. His chest went tight. His lower body responded.

'No.' He shook his head. 'Not in this lifetime.'

'Then in which lifetime?' He froze and she scooted in front of him again, lifting her hand to his cheek. He resisted the urge to turn into her palm. 'I've been half-dead for nearly three years, TJ.

Yet I've felt alive since the first day I saw you. Something inside me is healing. How can that be a bad thing?'

Because that's what happened just before the downhill run into disaster. 'It is. Trust me. You don't know me.'

She tilted her head. 'I want to know you. I think you're lost in a dark place, too.'

He turned his head away so she couldn't read his need.

'We're both consenting adults,' she said. 'You thawed me back to life. Maybe I could help you, too.'

He understood she wasn't just talking about the sex – she'd be in it for the long haul. 'I don't want you to know me that well, Belle. You won't like what you find if you dive into my darkness.'

'I see the damaged man. So many walls. How long will you stay in the dark, TJ?'

This woman was begging him to take her to bed. Let her in as she let him in. What sort of insanity had happened here in the last ten minutes? It had him floundering. Bringing her on this trip had been such a disaster.

'I'm a doctor.' She said it like it was sort of a joke. 'Maybe I could heal you, or at least start you on the road to recovery.'

He snuffed a pained laugh. 'Through wild monkey sex?'

She grinned. 'Not the worst idea in the world. If that's what it takes.'

He needed to escape before he took what she offered. 'Go heal someone else. Get on with your life without me.'

'And what if I don't want to get on with my life without you?'

No. No. No. 'Thankfully, we are not in that place.'

'Yet . . .' she trailed off before finishing quietly, 'I suspect it could be amazing.'

He muttered, 'Terrifying.'

'Kiss me again, TJ.' She had that same 'I dare you' note in her voice he couldn't resist.

And just like that his hand snaked around her waist and pulled her in and she hit his body, slamming heat into his rib cage.

Again, his mouth slanted down, hovered to see if she'd pull away – which she most certainly did not – and finally sealed hers in the slide of silk and taste that was her.

Again, he seduced, didn't take. Gently building a rhythm.

Breathing her in. Building pressure. Building sensations until her fingers dug into his shoulders like she would fall off the edge of the world if she didn't hang on. He pulled her closer.

His tongue duelled with hers and the world again disappeared around them.

Trying not to pant, he untangled her arms and stepped back.

His heart hunted and haunted. Hurting.

There was so much want and warmth and wonder in her eyes.

To give himself time to recover, he stepped back further.

'You are a dangerous woman, Belle.' The earth still shifted under him.

She shook her head sadly. 'You're a hard man to seduce.'

'Is that what you're doing?' Those words were like an emotional trigger that should have a warning. 'I've never met a woman like you.'

'Good. Don't blow it.'

Which helped him right himself. Feel his feet. And his brain.

'There you are. Smart. Determined. Driven. Capable of grabbing anything you want. I'm not going to allow you to destroy yourself, Belle. But I will find out what happened to your brother.' He darted sideways, past her. 'People to see. I'm out of here.'

TJ pushed open the screen door and bolted. Left her alone in the cottage and drove into Broken Hill, looking for a bad man while escaping from a good woman.

Chapter Twenty-Two

Bella

Bella leaned into the closed door with her forehead to the cool wood. Breathing. Well, that ending sucked big time.

It would be embarrassing if she let it, but no, she wouldn't be embarrassed, because she didn't regret one second of TJ's trans-fusion of life, considering how anaemically she'd been living since William had gone. Something she'd think more about when she got home, to the Ridge, and this mission was behind them.

The timing sucked.

She'd seen the want in his eyes. Seen his desire to toss her on the day bed and climb after her. Helped by the fact that the small day bed held no past, no future – a moment out of time they could leave behind if they wanted to. Yep. She'd been all for it.

Of course he hadn't gone through with it because of some moral dilemma he refused to tell her about.

Damn him.

But it was his choice.

She wouldn't push again. At least not until they were back in the Ridge. There was no doubt she'd been playing with fire, but it felt so freaking good to feel anything that momentous after the last dark years, let alone such an unexpected world of shifting, shuddering lust.

Still, she'd always be grateful to TJ for awakening her from the echoing hell she'd been trapped in.

Down the track, maybe she'd fight again for a chance to see what really lay between them, but he had some powerful internal fences and he was going to have to be the one to open the gate next time.

If he'd just wanted sex, they would have been there and done, no doubt, so something hugely important had to be holding him back.

Strange to think that such a powerful man had the most to lose if they went to bed – as if he was the fragile one. She understood that two people needed an emotional power balance in the middle for a relationship to work. But the man had such deep-rooted issues, she wasn't sure she could help.

And then, of course, what if she wasn't the one TJ wanted? Was he in love with someone else – past or current? With him kissing her like that, she didn't think so but . . .

She wasn't pushing further until he was ready.

On her side, she could see amazing potential with TJ, but was the Ridge her forever home? What if they found something about William that she could never forgive the Ridge for? She'd have to leave, and that wouldn't be fair to him either.

So back off, Bella, she told herself. Wait. Think about William.

TJ arrived back at the cabin at p.m. He opened the door and just stood there for a few seconds while her heart rate bumped like an idiot and her face heated.

She'd left a dim light on in the corner of the room near the bathroom door, but she kept her face to the wall and her shoulder to him from her curled up position in her swag. Pretending to be asleep.

The door clicked shut and she could hear him walking around the verandah. No doubt setting up his own swag. She'd thought of doing it for him, but since it was outside she didn't want to encourage any biting wildlife to bed down in there before he did.

Plus, she was determined to keep her hands to herself.

Bella dressed before TJ in the morning after another speedy shower and pulled out a couple of coffee sachets she'd brought with her, along with a mini carton of long-life milk. Back to square one, making him coffee. She smiled grimly to herself as she turned on the kettle and put away the clean dishes that had dried overnight.

'Morning,' he growled as he stalked inside with his clothes.

'Morning,' she replied easily, resisting the urge to watch him disappear into the bathroom.

She heard the shower turn on. Decided it was a good time to roll up her swag while she waited for the jug to boil. Managed that full body struggle to compress it on hands and knees after dragging it to the floor, then hoisted the bulky roll out the door and dropped it beside TJ's on the verandah.

By the time she was back at the kitchen sink filling the Yeti mugs, the bathroom door opened. She didn't turn around.

'Leaving in ten.'

'Okay. Coffee will be there.' She indicated the table behind her and finished the task.

*

After the first hour of monosyllabic answers, Bella had had enough.

They didn't have to be lovey-dovey, but surely they could *talk* in the next ten hours. She pretended to punch TJ's arm, which felt like tapping a brick, and said, 'For goodness' sake, stop worrying. I won't molest you.'

'Never doubted it,' he said with a straight face and then rubbed his arm. 'Violence is an issue, though.'

She snorted. 'My apologies, but I can't stand the silence. Tell me about Coober Pedy. You said you've been there.'

'Coober Pedy.' He drew in deep breath, chest expanding, and shrugged his big shoulders, everything rippling as if he was relieved. She looked away. *Think about William, Bella.*

TJ continued. 'Spent six months out there mostly underground.

Good opal. Summer temps are ridiculous, though. Over fifty degrees.'

He shrugged his shoulders again and she narrowed her eyes, wondering if he was flexing as payback. There did seem to be a twinkle in the eye she could see.

He went on, saying blithely, 'I prefer the cooler weather of the Ridge.'

'Ha, ha. Did you live underground in Coober Pedy?'

'Yep. About sixty per cent of the population do. The area's sandstone, so they carve shafts for mining as well as rooms out of the sandstone. They call them dugouts. With the houses and businesses, they're saving on aircon.'

'So, it's cool under there?'

'The temperature underground sits between about nineteen and twenty-three degrees, so warm in winter and cool in summer.'

She thought about confined shafts and closed rooms. 'Does the air get stale?'

'Ventilation chimneys help, which is what you see above ground if a dwelling is beneath it. These aren't just homes in the ground – they're clean-lined rooms and hallways, because the sandstone here stands firm without cracks and weak spots like in Lightning Ridge. Families can spread out properly underground.

When they need another living space, in comes the tunneling machine, except you're carving it from the earth. Ventilation shafts pull the air through, and ceiling fans do most of the cooling work.

Some do put in aircon but most don't bother. Miners here wear masks to avoid silicosis. Because that's actually what an opal miner is looking for – silica deposits.'

The kilometres flashed past. They went on to talk about the town, the type of people who could survive out there, and, of course, the opal. Even about movies – *Mad Max* was shot in Broken Hill and *Mad Max Beyond Thunderdome* was shot in Coober Pedy, apparently.

Towards the end of the long day, driving into the deep orange around Coober Pedy felt like driving on the surface of Mars. Not that she'd ever been planet side, but judging by that time she'd watched Matt Damon in *The Martian*, it was similar. Red dust and sandstone with white anthills of opal dirt marking the ground like pale pimples.

Finally, they hit another classic signpost – a mounted truck on the main road leading into town saying they'd arrived at their destination. What was with these opal towns and their vehicular signs? Instead of Lightning Ridge's cement mixer, this one was a black ute with a crane, on steel poles, that declared their arrival in Coober Pedy.

She gestured at it with her head. 'You'd like that one.'

'I do.' Another smile. She enjoyed the brief moment of camaraderie.

The outside temp read thirty on the F truck's dash, so not too hot today, but she was disappointed to see TJ pull into an above ground motel instead of one of the dugouts she'd heard about.

As if he'd read her mind, TJ said, 'We'll be leaving as soon as we're done. Ready to go. I want the truck outside our room.'

For a quick getaway? Made sense. 'Fine. I'm guessing you're going off for a walk while I stay here?'

'Nope. I'll sort the accommodation and put my head down.

Hoping for a few hours' sleep to bank some z's. We won't be stopping on the way back to the Ridge.' His implacable look said no negotiation would be possible.

Ouch. And she didn't mean nineteen hours in the car seat.

He was that desperate to not camp anywhere with her overnight.

She didn't bother arguing. *This is about William*, she reminded herself.

'Then I should go for a walk.'

'There's tourist attractions and places to eat, some of them underground. Meet you back here at six.' He caught her gaze and said quietly, 'Be situationally aware, please. It's a little more Wild West than the Ridge.'

He glanced at the obvious mining paraphernalia across the road from the motel. Trucks of all sizes. Tin sheds. Dead cars. Few people.

She was here for William, not sightseeing, but she needed to walk. TJ's sleep plan made sense, especially if he wasn't going to let her drive on this trip. She'd asked him twice on the way from Broken Hill, but he'd declined the offer.

'Okay, then. I'll stick around for a quick shower, then go safely exploring.'

Yes, Bella thought, as she walked the dusty streets. Coober Pedy did feel different to the colourful eccentricity of the Ridge. Even now, in the afternoon, she got the feeling the South Australian opal fields were rougher and rowdier. But then, it was a place of extreme temperatures, and the nearest city, Adelaide, was nine hours' drive away. You had to be tough to survive out here.

When she returned to the motel at five-thirty, she'd perused the few shops, enjoyed good coffee and a late lunch underground at a hotel. The most fun she'd had was when she'd browsed for nearly an hour in an opal emporium run by a wonderful woman of Greek heritage who'd moved to the area fifty years ago, she'd told Bella. She had passion, like Meesha, about her opals, and Bella had watched her make everyone who walked into the shop feel welcome and special.

Back at the motel, she guessed TJ had recently showered, judging by the steam in the air, and it was probably for the best she'd missed the tempting event.

He looked up from a map he studied at the table and nodded at her.

'Did you sleep?'

'Enough.' His dark brows furrowed. 'How'd you go?'

'Good. I wasn't sure whether you wanted me to bring back food, or if you'd fill up when you went looking for Bane.'

'I'll eat out.' He smiled. 'Thanks for thinking of it. You?'

'I've eaten, thanks. Brought home a pie and bottle of water for later, in case I have to stay in for the night until you find him, like in Broken Hill.'

'Good. That's for the best. Be packed and ready to go. When I find him, I'll work out a way for you to ask your questions, then we'll leave. There's phone service in town, so I'll text when coming back for you.'

'Do you have any ideas?' She suspected he would have, based on his past performances.

He glanced at his phone. 'It's Thursday, prime "mark time", so he should be out looking for people to con, though I don't expect him until dark. He's the kind of person who likes the anonymity of the night.'

'Sounds charming.'

'Sadly, he can be.'

Bella looked at her watch. 'It's a long time till dark.'

'I want to be ready when he arrives. If he's even here. I've got a list of questions for you to check, so you can use it when you talk to him, in case you go blank. Add anything else you can think of. While you're doing that, I'll drive around, then hit the pub and wait.'

Chapter Twenty-Three

Meesha

On Friday at p.m. Meesha walked along the footpath with Luci to the Lightning Ridge Ladies night. Her shop had been securely locked after a successful day, and the late afternoon felt pleasant in the warm breeze, even though the sun hadn't gone down yet.

They strolled arm in arm towards the servo with Pluto at Luci's knee. 'Another children's book arrived today.' Luci grinned. '*Hairy Maclary from Donaldson's Dairy*. That's six braille picture books I've bought now. I put braille stickers on each spine so I can find them easily. I'm so excited.' She laughed. Then added quietly, 'You know, Meesh, I've always wanted to have a baby.'

'I know.' Meesha squeezed Luci's arm. 'Soon.'

Luci squeezed Meesha's arm back. 'I can't wait to be a mother.'

Bumbling Batte was good for something, Meesha thought. Out loud she said, 'You'll be a wonderful mother. You should buy even more books.'

Luci laughed again and the sound made Meesha's chest ache with love. 'I read the new one to Eric and he said he can't wait to hear me read it to the baby.'

'You and Eric seem to enjoy each other's company,' Meesha teased.

'He's sweet.'

'He's sweet on you.' Meesha glanced sideways and her sister's cheeks slowly pinked.

Luci tilted her chin. 'I'm not rushing into anything.'

Of course. But . . . 'So . . . he's just handy with a hammer?'

She waited and finally Luci murmured, 'He's more than that.

A lot more. But I'm not ready.'

Ah, nice. Her sister deserved happiness. 'And nobody is pushing. Least of all me.' She changed the subject. 'I can't believe it's only four weeks till your baby's due.'

Luci turned her face Meesha's way. 'I know. And you have the big designer awards next week. When do you leave?'

They turned the corner and walked across the servo edge towards the back gate of Desiree's yard. Meesha not guiding Luci on one side, Pluto doing the work on the other.

'I'll drive to Brisbane Friday. If I leave at eight in the morning, should be there by four-ish depending how long I stop for on the way.'

'Staying at the conference hotel.' Luci nodded. 'There's more on as well as the awards, isn't there?'

'Yes.' Meesha laughed. 'Buyers and sellers at lunch and the conference itself is Saturday and Sunday. The awards are on Saturday night.'

'So when do you come home?' There was something in Luci's voice she couldn't pick. Not worry. Not disagreement. Meesha couldn't place it.

She replied carefully, 'Monday afternoon, depending on what time I leave. Gillian said she's fine to have the store until Tuesday.'

'She's good people.' Luci frowned. 'Don't you usually stay a few more days in Brisbane, after the conference? Don't you have other suppliers there to see?'

'I do. But not this time. I want to come home right away.'

Another long pause and then Luci said quietly, 'For me?'

'What's wrong with that?'

'You can't put your life on hold for me, Meesha.'

'Silly. I'm not.' *More change of subject needed*, Meesha thought, as they came up to the back gate. 'Did I tell you Bella said I could show her necklace? I'd hand it in Friday night in Brissy for finalist judging.'

'That's wonderful! Hope you win. Mum and Dad would be so proud.'

Meesha felt the pang but also the warmth of knowledge that it was true. 'I think Grandpa would be the happiest.'

They both smiled at that and Meesha pushed open the gate.

'Welcome, girls.' Greta came up and touched Luci's shoulder, then patted Meesha's arm. 'Lovely to see you both. Desiree was just wondering if you two were coming. We're all talking about next year's Lightning Ridge Easter Festival, after this year's was such a success.'

Meesha leaned forward, excited to be thinking about next year, which would be even better with Luci and the baby, Bella and the ladies, all in her life.

CHAPTER TWENTY-FOUR

TJ

TJ shut down all thoughts of Belle as he drove around the outskirts of Coober Pedy. His scattered memories of his time here, not long after Ree's death, reminding him of directions, semi-familiar yards of tin and derelict vehicles the further he went towards the mines.

There seemed more ordinary houses than he expected, since most people lived underground.

Back in the main part of town, he passed the school, the health centre, the library as he reacquainted himself with the layout of the streets, the local pubs and places to eat. He drove past the bottle shop, the second place you could buy a beer here, until eventually, he parked outside the entrance to the hotel most popular with tourists.

As he'd said to Bella, Bane wouldn't be out until dark. From what TJ knew of him, the man liked to be able to disappear into the night. TJ had kept to himself in Lightning Ridge, avoiding the criminal element, until William came along, but he'd known Bane had no morals about robbing anyone weaker than himself. Out of the force, TJ had made himself turn away, not get involved unless it directly affected him, like the ratters, because that would have outed his past faster than Desiree could have.

When TJ walked into the tavern, he could see he'd been right that it was the place for new miners to congregate. The pretty, bleached-blonde barmaid confirmed with a wrinkled nose that she knew the fussy little man he described, and sadly, yes, he'd lived in town for a long while now.

TJ thanked her, suggested mildly she could forget he'd inquired, ordered a beer and a steak and settled in the corner as the pub began to fill with new hopefuls.

He leaned back against the fly-spotted wall in the shadows, thanked the waitress for his meal when it came, and watched the walk-ins as he ate.

His mind stewed over Bella's apparent ability to get over his dramatic knock back, tried not to think of her sitting alone in the motel unit waiting for him, and shook his head at his loss of control despite his best intentions. Best case scenario, this whole wild goose chase of hunting Bane would mean the man had had nothing to do with William's disappearance, and they could all move on.

Around p.m. a short, dapper man, brown-haired and clean shaven in a western-style shirt and polished boots, one who obviously considered himself quite *the thing*, began to circulate the room. Bane. TJ's shoulders relaxed.

Gotcha.

Bane ingratiated himself with the new chums, those with clean clothes and soft hands, all the while probably sowing seeds of bonhomie, largesse and deceit.

There you are, you little worm, TJ thought, his mouth flatten-ing. He settled deeper into the shadows, pretending to read his phone, but in fact he angled it to video the action just in case the man was up to what TJ suspected were old tricks.

Yep. Bane attached himself to a pimply youth, and TJ watched for the sleight of hand he hoped wasn't coming.

And there it was – powder slipped into the victim's drink amid genial backslapping to disguise the action.

At least he'd caught it on his phone. He would make sure somebody brought the dog down. It would be good insurance as well, but inside a slow hum of anger burned at the fact that Bane had proved to be that low.

Within half an hour, Bane solicitously assisted his wobbly new friend to his feet, laughing and cajoling him outside, where no doubt the lad would be relieved of his money and phone. TJ's ire spiked again. Had that been what happened to William? A robbery gone wrong? No, Konrad had confirmed the note was his brother's handwriting.

Even though the victim would no doubt wake with a headache, lost goods, and a poor recollection of what had gone down, Bane would keep him alive to prevent any serious repercussions, but he would not feel a moment's remorse.

When the door closed behind Bane and his new 'mate', TJ rose and slipped out after them, reaching the barely lit road in time to see the headlights of a dusty utility disappearing towards the town outskirts.

TJ palmed his keys and quickened his pace to his own vehicle, where he slid behind the wheel and followed, keeping well back and, to his approval, with another random vehicle pulling out in front of him to head in the same direction. TJ followed Bane towards the heavier scatter of disused equipment and old mines he'd passed earlier that evening.

The moon was up, which would help a lot when he had to turn out his lights, and as TJ continued, the terrain grew familiar.

When Bane stopped, and the other car went on past him, TJ slowed until the victim's ute had turned off the main road.

Extinguishing his headlights, TJ hung a slow left after them and crawled along the dirt track through the outlying camps, the detritus of rusty disuse casting dark shadows and bizarre shapes across the road in the moonlight. The ute turned into a deserted miners' yard. This approaching dead end would be a good place for Bane to do his dirty work.

And for TJ to have that first chat.

Fifty metres before the road ran out, TJ switched his ignition off and let his car roll up behind an ancient tow truck, coasting to a stop without flaring his brake lights. The broken tower's tall winch cast a triangle of darkness across his windshield. The leaning and rusty doors of the wreck were all open, as if ghostly people had just stepped out.

Other ancient vehicles crouched like sinister beings in the shadows, and behind him the moon hung over it all, casting an eerie feel to the desolate place as he waited for a cue.

The headlights ahead extinguished and the cabin light lit up.

He reassured himself Bane wouldn't do anything terminal to the poor bloke. Thanks to the moon, TJ saw the moment Bane stepped out of the vehicle with a handful of small items and kicked the door shut.

TJ suspected the young victim had become unconscious from the drug and been well rifled for his possessions. He scanned the area, but it was too dark to differentiate new vehicles from old.

Bane must have his own transport stashed around here somewhere; he had to get back to town after his night's work.

A cloud shifted and the waiting motorbike flickered into view the same time as Bane turned towards it. TJ hit the F-'s switches for power and high beam and swung out of his hiding spot to roar down on the well-dressed creep. He snarled as Bane froze for a second like a spotlit fox on a rifle range, a shocked and terrified gaze lasting only a second before he streaked towards the bike tucked beside an oil drum, bent on escape.

'Oh yeah, buddy, not happening.' And that feeling, that cop-with-a-quarry-in-sight feeling rose unexpectedly. The familiarity took hold – how many times had he thrown his body into apprehending a lowlife, into protecting an innocent? The muscle memory left him ferocious and focused, useful in this situation, and it was not an unpleasant memory. TJ wasn't sure whether that was a good or a bad thing.

His vehicle roared down to the left behind the sprinting Bane, passing him and knocking into the bike, sending it flying, probably buckling it, he hoped.

TJ jammed on the brakes, pushed open the door, and despite the little man's swerve, he caught Bane around the shoulders and spun him, both of them ending up face to face with a clack. The objects in Bane's hands fell to the ground as TJ's fist punched him in the solar plexus. Hard.

Once was enough.

Bane gasped and fell, spasming. Wheezed almost silently as he tried to breathe. Didn't succeed.

In the zone, TJ leaned over and pulled out the plastic ties from his pocket, snapping them to Bane's wrists and ankles. Bane's eyes widened and he seemed to recognise TJ. The fear leached out, instantly replaced with outraged fury.

TJ ignored the shock as he secured Bane's limbs. Once done, he walked back to his truck, removed his torch and took himself over to the other vehicle.

The young victim lay boneless in the passenger seat, his head against the door, pale and breathing – thankfully deep and regular.

TJ straightened him out on his side to keep his airway clear and left the driver's door open with the light off. He'd frisk Bane, drop the young bloke's cash and goods on the ute's floor and contact the police once they were done here.

He pulled out his phone and texted Belle, his mind clicking through the logistics of keeping her safe. A story he could fabricate. The video of Bane's offence at the pub should be enough to keep him quiet afterwards, at least until the police picked him up.

I'll be there in ten. Be ready to go.

Now to put fear into Bane, to hopefully scare him enough to tell the truth. It wasn't seeming such a great idea to have Belle near the man, but if TJ questioned him alone, it could turn into a slug fest that ended with Bane not talking at all. And something told him not to underestimate Bella like he'd underestimated William.

Still, Bane knew TJ wouldn't kill him. Hell, he'd robbed TJ's mine and got away with a beating.

So, TJ had to make him believe there was someone bigger and badder than himself, someone TJ was afraid of. Almost true.

By the time TJ had a piece of silver tape cut and hanging from his fingers, Bane managed to gasp air into his lungs in partial recovery as he lay in the dirt.

'TJ?' Gasp. 'Why?' Gasp. 'Can't do this,' he wheezed.

'You get paid to do things. So do I, now. Big bucks. And the woman I work for might just decide to end you herself.' Patiently, TJ waited until Bane's breathing had returned to the life-sustaining kind before slapping the tape over the man's mouth.

After what the lowlife had done to the young bloke in the ute, TJ wished he could tape his face. Bane's sudden nasal inhalation led to a snort loud enough to scare the birds, and TJ tried not to enjoy the sound too much.

The guy was a douche and would be no great loss to the world, but Belle would hear what she needed before TJ released him, hopefully to the police.

He stared down at the man's wide eyes. 'Yeah. Deserved. Think about the answers you want to give her when she comes. I won't be able to save you if she doesn't like what you say.'

He'd considered telling his prisoner what the-person-who-wanted-answers would ask – but he decided the man was so devious that giving him time to think and manipulate the situation wouldn't help Bella find the truth. Let him think TJ had been paid to capture and hold – and possibly end – him. Hopefully he sweated over it.

Without speaking again, TJ picked Bane up by his belt and swung him less than gently into the back of the young man's ute, out of sight until he could return with Belle. He scooped up the victim's possessions Bane had pilfered and tossed them onto the floor of the utility.

As he walked away, he could hear Bane kicking uselessly against the tray of the ute with his fancy boots. The tinny noise wasn't loud but might carry and attract attention. He didn't want anyone investigating yet.

TJ paused, then went back. 'Stop. Or I'll roll you in the tarp to shut you up.'

The kicking continued.

TJ sighed. He lifted a folded tarp out of the back of his truck's tray and opened it longways on the ground. He picked up Bane by the waist again, the man hanging like a wiggling bag of concrete, heaved him over the side of the ute and dropped him in the centre of the tarp.

Air rushed out of Bane's nose as he groaned and sucked oxygen in and out loudly through his nostrils.

'Warned you.' TJ rolled him up loosely in the tarp with just his face poking out, then lifted him back into the tray of the ute.

Silence. Sweet.

Bane was lucky TJ was a law-abiding citizen. Mostly.

Before he drove for Belle, TJ checked on the young victim again. Still sleeping heavily in his car.

'Back soon, mate,' he said and climbed into his truck, pulled off his gloves, started the engine and drove sedately out of the deserted mine yard and towards town.

When he pulled into the motel, Bella opened the door. In the light from the room, her face looked pale but determined, and he reminded himself she was a doctor.

He'd made an oath too. Though discharged from duty, he'd agreed to serve the Queen – though it was the King now, he supposed – to uphold the law and keep the peace. He was doing most of that, albeit in a roundabout way.

'I'll just be a sec, then we'll head off.' TJ went past Bella, cleaned his teeth and used the facilities. Made sure he'd left nothing behind, picked up the prompt sheet he'd left her, and grabbed the bags. Explained about what he'd seen Bane do and what was waiting for them.

'Let's go.' He pulled the door shut. 'Can you drop the room key into the after-hours slot?'

Bella nodded. 'Yup.'

He appreciated her easy compliance considering it must have been odd to be left here all evening and then gone within minutes.

He wasn't surprised she made a good partner, the thought skit-ter-ing seductively, but he pushed it away. That thought came with more than he needed to think about right now.

Chapter Twenty-Five

Bella

As they drove out to the deserted spot where TJ had stashed Bane, Bella scanned the surroundings, all the spooky mechanical shapes illuminated by the truck's headlights, and TJ explained the events of his evening.

When he'd finished, he added, 'You can check the victim first.

I think he'll be fine. But we'll send the police out to the young guy as soon as we're done.'

He reached into the glove box and stuffed a long piece of material into his pocket. Maybe a scarf.

She peered around his arm. 'What you got there?'

'Blindfold. Probably won't need to use it – I'll set him up so you can interview him with the light in his eyes. I'll blindfold him if the light doesn't work. Don't want him seeing your face.'

Bella grimaced. 'What detective show have you been watching?'

'I'm not kidding.'

Softly, she said, 'That's not going to work when I ask about my brother.'

He ignored that. 'He can't see you, but you'll see his face. I'll make sure of that.'

She blinked at his fierceness. 'What did you do before you were a miner?' When he didn't answer, she went on. 'Who are you?

What's your real name?'

Another of those grim smiles crossed his face. 'I could tell you but then I'd have to kill you.'

'Or I could medicate you so you'll answer me.' She snorted.

'Because this does make me more curious.'

He blew out a frustrated sigh. 'So be curious. You're not taking this seriously enough.'

That sobered her up. He was right. This wasn't just TJ's 'bad boy' games, this was about William. Her dead brother William.

And criminals TJ worried could hurt her. All the humour fled.

TJ looked over at her and nodded. 'This is how it's going to work. Bane'll be restrained, but don't worry, I'll leave him unhurt when it's all over.' There was something in his face that hinted at a struggle with that concept, and she called him on it.

'You sure about that? No accidents? It's Hippocratic oath and all that for me.'

He nodded again. 'He'll be able to walk back to town from there.' But his look added the unsaid, *at some stage*.

Crikey. Now he had her worried. 'Okay. So, how about you reassure me you don't "off" people. Even criminals?' She had to know, because the alternative would be seriously alarming.

'Breaking that promise would not make me happy.'

'I'm a law-abiding citizen, promise.' He shook his head at her.

'You ask the questions and watch his expressions. The guy's an accomplished liar.'

She nodded and he looked satisfied.

'William liked James Bond movies. Do you?'

She looked at him quizzically and nodded again.

'So, channel M, Bond's lady boss. I'm aiming for Bane to think someone bigger than all of us wants the answers.'

Good grief. Secret agent stuff as well? 'Is this really necessary?'

'When it's all over, I don't want him to know you're William's sister. Try not to give it away when I've gone to all this trouble.'

Her back stiffened and she glared at him. He'd gone to all this trouble, had he? She was right here beside him, in it together.

Although, she guessed he had organised it all and bent a lot of rules if he'd restrained the guy.

So, yes. Maybe he had gone to the trouble. She could do this.

For the truth about William. Konrad would never have agreed to this, so what did that make her? 'Okay. You have no idea how tough I can be.' She raised her brows. 'I have an IQ of one hundred and forty. I should be smart enough to outwit a petty criminal.'

'Yeah, well, think of it as roleplay, and don't forget to play the role,' he joked, but there wasn't a lot of confidence in his tone.

It forced her into remembering this interrogation was for real.

She might find stuff out, possibly in gory detail, about William's final moments she hadn't wanted to learn. 'You're right to drive straight home after this. I suspect I'm not going to be able to sleep when we're done.'

But this wasn't about her. This was all about William and the answers she might not want but needed, so she pushed aside the little girl lost and the stupid games – games she was probably using to hide anyway – pushed it all away. 'I'm sorry. Of course. You've gone to a lot of effort. I do appreciate you doing all of this for someone you barely know.'

His rugged face twisted. But could that be a hint of regret she read on his face before the stone wall slammed back into place?

'Mind on the game,' TJ instructed. 'Let him think. Let him sweat. Let him trap himself.'

'I can do that.'

'I'll address you as Ma'am.' He passed her the handwritten sheet he'd given her earlier. He must have picked it up from the motel table, and she couldn't believe she'd just left it lying there.

She'd make a hopeless secret agent.

Nerves bubbled up and she hugged her stomach, feeling sick.

Cold. She rubbed her arms. 'We're technically doing something illegal. Could I go to jail for this?'

'No.' He didn't elaborate.

She thought of the questions, and her nerves escalated. This *was* illegal. There was no whitewash about it. Plus, if TJ felt they needed this many precautions . . .

What if she found out William had been tortured, or horribly maimed before he died?

What if he had lain for days dying? In pain? Nausea swirled in her gut and she wished she hadn't eaten that pie. Did she really want to live with that sort of knowledge forever?

What if she was wrong about all of this, and he really had committed suicide?

The fear in her eyes must have shown, because after TJ glanced her way he said, 'If it goes down an unexpected track, one that will put you in danger to hear, I'll stop it. You'll leave and I'll finish up without you. You have to agree to that before we start.'

Relief surged and she fought it back. Killed it. Lifted her chin.

Blew out the dread. 'No. If William's gone through anything, then the least I can do is be present for it. He was my twin. I'm not going to be protected. I'll do what I need for answers.'

Silence from the driver's seat until finally TJ said, 'Yeah.' An expression she couldn't read crossed his face and then he nodded.

'I can't fight with that. Your call.'

When they pulled into a deserted yard, packed with dumped machinery, rubbish and vehicles in disarray, Bella eased open her door to see a modern utility parked in the shadows. It was bouncing as if someone moved around inside it or in the back. TJ turned the engine and lights off.

'Give it a minute until our night vision readjusts.'

So, they waited, and finally she could pick things out in the more than reasonable moonlight, possibly even walk around without tripping.

'Don't step off the driveway area,' TJ warned. 'There's shafts everywhere here when you go into the paddock.'

TJ slipped out of the truck and around to Bella's door in three quick strides, looming up out of the darkness.

'Just give me a few minutes, then you can have the torch and check on the young guy. He's in the front cab.' His voice floated across her skin, and she could see he was running on fumes.

Determined. Bossy. All that gathered from a glance and the tone of his voice.

Darkness blanketed the old yard, except for the moon's patchy generosity. 'I have a torch.' She reached into her backpack and rifled around until she lifted it out. 'You keep yours.'

'Okay,' he whispered, 'but give me a minute to shift our bad guy out of sight.' He strode over to the back of the ute and she waited as he removed a long roll – carpet, maybe? – from the back.

The roll moved as he lowered it onto the ground, dropping it when it was only a few inches from the dirt.

He held onto one side of the tarp – she recognised what it was now – and suddenly a body spilled out into the dirt. Lay still.

Bella sucked in a breath. Oh no. Please don't tell me he killed him.

Then the body jerked and wriggled. Made violent noises.

She heard TJ say conversationally, 'That's quite an impressive look of hate. If I was you, I'd figure out how you're going to get back to town later if I have to hurt you.'

He hauled the man up as if he were a child and pushed him to stumble behind a large container. She thought she could hear more mumbling noises, but then they died away.

Once they were out of sight, Bella switched on her torch and hurried across to the cab of the other utility. At the sight of the even breaths rising from the drugged man, and the occasional mumbling in his sleep, she allowed herself to pause and study him. Breathing not too slow and deep. She reached in and felt his pulse – slow but even. Skin temp neither too hot nor cold.

Bella stepped back. She'd seen Rohypnol victims before. It seemed this was something like that. Time would help it wear off.

TJ appeared from behind the container and gestured for her to join him.

Taking a deep breath to settle the snakes in her belly, she followed him around the corner and stopped. The small man, Bane, sat on an upturned drum, his hands pulled to the left and secured to a rusty door unconnected to anything. Just a random big door on its side, leaning up against the drum. He wouldn't be walking anywhere easily with that anchor on his wrists.

TJ had secured the torch to an old pole directly opposite Bane's face, and Bane's head was down as he avoided the light between him and Bella.

TJ stood behind him, out of the beam but in easy reach of the prisoner – because that's what he was. Good grief, what had she become involved in? Drugged victims. Secured prisoners. A dead brother.

That last thought stiffened her resolve. Damn it, she would find out the truth of how William died, and if this man didn't know anything, they would let him go. But if he did . . . he deserved this.

Aaaaand then she'd go to hell.

She had no idea how releasing the prisoner afterwards would work, but that was TJ's problem. She'd forced him to bring her on this run, so it was only fair to trust him now.

It was easier than she expected it to be. Especially as TJ caught her eye and nodded. The sooner she started the sooner they could leave.

From the first time she saw Bane's face clearly, she recognised the lack of morality in his eyes. Oh yeah. This guy was a lowlife.

What on earth had William been doing to be associated with him?

'Ma'am?' TJ prompted.

Ma'am? Ah, yes. And she'd said she was bright. Sheesh. Okay, time for roleplay. She was M. Bella blinked, drawing on her photo-graphic memory to bring back the questions on the sheet of paper clutched tightly in her hand. She forced herself to loosen her fingers and ask the first question in the light from TJ's torch.

She spoke slowly, with a faked boredom. 'Your name?'

Bane scrunched his mouth shut. TJ closed his hand on the man's shoulder and squeezed. He tried to shake him off, then finally spat,
   'Bane.'

Oh my goodness, they were all going to hell. Bella forced her voice to remain even. With a bite. 'Full name, Bane.'

He glanced furtively to the side as if he could escape, or to try to see her face. TJ waved his hand at him, and Bane answered sullenly. 'Francis Eric Bane.'

'How long did you live in the Ridge, Francis?' *M*, she repeated to herself. Resting bitch face. Calling him Francis made her feel just that little bit more in control, keeping him at a disadvantage, even if it was a tiny one.

'Five years.'

'And where were you before then?'

'Coober Pedy,' he said, more sullen than before. 'Like now.'

'We . . .' She paused at the word. What did TJ mean by 'we'?

Then she hurried on before it became obvious she'd been side-tracked. 'We are interested in a man you knew three years ago. He disappeared. You've been tracked as part of our investigation into that disappearance.'

This whole thing felt surreal. Like suddenly a curtain would fall and an audience would clap. Or boo.

'How would I know what man?' Bane sounded belligerent now.

Bella tried to keep the words level. Unemotional. 'William Grey.' She managed to get the name out but her heart pounded.

She watched Bane's face – easy with the brightness shining on him – and she caught the moment his eyebrows drew together as the memory hit him. Then he looked away. Not to TJ. Away to the right and then down to the ground, avoiding eye contact. 'Don't remember that name.'

The lie was as plain and clear as the container in front of her, but she guessed she expected that. Even before he'd started to answer.

TJ's big hand came down on the man's shoulder again and Bane jumped. In his deep voice, TJ growled, 'We all know you knew William. Don't start with a lie.'

Bane shrugged TJ's hand away, but she guessed he had loosened his grip or he wouldn't have been able to. Bane's close-set eyes narrowed even further as he stared at Bella through the blinding light. Trying to see her face.

'So, what's there to remember? He was just another loser in town who drank too much and necked himself.'

Belle sucked in her breath, though somehow she managed it quietly. Forced herself not to say anything as she remembered TJ's words.

Let him think. Sweat. Trap himself.

She could do this.

She looked down at the sheet of paper gripped tightly in her fingers. After that last question, TJ had written in bold, capital letters: *BE CAREFUL HERE. No matter what he says.*

She quietly blew out the held breath and said slowly, 'What makes you think he' – she forced herself to finish – 'necked himself?'

'Left a note, didn't he?'

She paused. Remembered TJ saying he'd only shared that detail with Konrad.

Bella asked, in two slow, deliberate syllables, 'Did he?'

CHAPTER TWENTY-SIX

TJ

Oh, you clever girl, TJ thought with relief, because he could imagine the strain for Belle in navigating this huge emotional hurdle. He'd worried about this situation asking too much of her, even while his ears pricked up at the note reference. He was pretty sure William's suicide note had never been mentioned in town.

TJ himself had slipped the note quietly to Konrad after he found it at his camp. Even Desiree hadn't known about that, which made Bane's knowledge suspicious in the extreme.

'Tell me about the note.'

Belle's demand took them both by surprise. Bane actually twitched and TJ wanted to cheer. His Belle was good at this.

No. Not his Belle. William's Tinkerbell.

The next few minutes would tell if all this drama of catching Bane had been worth it. This whole plan had been rife with dangerous repercussions.

When Bane didn't answer, Belle asked more insistently, voice gravelly, 'What did it say?'

Bane flinched. 'I dunno.'

TJ added incentive. 'Answer the question.'

'I dunno! Just a note. That he was necking himself and they wouldn't find his body.'

Calmly, Belle said, 'Who forced him to write the note?'

This time Bane physically jumped, as much as he could in his restrained position, and TJ knew they'd broken through. Who would have thought sweet Belle Bird had it in her? Though, she'd had him on the ropes a few times, and that was when she was playing nice. Now she definitely was not.

She wasn't finished. 'Were you there when they forced him to write that suicide note? Did *you* force him to write the note? What did they threaten him with?'

Bane shifted urgently in the chair. Sweat beaded on his forehead and his gaze shifted side to side. 'It wasn't me.'

'But you were there.' This time there was no question, just a sharp statement of fact.

Bane's head swivelled as he looked for escape. 'He annoyed people. Asked about opals disappearing. Knew too much.'

'And . . .?'

'They wanted him silenced.'

'They? And the threats they made?'

Bane said, 'The usual. His family. The bloke had a twin, a chick, and once they threatened her' – Bane snickered – 'he wrote that note pronto.'

'Then you threw him down a deserted shaft and left him to die?' The tone that came out of Belle's mouth lifted the hairs on the back of TJ's neck, and Bane flinched.

'It wasn't me! But . . .' The man hesitated before continuing.

'I don't think he died. Or at least not then.'

Silence from the interrogator.

Bane waited, sweating profusely now. But still no questions came. After a long, long time, during which TJ worried about Belle and Bane began to struggle and pull at the door as if he could shake it off, the small man cracked. And the words tumbled out.

'I didn't throw him, okay? Someone else did. I just checked on him afterwards.'

'Was he conscious when you threw him down?' Belle asked.

Silence.

'Was he conscious?'

'Yeah, but he'd had a rough afternoon. He didn't make a sound after he hit the bottom.'

Belle didn't speak and TJ didn't think she could. So he took over. 'How did you get down to check on him?'

'I came back in daylight and had a winch on the front of my car.'

'Who were you working for? Blackjack? Rigger?'

'No. Much bigger. Bad guys.' He was sweating again, or perhaps he'd never stopped. 'Not worth my life to tell you.'

TJ laughed but it wasn't a friendly sound. 'Your life isn't worth much.' He could have pushed, punished the man more, but he didn't need to know. This was about finding William . . . or his body. He wasn't a cop anymore, and the rest was just backstory.

Bane sneered right back – fake bravado considering his obvious nerves. 'Yeah? Let's see if it's worth anything after I tell them what you've been asking me about.'

'Tell them whatever you like,' TJ snarled, disgusted.

Bane snapped, 'I went back. I'm not a model citizen, but I don't do murder. I went back to see if he was alive.'

He looked up, straight at the light. 'His body was gone. I'd seen it there at the bottom of the shaft after they pushed him. But it was gone. He could have crawled further into the mine and died there, maybe, but I sent a drone in. Couldn't find the body. Found some blood. And maybe some scuff marks where he could have climbed out. Or someone helped him. He could have lived, but he wasn't anywhere that I could see in that mine.'

Silence.

Finally, Belle said flatly, 'You're sure?'

'Was the job. The searchers aren't s'posed to find the body.

I was s'posed to make that happen. No body. Big mystery. Didn't want to get caught up in it, so I left town.' He glared with hatred at TJ standing immobile beside him. 'Until *he* kidnapped me.'

Belle's voice returned. Soft. Menacing. Implacable. 'There's a chance you can still walk away, Francis.' A chance, but the tone suggested a slim one.

Bane strained to hear how he could save himself. Breathing heavily. Anxiously.

Belle spoke again. 'Explain to us, now, how to find the correct shaft. Then, answer any other questions TJ has. Only then, I might let you go. You'll forget we were here. We'll keep the video of you drugging that boy as insurance.' The menacing tone bit through so coldly even TJ wanted to shiver.

He'd created a monster. But TJ knew now was the time to get the information, while the man was off kilter from the interrogation to get the truth.

Bane didn't answer. Rock and hard place. If TJ found the body he'd missed in that one search, he was the last person to see William alive. He'd be blamed.

'Which mine?' TJ's own voice was sharp, demanding, and he snarled, 'Tell me.'

Bane jumped. 'Coocoran.'

TJ leaned back, surprised. They hadn't considered Coocoran Opal Fields when they'd first searched for William. Twenty kilometres out of the Ridge, there would be another fifty or so named opal fields out there. That wasn't counting the hundreds, if not thousands, of shafts. Hell.

But it was time to end this before someone nosey decided to see why there were lights out here in no man's land.

Bane had worked himself up into quite a state. 'Why the sudden interest in William Grey after all this time?'

TJ considered misdirection, then compromised with, 'I'm paid to do a job, just like you've been paid to do your filthy work.

Where in Coocoran? And I will track you down if you lie.'

Bane had his head down. Shaking and twitchy, like he knew he'd said too much for his own health. 'Jesus. Give me a break. Johnson's old mine. The one that kid fell down that time and they locked it up.

We reopened it. S'posed to close it after, but the body wasn't there when I went back. Closed it anyway.' Bane looked up and his eyes were wide and panicked. 'They don't take failure well.'

'Who?'

Bane shook his head. 'You might kill me. But they will.'

TJ met Bella's eyes and she nodded.

They'd both heard the truth. Which just created more questions about what had happened to William's body.

'I'll finish up here, Ma'am.'

Bane started to shake his head, but TJ ignored him. All his concern was for Bella. She looked at him as if she hadn't heard,

and then she nodded, once, and walked away without speaking again. His heart followed her, because despite the expressionless face, in posture she'd looked shattered.

He sent video footage of Bane to an ex-colleague in Vice to liaise with the local cops in Coober Pedy. The video clearly showed the sleight of hand over the drugged drink and Bane leaving the bar with the staggering youth. The photo of the young man unconscious in the front seat of his car should seal the deal.

Enough to get the kid checked out, probably not enough to hold up in court, but at least it captured a scenario the department could use against him if they wanted to set up for a later sting if Bane got away tonight. Or turned up causing trouble in another town.

Bella was back in his car – she'd satisfied her doctor instincts after checking on the victim once more, while he sorted Bane. The man's hands were still bound but no longer anchored to the heavy door, and he'd been pushed out onto the road and sent walking into town. TJ didn't want him here with the sleeping victim until the police were on their way.

TJ had no doubt the weasel would hide if the police came while he was still on the road, too. And he would easily find a piece of sharp metal and free himself from the plastic ties.

They were done here.

He started the engine and turned out of town into the night.

They passed Bane walking on the side of the road, but didn't slow.

Still shaking his head at Bella's ability to sink into the role of bad cop, TJ tried to equate her recent actions with the woman who had kissed him in Broken Hill. He couldn't.

He *was* worried about her. 'You okay?'

'I don't think so.' Her voice came out of the darkness beside him and his stomach sank. He didn't like the despairing note it contained. 'What we did tonight was crazy and wrong.'

He guessed he'd expected that.

But she wasn't finished. 'I know there are weak and evil people in the world. And my foolish, darling twin was mixed up with them. I didn't think I was naive.' She shifted in the passenger seat and turned to face him, her gaze locked on him as the road disappeared behind them in the night. 'I just didn't know evil could infect me and make me feel this contaminated.'

Ah, hell. He'd done this to her. His gut twisted in remorse.

Finally, quietly, he said, 'I'm sorry I made you feel that way.'

She tapped his biceps with her fist. 'Not you, idiot, though the other side of you is a tad scary.'

She shifted again, leaned towards him. 'What worries me, TJ, is that I'm not sorry we frightened that man and made him tell us things he didn't want to share. That I was complicit, agreed one hundred per cent, to restrain and threaten him to get those answers. And what's really scary . . .' She let that hang for a minute. 'I would do it again.'

That he hadn't expected. 'You did it for William.'

She snorted. 'That's crap. I'm having a little revelation about myself over here. I did it for me.' She waved her hand in the air.

'Oh, I can be noble and say I did it for my parents, and Konrad, and everyone else who wants to know what happened to William.

But that's not true. Once I knew that man had been standing by when William was pushed down that shaft, had been a part of the evil that took my brother, I didn't regret being there.'

'Okay. But that's not a bad thing.'

'It's horrific.' She stared ahead now. 'I'm a doctor. Do no harm.'

So? They hadn't. 'Bane walked away. Let's get real here. That lowlife was probably the last person to see your brother alive.

He had clues you didn't have prior to coming here. So, I agree.

I don't regret we came.' Time for a diversion. 'Where do you think William's body could be, then?'

She sagged in the seat. Her voice trailing off. 'I don't know.

And my head is exploding with tangents and wild ideas and the worst headache I've had for a while.'

'Then how about you close your eyes? I'll put quiet music on.

And we'll both be better for the break from thinking.' He glanced across at her as she rubbed her brow. 'When we get home, we'll sort this out.'

'Let's do that.' She reached across and touched his thigh, and he felt that gentle caress go through his whole body. 'No matter how this ends, TJ – thank you. I'll always be grateful to you for putting yourself at risk for me.'

He wanted to put his fingers over hers and hold her hand, but she lifted it away before he could and reached down to hoist her backpack onto her lap. He heard the rustle of foil tablets being popped out.

'I don't think I'll sleep, but I'll try.'

Belle gently puffed in sleep an hour outside Coober Pedy, her head on her backpack jammed against the door frame, while TJ drove into the night.

Heaven help him, he admired this woman so much. Was so proud of her strength in Coober Pedy. And awed by her. He smiled as he remembered snippets of the last two days. Maybe he needed to ask more about what she'd been like before she'd become a doctor. Still tough, he'd bet.

He wished, once they found out what had really happened to William, he could investigate that tough side of her a bit more.

If only in his dreams.

Shortly after sunrise, TJ pulled over at a truck stop on the outskirts of Broken Hill. They stretched, washed their faces and ate a quick breakfast of muesli bars. When they returned to the car, Bella stood in front of his door, her fingers over the handle.

'I'll drive. You're wrecked.' Before he could refuse, she said simply, 'I don't feel safe in the car with your fatigue.'

He wanted to fight about it, but it was the perfect argument; he couldn't put her at risk. She was right. She'd slept most of the night, and he'd been drifting the last hour. Now with food on board, and his stomach stealing the blood from his brain, he'd be worse.

She drove for nearly five hours, stopped at Cobar for fuel and they swapped drivers again.

When they arrived back in Lightning Ridge around p.m. on Saturday afternoon, he pulled the car in by her unit to drop her off.

She climbed out of the F truck wearily with her backpack, turned and just stared at him from the open door. 'Are you going to bed now?'

'Soon. There's a couple of hours of light left. Might try to find that old mine out at Coocoran Bane mentioned.'

'Do you have to do that right now?'

Neither of them expected to find anything there, and he knew she was too mentally exhausted to go with him.

'I just want to set the place in my mind. I've got maps of the fields at home. I'll grab a rope and the drone from my place. I need conclusive proof he's not there, Belle. But I want to see it now.'

She nodded. Climbed back into the truck. 'You can't go into a deserted mine alone. I'll stay up top while you look.'

He stared at her. 'You sure?'

She raised her brows at him. 'What do you think, TJ?'

Twenty-one kilometres out of town, TJ stopped his truck at the site of an abandoned lease set well back from the road. The camp had fallen into ruin, and struggling grass covered everything. But several half-covered shafts lay exposed in the evening light – so many shafts, but only one blocked off with boards. He drove the truck right to it, winch facing the shaft.

'This one,' he muttered. Before he'd left Belle's, he'd quickly searched Google for the photographs he'd known were taken when that child had fallen down the mine. It had rocked the Ridge.

He worried about Belle as she undid her seat belt. 'There are old mines everywhere. Watch every single time you put your foot down. Do not walk backwards. I do not want to have to haul you out injured or dead.'

'You sound like a police officer. Sheesh.' She was looking around the site so missed his jolt of surprise, thankfully. Although, he guessed that secret would come out soon enough, anyway. Just not now.

'Me neither,' she continued as she climbed out carefully, looking at the scatter of holes. 'I hear you.'

TJ blew out a relieved breath and headed for the tray. He removed the drone box, his headlamp and spare torch, his climbing gear and his two-way set.

He explained about the winch, and how she would need to turn it off and then on again when he called her. Typically, she understood the concepts quickly.

Chapter Twenty-Seven

Bella

Bella watched TJ pull the boards off the top of the shaft with his gloved hands, muscles straining, face intent. Every few minutes another crack broke the silence as a board was torn free and tossed aside.

This place was deserted. But she'd had to come with him.

This was the shaft William had been thrown down.

Not fallen down.

Not jumped down.

Thrown down. Which meant, after their little kidnapping escapade, they were interfering with evidence of a murder case.

They were definitely going to prison.

She told herself to chill.

If they hadn't found Bane, there would be no case. No place to search. She had to trust that TJ knew what he was doing, and technically, even if she didn't have muscle memory to guide, she knew what she would be doing with the winch. Making sure TJ got out alive.

'I have to run the truck's engine, so my battery won't go flat.

It won't hurt to keep it running until you bring me back up.'

TJ sounded a lot calmer than she felt. 'Okay, I'm ready. Turn the car on and lower me down slowly.'

She blinked herself back into the present. She'd missed him picking up the two-way. Missed that he'd slung the drone bag over his shoulder. Missed him moving to the side of the mine with the end of the winch on his boot and his headlamp sitting on his forehead.

'Right. Yes.' She climbed into the driver's side and started the engine, leaving the truck in park, then went back to the front of the vehicle where she could see TJ, and picked up the hand control he'd explained. Simple. Safe. Scary.

She pushed the button and TJ began to lower into the mine.

It seemed to take a long, crawling time, and yet not long enough, until his head and extended arm holding the cable disappeared.

He'd said it was sixteen metres deep and there was only one hori-zontal shaft that went in a long way down.

Ninety seconds later, his voice came over the two-way. 'Stop the winch. I'm on the bottom.'

She hit the button to stop. Crap. They were about to find out if William's body was there.

'I'm sending the drone along the floor to check for other shafts.

Then I'll follow that as far as I can.'

'I'm here.' That was all she could say.

Twenty minutes later TJ called again. 'Nothing, sorry. I'm ready. Bring me up slow.'

Bella forced her mind to concentrate as she worked the controls. Tried not to think about what TJ said until she got him out. Nothing? No William? Had someone come and retrieved the body? Changed their mind about it being found?'

She saw TJ's hand and arm first, and then the rest of him appeared out of the shaft. She followed his instructions and stopped the winch as his foot, held in the loop of cable, came level with the ground.

By the time they made it back to Lightning Ridge, Belle's mind was whirling. Her brain felt stuffed with so many thoughts and scenarios of where they could go from here. Images of William's body down a shaft, wilder thoughts that possibly William was alive somewhere, or had been, at least for a little while before he'd suc-cumbed to his wounds. He hadn't intentionally left her. She felt a twisted sense of relief that he hadn't committed suicide, that leaving her hadn't been his choice, but that feeling was tempered with the pain that someone might have murdered him instead, that William had spent his last moments afraid and alone. She felt she was going to splinter into a million pieces. Thank heaven TJ was still with her because she didn't think she could feel this on her own and not crumble.

They'd agreed to hold off discussing the findings until they arrived back to Bella's unit. But if TJ thought he was escaping that talk until tomorrow, he had another think coming.

'Come in,' she said as she stepped out of the truck into the deep-ening dusk. 'You can't go yet.'

Even through the open door of his truck, he looked big and reas-suring, not dark and dour like she was used to, and she needed him and a brandy to settle her agitation. Needed to talk about the infor-mation that her brother hadn't suicided, that he'd been murdered, or the even more tantalising hope that William might have escaped. But that didn't make sense. If he had he would have contacted them? And how could he have got away?

She shut that thought down before it could fully do her head in.

TJ hesitated, holding onto the wheel with both hands. Then he sniffed under his arm. 'I need to go home and shower.'

'I can't wait longer for you to come back.' Besides, he always smelled good to her, but she wasn't saying that. 'Use mine. It's big enough, even for you.' Or two.

His brow creased as he considered it.

She waved him over with her hand. 'Just do it and stop complaining. I'll get you a towel.'

Looking at her from under his brows, he muttered as he climbed out, 'I think this interrogation stuff has gone to your head.

Created a monster.' He blew out a breath. 'I'll just grab some clean clothes from my pack.'

She smiled as she keyed open the door to her unit. A win, finally, even though she didn't feel like anything was a win at the moment. She didn't know what to feel. Not until she knew more.

As TJ came through the door and closed it behind him, he didn't look at her. 'Which way?'

She gestured through to the adjoining room. As he walked past, she whispered, 'William might be alive?'

TJ froze. Bella's breath stopped as he turned as if to step forward and take her in his arms, but then he straightened and sighed. She let out a shaky breath.

'Don't get your hopes up. I saw the place. It was a deep shaft.'

Then he disappeared towards the shower she had pointed out and very soon she heard the water running.

Unless TJ had jumped in fully dressed, she could imagine all that inked skin slick with water, his muscles and sinews and angled bones glistening from the water streaming down. If she had more fortitude, she'd strip off her clothes and slip in next to him.

After all, what would he do once they were skin to skin?

She'd seen the look in his eyes after they'd kissed, could read so clearly what he couldn't say to her face.

She pictured herself following him to the shower, imagined herself stepping in. Feeling his skin against hers as his arms clamped around her.

Stuff it. She needed to be wrapped in his embrace. The emotional havoc wreaked by the interview – the thought of her brother's body hurtling over the edge of a mine, the thought he'd been hurt and alone – still haunted her. And now, a tiny glimmer that he might have been alive, could still be alive somewhere – amnesic, a prisoner, who the heck knew – but after all the years, months, weeks of suffering, it made her want to scream at the concept.

She wanted to slap her hands against the wall, punch a hole through it, let the frustration out.

But right now, she needed TJ, his presence, him holding her. That was one thing she knew would help. And he was here, in her shower, naked, solid, comforting, and yes, as good as a man could be.

Bella reached for the hem of her T-shirt, undid the buttons of her trousers, pulled off her bra and panties. She pushed through the bathroom door, stepped into the open-ended, long shower recess and into the steam. Slid in behind him, and wrapped her arms around his waist.

'Don't get soap in your eyes,' she murmured.

He was still washing his hair, soap dripping down, and when he tensed, felt her, turned, he closed his eyes when the suds stung them. Or to block her out.

'What are you doing here?' he growled, sounding half-crazed, half-amused.

She rubbed up against him. 'Taking advantage of you. I couldn't stay away. I need you to hold me. After everything . . .'

He sighed, and under her hands, she felt the stiffness ease out of his muscles, tension falling away as the water did. As she watched his broad chest rising and falling with each deep breath, she hoped he wouldn't push past her and leave . . .

He didn't, he spun, yanked her against his chest and pulled her tighter, crushing her to him. 'Too late now,' he whispered into her hair.

She turned her ear against his chest, listening to the rhythmic pounding of his heart, pounding like hers, fast but steady as a drum. 'Too late now, TJ.'

When she lifted her head to look at him, his mouth came down over hers, and everything else faded away.

The kiss lasted forever, his mouth everything she remembered, and the crazy feeling built, the need surged and cried out for more until TJ turned off the shower, wrapped her in a towel and carried her to her bed. Their very, very clean skin melded together. Sliding and slick. As she'd known he would, he worshipped her, marvelled over her, and finally made slow, gentle love to her. Changed tempo, less finesse and more demand, and started all over. Then turned gentle again, until they both fell asleep, exhausted and entwined, a few hours before dawn.

Morning came too fast, though it was a.m. by the time they woke. Bella heard that shower turn on, so she shifted to the kitchen. It was probably only a few minutes before he reappeared, yester-day's discarded clothes bundled under his arm, but mean-while she'd whipped up a fast plate of scrambled eggs and toast, piled high and set at the table for him.

'Protein won't hurt.'

She scored a crooked smile for that. 'You really want to feed me, don't you?'

Tried a sultry look. 'Not feeling maternal here.' She held up her hands in mock protest. 'Promise.'

He actually laughed at that. 'Lucky. Because that horse has bolted.'

She really did enjoy his infrequent sense of humour. 'Eat. I'll show-er and then we'll talk.'

Minutes later, she was back. 'So, what do we do now?' They hadn't talked at all about William. They'd been busy. Had escaped from all the scenarios in mutual release. Now her brain felt sharp and clear. Thank you, TJ.

He glanced at her from the microwave eggs he'd made for her in return, gesturing with his head for her to sit while he put his freshly washed plate in the drying rack. 'Food was great.'

'Good. And thanks.' She sat. Ate, suddenly ravenous, and smiled into her eggs. His might be even better than hers. When she'd fin-ished, he took her plate, washed it and dried his hands as he came over. Drew her down onto the lounge so she was in his lap, and hugged her. 'Let's work it out.'

Her heart eased as she savoured his arms around her, turned to rest her head on his chest and stare up at his profile. 'Where could William have gone, TJ? If he lived?'

'I have no idea.'

She shook her head. 'There are so many possible scenarios and questions, and I don't even know who to ask. We know so little.

When should I tell my parents? Konrad?'

He stroked her shoulder. 'What do you think happened now?'

'What can I think? He managed to climb out. Stumbled away and died and nobody found the body?' She shook her head. 'Maybe a head injury with amnesia and he doesn't remember who he is? Still doesn't? Or why would he stay away for nearly three years?'

'Or. He decided not to come back for reasons we can't even imagine.'

She looked at the concern in TJ's face. Concern for her. She touched TJ's cheek. 'What do you think?'

TJ stared at the front door. Finally, he said, 'It suggests somebody in town might have helped him.'

Bella searched his face. But she couldn't see even a glimmer that said he knew who. She racked her own knowledge of the Ridge inhabitants. 'We have to find out.'

'Damn sure it's someone who can keep a secret. For almost three years.'

She nodded. Clasped her fingers in front of her face, rubbing her nose. 'Somebody with their finger on what's going on in town,' she said.

He looked back at her. 'And knows who's coming and going, because if William *is* alive, he's probably been spirited away from the Ridge by somebody, maybe somebody no one would take any notice of leaving town, if those after him thought he was dead.'

'Any ideas? Suggestions? Who knows everything in town?'

They looked at each other. A few seconds later, they both smiled grimly and said together, 'Desiree.'

CHAPTER TWENTY-EIGHT

MEESHA

Meesha liked the idea of Gillian working two days a week at The Iridescent Opal, so she'd asked her to drop in at the store today to discuss a more permanent part-time arrangement. She could afford this. Could listen to sisters and friends who said she needed balance. She could change.

Gillian loved bright clothes, too. Fitted the store's vibe of creative and classy. Just as they were getting into logistics, Bella walked in, and the intense, harried look on her face had Meesha tilting her head.

'I think she wants to talk to you.' Gillian flicked her copper-top ponytail as she turned in Bella's direction.

'Me too.' She crossed the showroom to her friend. 'Hey, missy. What's up?'

Bella was speaking before she came to a stop. 'Sorry, Meesha.

But I need a big favour. Can you shut the shop and come with me to see Desiree, please?'

Meesha stared. 'Umm.' She glanced over her shoulder at Gillian, who'd obviously heard the request. The other woman waved her on. 'Okaaay. Gillian's here, though, for an interview.

Why do you need me to come?'

'It's a long story, but . . .' Bella's voice dropped to a whisper Meesha could barely hear. 'I think Desiree might know something about my brother's disappearance. Something that she's kept secret all these years.'

'Whoa.' Meesha considered that bombshell. She should have had two coffees with breakfast. 'That's a big accusation.'

'It is.'

Meesha searched for any doubt in Bella's face but couldn't see a hint of hesitation.

Okay, then. Friend duty first. She glanced at Gillian who gestured for her to go ahead.

Meesha nodded in thanks, then pulled Bella through the shop and into her workshop. She wasn't saying she wouldn't go, but she might need more convincing if Bella wanted her to play wing-woman while she upset Desiree, a woman enormously respected in town. And who provided access to the Lightning Ridge Ladies, and company Meesha enjoyed.

When the door between shop and workshop was shut, she asked, 'Why do you need me to come with you? Why wouldn't you take TJ? I'm guessing you guys found something out while you were away?'

'Yes, we did, and I thought it less confronting if you came instead.'

Meesha wasn't so sure of that.

'Plus, he's going back to the area we think William disappeared from to look for more clues. I need someone to come with me. And you said I was your friend, right?'

Meesha noticed Bella's dark circles under her eyes that stood out like a panda's on her pale face. Along with that hint of desperation in her gaze. 'Quick question. Have you slept at all?'

'Four hours this morning after we got back, but that's not important. Will you come or not? TJ says she shuts the servo at twelve on the weekend, so we need to hurry if we want to catch her in time.'

Bella looked just a little wild, and accompanying her might be a good idea for everyone's sake, Meesha thought. She nodded. 'Sure. What's been happening? Was it the Bane bloke you spoke to?'

'I'll tell you as we walk,' Bella replied and turned back the way she'd come.

Meesha glanced down at her clothes. She was decent. Besides, she was dying to find out what all this was about. Did Bella really believe Desiree knew something about what had happened to William?

Bella hovered by the door that led back into the shop. 'Plus, you know Desiree better than I do. It would be helpful to have you there, in case things get tense.'

'Greta knows her better than me,' Meesha corrected, her brain finally clicking into gear. 'I think we should ask her to come, too.

She's Desiree's friend who also adores you and could be good back-up. And, you know, an all-round pacifier person if things go south.'

They ended up as a posse of three, corralling Desiree when she backed out of the service station, pulling the door shut behind her,

preparing for the weekend. She glanced at them from beneath her snowy brows and snapped the lock on the door shut.

'You three look like you mean business.' Desiree wrinkled her forehead, scanning their faces before settling on Greta. 'What's all this about? And what's with the support team?'

'Bella's come across some information about her brother William.' Greta's voice stayed low but firm, which told Meesha she believed in Bella's intel. 'She thinks you might have more to tell us and asked me to come with her as your friend.'

Desiree's face didn't change but she stilled. Meesha sucked in a breath quietly. Seriously? Desiree *did* know something.

The older woman stabbed a finger at Meesha. 'What about her?'

'She's here as my friend,' Bella said.

Desiree turned to Bella, eyeing her carefully. Scanned the vicinity as if checking that nobody else was in earshot. 'Well, you have me. I'm not happy, but ask your questions.'

'I think someone in town helped my brother disappear when he was injured, not dead, and' – she paused and sucked in a breath, before continuing more quietly – 'that he didn't try to kill himself.

Someone tried to kill him. I want to know if you know anything about that.'

'What makes you think I do?' Desiree shot back.

Meesha spoke the same time as Greta did. 'Because you know everything.'

The older woman shook her head in exasperation and . . .

Meesha wasn't sure, but was that a shudder of guilt? Good grief.

Meesha's mouth wanted to drop open. How could Desiree have kept this massive secret and caused so much pain to William's family? To Bella? Man, she couldn't believe how Desiree could have looked Konrad and Bella in the eyes if she really knew William hadn't committed suicide.

Desiree muttered, 'You'd better come round the back, and we'll talk.'

She led them around the side of the now-closed fuel station, Meesha blinking rapidly, one hand holding her chest in shock. She had not expected this when Bella came to her door today.

They followed Desiree like schoolgirls through the back gate, a spot usually unseen except on Friday nights, and into the yard where they all sat down in the shade of the pergola. It missed that touch of magic without the night-time and twinkling fairy lights and laughter. Or maybe it felt harsher and less comforting in the light of day and in the heat, given what they were about to discuss.

Meesha watched Desiree blow out a pained breath and glanced at Bella who looked as though she might beat the truth out of Desiree if she didn't offer it. Whoa. She was so glad Greta was here.

'Nearly three years I've carried this. Scared of the damage I'd do if I told anyone. And don't think I haven't suffered to know your family suffered.' Desiree's eyes were suspiciously bright and her hands shook. 'Poor Doc Konrad . . .'

It struck Meesha at how the impossibly strong Desiree suddenly aged, looked almost broken, verging on distraught.

'I had to watch a man I admire so much almost break with the pain. But William insisted it was the only way I could keep his family safe.' She glanced at Bella. 'Especially you.'

Greta sprang up and then crouched by Desiree's chair. Put her arm around her shoulders. 'Oh, Desiree. How awful for you. You haven't been yourself for a long time, have you?'

Desiree patted Greta's hand and straightened her back. 'Thank you, Greta. You just sit down in that chair. Don't go hurting your knees. I'll be fine.'

Greta smiled and did what she was told. Desiree's chin went up, but her voice had dropped to quiet and resigned. 'What do you want to know?'

Meesha blinked. Looked between Bella and Desiree. Caught by the lack of surprise on Bella's face and something that vibrated in her friend like tension. Stress? Excitement?

'I want to know all of it,' said Bella, and Meesha could see she had herself well under control, now, thank goodness.

Desiree ruffled her hair. 'It's a long story.' She sighed as if not knowing where to begin. 'There's a woman who comes through every few months in her mobile home, one of those trailer units with a Suzuki soft-top, you know those tiny cars, hitched to the back. She'd stay a couple of weeks, do a bit of noodling, then head back to Perth. Used to be in the army as a medic and then in the police force.'

She gazed off into the yard as if seeing the past. 'Carol. Made detective, she told me – Detective Carol Wood. Supposedly retired.

Strong woman. Takes no nonsense.' She looked up and locked eyes with Bella. 'Good person.'

Meesha vaguely remembered an ex-policewoman who came and went every couple of months. She'd popped by The Iridescent Opal once or twice, but in those early, chaotic days when Meesha couldn't recall all the details.

Desiree sighed at everyone's eyes still fixed on her. 'The same day she was leaving that year' – she focused on Bella and clarified – 'when your brother disappeared, a bunch of yobbos pulled into my

servo for some petrol. Not a brain among them. That Bane was with them.'

Her gaze wandered to the fence separating the outside world from her backyard – towards where her fuel pumps would be – as if she could see it all happening again.

'I caught a glimpse of William in the back seat, between two big blokes I didn't know. He didn't look right, but he didn't ask for help, so I couldn't call them on it.'

Meesha caught the apologetic look Desiree sent to Bella and unobtrusively slid a supportive hand into Bella's. Her friend gripped her fingers back.

'Anyway, Carol – Detective Wood – was just filling her little Suzuki before she put it back on her trailer, and I had a word with her about being worried for your brother. She'd met him at my place out the back. They chatted. So she followed them, to see what was going on. Turned out later she already knew young William. Except.' Desiree's face twisted in disgust. 'Turns out more happened than she expected. Because she was on her own, and she couldn't stop them doing what they did. She couldn't stop them throwing William down an old mine shaft.'

Meesha glanced at Bella. Her friend's eyes were wide in dread but not quite surprise. Did she know this already? Meesha didn't understand but her fingers were almost crushed in Bella's hand.

Desiree went on. 'She did, however, check on your brother soon as they left.' She looked at Bella.

Bella nodded, but Meesha just stared at Desiree, blown away.

She really knew what had happened, that William hadn't killed himself? All these years, and not a word. Why?

'To Carol's relief,' Desiree continued, 'he wasn't dead, just confused, concussed, a bit broken. But she threw him a rope and got him out. She stuck him in her car and brought him back to me, on the quiet. He was raving about how if they found out he was alive, they'd kill his sister – you – or his brother, Doc Konrad.'

'Ahhh,' said Bella quietly as her shoulders slumped and her hands came together almost as if she were praying. 'He was alive.

And that's the reason for silence.' She lifted her chin and speared Desiree with a look. More loudly, she asked, 'Is he still alive?'

Desiree nodded. 'So, I swore not to say a word, and Carol took him with her.'

'Where?' Bella's voice more strident.

'They didn't say. But Carol's from Perth.' Desiree glanced at Greta. 'But I knew it left us with some scary people in the Ridge who needed stopping. Turns out, ones with fingers that reached much further than our opal fields. William and Carol had been working on it the whole time.' She sat back. 'I'd heard the whispers of ratters, of course, but thought they were the usual lone wolf types, all out for their own gain. Guess I didn't know everything after all – there's a whole network of them, targeting mines together, to this day.'

Bella's eyes were narrowed. 'So . . . the people who tried to kill William threatened me and Konrad?'

'They did. He'd clearly learned information the bosses didn't want known, things he and Carol had been investigating all along, under-cover. Still are, far as I can tell. But you know he's alive now.'

She shook her head. 'I just hope you haven't stuffed up years of work for them,' Desiree finished. 'After all this angst – you better not get yourself killed.'

They all sat in silence. Bella touched the opal necklace again, like it was a talisman for her brother and could keep him alive.

Meesha's mouth made an 'O' at the truth bombs that had landed.

Finally, Bella whispered, 'So William's really alive?'

Desiree nodded. 'Last I heard. Killed me not telling Doc Konrad. Even harder lying to you, William's twin, when you arrived. Gave me a start to see you looking just like him – the exact same eyes and hair. But I promised him. Life or death. That's the reason he hasn't come back, and not because of his health, or that he didn't want to. All about *your* health. To keep you safe.'

Bella's gaze was glued to Desiree's. She whispered, 'So how do I contact him?'

'You can't. Best I can do is contact Carol, tell her you know, and get him to reach out to you.'

'William's alive,' Bella repeated, her voice breaking. Tears slid silently down her cheeks until she put her face silently into her hands.

Oh my heaven. Meesha put an arm around her friend and pulled her close. How did anyone process this? The last three years of her life had been based on a lie.

'Oh, Desiree.' Greta put her hand out to her old friend. 'This must have been so hard for you.'

'Yes, but . . . I put myself in the firing line. Sticking my nose in.'

Bella stood up. Nearly knocked her chair over in the rush.

'Desiree!' She threw her arms around the woman but stopped when Desiree stiffened. 'Thank goodness you did. Thank you.' Bella managed a shaky laugh through her tears. 'It's going to take some getting used to. But he's alive!' Her exuberant face morphed into something else. 'Oh my stars, I'm going to kill him for not telling us.'

'Thought you might feel like that,' Desiree said gently, 'but I'm sure Carol and William have a good reason for keeping things quiet. Don't go spreading the news until you hear from him, or he might end up dead. Or you might. Or you'll ruin the whole case they're trying to sort out. These guys are way worse than your average ratters.'

Greta asked, 'So you still keep contact with Carol?'

'Every week. Someone has to pass on the information that brings this group down. I see everyone who comes and goes.

Waited for a knock on my door every night for three years from the criminals but it hasn't happened yet. See that it doesn't.'

Desiree the undercover spy, Meesha thought. In danger all this time, but trying to do her bit to protect the Ridge.

They all nodded. Vehemently.

Greta stayed behind with Desiree, and Bella didn't let go of Meesha's hand as they walked back to her house, the weight of the news sinking into both of them with every step.

CHAPTER TWENTY-NINE

BELLA

Bella's head swam. Her heart thudded and she didn't know whether to laugh or cry or even if she was game to do either. In case it all changed again. William was alive. Desiree had known. Yet his own family hadn't. How could that be?

Her twin was alive! Somewhere. Where?

Bella's eyes snagged on TJ leaning against the side of the medical centre in a patch of shade, waiting for her, and some of the weight fell from her shoulders even though the shock still coursed through her.

TJ was in her corner. He'd help her deal with this. After their night together, there was no doubt. She still wasn't sure if they'd make a couple, but that would have to wait. Right now, he looked solid, reassuring, and worried. About her.

While her mind flew in all directions with the William bombshell, she glanced down at Meesha's hand still held in hers. Bella squeezed her fingers. 'Thanks, Meesha. You were there when I needed you. I'll never forget that.'

'Happy to be.' Meesha tilted her head towards the man ahead.

'Don't need me now, though, with the big boy here, do you?' she said with a grin, dropping her hand and nudging Bella's shoulder with her own.

'Doesn't mean you have to leave. You're welcome at my place anytime.'

'Nah. I gotta get back to work. Talk to Gillian.' Meesha lifted a hand. 'I'm out of here. And I need another coffee.'

'Thanks, Meesh.' TJ inclined his head at her.

'He has manners,' Meesha teased, and Bella laughed. A weird, crazed laugh and she shut her mouth.

'He pretends he hasn't,' Bella said more calmly. 'But he's a gentleman, through and through.'

TJ didn't comment, just lifted a finger in farewell and followed Bella into the unit, his bulk looming reassuringly behind her.

As he reached her, she touched his corded arm. She had no idea how he'd come to make such a huge impact on her life, but he was someone she wanted to hold on to right now. The solid in her unstable world. Maybe even her future.

'I have news. Confusing but wonderful news.'

She smiled, more centred now that she had him by her side again. But glancing at his face in the light through the window, she noticed the lines and shadows. 'You look as worn out as I feel. Did you find anything more at the site?'

'No. Not that I expected to but wanted one more look. I'm more worried about you at the moment,' TJ replied. 'And ready to explode with curiosity. What did Desiree say?'

He was worried about her. Had allowed himself to care. In fact, hadn't he done everything to ensure her safety the last three days?

But right now he was waiting, so she gathered her thoughts.

'In a nutshell, Desiree helped some female ex-detective – or maybe not ex – spirit William away to Perth on the night those men threw him down the mine. Wounded but alive, and he's been there ever since while they try to shut down the criminals through a country-wide task force. She warned me not to tell anyone until she can contact this woman, Carol. He stayed hidden because they threatened my life and Konrad's when they kidnapped him.'

'Damn.' TJ shook his head in disbelief and his eyes narrowed.

'But three years of silence?'

Bella sighed. 'I know. It's hard to wrap my head around, too.

But Desiree said she'd contact Carol, who helped him escape, let them know we know, and get William to contact me. I gave her my phone number in case he hasn't got it.'

She then explained the sequence of events that Desiree had shared with them, until her voice trailed off. Suddenly exhausted by the momentous findings. Emotional overload setting in.

She choked out a laugh that sounded more like a sob. 'You want a cold water?' Turned her face away to peer into the fridge, her head whirling. 'I don't know what to do. I'm stunned. I just want to hear his voice.'

'Love a water,' TJ replied from much closer than she expected.

'Hot outside.' His hand slid around her waist, and he pulled her into him. 'You need a hug.'

'I so do.' She leaned her shoulder back into him as she put the water bottles on the kitchen bench. Turned in his arms and slid her hands around his waist.

'I'm buzzed from lack of sleep and adrenaline. And other things.'

'So, what are you going to do?' TJ asked, as he rested his chin on her hair.

Bella sighed and slid one arm free to pull her phone from her pocket. 'I guess we can't do anything until this Carol contacts us,' she said, closing her eyes. 'What sort of woman follows suspected criminals into deserted opal fields on her own? And saves my brother while she's at it?'

TJ smiled grimly. 'Dangerous for anyone. You sure this Carol isn't related to you, Belle Bird?'

Bella frowned. 'How'd you reach that conclusion?'

'Balls of steel,' TJ said dryly.

She laughed and it came out as a half-sob again. She needed to get herself together, but it felt impossible when her brain still reeled from the concept of William not being gone. She didn't think she'd survive if something had happened to him, now, now she'd heard he was alive.

Bella's phone rang, and they stilled. Stared at the screen in silence.

TJ moved behind Bella, peering over her shoulder. 'Unknown number,' he growled. 'For once, I'd say answer it.'

Bella jumped, fumbling with the phone. 'Yes, yes, of course . . . Hello? This is Bella,' she said, and even she could hear that her words trembled as she waited.

'Tinkerbell!' said the voice on the other end. Bella nearly dropped the phone. Her hand covered her mouth and she shoved it against her lips to stop the scream escaping.

That familiar voice. A voice she thought she'd never hear again.

Clear and unmistakable. Thick with emotion. 'It's amazing to hear you, sis.'

Bella's throat closed, words catching there. She handed the phone to TJ, waving her hand in front of her face, before she buried her nose in his chest and a raw sob erupted and felt like it ripped her chest in half.

TJ switched the phone to speaker mode. 'This is TJ,' he growled. 'Give your sister one good reason for not contacting her for nearly three years, you little monster.'

A gasp at the other end. 'TJ? Man, it's good to hear you, too.'

There was a brief pause before William sighed. 'The only reason there is. They threatened to kill Bella and Konrad.'

Bella watched TJ close his eyes and she sagged against him.

Tried desperately to swallow. Reached out for the water bottle on the bench, gulped a mouthful of it and swallowed past the lump.

Put the bottle down and waved her fingers at the phone.

'William. You're alive,' she managed to say. 'That's all that matters.' Distantly she supposed she'd have stayed hidden, too, if it meant William was safe.

William's voice cracked. 'I've wanted to hear your voice for so long. So many times, I almost called, despite knowing it might jeopardise you and the case against the criminals. But I didn't.'

The desperate emotion in William's voice, the remorse, came through clearly. 'It hasn't been easy. Tinkerbell. I've missed you so much.'

Her heart felt so big, her throat so closed up, she could only nod and squeak, 'Yes. I'm here.'

TJ pressed closer and Bella smiled as she strained to soak in her brother's voice. He was *alive*.

TJ said, 'That's good for a few months, but almost three freakin' years? Is there a plan for you to come back now?'

'I can't tell you all the details today,' William replied softly.

'But I will. Soon. Your timing sucks. Can you leave everything as is,

without opening more cans of worms? I'll leave for the Ridge as soon as it breaks.'

'Considering I've just hauled your sister out to Coober Pedy and back after we kidnapped and threatened Bane, that might be tricky.'

William groaned. 'You didn't? Damn it, TJ. You don't know who we're dealing with here. They won't stop if we don't stop them. These aren't just ratters, out for themselves and some quick money. This is an organised group, stretching further than Lightning Ridge. They won't stop if we don't stop them.'

Bella took the phone back, 'I get that, but what about Mum and Dad? What about Konrad? They deserve to know you're alive.'

'You can't tell anyone, Tinkerbell. Please, just hang in there for another few days. I promise I'll explain everything. I'm desperate to. I'll tell Mum and Dad and Konrad as soon as I arrive.

I promise.' He was rushing. 'Everything will be okay.' He paused. 'But only if we leave nothing undone.'

'Except we all thought you were dead.' Bella's voice broke again.

William said quietly and urgently, 'I'm so sorry. I've been watching from afar. Desiree's been passing along updates when she can. Nearly broke me.' His voice croaked with emotion. 'I'll explain later. I didn't expect you to move to Lightning Ridge. I'm not sure you're safe.'

Bella gathered her thoughts. She couldn't think of the last years of pain. Right now, it was unimportant compared to the incredible truth of William being alive. 'Umm. Konrad's having a honeymoon. *I took over the surgery.' And I was trying to learn to live again.*

'I heard. And TJ? How come he's there?'

Of course he'd heard. Desiree. He'd just said that. She looked at the man standing so close she could feel his heat. She lifted her hand to his face. 'Well, TJ's been keeping me sane.'

'She's safe,' TJ spoke into the phone and drew her hand down and held it in his.

William said, 'I have to get onto my superiors. We need to move the closure of this operation forward. It's big. Dangerous.

We're about to move on the people we think are running the whole ring. If we lose them now, we won't get another chance.' A voice in the background made a muffled comment and William added quickly, 'Bella, I have to go. I'll try to ring you tomorrow.'

He hung up and there was silence.

Suddenly it was all too much. She stepped back into TJ's embrace, buried her face in his chest and began to sob.

CHAPTER THIRTY

TJ

All TJ could do was hold Belle and curse her brother for causing them all so much pain. From the little William said, TJ suspected he had been undercover the entire time he'd known him. Probably since Bella said he'd left the force – most likely a ruse to get him on the ground in Lightning Ridge.

The man had obviously created the persona that would make him attractive to Bane, his goal being to infiltrate the criminal elements TJ had suspected existed in the Ridge, but hadn't wanted to know about, stuck in his own private hell as he had been.

He'd retired. Buried himself here, in his mine. Hidden like a coward. Maybe if he hadn't pushed it all away, Belle would have had her brother back sooner.

William had suffered, no doubt, had to have knowing he had destroyed his family.

Some of the inconsistencies TJ had noticed in Belle's brother now became clear. With irony, he wondered if he'd been one of the original suspects in William's undercover work. Probably.

It made more sense then that William had pursued a friendship despite TJ's efforts to keep him at arm's length.

Well, he guessed he'd find out eventually. But so much for friendship. For almost breaking himself with guilt over the guy's supposed suicide.

Sadly, in the context of undercover operations, he got it. But it was harder to forgive William for what he'd done to Belle.

Until this moment, Belle had needed him, but soon she wouldn't.

Not when she had her brother back. He got that. She'd only come to him looking for information on William.

When she had him back, she wouldn't need a man with his enormous suitcase of emotional drama. She would want security, family and the mending of wounds.

He wished last night hadn't happened for her sake, but for himself he knew he'd never stop reliving those moments when she'd given herself to him so completely.

As if in response, his fingers tightened their hold on her and he rested his chin on top of her head. Closed his eyes and breathed her in. Savoured the moment, before he had to lose her forever.

'I guess we can all stop feeling guilty for not being there for William,' Bella mumbled against his chest, with a tightness to her voice that made him lift one hand and smooth her hair.

'So, it seems,' TJ muttered, then he pulled back. 'But he is alive.

You've found him. Now you can start living again.' As much as he didn't want to leave, he needed to start rebuilding the distance.

'You okay, now?'

She blew out a breath and straightened her shoulders. Looked up at him, her eyes still red, her nose pink. 'No, but I've been worse. Though I may strangle William when he finally turns up.'

TJ smiled grimly. Edged her further away from his body.

'Might be a line of people waiting to do just that when William gets home. After they all hug him to death.'

Belle sucked in a breath. 'God. Konrad. The guilt he suffered.'

She shook her head. 'My parents. William might die yet.'

But they both knew her missing brother would be welcomed back like the prodigal son. It's what families did. Or so he'd heard.

Belle groaned. 'What do we do now? Today? Just sit around and wait until he contacts me?' The lost tone in her voice made him want to gather her to him again. But he couldn't. For her.

Starting right now.

She needed to not need him.

He had to pull back before he did more damage. 'I think you should go down and see Meesha as soon as she shuts the shop.

Spend some time with her and Luci. I've things I need to do at my camp after being away the last few days.'

He saw the moment his words registered and she stepped back.

'Oh. Of course you do. I'm sorry. You go.'

Go. That one word felt like a punch to the centre of his being.

Her eyes searched his face, a flash of what looked like insecurity crossing hers. But this was Belle – she didn't have insecurities.

More likely it was an apology for keeping him from his own life he'd just declared he needed. He tried to keep his expression neutral.

Quietly, she murmured again, 'You go. Thanks for staying last night. Afraid I didn't give you much choice there.'

Damn. He'd hurt her but, hell, that was all there was in the future if he didn't put those walls between them again.

He shrugged, pretending it was all good. 'Hard to knock you back when we were skin to skin in the shower,' he said, trying for light ness but sounding more like a dick than he'd meant to.

He cursed himself when redness flooded up her cheeks. Now he'd embarrassed her. He needed to get out of here before he did more damage.

Despite the blush, she lifted her chin and gave him a wobbly smile. Damn, she was amazing. This was his Belle. Tough as they come, and again he had to clench his teeth to stop himself from reaching for her. No. Not his.

'It was an amazing night,' she said, her eyes tracking his features, searching and not finding what she was looking for. She sighed. 'Maybe we both need some sleep.'

'Right.' He took another pace backwards. Ensuring he couldn't embrace her. 'We go on like before and pretend that we didn't know any of this stuff until William comes home.'

Get out, get out, his brain chanted.

He spun, wanting her, not trusting himself with a last look, so he opened the door and let himself out, moving faster than polite.

Once in his F-, he roared down the street, took the corner hard and turned onto Three Mile Road. He slammed his palm on the steering wheel. Slammed it again.

'Such a freakin' idiot,' he growled to the windscreen. 'Should've stayed out of that shower.' But no way would he ever forget the gift she'd given him last night. Not until he was old and deaf and doddering. Maybe one day he'd wish he could. But not today.

When he unlocked the gate to his camp, the place sat untouched – no one had entered since he'd left. The trip lines were still in place. Good to confirm it in real life and not just on camera.

He parked in the garage – he'd clean the travel-stained vehicle later – but right now he needed to process everything that had happened. And what shouldn't have happened.

Hard to do when all he could see was Belle's stoic face as she tried to smile as he left her. God, she was so brave, so open.

Offering him the world. Not like him, offering her nothing but locked walls.

If he was a better man, he would've walked away sooner. Or been worthy enough to stay with her forever. Seemed like all that fear of getting too close to Belle hadn't been any use, because he had feelings for her that even the love he'd had for Ree hadn't touched. Knew, deep in his gut, his soul, he loved Belle.

He strode to the door of the house, stomped inside and threw his kit on the table, but all he could see was Belle sitting there demanding he tell her what he knew. Belle handing him coffee.

Belle unwrapping the foil of a bacon and egg roll as she gently harassed him.

He shook his head. She'd never been inside his bedroom, but he could see her there, too, as plain as day, her arms reaching up for him.

TJ spun around and strode outside to the mine. Maybe he just needed to work off this angst. He pulled his big keyring out and began unlocking everything, head down, determined, pushing back all the feelings as the familiar routine tried to mask the anguish in his heart.

He switched on the generator so the lights down in the mine would be waiting, threw back the grate, jammed on his helmet and disappeared down the ladder until he was back underground where the world couldn't touch him.

Chapter Thirty-One

Meesha

The Iridescent Opal had been shut for hours. Meesha put down the opal pendant she couldn't seem to concentrate on as she sat in her workshop. Ground her teeth. It was too hard to try to create a new masterpiece for her depleted stock when she still couldn't help worrying about Bella and the roller coaster of emotions she must be feeling after visiting Desiree.

She tried again to fix the end of the silver drop to where she wanted it but couldn't make it stick. She needed to stop making mistakes with the setting or put the whole thing down. Sighing, she lifted her head and stared at the same door she'd dragged Bella through earlier today.

Bella had clearly fallen for TJ, but it was still all pretty new.

Meesha hoped he was the rock he really looked like, but she suspected he carried his own dark past. She just hoped he didn't make William's sudden reappearance a reason to back away from Bella and break her heart.

She heard the back door creak open, and Pluto nosed his way into the workshop, followed by her sister.

'Hey you,' Luci called. 'You didn't come in when you came home from work.'

Heck, she'd forgotten she'd said she might go next door. She'd gone straight to her workbench after work to soothe her mind. But Luci needed her, too.

Luci's voice brought her back to the present. 'Something wrong?'

Meesha opened her mouth and closed it again. She wanted Luci's input; her sister had always been the wise one, but did she have the right to share Bella's secrets? Though, Bella had shared most of it with Luci already.

'We'd better sit down.' Meesha touched Luci's hand and they went over to the table and two chairs set back against the wall.

'Bella told you about Bane and how she wanted to ask questions about her brother, didn't she?'

'Yes. Why? What's happened?'

'You can't tell Eric or anyone.'

Luci turned her way. 'Of course not, if you say so.'

Meesha chewed her lip. 'I think it might even be a life or death thing.'

'What?' Her sister sat up straighter. 'What are you involved in?'

Meesha quickly recounted everything Desiree had revealed about William. She could see the same shock on her sister's face that she'd felt.

'William survived? And he didn't tell his family? How could he do that?'

Huge unexplained mystery, that one. 'I don't know. But you can imagine what Bella's like at the moment.'

Luci nodded. 'I'm glad I'm sitting down. So why aren't you with her?'

And that was the crux of it. Meesha needed advice. 'TJ's there. I'm just worried he'll leave and if she needs me, she won't ask.'

'Ahh.' Luci nodded. 'You guys are good friends, but Bella's a tough cookie. Maybe even if TJ does leave, she might need time on her own to work through the implications. Everything she thought she knew was a lie. Why don't you text her and say you're here if she needs you. Give her space as well as support.'

Meesha blew out a breath. Now that made sense. She sent the message and felt an instant easing of tension. Bella might feel comfortable enough to ask now, if and when she needed a shoulder or a sounding board or a drinking buddy. 'And that's another reason why I love having you here, sis. Thank you.'

'You're welcome.' Luci reached for Meesha's hand, grazing over the table until she found it. 'Which brings me to something I've been worrying about. It's been on my mind, and I just need to ask. Are you sure you're happy to have me here bringing my baby into your busy life?'

Meesha sucked in a breath. Where had that come from? She must have dropped the ball with supporting her sister. 'You're kidding me. Having you here is one of the best things that's happened to me this year.'

'Yeah?' Luci still sounded sceptical.

'Hey. You and Bella are changing my life for the better. I was a workaholic before you guys came and didn't realise how much I needed my own tribe.'

'So, I'm your tribe?'

Meesha squeezed Luci's fingers. 'Chief of my tribe. And I asked Gillian to work every Saturday and Monday for me. What do you think of that?'

'Now that is excellent.' Luci smiled and Meesha bumped her shoulder gently.

'I can't wait for your baby to arrive. To watch my sister be the best mother there is while I get to be the fun aunt.'

Luci chewed her lip before saying softly, 'I hope so. That I'm the best mother, that is. I know you'll be the most fun aunt in the world.'

Meesha frowned. 'Where has this doubt come from?' She needed to keep a closer eye on her big sis if she was going to have these thoughts. 'I know it's true.'

'No idea. Crazy thoughts.' Luci rubbed her forehead. 'It snuck up on me. I guess I'm nervous. It's getting close.'

'You're not doing this on your own, Luci. I can't wait to help, and I know Bella's the same, and not just as your doctor. Heck, even Eric would walk on hot stones for you.'

Luci nodded. 'Okay. Sorry for the pity party. That's enough about me.'

Meesha squeezed her sister's hand. 'Never enough about you.

I hate that you were thinking like this. Tell me earlier next time if the gremlins get in your head.'

'I promise.' Luci waved the subject away.

But Meesha hadn't finished. 'I don't have to go to Brisbane.

I can try for the US shows next year. It's very close to when your baby's due.'

'Don't even think about staying for me. I want to see you showing your designs to the world, too. This is your big chance.'

She stared hard in Meesha's direction.

Well, that was a direct order from her older sister. Meesha smiled as Luci went on.

'But back to Bella. I'm gobsmacked that Desiree kept a massive secret like that. I hope it doesn't cause problems for her when the other ladies hear. She doesn't deserve that.'

Meesha was seeing the enormity of Desiree's burden, too.

Hopefully, when it got out, it wouldn't change people's perceptions of her. That wouldn't be fair. In her way, Desiree had helped save William's life. And maybe Bella's. Meesha thought about Greta's instant sympathy for Desiree. 'I don't think it will. We're all blown away. Greta's first thought was for Desiree. And now that I think about it, Desiree was in a tough spot for a very long time, carrying that secret. We'll support her, too.'

Luci nodded. 'She's strong.'

Meesha only now understood how strong. 'She had to be. Man, I would hate to be in her place. If the people who tried to kill William found out what she'd done, then she'd be in major danger as well. Let alone swearing to keep secrets that she wanted to share with Konrad.'

'Konrad's Bella's brother, the doctor here, wasn't he?'

'Yes. Must have been a good reason she wasn't allowed to share.'

Luci leaned down and gently smoothed Pluto's ears as if she needed the comfort of touch. 'All this in a sleepy, quirky little mining town. Makes you wonder, doesn't it?'

'True.' As far as Meesha was concerned, Desiree had saved William's life, putting her own on the line by interfering. And maybe Bella's and Konrad's too. She'd be backing Desiree all the way.

'Just like Bella, Desiree's a pretty tough cookie,' Luci said thoughtfully, and Meesha took some comfort in that.

'She is. And apparently the woman who whisked William away was a detective who comes to the Ridge a lot. I guess she could have spoken to her about it all. I just hope William rings Bella soon and takes away the doubt.'

Luci winced. 'She'll want to kill him all over again for the pain.'

CHAPTER THIRTY-TWO

BELLA

Bella stood at the open door, her fingers curling to grip the metal frame as she watched TJ's F truck disappear.

'Damn you, TJ,' she whispered. 'I need you, now.'

How did TJ mean that much to her already, after just a few weeks knowing him? And now, she needed him even more desperately since last night had changed her world. Her other hand lifted to where a physical pain gnawed in her chest, reminiscent of when she'd lost William, but different.

William who wasn't dead, William who had stayed hidden to keep Bella safe.

How could he? And how could he ask her not to share the news with their parents and Konrad? Too many unresolvable questions were spinning in her head and, until she actually touched William, she wasn't game to crack open the pain and let it all out.

For now, she'd just concentrate on the fact she'd heard his voice.

She needed distraction from something she had no answers for.

She rubbed her sternum then wrapped her arms around herself as if it would help her remember more clearly the feel of TJ's embrace. When she inhaled, she could smell the scent of his skin on her biceps, just faintly, making it hard to think.

Bella blew out a disgusted breath. Staring at the empty road achieved nothing, so she pushed herself inside to the coffee machine to make a coffee she didn't want.

Yet, standing there with her back to the bedroom and with her hands busy, she could almost feel the warmth of his skin against her bottom as she tried to process why he'd left her to grapple with William's reappearance on her own.

It wasn't to do with his camp needing him. She knew that much. She also knew she hadn't wanted him to leave and maybe she'd been too quick to agree. Should have asked him to stay if he needed that. Especially after last night. He'd been as perfect a lover as she'd known he would be, once he'd given in. Since she'd seduced him, really. Poor guy.

Had she been wrong?

Hard to think that when he'd been so tender and responsive. So openly delighted in her. So different to the exterior he presented to the world. This was the man she knew hid inside him. Holding her like she was the most precious woman in the world in his strong arms. Worshipping her with his mouth and his hands and his body.

And she'd done the same back. She'd thought she'd shown him what he meant to her.

My heaven, his body. She closed her eyes as the images burned across her skin.

Despite his strength, she'd felt protected and extraordinary.

Almost sacred. And that vulnerable look she'd seen – the one he tried to hide but couldn't help expressing in those unguarded moments when they stared into each other's eyes. He'd felt it too – she knew he did, and she drew some comfort knowing that even if he never let her in completely, at least she knew he cared.

They were two halves of a strong force. She had to believe that.

No man had ever touched her heart and soul like TJ had. She suspected it was the same for him, if only he would admit it.

She picked up her phone to call Meesha but put it down again.

Meesha had become a major part of her life here, too, but she needed to work TJ out for herself first. A diversion from William.

She could at least try to look at this analytically. She sipped the hot liquid, trying to process his actions from a professional per-spective. She could do that. She'd topped her psychology degree, for pity's sake.

Bella carried the coffee mug over to the table and sat frowning into the mug.

'Okay,' she said out loud. 'Analyse this, Dr Grey. What are TJ's dilemmas?'

That one was easy. Protective instincts. Possible previous loss.

Perceived failure for not saving William.

Plus, his unfounded concern she'd be tainted in town by associat-ing with him – which was just crap.

Before her arrival he'd been gutted by William's supposed suicide – that could explain some of his wanting to keep her safe.

But even before William had disappeared, Meesha had said TJ had been self-isolating because of some past he didn't want to talk about.

Bella suspected his past had included the loss of loved ones, and she just wished he'd open up to her about it.

But that didn't help unless she could love him despite the damage.

Could she do that? Well, yes. She already did.

But if he didn't want help to process his past, could she leave well enough alone and not try to fix him? Could she accept that?

Was she strong enough to keep offering a love he might never be able to accept?

She didn't know that one. It depended on his reason for pulling away. If it wasn't about him loving her – maybe it was about his fear of losing her. Or she could be way off beam.

Bella drained the cup and took herself for a cool shower, except that standing in there brought back everything they'd done last night, and by the time she turned the water off she was just as hot as she'd been when she stepped in.

When she was dressed again, she stripped the sheets from the bed, something she needed to do if she wasn't going to lie awake tonight and hug his pillow. But as she tucked in the corners, she remembered TJ's hospital edges in his camp. And damn if she didn't wish she was there right now.

Okay. Enough. She couldn't do anything about loving TJ – her feelings were a force of nature – but if it didn't work out between them, she couldn't change that either.

She wasn't going to shut down like she did after William disappeared.

But today, while she knew now William was okay, she also knew she'd survived the worst thing that could have happened and come out the other end. She would make a life in Lightning Ridge and maybe one day TJ would share it with her, because out of all this drama she had found a place to call home. Her place. She guessed she was in the Ridge to stay.

Thankfully, she was a whole lot stronger than when she arrived.

She had Meesha, Luci and the Lightning Ridge Ladies.

She had work.

She even had her opals to cut.

And if she still dreamed that maybe it would all work out with TJ, she could hug that wish to herself. But she'd survive even if it didn't.

I'm not going anywhere. The opal-coloured ball's in your court, now, TJ.

CHAPTER THIRTY-THREE

TJ

By the time TJ had shovelled five days of sandstone and dumped it on the sorting table in his yard, he knew his decision to stay away from Belle wasn't cut and dried. Or forgiving William when he came back.

As he climbed down the ladder for the third time that day, he knew it was going to be impossible to walk away from either of them. Especially Belle.

He'd tried pushing himself as hard as he could to drown her out of his thoughts. It wasn't working. At all.

He'd come to realise that solitude down in his mine wasn't peace – it was hiding.

He had a sudden stabbing vision of four years ago when that man had loosed a hail of bullets. Of Ree sprawled in a pool of blood and the team wounded on his watch. It had been tough. Devastating.

He'd chosen to block it out. Run away.

He stared at the opal dirt on the table in front of him.

That mode of dealing with it hadn't been much of a success, had it, Bozo?

He thought about William having to wrestle with watching his family from afar, break their hearts, knowing his twin would be suffering the ultimate pain, and shook his head. That took a special type of guts. He didn't believe William was a callous mongrel, so it must have been excruciating for the guy.

TJ wasn't the only person in the world to deal with difficult decisions and trauma. It was time to work out if he was going to let his past affect the rest of his life, or if he should finally let it go of the damage that crippled him.

He picked up the jackhammer he'd once thought Bella resembled and shook his head. She'd had his walls crumbling on day one, and any peace he might have found down here was transient.

It was well past time he manned up, or he might just lose the best thing in his life.

He wanted Belle. Chose Belle. Loved Belle.

His only concern now was: would she accept what he offered?

CHAPTER THIRTY-FOUR

BELLA

The day after she spoke to him on the phone, there was a text from William – from a private number – just a heart and a fairy emoji like he'd used to send her all the time. *William loves Tinkerbell.*

'Damn it, William,' she cursed. 'How could you? Just hurry up and come back so I can smack you upside the head.'

She received an emoji text every morning through the week from William but no calls. Damn her twin. But slowly she was easing into belief that she would see him on her doorstep one morning.

On Friday afternoon, Bella's mobile phone vibrated in her pocket but stopped before she could salvage it as she smiled at her departing patient. She checked no one else was left in the waiting room that she'd missed on the appointment screen. The caller would surely leave a message.

Her mother had spoken to her last night and confirmed she and Bella's dad were coming tomorrow lunch time. Avoiding any mention of the true reason, Bella had invited them to visit the Ridge to see how well she'd settled in. Bella hated the idea that she knew William was alive and her parents didn't, and their arrival here wouldn't make that any easier. She hoped William would have sorted everything by then, or she'd just have to deal and keep up the ruse. Konrad and Riley still weren't due back for a couple of weeks.

When she did glance at her phone and saw the missed call came from TJ, she sucked in a breath. She'd almost given up on him.

And he hadn't let it ring very long. Damn him. But maybe he'd thought she was with a patient?

She pressed the call-back button, and one hand lifted to the centre of her chest as she composed herself, feeling her heart thumping. She moistened her lips as she waited for him to answer.

When he did, she drawled, 'You phoned, stranger?'

'Yeah.'

'And?' She was not going to make it easy for him.

'Sorry for the radio silence. I had some thinking to do.'

Bella didn't answer immediately, and the silence stretched like hot tar on the road between them. A bit like on the way to Coober Pedy after Broken Hill. She let him stew until she finally said, again, 'And?'

'You busy tonight?'

Her pulse rate jumped ten beats, and she struggled to bring her voice under control. 'Yes, I am.' He was such a conversation-alist. Not. One of them had to use words. 'It's Lightning Ridge Ladies night. Meesha's driving to Brisbane and won't be back until Monday – she has my necklace with her. I'm going to Desiree's with Luci.'

There was a long silence, and she wished she could have said, *Come anyway*.

Finally, he asked, 'How about tomorrow? Breakfast?'

'At your camp? How about you come here? You can make breakfast for me.' She could feel delight uncurling in her belly at the thought. Not the food.

'Yep. I can do that.' There was genuine amusement in his voice.

'I know what you like.'

That he did. In many ways. 'You're on. What time?'

He drawled, 'The usual time you wake me up on a Saturday.'

She laughed. 'I have to be finished by lunch time, because my parents are coming.'

'We can do that. And Belle? When you get home tonight, from the ladies, sleep well.' The last words were so low and deep she felt her body tingle from the toes up. This man. He could turn her into flames just using her name.

'I probably won't, now,' she said, pretending to grump.

'Me neither. Let me know if you need some help.'

He still sounded amused as he cut the call. She shook her head at her phone, but she couldn't help grinning. TJ was coming over, and it sounded positive.

'You look happy.' Mel's voice called her back to the present and she looked up. Her admin wore her crossbody bag, ready to go.

'Yep. You're off then, Mel?'

'Unless there's something you want me to do?'

'Nope. All good. Thanks.'

'I put your takeaway in the fridge. Greta made Thai chicken salad tonight.'

'Yum, can't wait. See you Monday.' She lifted a hand and began to shut down her computer.

'Have a good weekend,' Mel called back as she disappeared.

'You, too.'

A few seconds later, Bella heard the front door close. Hopefully a stellar weekend. Oh, yes. She was planning on having a great Saturday morning. And if William's news broke by the time her parents arrived, that would be the best weekend ever.

It turned out, William's news broke while Bella was at her unit changing into a blue jumpsuit with flowers on the hem before leaving for the Lightning Ridge Ladies night. No idea why she'd thrown that outfit in her bag when she moved here, but it had no sleeves, which was good for the heat, and the flowy style made her feel pretty and happy.

That's how she felt, right up until she walked past the p.m.

news broadcast on the TV and recognised the photo of the blue cement mixer with the Lightning Ridge sign, followed by Coober Pedy's black truck. The news headline read 'Opal fields crime syndicate captured!' and Bella turned the volume up to hear the newsreader's announcement.

'A three-year multi-state task force captured the leaders of an Aus-tralia-wide theft and smuggling operation preying on outback min-ing towns. The alleged perpetrators are accused of siphoning off local opal and gemstones using violence and threats. The four men, long wanted by the police, have been apprehended and are in custody, where they will face charges.'

'William,' Bella breathed. 'Oh my stars, it's over. And thank you, Desiree, and Carol, whoever you are.' The Lightning Ridge locals would be agog with the excitement and lots of questions.

And for Desiree, the end of years of secrecy would be a huge relief, she imagined.

Looking at the list of towns involved, she felt sick at the magnitude of the operation. Wondered how many casualties like William there had been that nobody heard had about. Other families deal ing with the same grief as the Greys. How many hard-working business people like Meesha had been affected? And to think she and TJ had blithely captured a minor player and interrogated him just before it all went down. No wonder William had been horrified when TJ told him they'd threatened Bane.

But now it was all out. Hopefully finished. She had to assume she would hear from William soon.

She glanced at her watch; she needed to meet Luci.

Luci had heard the news, too – she liked to keep up to date with things by checking the news on her phone, and she nearly always had the radio chattering in the background at her place – and when Bella arrived to share the walk along to Desiree's, Bella explained the rest as much as she knew.

'You must be desperate to see William,' Luci said with such empa-thy it made Bella grateful again for her friends.

Walking in to the party behind the servo together, Bella sensed a strange vibe – the noise level seemed lower, the music hadn't yet started, and Desiree sat on her own while the others gathered across the room.

Sylvia waved to Bella and Luci, and Elsa raised and lowered her brows a few times in a silent commentary about the vibe she'd clearly noticed too. Things seemed awkward with Desiree.

Greta fidgeted in her own chair near the door, almost wringing her hands as she tried to appear normal. Across the yard, at separate tables, the other ladies watched the two women with gimlet eyes.

'Some odd facial expressions here tonight, Luci,' Bella murmured. 'Everyone is looking at Desiree. As if waiting for something.'

'Sounds quieter,' Luci agreed, lifting her face. 'Feels tense.'

It was true, Bella thought – the other ladies looked as if they were preparing to pounce.

As Luci settled in her chair and Greta came over to say hello, Bella whispered, 'I just want to check Desiree's okay.'

But as Bella moved to take Desiree aside to ask, Sylvia wandered over, closely followed by her cousin and Gerry. 'Hey, you two.

Before you go into a huddle, did you see the news tonight?'

Bella stopped and Desiree grimaced. 'Yeah.' The white-haired woman huffed out a weary breath. 'I guess you all did, too?'

'Yes, we did.' Gerry waved a piece of paper in front of her.

'Printed this out from the online news.' She glanced down at it, but Bella suspected it was more for ingrained theatrical effect than need to read the type. 'Seems they busted a crime syndicate that mentions Lightning Ridge. Says investigations have been going on for three years. You wouldn't know anything about that, would you, Desiree? You know. Because you know everything.'

'Yes, Desiree.' The chorus went up. 'And if you did, why weren't we included? Don't you trust us?'

'All right. All right. Give me a break,' Desiree pleaded.

'Dangerous secrets I could've done without.' She huffed a flustered breath and glanced around at the almost accusing faces and threw out a hand. 'Would've been happy to change places with any of you. You wanna keep a secret like that? Lying to everyone, to keep people safe?'

From Selena. 'A secret like what? That the whole town was under investigation? And nobody knew?'

'A few were being watched.'

'You gonna tell us more, now?' Sylvia asked with just a bit of snark.

'Can now.' Desiree glanced at Bella. Some of the tension seeped from the group. 'Though most of it's her story.'

Bella decided that was enough heat for the woman who protected her family. 'Desiree saved my brother, William, when he was kidnapped and almost murdered,' she declared.

'William's not dead?' The question came from Elsa, and the others stared on, open mouthed.

'Thanks to Desiree. She made sure he got away in secret from the criminals who would have hurt me if they knew William survived.'

There was a hushed silence.

Bella circled her gaze around the group of slightly hostile ladies.

'Desiree has had to live with the knowledge of my twin being alive all this time. And you all know how much that would have hurt her, to keep that from my brother. She admires Konrad.'

Sylvia stuck out her chin. 'She could have told us on the sly.'

'Protecting me. And Konrad. Not when the criminals had already threatened us. I don't think Desiree's had it easy at all.'

Surprisingly, and to everyone's horror, Desiree rubbed her wrist across her eyes and turned her head away. Greta scooted over to her, blocking everyone's view, but they all heard the gruff, 'Rather not talk about it now.'

Bella's throat tightened in sympathy. She said distinctly, so the others could hear, 'You know my whole family will always be indebted to you, Desiree. The whole town should be indebted, because you've helped the task force for almost three years at great personal risk.' She turned to give the woman a quick impulsive hug, but Desiree stiffened uncomfortably so she settled for patting her arm.

Still not a hugger, Bella thought with a smile, as she stepped back. Softly, she said to her, 'If it wasn't for you, William wouldn't be coming back to us at all. So, thank you.'

Desiree grimaced. Shook her head, her mouth pursed as if in pain. 'Hurt me real bad not telling Doc Konrad.' She glanced at the other ladies who still wore expressions of incredulity. 'Lives were at stake.' She lifted her chin, and yes, there was dampness in her eyes, as if she had to get that point across to Bella after stewing on it all week. 'Wanted to tell you, Bella. It upset me so much to see you that first day at the servo, in such pain.' She gave a huge sigh.

'Couldn't make trouble right at the end, even though you were here now. Your twin was determined.'

Bella nodded. 'That he is. Everything you did, you did for the best reasons. It's not your fault, Desiree. Not your problem anymore, either.'

Luci's clear voice carried out across the yard. 'Must have been so hard for you, Desiree. You're a champion.'

At that came twitters of agreement as the mood changed and the others moved closer, enveloping Desiree in comfort rather than hostility now. The chatter grew louder.

The beleaguered woman patted Bella's shoulder. 'Thanks. You're a good sister.' She straightened, less tense now and said a little louder, 'Hear you're a good doctor like your brother as well.'

Bella smiled as they turned back into the fray. 'I'm enjoying my clients.'

'And the Ridge?' asked Desiree.

'And very much the Ridge.'

Maybe to change the subject away from Desiree, Luci added, 'Did you know Meesha's teaching Bella how to cut opal, Desiree?'

'Is she?' The older woman swivelled her head to Luci then back to Bella. 'Why would she do that?'

'She can't just be a doctor all her life,' Luci quoted her sister with the same familial mischief Meesha would have had. Bella's heart swelled – she loved these girls.

Desiree stiffened. 'Nothing wrong with being a doc. Doc Konrad is one of my favourite people. And Doc Riley.'

'Nothing wrong with being an opal cutter,' Luci rejoined.

Bella rolled her eyes. 'I'll leave you to it. I'm off to see this mob over here. You coming, Greta?'

After that conversation, the night flowed easily and the laughs grew more frequent. Bella knew the other ladies were avidly curious to hear more from Desiree, and she guessed they'd find out everything in due time.

But Desiree had survived, and Greta had her back, just like Bella would have Desiree's back, forever.

Around p.m. Bella walked Luci and Pluto home, with Luci citing tiredness and Bella eager to phone a certain male friend about her impending insomnia.

Once Luci had slipped inside her duplex with her furry companion and the door had safely shut, Bella pulled her phone from her pocket and pressed TJ's number. She strolled up the street towards her house, the warm glow in her chest making her heart flutter.

'Bella? You okay? I saw the news.' Just the sound of TJ's voice fluttered her nerves.

'Yes, I saw. Hopefully William will be here soon. Actually, it's all a bit overwhelming, and I think I have a problem.' She glanced up at the stars, grinned at the twinkling sky. 'I can't sleep.'

'Really?' She could hear the warmth in his voice. 'Where are you?'

'Just walking home.'

'Should I come tuck you in? Help with that sleep problem?'

'As long as I get to hear why it's taken you a week to think about calling.'

'That seems reasonable. I'll be there in ten minutes.'

TJ pulled up exactly ten minutes later. He must have hurried, Bella thought happily to herself as she opened the door.

It had been less than a week, but it was as if she'd forgotten how tall and broad he was as he blocked out the new motion sensor light Mel's husband, Toby, had installed that Monday morning.

'Did you tell Toby to put that sensor light in?' she asked. Toby had said it was something he'd meant to do earlier and hadn't got around to.

TJ frowned at it as if the question offended him. 'Yeah. You needed it.'

'Bossy.'

'Among other things.'

'What other things?' she teased as she stepped back, letting him into her flat. What she really wanted to do was throw her arms around him, but if she did that, she wouldn't hear any of his explanations. And typically, he wasn't one to rush into body contact, she knew. Her belly fluttered and she suspected she sounded as flustered as she felt when she said, 'Would you like a tea? Or a beer?'

'Or iced water?' he asked, quirking a brow at her.

Her lips twitched, suddenly more at ease with his teasing.

'Would you like an iced water, TJ?'

'No, thank you.' He shook his head with a strange expression on his face. 'You look good, Belle.'

'You look good, too. Take a seat. You're looming over me.' She wanted to pull his head down and kiss him.

He opened his beautiful mouth and closed it again, as if now wasn't the time to say what thought had just run through his brain.

She couldn't help the twitch of her lips. Of course he gestured her to a seat first, so she sat on the recliner opposite the settee. Once she sat down, he did the same.

She fixed her gaze on his strong face. Trying to read the blank canvas there and not achieving much. 'I'm listening.'

'I want to tell you a story.' He leaned forward and clasped his hands between his knees. Stared past her at the wall behind her head. 'Four years ago, I was the lead in a Tactical Response team in Sydney.'

'Police or army?'

'Police.'

Ah, now that made sense, she thought as he went on slowly.

'On my last case, my partner – my girlfriend – was killed and the rest of my team were gunned down when a perpetrator sprayed the lot of us with bullets.'

Her heart squeezed. He could have died. 'Were you injured?'

'Scratched. I killed him.' He shook his head. 'Several times, in fact, but too late to help anyone.' His voice roughened. 'I should have taken the bullet for Ree, but that's not how it works.'

She wanted to deny that but kept her mouth shut. As a doctor, she knew and agreed – that wasn't how life, and death, worked.

'They pensioned me out with PTSD. When I moved out here, I went to ground. Literally.'

She understood so many things about him now. 'Until I dug you out?'

'More like jackhammered,' he said, glancing up at her with a brief smile. 'Anyway. The first person I really made friends with after that case – as in, spoke to without necessity – was your annoying brother William. He's a good actor. I didn't pick him as undercover.

Hope you're not as good a player as he is.'

She gave him a wide-eyed look. 'I'm not playing at anything, TJ. I'm just being me.'

'I did think that.' He grimaced. 'I'm trusting in that.'

Wow. That was big. 'I'm glad you believe me.' She paused.

Just how much would he share? 'So why did you walk away last week?'

He blew out a breath and, looking up at her with those dark eyes, said very softly, 'From the beginning I've been trying to protect you from me.'

She wasn't surprised. She'd thought it had been something like that. But she was shocked when he added, 'People die around me, Belle. My dad before I was born. My mum in the car when I was a kid sitting right next to her. My girl in the force. Four years ago, I came to the conclusion that anyone I cared about would come to a sticky end. So, I chose not to let myself care.'

It was a lot to take in. He was an orphan. And his girl had died beside him. TJ the protector. She shook her head. 'That's not a reasonable belief.'

He shrugged. 'My plan was to stay aloof. Keep my head down. Not to make friends or lovers. That way, everybody else was safe.'

He sighed. 'Until William came along. He's got a lot of charm, your brother. And he's persistent.' He glanced up at her from under his brows. 'A pest. Very similar to someone else I know.'

She smiled. 'Really?' Then more seriously, finally understanding, she said, 'So, when William apparently died by suicide, you decided it was somehow your fault? That you should have prevented it, just like you should have prevented your team being killed and injured?

Another person who died by associating with you?'

He nodded. 'Just about. And then you came along. And the last thing I wanted to do was bring you into the fold of people who get hurt around me.'

'Oh, TJ, that's not how it works.'

He held up a hand to stop her speaking. 'Please let me finish.'

Bella faked zipping her lips and his expression softened. Her beautiful, damaged, darling man.

'You see, my Belle Bird, I fell for you the first day I saw you. And that just made me want to run.'

She leaned back. He was giving her so much more honesty than she'd expected or even hoped for. 'You speak well when you get going,' she marvelled. 'And thank you, that explains a lot. Except why you're here now.'

'You left me with a dilemma.' There was so much heat, desire and pure damn want in his eyes she felt her belly melt into a volcanic puddle. She pulled her collar away from her neck. Phew. Hot in here.

'And what dilemma would that be?'

'How do I protect you by staying away when I need you so much?'

Typical man. 'I don't need protecting, TJ.'

He laughed at that. 'Maybe, maybe not.'

She gave him the same look he was giving her. With interest.

'Maybe you're the one who needs protecting. Or maybe we're both stronger together. Sharing the world.'

He smiled then. The wide, rare smile she would sell her soul to see every day for the rest of her life. 'It's a thought, Belle. One I'm leaning towards.'

She tilted her head at him. 'So how about sharing what "TJ" stands for?'

He smiled again. 'Terence Judd Jefferies, at your service.'

'Terence, huh? I can see Terence. Or Judd. Can't see you as a Terry, though.'

'You'd better not. I've put some Terrys in jail.'

'I'm sure they deserved it.'

'To explain the name,' he continued, 'my mother was a piano teacher. She named me after a concert pianist she saw once. Terence Judd. He died young.'

'Ouch.' Bella raised her brows. 'Did you blame yourself for that one, too?'

'Maybe,' he said with a self-mocking smile.

Of course he included that poor soul in his list. 'Well, I'll have you, despite your string of bad luck.'

'Except I still think you're out of my league.'

'Who's out of whose league? That's a question we could debate.' She nodded thoughtfully. 'I could play you at pool again.

That will give us a winner.'

'You're so dreaming if you think there's any chance you'll win next time, Belle Bird.'

'How about you teach me about mining a shaft and I'll teach you how to manage past trauma?'

'And how are you going to do that?'

'It might take a while, a lot of intense physical therapy, but I'm pretty sure I can do it.' She knew he could see the wicked gleam in her eyes. 'We could start now, but we only have until morning when I have a breakfast date.'

'Won't Lightning Ridge notice my not-so-subtle truck has been outside your house all night?' He glanced towards the closed door.

'Should we move to my place?'

Oh no. He wasn't going to hide their connection from the world. 'No. I think it's about time Lightning Ridge saw your truck outside my house all night.'

He stood and reached down to take her hand, pulling her up until she was pressed against his heart. She could feel it pounding in his chest. She did that to him, she liked that very much, just as he did to her.

TJ lowered his voice and leaned in. Widened his eyes and showed her his soul. 'I love you, Belle. A lot. I've never felt about anyone the way I feel about you.'

She felt the tears prick her eyes at the vulnerability he offered.

Her tough TJ.

Then he spoilt it by saying, 'Though, sometimes I want to put my hand over your mouth and stop all the words.'

She mock-glared at him. 'How about you just put your mouth over my mouth? Then I promise I won't talk.' Her eyes sparkled.

'Much.'

His gaze darkened as he shook his head. 'I can see my life is going to change in many ways.'

'You have no idea.'

CHAPTER THIRTY-FIVE

TJ

Bella's phone rang just as TJ's lips touched hers, and they both groaned as she broke the kiss. In his head, he began to swear.

TJ glared at the phone as she took it from her pocket. Couldn't help himself from muttering, 'If that's your brother, I'm going to kill him properly.'

'No more killing people, officer,' she said as she opened her eyes and glanced at the screen. Her mouth fell open. 'It's Luci.'

By the stricken look on her face, this was not good.

'Hello? Luci, you okay?'

The other woman's voice came through clearly to TJ, even though Belle hadn't put it on speaker. 'No,' the tinny voice said.

'I think my water broke? And I can feel something odd hanging out.'

Okay. Good reason for an interruption. He saw Belle's lips mouth 'Oh lord' as she closed her eyes. TJ racked his brains for any obstetric knowledge, but he'd been trained mostly in straight trauma.

It could be a breech foot, he supposed, or a cord? They fell out sometimes when waters broke, didn't they? Or both. Neither could be good.

He heard Bella say, 'I'm coming.' And he looked to her as she took a breath and said calmly into the phone, 'Luci. Open the door so we can get in. Then crawl onto your bed on all fours, head down, bottom up, until I get there. If it is a cord prolapse, gravity will ease pressure off the cord for baby. Two minutes.'

Two minutes. Right. He felt for the keys in his pocket.

'I can do that,' Luci said, not sounding like herself at all.

'I'm coming,' Bella reassured her.

He guessed she couldn't think of anything more comforting to say. Neither could he.

She ended the call and spun away from him. 'Where's Riley the obstetrician when I need her?'

He guessed Hawaii, but knew she didn't want that answer.

'You'll be great.' And she would be. His Belle blew him away with her smarts. She was digging for something in the cupboard.

'Do you have obstetric training?' he asked.

'I've only seen one cord prolapse in my training, but it's burned in my memory. That was a caesarean birth.'

She pulled out the black doctor's bag she taken with them to Coober Pedy and had said she used for house calls, putting it on the floor while she searched for shoes. 'And I've been present at four births. That's it.'

'You want me to come?' TJ stood behind her as she reached for the big satchel and took it from her.

'Yes. A second person is always good. Plus, I'm guessing if you were in Tactical Response, you've had medical training?'

'True, but not obstetric. Though I can lift Luci if needed.'

'Absolutely. You can call the ambulance when I see her. I'll wait till then, just in case it's a false alarm.'

'We'll take my car. And the tray is empty and clean.'

'It would be.' She smiled grimly at him with that strange comment. 'I'm sure we could eat out of it, knowing you. But that's good. You can throw in a mattress and put her in the back if the ambulance is out of town.'

It took less than two minutes for them to pull up outside Luci's house, just down the street and around the corner a bit from Belle's unit.

Belle went around the back before TJ had even climbed from the car. The duplex's door stood open.

'Luci?' he heard her call out as she dashed inside.

'Through here,' came a steady voice.

Hot on Bella's heels, TJ felt relief at Luci's calm tone and slowed to a less frantic pace.

'I've got TJ with me,' Bella said as she looked back at him and smiled, 'but I won't show him any of your bits.'

'Oh, good to know.' He heard Luci laugh shakily. 'Though I almost don't care.'

Chapter Thirty-Six

Bella

Well, lack of modesty wasn't a good sign, Bella thought as she entered the bedroom. Luci had climbed on the bed with her forehead down on her crossed arms, and her bum up high, on her hands and knees, the position Bella had requested. She'd dragged the quilt back over her bare bottom.

Pluto lay beside his mistress minus his harness, big eyes worried as he gazed at her.

Luci began to breathe rapidly, and Bella felt her own tension rise. 'How often are the pains coming?' she asked quietly.

'Every couple of minutes,' Luci gasped when she could. 'Seem to last forever. Almost until the next one starts.'

Could be precipitous labour, Bella thought dismally, in which case it might all be over faster than she could have an impact on the outcome. Either way, they needed the ambulance.

'Step back into the other room, TJ, and call the ambulance, please. If they're not in town, start sorting out the back of your utility. We'll at least get her to the health centre.'

'Roger.'

Bella shut the door to the bedroom, leaving just her, Luci and Pluto in the room. 'I need to have a look.'

'Go right ahead. I can't do much in this position.'

When Bella lifted the quilt, the shiny loop of cord was easy to see swinging below Luci's bottom. She touched a loop gently through the sheet, felt the strong pulsation, held it gently for a few seconds and estimated around one-twenty beats per minute. She didn't want to cause it to spasm, but it was reassuring to know blood still travelled along the placenta to the baby, despite being exposed to the air. 'Okay, the cord has come first, which is what you felt, but good news. Nice strong pulsation there, Luci. Baby is managing. Heartbeat not too fast or slow.'

'Thank God. Will my baby be all right?'

'So far. Your best bet is to let go of as much tension as you can and birth this baby while we prepare to fly you somewhere for a caesarean section.' She placed the sheet back over Luci's bottom and stepped back.

Bella called through the door. 'What happened with the ambulance, TJ?'

'They're driving back from Moree after transporting a cardiac patient. Be an hour.'

Too late for them to transfer by road. Almost three hours' drive anyway. 'Okay. Phone the hospital emergency department here and tell them we're coming in. Precipitous labour and cord prolapse.

Thirty-seven weeks' gestation. Prepare for birth.'

A second's silence and then TJ said again, 'Roger.'

Luci's muffled voice came from the mound of blankets. 'Who's Roger?'

Bella snorted just a bit. 'TJ was a Tactical Response guy in a past life, but don't tell him I told you.'

Luci gave a tiny, strained cough of amusement and then she began to breathe loudly.

'How's that bed coming, TJ?' Bella called.

'Almost done.'

Her man was nothing if not efficient, she thought gratefully.

'Okay if we leave Pluto here, Luci, and TJ'll pick him up later, as soon as he's needed?'

'Yes. Just don't leave me until he's back with me.'

Bella agreed. 'I promise.'

'Okay. Stay, Pluto.'

By the time TJ carried Luci out to the back of the utility Bella saw the single mattress jammed in the back and a mound of blankets and pillows. Task achieved as required.

'Before you put her down, wait. It's too dangerous to transport her in the knee to chest position. Luci, you'll have to lie on your left side, and I'll sit beside you in the back keeping you steady.'

Bella knew the exaggerated SIMS position would be the safest bet to keep the pressure off the cord until they arrived.

TJ nodded and Bella positioned the pillow so TJ could place Luci lying sideways with hips elevated. 'Okay, Luci. Emergency department. Left side is great. Right knee and right thigh, draw them up high. The pillow under your hips is to help keep the pressure off the cord until we get there. It's less than a kilometre.'

Bella helped Luci position herself as TJ floated the quilt over the top of her.

'Okay,' Luci gasped between pants. The labour had progressed even more quickly than hoped, Bella thought with metaphorically crossed fingers. She couldn't imagine coping with this, but Luci held onto her control.

'It's not far,' TJ reminded them as he headed for the driver's side.

Yeah, let's get there quickish, Bella thought silently. If we can't do a caesarean, let's hope it's a very fast natural birth.

When they arrived, there was a trolley and two nurses waiting outside the door as soon as they stopped. TJ leaped out, ready to scoop Luci from the back of the truck.

'I'm going to pick you up now, Luci,' he warned her. 'I'll put you on a trolley and then they'll wheel you into the emergency room. There's two nurses here, as well as us. Belle's following.'

Bella heard Luci's soft, 'Okay,' he scooped her up and placed her on the trolley in the same position she'd adopted in the back of the truck.

A nurse draped a white hospital blanket over Luci's side and the trolley disappeared into the building. Bella looked back at TJ.

'I'll go lock up the house and bring Pluto,' TJ said. 'I'll return as soon as I'm done.'

'Thank you, Mr Unflappable.'

'You'll be amazing,' he mouthed, and Bella nodded as she hurried after the trolley.

When Bella walked into the room, Luci had begun to grunt with expulsive breaths, so an imminent birth could happen.

Only case scenario, Bella told herself as she accepted responsibility for the arrival of Luci's baby. She just needed to keep Luci calm and facilitate a safe birth.

No time for nerves and fruitless wishes that she'd had time to read up and refresh on the process, but she had a good memory of how a precipitous birth could go. The mother did it all, fast.

A nurse directed her to a sink to wash her hands and pointed to an open set of gloves.

'I'm Alice. I went for size six and half – is that okay?'

'Perfect, Alice, thanks,' Bella said and began to scrub. Glove size was not a problem. 'Great job there, Luci. We'll be ready when you are.'

She could see that the cord had lengthened considerably.

Hopefully this meant the baby had descended in the birth canal, even though that also meant the cord would compressed by the foetal skull in the pelvis potentially cutting off baby's oxygen-carrying blood supply. *Arrive soon, baby,* she prayed, as she pulled on the gloves and glanced at the nurse up the other end of the bed with the foetal ultrasound doppler. 'How's the foetal heart?'

'One forty.'

Phew. 'And resuscitation equipment?'

'We have the latest trolley Dr Riley sent us. And we've all done a refresher on neonatal resus.'

Bless Riley. 'Great news. If there's a problem, I'll intubate.'

She'd had good hands for airway assistance in her training.

Hopefully they were still good.

The nurse listening to the foetal heart said, 'I was a midwife five years ago. I'm happy with managing third stage if you need to leave mum.'

'We're sorted then.' Bella stepped up to the bed. 'Up to you now, Luci.'

'Lucky,' she groaned. 'It's coming.'

'Let it happen. Everything is good. We're all here for you.'

Still on her side, Luci gave a big push and then another, but at the lack of any progress, she swore and then sobbed once out loud.

Bella could see no progress either. 'Rest between the con-trac-tions,' she said gently.

Luci shook her head, cross and crabby. 'Bella. I need to turn over. Onto all fours again. This doesn't feel right.'

Frowns crossed all the watching faces and Bella winced. She hadn't delivered a baby upside down before, but she remembered something Riley had told her. *Always listen to the mother. She knows best in those final moments.*

She'd just have to listen to Luci. And the nurse with the doppler would have to contort. 'You do what you need to do, Luci. We'll adjust. You don't have to put your head down if you don't want to. Bring some extra pillows here for her head, please. On hands and knees is fine when you're pushing. Let's give this a go.'

Speed was what they needed now. She glanced around the room reassuringly. 'It's okay, people, let's help her move.'

Once again on all fours, Luci nodded her head. 'So much better,' she sighed, and then she pushed. Within seconds a shiny dome of head with a few fine blonde hairs stretched across it gently appeared at the introitus. Luci breathed out in one long slow exhalation until the head eased all the way out in a smooth, controlled push.

A small, squashed face rotated as the shoulder went through the pelvis.

Bella was torn between urging the mother to push with all her might and Riley's words about allowing the mother to do what she needed.

In the end it didn't matter, because in two more smooth pushes, Luci's baby curled out from the birth canal into Bella's hands with another, bigger splash of amniotic fluid and a long coil of thick cord.

Straight off. As though nothing was wrong. The baby cried.

Bella, the two nurses and Luci did, too. Or at least, tears chased each other down their cheeks.

'Oh, Luci, you champion,' Bella whispered, thanking her stars she'd not been away from town tonight. 'She's beautiful. Your sister is going to kill me for being here instead of her.'

A beatific smile spread over the new mum's face. 'A girl? She's a girl? Let me feel her.'

Bella laughed, crazily high on the fact baby was wriggling and bawling after such drama. 'Lucky there's a long cord. I think she'll reach up to your chest before we cut it.'

More tears trickled down Bella's cheeks as she watched Luci's gentle hands skimming over her daughter, reading her shape, caressing her little face and tracing the hollows and squashed nose, her tiny hands and feet. Checking to see everything was accounted for by touch.

Swallowing back the enormous lump in her throat, Luci whispered, 'She really is beautiful.'

'Just like her mum.'

Chapter Thirty-Seven

Meesha

Meesha stared at her phone, stunned, thrilled and a touch devastated.

The photo on the screen showed Luci sitting up in bed with her baby daughter against her chest. Meesha's niece. Oh my heaven, she had a niece. The smile on her sister's face made the tears trickle down Meesha's cheeks.

'Oh, Luci,' she whispered. 'You're so amazing. And I'm so sorry I wasn't there for you.'

On the one hand, the relief spurted like a dropped soft-drink can that both mother and baby were healthy, the birth was over, and that Bella had been there for them.

Poor Bella, right in the thick of it all, dealing with that on top of all the drama of her brother's impending reappearance. Meesha should have been there for her friend, too – but mainly for Luci.

She cursed her decision to dash to Brisbane even if the competition would decide which jewellers would be sponsored to represent Australia at the US trade shows. Though, she was excited to show Bella's necklace as her best piece.

She'd thought she had enough time before the baby was due.

That she had time to refill her jewellery supplies, sell some of her less spectacular opals and be there for the announcement about the sponsorships. Apparently not.

She loved The Iridescent Opal, but she'd just discovered, her business wasn't worth missing out on these precious moments in life. And the opportunity of being there at the birth for her as-yet-unnamed niece would never come back. Damn it.

This was exactly what she didn't want to do – let the business overwhelm her life. From now on, she would not let her work take over.

She planned to go home on Monday – instead she'd go Sunday, just wished it could have been today. Could she skip the announcement for the awards tonight? She'd miss out on more of the first few days of her niece's arrival, but Luci would kill her if she left. And she'd lose the chance for stall and accommodation at the Tucson show in the US. She had to be here in person to claim it if she won.

She had to stay. Would stay. But she'd go back to the Ridge on Sunday.

Her sister needed her, but Luci had planned well in advance for the right support.

Luci had this. The mothercraft nurse would pick her up from the hospital tomorrow in Moree, where Luci and baby had been admitted overnight just to check everything was fine.

Thank goodness they'd had Bella for keeping everyone safe. She would also be able to tell Meesha everything when she got home.

Bless Bella, the best of friends.

Meesha dropped her shoulders and let the angst go. Everything would be smooth now the baby was here, and with the mothercraft nurse staying in the Ridge for the first fortnight, Luci would have time to get into the habits of mothering.

As for herself, she could not wait to see her sister. And the baby. Her niece, thank you very much!

That night, Meesha sat drumming her feet at the awards dinner, dressed in a black sheath dress, poking at the impeccably presented meal in front of her. The people sharing her table were old acquaintances, people she'd met from other years, but she was the only category finalist on the table, and they seemed more excited than she was about her chances of winning. Her neighbour kept pushing champagne at her, but Meesha kept sipping her sparkling water, aware she had a big drive home tomorrow.

To see her niece.

She really wanted to be home but she wasn't – she needed to be present, now. She never would have thought winning wasn't everything but it seemed life was always a learning curve.

'Here comes your award, Meesha.' The woman next to her clinked her glass against Meesha's. 'We've our fingers crossed for you.'

Meesha lifted her chin, lips pressed together in nerves, and crossed her own fingers. She managed to squeeze out, 'Thank you.'

The MC's voice boomed across the tables. 'For the Most Original Design Award, sponsored by Tucson Jewelry Association, which means this award carries the added bonus of not only a prestige and prime position stand at the Tucson Gem Show and the associated media coverage, but also fully covered flights and accommodation for the lucky recipient. And the winner is . . .' The announcer paused, drawing it out.

Come on, Meesha thought. How had she even imagined this would be her?

Meesha couldn't look at the stage; instead she looked around the table of faces surrounding her. These people were cheering for her. That was pretty darn cool. If she didn't win, it was fine. Still major kudos to be a finalist.

The announcer breathed in. 'Tamika Kerrison.'

The crowd applauded, heads turning as they searched for the winner.

Meesha froze. Stunned. 'Oh my stars,' she murmured. She looked around at the disappointed, falling faces of her companions and grinned. They hadn't recognised her name. She stood up on shaky legs. Bent down and said over the applause, 'My real name is Tamika.' Their faces lifted with delight and it warmed her. These people actually cared that she won. OMG, she'd won!

Meesha grinned back at them and spun to make her way through the tables towards the stage. She couldn't wait to share the news with her family and friends back in Lightning Ridge.

CHAPTER THIRTY-EIGHT

TJ

On Saturday just before lunch, TJ heard a car pull up at his camp, then a loud knock on his gate. He hadn't been home long because, after the best morning of his life, he'd left Belle to get ready for her parents' arrival. It wasn't the sound of her vehicle.

He looked out his window at the man climbing from the late model car and sucked in a breath laden with relief and anger.

Larger than life.

Oh yeah, I've got a few words to say to this guy.

William looked good. Bigger than TJ remembered. Standing tall. He'd aged but it didn't detract. Yeah, well, a lot of people had aged in the last few years.

TJ pulled on his T-shirt and stomped across the kitchen to throw open the door and pound down the steps, across the yard, unlocking the gate. He swung it wide and stood there with his hands on his hips. TJ pulled the idiot into a quick, bruising embrace and then spat, 'I should shake you until your teeth fall out.'

'I wouldn't be as pretty if my teeth fell out,' William said, trying for humour with incredibly poor timing.

Yep. He was alive. TJ spun and walked away from him towards the house leaving the gate open.

He didn't hear William follow and turned back to see him waiting at the entrance to the yard. TJ paused at the door. 'Are you coming in or not?'

'Is it safe?'

Just, TJ thought grimly. He couldn't believe he'd actually hugged the guy. 'Your sister wants you alive.'

William crossed the yard with his hands in his pockets, a sheepish expression on his handsome face. A face that TJ could see glimpses of Belle in – the bright eyes, the determined chin. That blonde hair. 'Come on, man, you don't really want to hurt me.'

'Actually, yeah, I do.' He pierced him with a look that he hoped made it clear. He was serious. 'You put me through hell, and you put your sister and your parents and your brother through worse than hell. You've got ten minutes with me before you go and face her.'

William followed him inside. TJ stopped and faced him, crossing his arms over his chest. 'Start.'

William sighed. 'That ratter ring . . . while I was undercover, I learned the boss man's name. When they came for me, they said if I didn't go with them, someone would grab Bella in Port Macquarie. She's my twin. Someone else had Konrad lined up.' He shrugged, his face grim. 'So, of course I went with them. Expecting to die. Hoping I'd be able to talk my way out of it.' A humourless smile. 'Didn't work.'

'But you didn't die. Then. You couldn't give your twin a hint?'

He shook his head. 'The stakes were too high. They never found out I lived. I kept it that way working with the task force.

I had superiors who ordered me not to contact anyone.'

'And you agreed?'

'I asked them. Every one of my family, except me, is a doctor.

They keep secrets for a living. But my superiors wouldn't budge.'

'Was it worth it?'

William sent him a scathing look that reminded TJ this was a different man to the one he thought he knew. 'To keep Bella and Konrad out of danger? Yes. Absolutely. And on the side, the dark underworld we had hiding in Lightning Ridge and other mining towns has gone. We got them. That's good for everyone, isn't it?'

William leaned against the door as if he wasn't sure he should come in any further. 'We didn't know this group was working Australia-wide, not just local. When I was first sent to the Ridge, we didn't know how bad it was.'

He wasn't lying, TJ could see that much. Though he'd missed all the untruths the last time he'd seen William. Which made him wonder what he'd tried not to see, wrapped up as he had been in his own baggage.

William watched him warily. 'We didn't realise how many people had gone missing. Just because they stumbled across some aspect of the criminal organisation. Part-time miners, blokes without family, disappearing and never to be seen again. Anyone with a drone. And we don't think they were being recruited.'

Extensive, then. TJ had seen that before. It was never good.

'Dealing in what? Sounds too big just for opals.'

William shook his head. 'Mostly opals, all gems, stockpiling to drive the price up, but bigger. You know how crazy people get over opals – they're precious. And there are some who'd do anything for money. If it hadn't been for Desiree and Carol, my superior from WA, I'd be dead and buried along with the others.'

TJ did get that, even if part of him didn't want to. But what William had done to Belle and her family . . . 'You'll have to explain that to your sister.'

William's gaze hardened. 'Without my digging and the proof I'd found, which I've spent nearly three years amassing, that group would still be out here, killing, sucking the life out of the place. Bringing Lightning Ridge down. Other outback towns down. Hurting the wonderful element of people who make this place what it is. I'm the good guy here, so give me a break.'

TJ watched William. Listened to his spiel and believed most of it. Still didn't forgive him, though – that would take some more time for what he'd done to Belle, but he would. Probably. Eventually.

He could see Belle in him, and he could see the layer of toughness that he'd missed in the man before. Suspected Belle had it too, especially after seeing her at the interrogation of Bane. Only Belle usually focused it in a more humane direction.

'You're good. I'll give you that. A good actor. A bigger player than I suspected.' He tilted his head at this man whom he'd trusted like a friend. A friendship that had taken a beating. 'Did you honestly think I was involved in these illegal operations?'

William shrugged. 'I hoped you weren't. I liked you.' He threw out his hand in a placating gesture. 'Hell, TJ, you're your own worst enemy. You're big and mean and cranky. You live in a fortress. And you're hiding secrets from your past that nobody knows.' A quick grin. 'Though I do know some now. I looked you up. Man, when I first came here, you looked like a crim's dream henchman, and even I couldn't find anything about you back then.'

'Thanks.' But he noted the irony was lost on William and snorted. He added, 'Your sister likes me.'

'Yeah?' And that earned another hard look from William.

'What happened there? Talk about chalk and cheese.'

TJ shrugged. 'She came to me looking for you.'

William obviously didn't believe that. He shook his head. 'She thought I was dead. Why look?'

'True, but she wanted to know how and why. She never truly believed that alleged suicide note. Anyway, Belle decided I could help her. I couldn't get her off my back.' *And she wouldn't leave me alone.* But TJ didn't say that.

William looked thoughtful and nodded. 'She's determined when she gets the bit between her teeth.'

'Family trait,' TJ said dryly. 'Anyway. I picked up Bane, thinking that if she had a chance to grill him, she might not have a use for me. Then she could move on.'

'And how'd that go for you?' William shook his head and shot him a quirky grin. 'What were you thinking? What did you do, tie him to a crane in Coober Pedy?'

'Pretty much.'

William laughed. 'More detail later, please. Not that I care what you did with the little worm. He didn't try to stop them throwing me in that hole. And he's in custody now, too.'

TJ smiled grimly and William's eyes widened. 'With that expression, it's no wonder I thought you were the bad guy.'

'I didn't hurt him. Some cable ties. Some silver tape I enjoyed ripping off later. Rolled him in a tarp for a while in the back of a ute.'

William snorted into his fist. 'You crack me up. You did that for my sister?' He assessed him thoughtfully. 'Well, you must get under her skin too, 'cause she's not normally someone who hangs with bad guys.'

TJ raised his brows. 'Who says I'm a bad guy?'

William pointed one finger. 'You.'

TJ shook his head. He needed to finish this conversation and get William to Belle. 'How long have you been undercover?'

'Four years. I supposedly dropped out of the police force, was bumming around doing odd jobs. When, in fact, they set me up undercover to look like a weak link, to draw some of the elements out. When I got here, that worked a bit too well.'

TJ remembered the note. The pain. The remorse and guilt. He wanted to shake William again but settled for spreading his fingers wide instead of curling them into fists. 'I thought you were dead, William,' he said, his voice low and bitter. 'You have to live with the pain you caused everyone – including Belle.'

William looked away. 'What's with the "Belle"? It's Bella. Everyone calls her Bella.'

'She asked me to call her Belle the first night we met.'

'Oh, spare me. Not love at first sight.' William screwed his face up.

'Your sister was broken when she got here.' TJ narrowed his eyes. 'Been broken for nearly three years.' He paused. 'And you're the one who broke her.'

If he'd wanted to slap him, that did it. William's face paled.

'I didn't plan it.'

'Didn't fix it either.'

There was resignation in William's eyes now. 'I couldn't help that. I had trouble remembering anything for the first few months. By the time I could string two thoughts together, my family had had a funeral. It was too late. My superiors told me to stay in deep cover in WA. The syndicate had threatened to hurt Bella and my family and the upline knew it. They held that over me.'

TJ nodded grudgingly.

'If I came back alive, they would have held my family until I turned myself in to them because I *did* have the intel. Then they would have killed us all. Would you have saved us?' He raised his brows. 'Didn't think so. And you know, if I had to do it all again, I would. For Bella.'

And there was that same determination William's sister had, the same driven strength of will. And when he'd been in Tactical Response, TJ guessed he would have felt the same.

TJ blew out a big breath. He hated that the words resonated.

But yes, he knew what it felt like when duty called. He understood, but he didn't have to like it.

'Go see your sister, William. Your parents will arrive this afternoon. She's in the last unit behind the surgery. Number three.'

Chapter Thirty-Nine

Bella

When Bella opened the door to the unit, her hand went out to steady herself on the doorframe. The breath sucked into her lungs and for a few taut seconds she couldn't force it out. Even though she'd heard his voice on the phone, it didn't feel real. The blonde man standing in the sunlight with a worried expression was the twin she'd never thought she would see again.

Harder, older, remorseful. But William in the flesh. Bella pressed her lips together to hold back the sob but couldn't stop the tears from rolling down her cheeks.

'Tinkerbell,' William said, his voice cracking. 'Oh, Tinkerbell. Look at you.'

Bella stood there unable to make her feet move, so overwhelmed by the reality of his dear frame in her doorway until William stepped forward himself and put his arms around her.

Tall and muscled. William. She squeezed him. Squeezed again. He was real.

'I'm so, so sorry I couldn't tell you.' He pulled her head down against his chest and suddenly she was sobbing. Deep, racking gulps of air and pain ripping from her chest, soaking and probably snotting all over his shirt. Her chest ached and tore with the raggedness of it.

It went on for a long time until finally her sobs slowed, and she could whisper hoarsely, 'You're here. It's been so hard, so unbelievably hard to think you were gone.'

'I missed you so bad.' He slid his hand up and down her back, soothing and stroking. Not hurrying her. Smelling just the same.

Sounding just the same. Solid. 'I'm so, so sorry, Bella. So sorry. But they threatened to kill you. I couldn't risk that.'

She lifted her head, used the back of a hand to wipe her eyes, dug a tissue out of her bra to blow her nose, and drew another shuddering breath. She focused on him. On his words. On the mess on his shirt.

Mum and Dad were coming tomorrow. Thank heaven she didn't have to keep this secret while facing them. She'd have to do her make-up all over again and yet she felt almost gratified to see her emotion smeared all over her brother's shirt. Her brother. Her twin. Who was apologising for causing her the worst pain in the world.

'William.' She sucked in a calming breath. 'We thought we lost you. The world stopped and we all died a little. I died.' She leaned back and looked at him, her throat catching again as she whispered, 'You let us all suffer.'

William stepped back, too, watching her face. 'I'm sorry . . .'

Her head came up along with the rebound angst. 'Sorry doesn't cut it.' She pushed him in the chest with one finger. Then repeated the gesture, twice. 'You couldn't whisper to your family you were alive?'

'I need you to—'

'To listen? No,' she interrupted. She dragged him inside and shut the door. With force. Not even realising she was finishing his sentence the way they'd used to do. 'I don't care what sort of work it was or is, or what the risks to us were, William Grey. I'll never understand how you could let us suffer like that. For so long.'

He was shaking his head. 'It was to save you.'

'I'm your twin. You died! How would you feel if I died?'

'Bella . . .'

'Don't "Bella" me. William. We buried an empty coffin.'

That caused his chin to lift. 'Exactly. I would have died if you died. And those criminals did threaten to kill you to get me to go with them. I couldn't pop back up alive so they could use you to grab me. Damn it, Bella.' He put his forehead against hers. Leaned into her. Breathed into her face. 'They would have killed you, our whole family, to catch and silence me, and I wasn't risking that.'

And suddenly she did understand. Had already thought once she would probably do the same if their roles were reversed. But three years? 'Oh heavens, William.'

He pulled back until he could see her eyes. 'I can see how bad it was. I wish it had never happened.' William's chin lifted. He tapped his chest. 'Undercover cop. Bringing down the bad guys. If they found out I was alive after I escaped, they would have come for you until I gave myself up. And I would have in a heartbeat to protect you, but it wouldn't have saved you. I had to keep silent.'

Bella thought about that. About William at the mercy of people who had no hesitation throwing him down an abandoned mine shaft. Where he could have died but hadn't.

'Tell me how you survived the fall.'

He dragged his fingers through his hair. 'Desiree sent Carol to look for me. If she hadn't . . . Carol helped me out of the mine. She couldn't believe I'd survived either.'

She remembered. 'I've seen the mine. How?'

'Apparently, I got tangled up in an old piece of ladder, so I fell down in stages. Not the whole however many metres in one go. I was in hospital under an assumed name for the first three months with a scrambled brain and fractures. It wasn't pleasant, but I eventually recovered from the cerebral oedema and loss of memory, along with my broken arm, cuts and bruises.'

'You said memory loss?'

'Yeah, they'd put me under the care of a police psychologist to deal with angst and guilt once I woke up enough to understand that everyone back here thought I'd suicided.'

He stared at her. Leaned over and touched her cheek. 'Contact with you was denied, Bella. That was the hardest. They ration-alised it as essential due to the risk to you all of being used as hostages against me. The whole operation was at risk.' He shook his head. 'I had no answer to that. Except to continue on until the criminal organisation could finally be brought down. They kept saying it would happen soon, and I'd be saving lives which otherwise would have been lost.'

'What about when you came out of hospital?'

'Eventually I was allowed to return to the task force. If I stayed in WA and worked with Carol Wood, the not-actually-retired detective, as my senior, I could remain on the federal investigative team.'

'So, you worked while we grieved.'

'The more I worked the faster I could come home.'

She imagined William, while not allowed to participate physically on the ground, would have thrown his entire life into digging up every morsel he could from intelligence gathered, the internet and his contacts – including Desiree – over the long investigation.

Working towards coming home to them. And they'd done it.

His eyes narrowed with an intensity she'd never seen in him.

'We did get them. Every single evil one of them. Our bosses are ecstatic. Carol's talking about real retirement, but I just want my family back. I want you back in my life. Mum and Dad and Konrad. And to thank Desiree.'

'How were you involved from so far away?'

'The ringleaders were in four states. While Carol monitored the Ridge with her three-monthly visits, Desiree continued to share what she saw and heard at the servo and kept our team updated of suspicious activity.'

She shook her head. 'That's a lot of personal risk for a woman in her seventies – for any civilian, in fact. How do you justify that?

Desiree had a lot of responsibility.'

'There were contingency plans to whisk her and her daughter's family away from the Ridge if needed, but the woman could have been born in the resistance in WW, she's that good.'

'Because she kept a secret?'

'Because one of the criminal leaders moved headquarters to a nearby sheep station, and she'd been the one to point that way.' He shuddered. 'When I think how close you and TJ came to tipping off the ringleaders, or getting Desiree killed – what possessed you to even think about abducting Bane and questioning the man?'

She glared at him. 'I wanted answers and Bane had them.

I don't regret that.'

'We only just found out fast enough to move the raid forward to still get the desired result. But it was a close call, Bella.'

She said quietly, 'You're lucky Dad didn't have a heart attack when he heard about the suicide note. Or Mum. They've aged.'

William winced.

'It was all part of the set-up, wasn't it?' He didn't answer so she went on. 'We thought you were depressed. Konrad was so worried, he followed you out here and stayed at the OPAL

centre. He stayed here suffering for the next two years of his life, at least until he found Riley. It destroyed him when he read that suicide note.'

'They forced me to write the note. And I didn't ask him to follow me. Though it worked in my favour when he added more fuel to the fact that my family was worried about me.' His eyes pleaded with her. 'I never left the force. I've been undercover most of my time there. That's the truth. I'm sorry, Tinkerbell.'

She watched his eyes plead again and she closed her eyes.

'I think I get it. I have to get it. It might take me a while to trust you again, William. But I love you. Don't ever lose touch again.

Don't put your precious duty in front of us all again.'

She was overwhelmed by the fact that William was really there in front of her. She blew out a breath. She needed to stop blaming him, but she had so much emotion to vent. Then she glanced at her watch. 'Mum and Dad will be here at two. Another hour. And I have a house call I have to make before then.'

She wiped her eyes again and blew out a breath. 'I still don't know what to think, but I'll stop shrieking at you. Might need my defibrillator handy when the parents walk in and see you, though.'

She squinted at him.

He looked distraught at that. 'I get it. I'm sorry. Can you try to focus on the fact I'm alive? I very nearly wasn't.'

This time, she nodded. Understood how fortunate she was that her twin stood here in front of her at all. She grabbed his shoulders and shook him, then kissed his cheek. 'Oh lord, I'm so pleased you're here. But I have no idea how you're going to tell Mum and Dad. And Konrad.' She thought of their older brother. 'Oh, William. I'm not sure what Konrad's going to say when he comes home, and I don't want to be there for it.'

William stepped back, a look of dread crossing his face. 'If it goes as badly as this, I don't think I want to be, either.'

She glared and he held up his hand. 'Sorry. Joking.'

'It's not a joke, William.'

His face stiffened. 'I never thought it was, Bella. You might not believe me, but it's been hard, incredibly hard on my end, too.'

She guessed she'd get there. Eventually. 'Where have you driven from? Have you slept?'

'A few hours in the plane. Flew in from Perth on the red-eye and drove here via Brisbane. I came as soon as I could. I was going to get a cabin. Maybe Chasin' Opal.' He named the accommodation complex down the street.

She glanced around. 'Take the lounge here. It's a fold-out. Unit two is Konrad and Riley's. Mum and Dad will go in number one.'

William was alive. She hugged him again and then stepped back. 'Have you seen TJ?'

'Yeah. He told me where to find you. After threatening to shake me till my teeth fell out.'

For the first time since she opened the door Bella felt like smiling. Then she glared. 'You mean you went there first?'

'I could handle it if he threw me out.' His eyes pleaded for understanding. 'But I didn't think I could if you did.'

She shook her head and embraced him again. 'I've missed you so much. Don't ever do that again.'

He hugged her back fiercely. 'Love you too. So much. Will you help me tell Mum and Dad and Konrad?'

Bella sighed. And there was the twin who always asked her for help when he got himself into a scrape. Except this wasn't a childhood scrape. This was a mammoth adult drama with broken hearts littering their family.

She shook her head. 'Not this time. I have no idea what you're going to say or do to make it up to them, but *you* have to do this.

And the sooner, the better.'

William's eyes were shiny with his own emotion. 'It's going to be even worse with Mum and Dad, isn't it?'

'A hundred times worse. Gird your loins for it.'

'Seems it was easier to look at your own death than to view it through the eyes of the people who love you.'

'Believe it.'

'I'll make it up to you all, somehow. Right now, I need a shower and a change of clothes. I have to see Desiree, too. She saved me, sending Carol. I owe her.'

'I know. I'll go to Desiree with you, if you like. She shuts the servo at twelve on weekends and will probably be home. After that, I'll go see my patient and then we'll have lunch.'

Bella curated him a cup of coffee using the unit's state-of-the-art coffee machine and put it on the table. 'You shower. Then we'll see Desiree.'

*

Bella and William walked into the backyard of the service station forty-five minutes later, and with relief saw the place was empty, except for the snowy-haired woman sitting beside the rustic bar.

Desiree looked up and grimaced. 'So. Finally. You're still alive.'

Bella let William go ahead of her. 'Thanks to you, Desiree.'

Oh dear, she didn't look too pleased to see him. Another casualty of his non-contact. 'Yeah, well, that secret caused me a bit of angst over the years,' she said, a massive understatement.

Bella admired the tough older woman's acerbity as she narrowed her eyes at her brother.

'I apologise for that.'

Oh William. He was saying that a lot today, and Bella doubted he'd finish repeating it any time soon.

'Not me you need to be sorry to.' Desiree's tone dry and caustic. 'Doc Konrad took it hard. Hated lying to him. And your sister.' She glanced up Bella. 'You forgive him yet?'

'Mostly. I'm just glad to see him alive.'

Desiree huffed at William and shot him another dirty look from under her snowy brows. He was getting a few of those today as well.

'I know. I know.' He held out his hands. 'But if you'd spoken up or I'd turned up kicking, they would have held my family until I gave myself up. Tough on everyone, but if you hadn't sent Carol to follow me, I wouldn't be here at all. So, thank you, Desiree, for putting yourself in danger for my sake.'

'Yeah, well, did it for your brother more than you. But I also didn't like the nasty element growing around here. We've always been a town that backs each other, no matter how rich or poor you are, and that outsider scum were changing everything.'

She glanced thoughtfully around the yard. 'Carol tells me they're all gone now. Locked up. We can get back to being ourselves.'

William waited until she looked at him. 'You saved a lot of future lives, Desiree, and not just mine.'

'If you say so.' She didn't look impressed – or that might just be she wasn't impressed with him. Bella hid a smile. Poor William.

'So, what you gonna do? You told your parents, yet? Doc Konrad?'

Bella's guilt crashed in again. She was as bad as William. Neither of them were looking forward to any of those conversations – her twin might have kept his secrets for longer, but she'd been lying to her family recently, too.

'I've told Bella.' William glanced over his shoulder at her. 'The parents today.'

'That sister of yours is good people.' Desiree sent a look at Bella, and one to her brother that said he might not be fit in the same category. William shifted uncomfortably.

Oh dear, Bella thought, hiding another smile.

Desiree went on. 'I think she's got her heart set on TJ. That's your fault, too.'

William smiled ruefully. 'Everything is my fault, it seems. But TJ's one of the good guys. Always has been – always will be. He puts on a front.'

Desiree scowled. 'Maybe. Might've got him wrong. We'll see. So, I can ring Greta and tell her you're here?'

'Tell anyone you like. I'd rather not have to explain myself every two minutes.'

'Oh, you'll have to do that anyway.' There was a malicious delight in Desiree's voice. 'Good to have you home, kid.'

Bella decided it might be better to let Desiree say everything she wanted to William without his sister hearing it. 'I'll meet you at home, William.'

William threw her a panicked look and sidled her way. 'Anyway, thank you, Desiree. That's what I came to say, and I really mean it. Just let me know if there's anything you need me to do. I owe you. Call and I'll be there with bells on.'

She stared at him, her white brows drawn together. 'You mean that, do you?'

Bella watched as her brother nodded. 'I owe you big time. I do.'

Desiree narrowed her eyes and her mouth curved in a way that made Bella wonder what she could possibly ask him to do.

'Good. Think I might go away and do one of them world trips. You can run the service station while I'm gone.'

William laughed and glanced in the direction of the pumps.

'You reckon I could learn that?'

She was joking, Bella thought, grinning as she left them to it.

'Not joking,' Desiree said, and William's face fell. Bella walked away.

'You let me know,' she heard as he backed out of the yard and Bella turned to walk up the hill towards the OPAL medical centre, trying not to laugh as William broke into a fast pace.

'Slow down! She's not after you.'

At first he didn't slow. But then he stopped. 'You know. I think I might drop into the bottle shop and bring back a bottle of wine for Mum and Dad. I have a feeling they might need it.'

She smiled. 'You do that. All Konrad has is red.'

CHAPTER FORTY

MEESHA

Meesha pulled up outside her house in Lightning Ridge early on Sunday afternoon, glad to be back. She'd left Brisbane first thing in the morning and been tapping the steering wheel all the way home, impatient to see her sister and niece.

The door opened and Eric strolled out, offering a huge grin when he saw her.

'It's Aunty Meesha.'

'Uncle Eric,' she retorted, laughing. 'What are you doing here?'

'I'm the three wise men all rolled into one, bearing gifts. Now I've been sent shopping.' He waved a piece of paper. 'Matilda is to be obeyed.'

'Is she scary?' Meesha hadn't met the mothercraft nurse, but Luci had said she was an absolute sweetie.

'Nah, she's a doll. And so great with Luci and the baby.'

'That's good. Phew. Still no name?'

He grinned. 'I think they're waiting for the aunty to come home.'

'As they should.' But secretly, Meesha warmed with delight. 'That's sweet.'

Eric waved his list and departed in a jaunty walk, leaving Meesha to shake her head at his besottedness. Then she took a deep breath and pushed open the door to her sister's duplex, poking her head around the door. 'Hello, Luci? You there?'

'Meesha! In the lounge on the recliner.' Her sister sounded happy and relaxed, and some of the tension Meesha had carried all the way from Brisbane left her neck.

A brown-haired, brown-eyed, medium-height woman with a warm smile came from the rear of the building. 'Hello! Meesha is it?' she asked as she held out her hand. 'I'm Matilda Humphries. Your clever sister is in the chair, breastfeeding.'

'Nice to meet you, Matilda. Finally.' She returned the smile.

'How are they doing?'

'Both wonderful. Luci gave her a bath this morning, too.'

Meesha stepped through to the lounge and the sight made her eyes fill with tears. 'Oh, look at you two,' she said as she fell to her knees and carefully hugged both mother and baby. She peered down into the tiny face and big dark eyes of her niece, then looked back at her sister in awe. She shook her head, too choked to speak for a few moments.

'I'm so proud of you,' she whispered and leaned over and kissed her sister's cheek. 'Your little one is so beautiful.'

'She feels beautiful,' Luci said with a contented smile, touching her baby's cheek with one soft finger. 'But the birth was pretty scary.'

Meesha's chest tightened. 'Must have been horrible.'

Luci frowned. 'It wasn't horrible, just scary until I knew baby would be fine.' Luci tilted her face towards Meesha. 'Bella was there. And TJ. He carried me around like I was a feather – and I know I'm not such a lightweight.' She laughed at the memory.

'And he warned me when he was about to pick me up and put me down, like an old hand.'

Meesha had to smile at that. She could imagine how small her sister would look in TJ's arms. *Go Bella and TJ.*

But she should have been here.

Luci felt around for Meesha's hand with her free one, as if sensing her angst. 'The nurses were wonderful in the emergency department and at Moree. Matilda picked me up yesterday and we all had a good sleep last night between feeds. Eric's going shopping.'

'I saw him. He looks pleased with himself.' Meesha had missed it all. 'I'm so sorry I wasn't here for you.'

'Don't be silly. None of us knew it would happen so quickly, and Bella came so fast I was barely alone.'

Meesha knew that. Had to accept nothing could be changed.

'I know. It's such a blessing everything worked out well.'

She sat back, pulling her composure to herself. *Less angst more joy*, she told herself sternly. 'So, do you have any idea what you're going to call this young lady?'

'I thought I'd call her Rose after Mum,' Luci said, her head tilted Meesha's way.

'That's so lovely.'

'And' – there was a pause as Luci looked towards her – 'I thought her middle name could be Tamika after her aunty.'

Meesha felt her heart swell with delight and love. 'I'm honoured,' she said in a choked voice. 'If you're sure?'

'I'm sure.'

'Well, I'd love that. Rose Tamika Kerrison is a lovely name.'

'So, we have a name,' Matilda murmured as she returned to the room with a full bottle of water she placed beside Luci.

'Remind her to hydrate when she's feeding,' she told Meesha.

'She's very bossy,' Luci said but she was smiling warmly in Matilda's direction. 'I'm feeling more confident every day.'

'By two weeks I'll be redundant,' Matilda agreed. 'But for the next six weeks I'll still come back once a week to stay two nights and give you a break.'

'Sounds perfect,' Luci said, and Meesha realised her sister really did have this sorted. 'So, how was Brisbane?'

'The opal business is not as exciting as everything that happened here. But in good news, I won the trip to America . . . although I'm thinking I might put it off till next year.'

'Oh, no, Meesha. Because of me and Rose?'

'No. Because I'm selfish and I want to see you and Rose. I want to be here for you, and yes, I know you have this, but I want to be here for *me*.'

A concept she'd been playing with for a while suddenly felt even more attractive than when she'd first considered it. 'Instead of rushing to the US, I thought I might get into training staff for a year. I've enjoyed teaching Bella very much.' It really did sound rewarding. 'Consolidation before expansion. I need to build up support staff for when I do go away. And they need to be able to run the shop and share the passion I have for opals with our customers.'

'You sound like such a businesswoman.'

'I do, don't I? But I'm more than that. I'm also an aunty and a sister who wants to enjoy her family without rushing away this year.'

'Who knows, you might even have time for a man,' Luci teased.

Meesha held up crossed fingers at that. 'Good grief, no. That is one thing I do not need.'

Chapter Forty-One

Bella

Bella concentrated on the house call consultation to her patient who found it difficult to come to the surgery. Keeping her focus all the way through the twenty-minute appointment. Funny what you could do when you had to, she thought, but the exhaustion of such emotion after seeing William was creeping in.

She really wanted to talk to TJ again. She guessed he was worried about her as well, since he'd made the call when she'd been driving to her patient, and she'd reassured him she was okay.

She glanced at the clock again. William had appeared exhausted after the visit to Desiree, too, but she just hoped he didn't disappear before she made it back home. Funny how she worried about that now.

There was a lot she needed to talk about, and they needed to work out how best to tell their parents without freaking them out.

She still worried about Dad's heart.

Driving home, she weighed options and decided the least trau-matic way of going about that would be to tell Konrad first.

Their older brother had always been the wise head.

She and Konrad could prepare their parents, and once they broke the news, William would be in the other room when they arrived.

She rubbed her forehead. The call would be horrid of course, but after that, it would be brilliant and emotional. She wondered if she could possibly have TJ in the background as support.

It was ridiculous, she knew that – now wasn't the time to think about the man in her life. But . . .

As she pulled in behind the units, Mel, wearing a red button-up shirt appeared with a carry bag, like Little Red Riding Hood and a basket of food. Bella sagged a little at the unobtrusive support she found in these people.

'Greta wanted me to drop off two lunches, one for you and one for William.'

'How lovely.' Bella took the bag gratefully. 'Of course she did.'

'I'm really glad he's alive.' Mel ducked her head shyly. 'Toby will be too. He said he always liked William.'

'Thanks, Mel. I'm surprised Greta didn't drop off three meals, one for TJ as well.'

Mel laughed. 'She did say if you wanted another one for TJ, she had a spare.'

Bella laughed out loud. *Of course*, she thought. 'I just might do that.'

'I'll tell her.'

Suddenly Bella wanted to hug her admin, but they'd never been like that. Heck, she wanted to hug everybody. 'It is a good day, Mel.'

Mel stepped in and made it happen, and Bella hugged her back.

'It is. See you Monday, Bella.'

'Bye, Mel. And thanks.'

Bella pushed inside with the meals and the door shut behind her as she pulled her phone from her pocket. Still smiling, she pressed TJ's number. When he answered she said, 'Hey, Terence, wanna come to my place for lunch with my back-from-the-dead brother?'

TJ said, 'I'll be there in twenty.'

'If you drop into Greta's café on the way, she'll have a meal in a box for you to bring.'

CHAPTER FORTY-TWO

MEESHA

Meesha couldn't wait to give Bella a great big hug for being there for her sister and baby Rose. It had been such a great day when her friend had first come to town. As she reached the doctor's surgery at the top of the hill, young Mel was just stepping away.

'Oohh. How are you going, Meesha? You tell Luci congratu-la-tions on her new baby.' Mel grinned with delight. 'Another baby born in Lightning Ridge.'

Ah, yes, Mel's baby had been an emergency birth, too, Meesha recalled. 'Will do. When they're older, Teddy and Rose Tamika will need to get together and talk about their exciting arrivals.'

'Rose Tamika? Nice name.' Mel laughed. 'They'll have to do that. Bella just got home, and I think she's on the phone.'

Meesha noticed Mel looking past her and saw her shy smile at someone coming up the hill. Then heard her say, 'William!'

'Melinda, isn't it?' a man said and Meesha turned around to see a tall, buff guy striding towards them. He had the look of Konrad and Bella, blond though wirier, and there was something deliciously hard and dangerous about him that made her eyebrows go up.

So, here he is, finally. Back from the dead.

Bella's brother just might be a bit of a hunk, Meesha thought, but not to be trusted if he could hurt his family that way.

Mel turned to include her. 'William, have you met Meesha? She owns The Iridescent Opal down town.'

'No. I haven't had the pleasure.' He put out his hand accom-panied by a charismatic, bad boy smile and Meesha touched his fingers briefly before pulling back.

He cocked his head at her. 'Don't want to shake my hand?'

She shook her head slowly. 'Jury's out. Damage to your sister and your family like you did is pretty suspect in my books. I am her best friend in town.'

His hand fell away and he grimaced. 'Yeah. It's been one of those days. I'm making enemies all over the place.'

Meesha wanted to soften towards him but held it in. 'Funny that. I'm guessing Bella's already seen you since you're walking around town?'

'Yep. Already been down to chat to Desiree.'

Meesha got that. And maybe she did feel a bit sorry for him, because Desiree'd had the raw end of the deal and she would have served him a good one – but Meesha wasn't telling him that.

'Which explains the "enemies" comment.'

Mel looked between the two of them. 'Why don't you knock and see Bella? I'm going home.' She offered them both a worried smile and hurried away from the awkward scene.

'After you,' William said smoothly and Meesha walked past him to knock on the door. Bella opened it as she put her mobile phone in her pocket.

She narrowed her eyes at her brother, but Meesha was too busy rushing towards Bella to be interested in understanding their sibling communication. 'Thank you, dear Bella! Luci said you were won-derful.' She enveloped Bella in a hug. 'You're not just the best friend but also the best catcher of babies in town.'

Bella grinned as she pulled away. 'Yes, well, lucky Riley's not here, or I'd have handed her over.' Her face lit at the memory, but Mee-sha suspected she sensed relief now it was done. 'It was an honour.

Your sister is a legend.' She glanced past Meesha at William. 'And TJ helped.'

Meesha didn't look behind her. 'Yes, Luci said, and the staff here and at Moree were great too. Of course I missed it all.'

Bella patted her shoulder. 'I knew you'd be devastated about that. But nobody could have predicted an early rupture of mem branes or a cord prolapse. Has your gorgeous niece got a name yet?'

Meesha couldn't help her glow. 'Yes, Rose Tamika Kerrison.'

'What a beautiful name for a beautiful baby.'

Meesha felt that joy again. 'I can't believe it. Can't believe she's here. Safe.'

Bella took her hands and squeezed them. 'So how come you're here? When your new niece is down the street?'

'I had to see you. To thank you.' She glanced back at William, who waited patiently. 'I was going to grill you for every detail but . . . that can wait.'

'I see you've met my brother, William.'

William answered before she could. 'Yeah. She's not impressed, sis. Any chance of you putting in a good word for me?'

Meesha watched Bella pause and saw the way she stared at her twin like still couldn't believe he was there. There were probably

going to be a lot of those moments in the near future for Bella, constantly having to reassure herself he was back.

'Best friend. Lost brother.' Bella pointed at Meesha. 'She keeps in touch.'

'Ouch.' William grabbed his chest. 'So harsh. I've been copping heat all day.'

'Not going to stop anytime soon,' Bella warned but she smiled and touched his arm.

Meesha decided to leave the two of them to it. 'Anyway, I might pick another time for talking about the adventures of my sister and Rose's arrival. You go and talk to William.'

'But—'

'No. I just wanted to give you your necklace back.' Meesha impulsively hugged Bella. 'I won. Thanks to that.' She pressed the box into her hand and cut off Bella's excitement, waving her away.

'I'll tell you everything later. But thank you. Now go, shoo. You have much bigger fish to fry.' She narrowed her eyes at William.

He folded his arms against his chest, propping his long, lean frame against the wall as he watched her like a lazy cat.

She did not just think that.

Best leave before either of them read something on her face she didn't want them to see. 'I'll catch you later, Bella.' She inclined her head towards the wall hanging. 'I'm even glad he's here. For your sake. Good luck.'

Meesha took herself out, careful not to brush against the man at the door, disappointed she couldn't have spent more time with Bella, but totally on board with the huge shifts the return of William entailed.

CHAPTER FORTY-THREE

TJ

TJ walked into the middle of a sibling fight, still marvelling that Belle wanted him there on her first day reunited with her twin.

They both swung their heads around and glared as he entered Belle's flat, then ignored him. His mouth curved into a small smile as he put his dinner from Greta on the bench.

William lifted his hand. 'I don't see why we have to tell Konrad first.'

'Obviously you don't.' Exasperation shimmered in Belle's voice as if this wasn't the first time she'd explained it. 'I think it would be better for Mum and Dad if it came from Konrad and me, rather than you just jumping out of the blue and appearing like a ghost.'

William blew out a disgusted breath. 'I don't think anything we do is gonna change the shock.'

'Well, I'm not surprised. In the last week I've had a lot more time to consider how to do this, and we should ring Konrad first.'

William threw up his hands. 'Fine. You always did get your own way.'

TJ suppressed a laugh. Maybe not well enough, because William turned on him. 'And what are you doing here, anyway?'

'Your sister invited me.'

Belle's head came up. 'TJ is my moral support.'

Her brother snorted. 'Since when have you needed moral support?'

'The last two and a half years.' Her expression changed. 'Since I lost my twin.'

William sucked in a breath and TJ considered it time for an intervention, before they said something they would both regret.

He crossed the room to Belle and wrapped his arms around her.

'Hey. Tough day? I just filled my car up down at Desiree's and she said she gave him a hard time, too.' He glanced over at William's set face. 'And apparently Meesha snarled at him as well.'

That caught Belle's attention. And William's. She studied his face. 'No way Desiree could know that.'

TJ would like to have known the story with Meesha, since she didn't usually take a dislike to people. Though she was loyal, so it was probably in defence of Belle's heartache.

He laughed. 'Get used to it, babe. Everybody knows everything in this town.'

'Not everything,' William said with a triumphant look.

Belle raised those beautiful brows. He squeezed her tighter, loving the feel of her in his arms. He felt his love vibrate under him. She waved her finger at her brother. 'Really?'

TJ had to laugh again. 'You two are like children.' Or twins.

'I heard you're an undercover cop from three people already.'

TJ enjoyed the dismay on William's face that he was currently the topic of conversation for the whole town. Lots of people would be looking for him to hear the story. But he had to tell the rest of his family first.

TJ picked up the Iridescent Opal jewellery box from the coffee table and opened it. 'Meesha brought back your necklace?'

Bella stopped glaring at her brother and looked at him. Her face softened and her shoulders dropped. When she held out her hand, he removed the necklace from the box and placed it gently in her palm.

'Hey.' William touched the opal in Bella's hand. 'That's my opal.'

'It's my opal and I love it.' She hugged him. 'Thank you, brother mine. It's beautiful. TJ gave it to Meesha to set, and I couldn't be happier you're here to see me put it back on.'

William touched it gently, too. 'Looks good on you.'

The siblings exchanged a look that made TJ almost wish he had a sister. *They'll be okay*, he thought.

'It is special. When I learned you planned to give it to me for our birthday, I knew you couldn't have committed suicide. So, it was the start of my hope.'

She slipped it over her head and her hand closed around it, gripping it tightly before she let it go to swing and glow as it caught the light.

Her sparkling eyes met TJ's. 'Meesha won the award.'

He felt the curl of delight in his chest. 'She deserved that.'

The call with Konrad didn't go too badly, TJ thought, at least after the initial stunned silence and some vicious swearing. TJ watched Belle's eyebrows climb as if she'd never heard her big brother explode like that.

Konrad and Riley made the snap decision to cut short the honeymoon and fly back to Lightning Ridge immediately. William was to pick them up from the airport in thirty-six hours' time. Or else.

Konrad also agreed for Belle to phone him as soon as their parents arrived. After they were warned about what was coming, William would step out of the other room.

Which meant TJ would get to meet the whole family today. He didn't know how he felt about that, but ready or not, he'd be there for Belle because she'd asked him to stay.

At least there'd be enough units to go around if Belle shared with her twin, while the parents took the first flat and Konrad and Riley moved back into number two. Seemed big families were complicated, but even he could tell how much they cared about each other. He squashed the young kid inside himself who was desperate for some of that.

When the time drew near for the parents' arrival, TJ sat out of immediate sight in the corner of the room, but close enough if Belle needed him.

His Belle had been through a tough couple of days, and if she wanted his physical support in her time of need, he'd be honoured to assist. The more she leaned on him, the more he allowed himself to dream there could be a future for them.

As an outsider to the coming drama, he was in a good position to observe and help pick up the pieces if needed.

Belle's parents didn't see him when they first entered the unit, which gave him a glimpse of her mother, Helen, white blonde and a hint to what his Belle would look like in thirty years' time – still a beautiful woman.

Her dad, Doug, was a craggy, big-shouldered bloke with white hair and frown lines TJ suspected had deepened since William's disappearance. His eyes were grey and tired.

Doug said, 'It's so good to see you, Bella. And what's this message about phoning Konrad right away? We've only just arrived.'

'Hello, and who's this?' Helen's eyes sparkled as she spotted TJ. 'More news?'

Belle came over and pulled him forward. 'Dad, Mum this is TJ, my good friend.' They all shook hands, and Belle's dad gave him a not unfriendly once over. Belle said into the little silence that fell after the gladhanding, 'TJ is also a friend of William's.'

She looked at TJ and he nodded. She must have drawn some comfort from him because she lifted her chin and continued.

'Because the news is about William. Which is why Konrad wants to video call as well.'

Both Doug and Helen paled as they stared at Belle.

'Please sit down,' Belle encouraged them, trying for a reassuring tone. 'It's not what you think. Just wait. And sit.'

They sat together at the kitchen table and TJ eased back out of the way. There, but not intruding.

Belle hit the computer speed dial and in a few seconds Konrad's face appeared on the screen. When Konrad spoke, TJ decided his face looked professionally caring, an expression he probably used on patients all the time.

'Hello, Mum, Dad. We've got news,' he said in a calm voice. 'About William.'

Belle's mother's hand tightened on the middle of her chest where it had flown at Belle's words. It was the same thing Belle did, too, TJ thought, when she was anxious.

He knew Belle was anxious now as she backed up against him.

He squeezed her shoulder in sympathy.

Doug reached over and took Helen's hand. Clasped it in both of his and leaned forward. Softly, he said, 'Did they find William's body, Konrad?'

TJ looked sideways to where he could see the tension in every line of William's shoulders as he stayed backed away out of his parents' sight in the other room. He spared a thought for how hard this would be for him and then shrugged it off.

Konrad didn't waste time, used to giving difficult news to people, TJ guessed. Part of being a doctor. Like Belle. And her parents.

Konrad said, 'No. Better than that. We've found William. Alive, not dead.'

Belle's father barked, 'What? You're telling us he's alive?'

TJ looked across to where William had his hand over his face and then saw him square his shoulders.

Konrad went on in that same logical tone. 'He's been an under-cover police officer for several years. There was an attempt on his life and he was severely injured and extricated. William had amnesia for the first three months. After that, if William resurfaced, Bella would have been in danger. So, he's remained hidden until now.'

'Alive,' Bella's mother whispered.

'Alive.' Konrad repeated the news. 'But now they've just brought down a large criminal syndicate that had been operating in Lightning Ridge and across Australia.'

'I heard about that on the news.' Still bristling, Doug ground out, 'You're in America. How do you know all this and we don't?'

'Because William phoned me, right after he went to see Bella today. He's in Lightning Ridge.' His face concerned, Konrad asked gently, 'You okay, Mum?'

The two parents clutched each other. Helen whispered,

'Where?' TJ's chest ached for the pain in their eyes and he wasn't sure this way was working. Helen continued, whispering again.

'Show me. I can't believe until—'

William stepped out from the other room and towards his mother. He stopped right in front of her, turned his head to his father. William licked his lips and said haltingly, 'Mum. Dad.

It's true. They were going to kill Bella – and Konrad, maybe all of you – if they found out I was alive.'

With a cry, Helen burst out of the chair and buried her face in William's chest. Doug came in over the top, hugging them both, his face pale but fierce grey eyes trained on William like twin lasers.

After several attempts to speak, Doug finally choked out,

'Alive, all this time? You've got a lot of explaining to do, son.' He rubbed his wife's back, never taking his eyes off William. 'It will take us a bit to get used to this, but we'll talk about it all.'

Konrad said from the screen, 'I thought you might say that.

Riley and I will be there tomorrow morning after we land and fly up from Sydney.'

'Good. We need you both here. The whole family.'

Pretty civilised, really, TJ thought, considering the magnitude of the disclosures. Belle moved them both back out of the way to give her brother and their parents some room.

His Belle leaned her head back against him and he kissed her hair, wrapping his arms around her as she sighed into him. These moments were the gold he was learning to love.

William was saying, 'I'm sorry, Mum, Dad. By the time I was sensible enough to know what was happening, you all thought I was dead. It was too late. And I—'

Doug growled, 'It was never too late. We all suffered. Your mother suffered.'

'I know,' William said, tiredly. 'I was scared for Bella. For all of you. I knew too much for them to leave my family alone if they knew I was alive. I'm sorry. I was doing my job.'

TJ winced as Belle sprang up and slapped her brother on the back of the head.

'Family over job every time!'

TJ winced. He'd thought he had it bad.

'Oww, Bella,' William said, as he rubbed his head. 'And just so you know, officially,' his eyes were brimming with tears. 'You are the people I love most in the world.'

TJ seriously got that. The absolute agony on Helen's face and the stoic despair in Doug's eyes must be ripping out his guts.

Helen admonished, 'Bella!' in the most mum voice ever.

Konrad laughed through the computer. 'Exactly what I wanted to do, Bella, but let's not get physical. Especially with his past head injury.'

But TJ could see Konrad grinning slyly and at least the horrible tension had decreased a notch. Konrad added, 'Riley and I will see you all on Monday around lunchtime. I'll phone you with a time for pick up, William.'

The party broke up after that, William and his parents going to the unit next door to debrief, TJ and Bella staying where they were until he'd given her the hug she said she needed. He'd been up for that, but he knew now she needed to be with her family.

When he rode his Harley back to his camp, his body still hummed with the feel of Belle in his arms.

He wouldn't go back tonight. The Greys needed to be together for the next few nights.

The enormity of what he'd seen today must have scrambled his brain because he dropped the keys opening his own gate. Ironic or symbolic, he thought – something about letting barriers down for the woman he'd tumbled into love with, despite all his kicking and screaming.

Belle was in his life for better or worse and he wasn't giving her up, now or ever.

But he needed to be a better man. More whole. For her.

Inside the house, his gaze fell on the tarp-covered pile in the corner and his eyes rested there for a moment.

Belle was here to stay. The past needed to stay where it belonged, too, and the mound in the corner was as good a place as any to start.

He tossed his overnight kit through the doorway onto the bed and walked over to the tarpaulin. Today he'd begin something he hadn't been able to do before Belle. Something he had to do now.

She deserved it. And apparently, as far as she was concerned, he deserved it, too.

Here goes.

He reached out and began rolling the tarp up and off the contents. Lifted the stool from the top of the pile and put it on the floor. Despite the covering, the black baby grand stood for-lornly, dull and dusty – and that wasn't what it deserved.

He huffed out a disgusted breath, muttered, 'Sacrilege,' and crossed back to the cupboard underneath the kitchen sink, pulling out a duster, some polish wipes and a buffing cloth.

It took him twenty minutes to rub the piano down, top and sides, smoothing the carved legs, and polishing the keyboard.

And all the while he worked, pictures from the past spun through his mind like an album on auto flip.

His mum proudly watching him play on their old spindle upright.

TJ as a man in the pub with his catcalling mates, serenading the sexy bird he fancied, with his fingers on the keys.

Ree and him together on the seat after she gifted him the Yamaha baby grand.

So many nights he'd played to her. So long ago, yet the poignant memories were much better than the shattered final ones with her he'd been replaying far too often, for far too long.

It was time to remember the good times. The beginning and the middle, not just the end of those days.

He rested his fingers on the keyboard and said quietly to the ghost in the room, 'You'll always be a part of my life, Ree, but it's time I moved on.' It sounded lame to his ears, mainly because she would have scorned his self-indulgent guilt and told him to do that years ago.

He depressed the middle C, and the sound rang clear in the room with the purity of a digital piano that didn't require the once or twice yearly tuning an old upright would have needed.

He didn't sit down and play, wasn't ready for that just yet.

Might never be ready, though he suspected the first time Belle saw the baby grand, she'd ask him to play for her. And he wouldn't be able to say no.

But not today.

The room looked better already with that tarp drawn back. Of course, the piano was too big for the space but it stood proud, shiny and waiting.

Soon, he promised.

CHAPTER FORTY-FOUR

BELLA

Bella ushered the last patient out into the reception area on Monday and checked her phone for the text she'd felt vibrate half an hour ago. TJ or William?

Not TJ. William, letting her know Konrad and Riley had arrived safely. Excellent. She wasn't exactly sorry she'd missed Konrad's first response to seeing William in the flesh. Her dear twin needed to deal with that all to himself. She expected William would have a big bruise on his left biceps, which was usually Konrad's way of saying, 'You stuffed up, little brother.'

She went back to her desk and closed her computer, taking a moment to stretch out-of-practice muscles that twinged after her recent night-time antics with TJ. A smile creased her face, and maybe her cheeks did tingle with heat. She'd known TJ could create magic and mayhem with her body, and she'd created some of her own back on Friday, until they'd both fallen asleep, exhausted and satiated. She'd miss him tonight – she missed him now, already.

Waking in his arms on Saturday morning had been stupendous, but she'd been disappointed when he refused to come back last night or tonight. Still, she knew this time he was right. William being alive was enough for her parents to think about for the moment. She turned off her consulting room light.

'You good to go, Mel?'

'Yes, thanks. Greta said she changed the sheets in Konrad and Riley's unit to make it even fresher for them coming home. She put new sheets on the fold-out lounge in yours and refolded it. William just needs to open it up when he goes to bed.'

'Dear Greta. She's a champion.'

Mel grinned. 'She is. And Toby dropped off the four double dinners. They're in the fridge. Greta said they all complement if you want to do share plates.'

'Fabulous idea. Thanks.' Her mum would want to cook soon, too, but couldn't do much yet with the lack of ingredients in Bella's fridge, so Bella had made the dinner order. Best to have a fait accompli by having the meals ready to go for when they'd all finished talking.

When she opened the door to her flat, her parents were sitting on the lounge with a pot of tea in front of them and William perched awkwardly on the recliner, watching their faces. Konrad and Riley were at the dining table with a glass of wine each. Bella put the containers on the bench as Konrad, looking more like a Viking than ever, reached out and wrapped her in a big bear hug. 'How's my little sister? You looking after all our patients in the Ridge?'

Before Bella could answer, Riley slipped in between them and put her arm around both their waists. 'Hello, dear sister-in-law. This must have been a crazy few weeks for you.'

William bounced out of the chair. 'Tinkerbell!' She could see the strain on his face and felt just a little mean for not wanting to share the angst of seeing Konrad and Riley at the airport with him. He took the takeaway containers from the bench to put in the fridge.

She touched his shoulder as she passed and leaned down to hug her mum and dad before they could get up. 'Stay there. I'll grab a cup and share your pot of tea. How was the afternoon?'

'Good to see these two back,' her dad said, inclining his head at Konrad and Riley. 'We didn't sleep much last night.'

'I'm sure.' She smiled at her mum. 'And how does William look today?'

'Wonderful. Older.' Mum tilted her head to the side and her eyes filled with tears. 'Alive.'

Bella's dad squeezed the fragile hand he held in his. 'He looks good.'

'That's what I thought,' Bella said, feeling the emotion well in her own chest. They all tried to ease it with chatter but knew it would take time. 'I didn't think we'd want to go out for dinner, so takeaway tonight. Greta is such a great cook. How about we do share plates and make William wash up.'

Dad smiled and even Mum sniffed and almost laughed at the task allocation.

They nodded and the silence fell. Bella added brightly, 'Now that Konrad and Riley are here, we can talk about what we want to do about cooking.'

Her mother nodded and silence fell again. Okay then. Bella tried again. 'You all settled in next door, Mum?'

'Yes, darling. We have everything we need.'

Dad added, 'Konrad's renovations are great. Showers seems big.'

Both she and William laughed, synchronised. Mum looked at them both and wiped away tears. Bella guessed that would happen for a while. 'Big shower. That's what I noticed when I moved in, too. You should have a good look around the Ridge while you're here, Mum. See Meesha's shop – it's so beautiful. And check out the tourist mines.'

William nodded. 'We could all go to the hot baths one night.'

'I haven't been yet, but I've been meaning to go with Meesha.'

She was babbling and needed to stop.

'Maybe we should,' Mum said, trying to help. 'We didn't feel like doing any sightseeing the last time we came.'

Silence fell again as they all went back to thinking about the horror of when William had been lost.

'Emotional minefields are everywhere,' William said tackling the elephant in the room. 'And it's all my fault. I know. I'm so sorry, I love you all, and you've all suffered so much.'

Bella stepped over and slung her arm around his shoulder. 'We love you, so much.' Maybe she should have insisted TJ come to help distract everyone – he'd certainly be a distraction for her. But she knew her parents just needed time to get used to seeing William every time they looked up. Let the live man sink in. Maybe hug him a few hundred times.

At least they had an excellent dinner to look forward to.

Tuesday night after work when Bella walked into the flat, she heard her mum's laughter, and her shoulders loosened with relief.

Things had improved, probably because Konrad and Riley were still here and everyone had plenty of time to settle in and catch up with William.

And they didn't even know about Coober Pedy. She'd have to mention she'd shut the surgery for two days at some stage. But it did feel extra good to be in this world of family support after the last few weeks of stress and angst.

'How's our patients?' Riley gave her that special warm smile she'd made her brand.

'Busy, busy, I can tell you. But luckily I've had Cyrus to keep my spirits up. He misses you.'

'Heard it wasn't just Cyrus keeping you busy,' Konrad murmured.

Riley frowned at him and flapped her husband away with her hand. 'How is dear Cyrus? He's a sweetie.'

Not the word Bella would have used to describe the large, bon-homie-filled miner, but he did make her smile. 'Well, he lost five kilos and when I mentioned that you'd be thrilled, he's taken up walking with a passion.'

Konrad grinned. 'Oh yeah, once he had Riley on the scene, he was never coming back to me as a patient. Though I'm guessing he'd be just as happy with his new doc.'

'Because I listen to him sing Riley's praises.'

It was Riley's turn to laugh and then her sister-in-law studied her more closely. 'You know, you do look fabulous, Bella. I love the necklace. You're a new woman since the last time I saw you. Lightning Ridge suits you.'

'Or is it a tall dark stranger who suits you?' Konrad murmured.

'Who has been telling tales out of school?' Bella mock glared at her twin. William had their mother next to him with his arm around her waist. 'How's your arm, William?'

William lifted his other arm and rubbed his biceps. 'Bruised.'

'Good.' Their eyes met in a sibling connection she'd missed like breathing. Yes. She was feeling better than she had in years – healing was a wonderful thing. Nothing could be better than having her whole family around her.

She lifted the necklace up again for Riley. 'William found the opal and Meesha from The Iridescent Opal designed the setting.'

Riley's eyes widened. 'Nice find, William.'

Yes, it had been. Now all she needed to make everything perfect was TJ, though she wasn't quite sure her man was ready for this much sibling and parental examination.

As if hearing her thoughts, her dad said, ever so casually, 'So, Bella. Tell us about this TJ who was here the other day. Is he someone special to you?'

And now they were all looking at her. Great job, William, she thought. Though Konrad had done his part, too, with his teasing.

The joy of having siblings. But even that thought there took away the sting of the annoyance. She'd rather have her siblings any day.

But all she said was, 'That was nice of William to mention my private life.' She raised both brows at her twin.

'Yeah, sorry.' He grinned, looking anything but. 'I was looking for a change of subject after all the scrutiny I was wearing.'

Bella knew it was time. 'TJ is a miner who used to be in the police as well.' She saw surprise register on Konrad's face. *Yeah, brothers, you're not the only ones with secrets.* 'He was a team leader in the Tactical Response group in Sydney. There was an incident and he lost someone close to him, so he moved out here and has been pretty much isolating himself since then.'

'So much tragedy in the world,' Mum murmured, but she was looking at William. He kissed her cheek.

'So how did you meet him?' Konrad asked. 'TJ isn't the most sociable guy, even by Lightning Ridge standards.'

'Meesha, you know the woman who owns The Iridescent Opal, had a party not long after I arrived. He's one of her suppliers.'

'I know Meesha,' Riley said. 'She's good people.'

'You think everyone in Lightning Ridge is good people.' Konrad hugged her to him with a smile.

'Well, they are,' Riley said stoutly. 'And Meesha does make beautiful jewellery. Bella's necklace included.'

'Anyway, I was invited to an anniversary party at the shop and was introduced to TJ, there. He called me Tinkerbell.' She glanced at William. 'Colour me suspicious.' Brows went up around the room. 'I'm guessing it's no surprise to most of you that one of the reasons I moved to Lightning Ridge was to find out more about the last few months of your life, dear risen-again William.

So, I followed up with him.'

'Bit between the teeth, Bella,' William teased, clearly hoping to keep the spotlight on her for a change. She narrowed her eyes at him. 'Poor bloke had no hope of escaping you.'

'Hang on. How did you pin him down?' Konrad frowned. 'He's a hard man to find. I know. I tried.'

Bella shrugged. 'I went to his camp. Meesha knew where he lived. I just knocked until he opened the gate.'

William laughed. Hard. 'That would have taken a while.'

'Doesn't he live in some sort of compound out on Three Mile Road?' Konrad looked even more unhappy and glanced at Dad.

'TJ's known as the dark dude around town.'

'Nope, one of the good guys,' William said. 'Moody blighter, though.'

'Not to me he isn't. Not now, anyway,' Bella said, her face curving into a smile. 'I'm persistent.'

Riley laughed out loud. 'This is why I love my sister-in-law.'

She patted Konrad to calm him. 'I bet he's a bit of a hunk.'

'Makes William look like a weed,' Bella said smugly, and the two women grinned at each other in the equivalent of a high-five.

Not missing any of this exchange, Dad said, 'Hang on. So, you're serious about this man? You didn't say that when we met him.'

Mum added, 'We should meet him properly.'

Bella nodded. 'You will. Soon. He's giving us time as a family to talk to William.'

'Sounds like he's a part of the family already,' Mum said. 'Why don't you invite him over tonight, Bella?'

Thirty minutes later, Bella heard TJ's motorbike pull up outside.

Her heart bumped ridiculously like a sixteen-year-old's. TJ was going to get the whole family in one go. But then, bar Riley, he had actually met them all individually. Mentally, she shrugged. He was a tough guy. He'd manage.

He pulled his helmet off and hooked it on the bike, his broad back turned to her for a moment, and she wanted to slip her arms around the leather-clad expanse of him and just rest her cheek on his shoulders.

But when he turned around and smiled quizzically at her, she wanted his mouth on hers more than anything.

'How you holding up?' he asked. 'You don't look too shattered.'

She could feel tension slipping off her like he was divesting his coat to hang it on the bike. 'I feel better seeing you.'

'Ditto,' he said and pulled her in for a kiss. His lips slid over hers possessively and she sighed into him. This. She needed *this*.

Finally, after a long, timeless interlude, she stepped back.

Suddenly eager to show him off. 'Come in to be officially welcomed to the family. My parents are still here. But you haven't met Riley, Konrad's wife, have you? You'll like her. She's smart and tough enough even for you.'

'Nobody's tougher or smarter than you, Belle Bird.'

CHAPTER FORTY-FIVE

TJ

TJ squeezed Belle's familiar fingers in his and tried to relax at the idea of meeting her family as her significant other.

The first person he locked eyes with was Konrad, frowning at him from the corner of the room where he stood beside a tall, confident looking red-head. At least she was smiling. TJ inclined his head that way, but Belle was dragging him across to her parents.

He held out his hand.

'Dr Grey, Dr Grey. I'm TJ. Terence.'

Doug took TJ's hand firmly and shook it. 'Good to meet you again, Terence. Bella speaks highly of you.' He turned to draw the other Dr Grey closer to his side. 'I'm Doug, and this is my wife, Helen.'

'Lovely to meet you properly, dear.' Helen, the woman who made him think of his Belle in thirty years, reached up and kissed his cheek. Her lips felt soft and gentle against his face, and he closed his eyes briefly at the acceptance he hadn't expected.

'Thank you.' It was all he could manage through a strangely tight throat.

Doug said, 'My daughter tells me you've been a big help in finding William.'

TJ looked at Belle. Did she now? 'Your daughter is like a terrier when she has her heart set.'

Belle grinned mischievously and he just wanted to kiss that smile until the mischief had changed to something else. But probably not the best decision while meeting her parents. 'I just went along for the ride.'

'Right mate,' mocked William from behind him. TJ turned and shook hands with him as William went on. 'I don't know that it's a ride if you drive all the way to Coober Pedy just so she can question someone.'

'What's this?' Konrad's frown deepened.

'For another day,' Belle said firmly, and TJ agreed heartily.

It was the last thing they needed to discuss, especially in front of Belle's parents.

Possibly with some reluctance, Konrad brought his wife over.

'TJ, this is my wife, Riley.'

He shook the tall woman's hand. 'Nice to meet you, Riley. Belle missed you.'

'Why, thank you, TJ.' She twinkled up at him before leaning over and kissing his cheek as well. What was with these women accepting him so readily?

Konrad looked even less friendly. Seemed the Greys were not so accepting on the male side, which amused TJ more than anything else.

'Something I'm curious about.' Konrad gave him another hard stare. 'Why all the secrecy with calling you TJ?'

The room fell silent, and TJ shrugged. Thank goodness he'd managed to share that with Belle first. He was beginning to see this family was all the same – blunt or bulldozer were two good descriptions for them.

After a glance his way and seeing his nod, Belle answered for him, saying serenely, 'Terence Judd Jefferies. But that's just for the family to know.' She glanced around to ensure she had agreement.

Not that he cared too much, but he appreciated that he understood his reluctance to shout it from the crane top.

'Terence Judd Jefferies,' William murmured. 'Well, there you go.' He pulled out his phone and typed it in to search.

TJ shook his head. Typical William, now he saw him clearly.

'Don't waste any time invading my privacy there, will you, mate?'

William just smiled without looking up.

On Saturday night TJ paced nervously while he waited for Belle to arrive at his camp. Last night Helen and Riley had wanted to go with her to the Lightning Ridge Ladies to thank Desiree and the ladies for their support of Belle and William. So she'd stayed in town.

Today Belle's parents had left to return to Port Macquarie for the weekend with William, while Konrad and Riley had flown to Sydney in Konrad's small plane. They still had honeymoon time planned together, before they both went back to work. Konrad was starting part-time at a local medical practice near Riley's work now that Belle had taken over the OPAL medical centre.

So, out of the six Greys, it was just Belle left in the Ridge.

With TJ.

He hadn't asked Belle to come out here while her parents were in town, but he did feel as if he'd been more accepted by them all than he'd expected. Her brothers had stopped teasing him. Or at least no more than they teased each other, anyway, and that made him feel included.

Konrad had stopped growling and Helen had made a fuss of him, which was weird but delightful as well. He'd often caught Belle's smile at the sight of him talking to Helen, as if his Belle knew how much it meant to him to be accepted into her family.

Towards the end of the week, it had felt almost easy mingling with Belle's family.

He glanced again at the shiny black piano in the corner.

He wanted to get this last bit over with.

Music had once been an important part of his life, and it might even become a part of his future, but he hadn't shared it with Belle.

At least the last few days had given him a chance to get used to seeing the instrument every time he walked into the house or woke up in the morning.

His fingers may even have itched with the urge to sit down and run the tips across the keyboard.

TJ heard her car pull up. He couldn't help the thrum of his pulse and the curve of his mouth as he stepped outside to greet her at the gate.

Belle lifted her face to his and he bent down until their lips met. It was coming home all over again. He slid his arm around her shoulder and pulled her against him as he locked the world out behind his gate.

'So, what is it?' His impatient Belle. She nudged him and he smiled. 'You said you had something special to show me.'

'Miss Curious. Although I must admit you've done very well waiting all this time.'

Her eyebrows furrowed in that cute way. Puzzled. Intrigued.

The aroma of cooking beef drifted out to greet them at the door.

'Dinner smells good,' she said.

'Pepper steak in pastry. My speciality.'

She turned, laughing back at him from the stairs. 'More bonus points you can claim later.'

'You can bet on it.'

'All these wonderful surprises,' she said as she went up the stairs, and he couldn't help the way his eyes landed on her backside and legs as she went past.

'Ohhhhh!' He heard the exclamation of surprise as he followed her inside and saw her turn to him with an expression of delight.

He'd suspected – hoped – this might be the case. 'You've been holding out on me.'

'Yes, well, you ripped off my bandaid. And threatened to look under there yourself.'

'I did not. Not until you said I could. But wow . . .' She walked over to the piano and ran one slender finger across the polished ebony wood. 'It's so beautiful. Like you. And you play.' There was no doubt in her voice.

He had no words.

She shook her head and came back to him, slipping her arms around his waist, hugging him to her. 'So, there's another side to big, bad TJ.'

'There are lots of sides, and eventually I'll show you most of them.'

She squeezed him. 'I'll see them all, thank you.'

He brushed his chin across her hair. Turned her in his arms so they both faced the piano in the corner. 'We'll talk about that, later.' He rested his eyes on his baby grand. 'What do you think?'

'I never guessed . . . never would have guessed.'

He smiled. 'What did you think it was?'

She shrugged. 'Maybe weight benches, or boxes of stuff.' She reached up and kissed him. 'I can't wait till you're ready to play for me.'

He blew out a laugh. There she was. His Belle. Understanding right from the get-go. 'If anyone's gonna help me be ready, it'll be you, my love. You'll be the first to hear it.'

She kissed him and went to look at the oven. 'How long before dinner? I'm starving.'

Again, she'd surprised him with letting it go, waiting until he was ready.

'I love you, my Belle.'

'And I love you, my big, beautiful TJ.'

EPILOGUE

Six months later on a Saturday afternoon, Meesha felt like the whole town had gathered for Luci's baby's christening.

So many people, she thought as she beamed at them all. It was so lovely to see the community behind her sister. Luci had always been Meesha's hero but it was heartwarming to see her become a part of these people's lives, inspiring them with her determination to live life to the fullest, no matter the challenges.

The well-wishing crowd in Meesha's shop flowed out onto the street where extra tables and chairs had been lined up and spilled over into the parking area next door. Rose Tamika Kerrison, her scrumptious niece, had grown so much in the past few months, snuggled and relaxed in Eric's arms right now, occasionally pulling at his new beard.

Rose chortled and said, 'Ba ba ba ba ba ba.'

TJ sauntered past with a beer and flute in his hand. Meesha watched him grin when Eric agreed absently, 'Yes, bababa,' as he jiggled the baby in one hand and sipped his beer with the other.

TJ waved Bella's flute of champagne at the man. 'You're doing well with that second language there, mate.'

Eric turned his head and gestured with his eyes at the glass.

'And you're well trained getting your girlfriend a wine. I hear you and Bella bought a house in town.'

'Yep.'

Meesha had loved that news, too. The thought gave her such plea-sure: Bella was staying, she and TJ were an amazing couple, and thank goodness Bella had been able to nudge her fiancé away from black fencing to keep the neighbours out.

TJ gestured at Toby, Greta's son, standing with a heavily pregnant Mel by his side. The couple were surrounded by the Lightning Ridge Ladies. 'Toby and I have big plans for the exten-sions. Any chance of you and Luci doing the same?'

'Plans are fluid but I'm working on it. Making slow progress.'

Eric jiggled the baby in his arms. 'Life's pretty good as it is.'

Meesha's mouth curved. Oh yes, Eric was making progress, though her sister was advancing at her own pace and wouldn't be hurried into anything.

Meesha looked TJ over. 'Dressed pretty flash there, in your new chinos. You still keeping your camp out in the sticks, tough guy?'

TJ glanced down at the sand-coloured trousers Meesha knew Bella had bought for him the last time they'd gone to Port Macquarie to see her parents. He'd also done the incredibly awkward old-fashioned thing of asking Bella's dad for his daughter's hand. So romantic.

Meesha wondered if Eric would ask *her* for Luci's hand one day. She snickered.

'Can't get rid of that. Mining's in my blood now, so, yeah, it's a decent lease. Nice colour. And Belle enjoys making jewellery from the opal I pull out.' He glanced Meesha's way, his lips curving.

'You've taught her well.'

The words warmed her.

Eric looked at Meesha, too. 'You're our star entrepreneur. The town's growing. Kelly's new shop's open. The Iridescent Opal's making a name for itself overseas, and the new girls you're teaching are giving you more time for the design pieces.'

'Life is good,' she agreed. And that's not even mentioning a certain man she was quietly interested in. 'That's because the Ridge is world class.'

It still felt incredibly humbling that TJ and Eric made no secret they admired her work ethic and her artistic flair. Though that work ethic had waned some since William had come back to the Ridge.

As if he could read her thoughts, TJ teased, 'I see you've taken up visiting the servo and the new pump princess.'

'Everyone needs petrol, TJ.' Meesha hoped her cheeks didn't look as warm as they felt.

Eric laughed. 'Desiree will be back. Interesting to see what William does now he's out of the police force.'

TJ grinned. 'More interesting to see what Meesha does.'

Meesha saw him catch Belle's gaze and she sighed at the tender look that passed between them. Love. Life. Future. Yes, she wanted what Bella had – but no hurry. She and Luci were very similar like that, she thought, as TJ moved on.

He raised the glass to Eric and Meesha. 'Better get this to my lady. She's waiting for me.'

Acknowledgements

Thank you so much for reading *The Lightning Ridge Ladies*.

I hope you enjoyed your opal-coloured view of Lightning Ridge through my fiction. I've used a lot of poetic licence, but the Ridge is an amazing place with warm and wonderful people – that's all true, and you really should see this iconic Australian outback town for yourself.

The first time I visited the Ridge I met opal-hunters and miners who generously shared the mining aspects for my newbie miner character, Adelaide, in *The Opal Miner's Daughter*. While there for that book, I met the charismatic and talented Vicki Bokros and her partner, Andrew, at the opal boutique Down to Earth Opals (down toearthopals.com.au). There are so many fabulous opal boutiques in the Ridge. It wasn't just the wine we consumed at the Bowlo, it was Vicki and Andrew's passion for finding, designing and sharing opals and their love of Lightning Ridge that inspired me to write this book. So here it is.

Huge thanks to Andrew Kemeny for the extra information on mining and polishing opal – any mining or opal-craft mistakes are not Andrew's, because the time he took to answer questions and help as much as he could after the book was written was golden!

For example: while Tucson does have a trade fair that includes opal, the prize I created is fiction. Meesha's imaginary world was inspired by Vicki's opal passion, but Meesha's journey is very different to Vicki's and is pure fiction.

My criminally created shortage of opal in Lightning Ridge is also all fiction and a little dabble for me in adding a flavour of mystery and crime to this book.

The setting for the doctor's surgery and units is again Fossickers Cottages: thank you, Jo Lindsay, and specifically the site of Harlequin Cottage where we stayed during the first visit. The units Konrad renovated out the back are my imagination.

Thank you to dear Di and your fabulous team at the Lightning Ridge Visitor Information Centre for all your support with launch-ing my books.

Thanks to Christine Hathaway for being my fabulous travel buddy on my latest visit to the Ridge.

Now Bella? Well, after *The Opal Miner's Daughter*, I always had a question about what happened to Konrad's brother, William, but I needed another book to find out. I didn't know the answer either before writing this book. Suicide is sadly a reality in the world: if you or someone you know needs support, it can be found at lifeline.org.au.

The Lightning Ridge Ladies is standalone because it's William's twin, Bella, briefly met at the end of *The Opal Miner's Daughter*, who moves to Lightning Ridge to find peace after loss and falls in love with that world. Everything is new for her, just like it's new for the reader. In the story, Bella's determined interrogation of the Ridge's toughest guy, TJ, is where the delight of imagination grabbed me. I loved TJ – the name inspired by my nail-ninja Kristie's husband. Great name but this TJ is my imagination. Bella and TJ's slow-burn romance were the first chapters I wrote, and they came so fast and funny I couldn't stop them bouncing off each other; their happily ever after drove me to the end.

The Lightning Ridge Ladies are fictitious, but we all know about classic small-town pillars of strength, and especially women like Desiree, who feels very real to me, but she doesn't actually run or live at the fuel station.

In my books I like to delve into medical challenges such as diabetes, epilepsy and, of course, a dramatic but inspiring childbirth. I guess you know this ex-midwife is addicted to birthing stories. This time I wanted to share some insight from Meesha's point of view about her sister's experience with blindness (seedifferently.org.au). The inspiration for Luci came during my last book tour, where I met a very spritely nonagenarian and passionate educator and advocate for people with blindness or low vision, helping sighted people understand the challenges for those with vision loss. This gorgeous lady made me think of things like traversing stairs and filling teacups with boiling water without sight, and she leaned very heavily on me to write a visually impaired character in my next book. I also have a lovely reader who has a guide dog, Major, and this is a blown kiss to her.

Online, I found the amazing Lucy Edwards, with the hashtag #blindnotbroken. How wonderful is that hashtag! Lucy Edwards is a blind disability activist and journalist, with a sister, and a notable figure in London who shares her experiences and insights on navigating the city and advocating for accessibility. She's on TikTok as well but I found her on YouTube and Instagram (lucyedwardsofficial).

Lucy definitely helped inspire me to write my Luci, but her story is not my Luci's. I love the real Lucy's determination to master make-up (I'm sighted and still haven't managed that) and choosing outfits. I listened to her speak about working towards pregnancy, and the midwife in me wants to hug any mum struggling with conception. Lucy's posts are where I heard about the Braille children's books, and I dream of her reading to her children for a long time to come. My thanks and much respect from afar to Lucy Edwards.

I've also salted some special names through this book, of friends and of winners in two separate charity raffles who won the right to add their names to a character in this book.

We have Matilda Humphries, who became the mothercraft nurse – and the idea for single mum Luci to engage such a helper comes from my admiration for these incredible women. (A nod to Zeb's mum here, who caught my attention fifteen years ago when I learned she would move into a new mum's house for a week or more at a time.) Sourcing a mothercraft nurse would usually come through an agency or private company, not the RBS.

Then there's Carol Wood, who became our clever and not-quite-retired senior detective.

We have Bruce Kerrison, (Meesha and Luci's grandfather), a man my husband admires greatly for his integrity and service to the NSW Police Force. Bruce holds fond memories of when he worked in Lightning Ridge for a time.

Helen and Doug, Bella's parents – well, that was a wave to you, Cookie, with love and gratitude for all your mentoring with obstetric emergencies. And to Luci, from Darwin and SA, who is a star. All real names turned into fictitious characters with a smile.

As always, I would love to thank the team at Penguin Random House Australia. My awesome publisher, Ali Watts, my wonderful editor, Shané Oosthuizen, who follows up all my questions, designer Nikki Townsend, Veronica Eze in audio and Laura Nimmo in publicity, who works so hard to let readers know my book is out in the world and waiting to be found. Thanks also to Sarah Fletcher for your insight and polish.

Special appreciation to my flight travel buddy, first reader and super-savvy writer friend Bronwyn Jameson for your amazing input with that first draft. I do love your sense of humour in dealing with me. You are a great mate.

To all the reviewers who do such an amazing job of sharing their thoughts on my fiction, I thank you. Writers know the best chance of their work being read is through word-of-mouth recom-mendations, and you share those words so beautifully.

Thanks to my agent, Tara Wynne, who is the person I turn to for career advice.

Thank you to my writing friends – special mention to Trish Morey, who always provides forward motion when I lose my way.

To Jaye Ford/Janette Paul for being my sounding board when we're at retreat, and all the WWOW writers at lunches for motivation.

Then there's my hero: my husband. No acknowledgement would be complete without the man who brings me back to earth and makes me laugh every day. Dearest Ian, my love, my best friend and my biggest fan – I am your biggest fan. Thank you.

All these people to write a book. That's what I love about writing – we give, we learn and we share so that we can create books that touch our readers, experience magic moments, and inspire the joy and satisfaction that comes from creating a story we love. I hope, dear reader, that you'll love *The Lightning Ridge Ladies* and want to visit this amazing small town. Our outback towns need you. Thank you for your wonderful support. xx Fi

ABOUT THE AUTHOR

#1 Bestselling Author - Amazon Medical Fiction & Australian Literature

Award Winner - Romance Writers of Australia RUBY and Romance Writers of New Zealand KORU Awards

With over sixty books to her name, former rural midwife Fiona McArthur weaves her medical expertise into heartwarming stories celebrating women, families, and rural Australian communities. Her tales feature strong heroines and kind-hearted heroes finding love amidst real-world challenges in remote settings.

"I live for those magical moments - the first cry of a newborn, the strength women share, and the beauty of our vast Australian landscape."

To her readers, Fiona promises stories that illuminate the extraordinary in the ordinary, celebrating the power of resilience, kindness, and love. Each book is an invitation to explore beautiful places while discovering that the world is indeed filled with wonderful people and endless possibilities.

Visit fionamcarthurauthor.com to find out more about Fiona's books!

This is the order of reading I suggest, but all books, and their common themes, can be read stand alone. Not all the books are connected but the ones that have characters popping back in common settings, are in order here. Enjoy.

Aussie Outback Medical Romance Series

The Desert Midwife
  The Opal Miner's Daughter
  Red Sand Sunrise
  The Baby Doctor
  The Bush Telegraph
  The Homestead Girls
  Heart of the Sky
  Mother's Day
  Midwife in the Jungle
  The Farmer's Friend
  As the River Rises
  Midwife on the Orient Express
  Back to Birdsville
  The Lightning Ridge Ladies
  Aussie Midwives: True Stories from Real Midwives (non-fiction)

The Aussie Doctors Series

The Doctor's Gift
  Dr. Bennett's Babies
  Her Doctor Prince
  The Doctor's Vision
  His Doctor at Sea

Midwives of Lyrebird Lake Series

Montana
  Misty

Mia
Emma
Christmas in Lyrebird Lake

Outback Brides & Outback Brides of Wirralong

Holly's Heart
   Lacey
   Maeve's Baby
   The Baby Whisperer
   The Midwife's Christmas Miracle

More Midwife Medical Romances

Medivac Midwife

Harlequin Romances

A Month to Marry the Midwife
   Healed by the Midwife's Kiss
   The Midwife's Secret Child
   Father for the Midwife's Twins
   Healing the Baby Doc's Heart
   Falling For The Single Mum Next Door